IN FULL VIEW

JOSEPH FATH

iUniverse, Inc.
New York Bloomington

IN FULL VIEW

Front cover design derived from a panel titled "*Reichskristallnacht*", one of nine panels from the series Y'mei Yehudim (Days of the Jews) painted by Joseph Fath 1995-2001.

iUniverse books may be ordered through booksellers or by contacting:

iUniverse
1663 Liberty Drive
Bloomington, IN 47403
www.iuniverse.com
1-800-Authors (1-800-288-4677)

ISBN: 978-1-4401-9039-1 (pbk)
ISBN: 978-1-4401-9041-4 (cloth)
ISBN: 978-1-4401-9040-7 (ebk)

Library of Congress Control Number: 2009911917

Printed in the United States of America

iUniverse rev. date: 1/5/2010

IN MEMORY

of the more than 11,500 Jews of the Frankfurt community whom the Third Reich deported during the years 1939 –1945 and exterminated in the death camps.

CONTENTS

	Preface	ix
	Acknowledgments	xiii
1	A Tearful Departure	1
2	Reflections on a Marriage	6
3	A Decade of Descent	16
4	Deception and Betrayal	29
5	An Unanticipated Opportunity	34
6	Coffee	62
7	Eviction	76
8	A New Face	97
9	Dinner and an Encore	109
10	The Darkness of War—the Feast of Lights	119
11	A Letter from the East	130
12	The New Year 1940	137
13	Victory in Poland	141
14	Another Cup of Coffee	144

15	Doubts, Further Deception, and Diversion	147
16	A Different Night—the Seder of the Remnants	170
17	1940—the War Nearly Over?	189
18	More Persecution	194
19	The Eastern Front Ignites	200
20	The Yellow Star—the Ultimate Deception	208
21	The End of an Imagined Dynasty	222
22	1942—the Other Shoe Drops	231
23	Goodbye, My Husband	250
24	Preparing to Leave	255
25	Leaving the Sanctuary	260
26	*Die Anstaendigen* (The Decent Ones)	269
27	The Witnesses	279
28	Final Blows—an Ill-timed Encounter	287
29	Why?	302
30	Verschollen (Vanished)	309

Preface

The annihilation and destruction of European Jewry during the Holocaust and its profound effect on all of human civilization has given rise to a massive volume of literature more than seventy-five years after the Nazi ascent to power in Germany. Much will continue to be written as further evidence is unearthed, including the recent release of millions of documents held in the German repository at Bad Arolsen. These materials will be examined in their original, factual form by historians and subjected to thorough analyses and interpretation. They will undoubtedly yield further insights into the incalculable crimes perpetrated in the name of the demonic ideology popularized and disseminated by Adolf Hitler.

The enormity of these crimes and the monstrous agenda Hitler had constructed to carry them out were fueled by a rage that had seldom seen its equal. He had recorded his intentions in 1923 from a cell in Landsberg Prison, where he wrote *Mein Kampf*, with predictions that at the time defied all credulity. His writings were disregarded by a troubled, self-centered Western world that could not remediate the enormity of the social problems it had created despite the carnage of World War I. The accuracy of his intent and prophecies have confounded and astonished the world ever since.

I have contemplated this history of horrors my entire life, because of my Jewish heritage and because, as a late (yet fortunate) escapee from Germany, I became a refugee in the fall of 1938 from that then perverted country of my birth. I came to the United States—the most wonderful land on this earth, despite its imperfections—which took in my family and let us start life over again in freedom to pursue endeavors of our own choice. I did not become an academic or a historian and have no expertise in these fields. Instead, I became a research chemist for the first twenty-five years of my career and a business executive in that industry during the second half, for a total of fifty years in my profession.

Therefore, I did, in fact, experience those times—that is, the period from the beginning of the Third Reich in 1933 until its total defeat and destruction in 1945. Although my experience is not as a survivor from the ovens of Auschwitz or Treblinka, I lived through that period of my life with my memory intact. Therefore, I feel it incumbent on myself to record material from the Nazi period—that is, my recollections and most indelible impressions of events from the middle of the 1930s to the 1940s—in as forceful a fashion as I can recall or reconstruct them.

My work is in a fictional form. I have reverted to that form against a background of historically realistic detail and accuracy with extensive resource material at my disposal. This has given me the freedom of compositing the lives of complicated fictional characters. The sum of each character's interactions and reactions is likely to have more substance than that of an individual who lived in Germany during World War II. Within that context, constructing these fictional, composite protagonists has permitted me to weave into their stories the human frailties, disappointments, conflicts, internal struggles, and tragedies better than those taken directly from sparse individual records.

The events leading to the Holocaust began in Germany. Therefore, that land contains its roots as they were nourished before World War II. From its outset, the Nazi regime began a systematic campaign to the drumbeat of anti-Semitism, of forced expulsion, ostracism, economic, cultural, religious, and physical depredation, degradation, and ultimately murder. Germany was its country of origin where its roots could be infused with evil to create a reality, nourished by the violence that was to follow. For that, the government needed to condition its citizens to the removal of legal protections, to create acquiescence and acceptance by a populace that developed a sense of helplessness, to suppress activism and moral awareness, and to foster the abandonment of all humanitarian and civilized behavior. At the same time, it developed massive propagandistic and public relations skills to lull the rest of the world into collective forgetfulness of what its prior history, including World War I, had been all about. It took only five and a half years to do that, an unbelievably short period of time, which culminated in the infamous Kristallnacht, the national pogrom on the night of November 9, 1938. This was the first instance of well-organized, major physical violence against the entire Jewish community in Germany. The forced exodus of some three hundred thousand people prior to Kristallnacht, about half the Jews living in Germany before 1939, was greatly slowed after the outbreak of World War II in September of that year. In the months thereafter it essentially slowed to a trickle as the initial conquest of Poland added an additional three million Jews to domination by the occupiers. The policy changed from a long-term strategy of annihilation to a short-term one of extermination.

The story narrated here does not treat the remaining Jews in Germany on a national level but rather focuses on a small family whose lives had previously been integrated and assimilated, as was frequently the case throughout the country. It focuses on those of its remaining members who were trapped in the process of preparing for their own exodus. The events take place in the community of Frankfurt am Main, where Jews had first settled some eight hundred years ago. Only at the beginning of the 1800s were they given some form of emancipation; the community was then destroyed after 1938. As it relates to the fictional family I have chosen to tell about, six were able to escape with just their basic belongings. Three were left behind to face suffering, deprivation, and psychological assault until their ultimate tragedy occurred. It is, therefore, as if I had zoomed in on a computer screen from a satellite photo taken from outer space to an intimate closeness from which the street signs of a neighborhood could clearly be read. The conflicts in the face of outside hostility, ghettoization into homes and special houses; and the deceptions, lies, hypocrisies, and isolation caused by an Aryan society had an inexorably degrading effect that I wish to examine and tell about.

The narrative covers a three and a half year period from mid-March 1939 to August 1942. As the Germans initiated their war during this time, what began with an initial sense of quick victory ended in a slow, grinding, horrendous defeat, which took another thirty-six months to complete. The Allied forces fought with incomparable valor and purpose as finally in 1941 the United States joined and led the Herculean effort to vanquish this unmitigated evil of Nazism.

Sixty million people were killed during World War II, of which six million were European Jews, or 10 percent of the total dead. This began in a country that, starting in 1933, had a Jewish community of nearly six hundred thousand, less than 1 percent of its own population then within its confines. What happens to the fictional Frankfurt family in this book epitomizes the power of hatred, ostracism, and indifference; the compartmentalization of fundamental moral tenets; the ever-hibernating beast of anti-Semitism; a parsing of convenient rationales; and all the remaining flaws in civilized behavior to corrode the human spirit.

I hope that readers will gain an added perspective from this work that will enhance their understanding for the need to comprehend the importance of the individual and personal transgressions of their fellow human beings. I also hope it will raise their consciousnesses of a firm obligation not to let these grave lapses ever occur again and to keep collective memory alive for future generations.

Joseph Fath

Acknowledgments

No manuscript is adequately tested without interchange and review by individuals, either expert in the subject or familiar with experiences on which the substance of the writing is based.

In my case, I have discussed the essence of the story with several persons whose judgment I highly respect and whose comments I have used to guide my progress.

They are the following:

Dr. Ernest Stock, Tel Aviv, for his generous analysis and encouragement to proceed with dissemination of the story. As a lifelong journalist and faculty member for some years at Brandeis University, our life paths have been different from one another but started out together as schoolmates in Frankfurt am Main in the same setting of the 1930s.

Professor Peter Paret, historian and Professor Emeritus in the School of Historical Studies at the Institute for Advanced Study in Princeton. I am grateful for his sage advice, excellent analytical insights, and reality checks, which have served me well as a sounding board and literary mirror.

Professor Esther Schor of the English department at Princeton University, with whom I had excellent and useful discussions regarding historically based writing and the special responsibilities and care that must be exercised in doing so.

Richard Larschan, Professor of English at the University of Massachusetts in Dartmouth, Massachusetts, for his editing help and advice on how to make the manuscript more reader friendly, concise, and appealing.

Morton Zachter, Princeton, author of a witty tome, on the amazing maze the publishing industry has become and how best to navigate it in its present state.

Ms. Hanna Fox, Princeton, for her diligence in editing and initial preparation of the manuscript as well as her encouraging comments.

Ms. Deborah Fath, Altadena, California (my daughter), professional graphic designer with many years of experience, for her artful assembly and tasteful incorporation of my painting "Reichskristallnacht" into an appropriate and dramatic cover design.

Most importantly, my dear wife and companion, Ruth, who has constantly read and reviewed my work while in progress, who guided me with wisdom and care and looked after me with gentle compassion while I was engaged in the many hours to complete this work.

I thank all of you for the contributions you have made to my work.

I A TEARFUL DEPARTURE

March 10, 1939: a damp and intense cold of winter's end relentlessly penetrated all who needed to be outside their heated homes. Carola Rossmann and her daughter Trudi stepped off the trolley car at the Hauptbahnhof, the main railroad station of the city, rushing inside quickly to avoid the chill that gripped those in the plaza in front of the building. They had each been lost in the silence of pain of their last hour together. All they seemed to be able to express had been said to each other during the beginning of their ride to the station. The haunting echo of love from the two remaining members of the Seidenberger family they had left behind an hour earlier in the dilapidated apartment on the *Unterlindau* reverberated steadily inside each of them. Once inside the station's track area, they embraced tearfully and held on to each other with the force of unconditional love between mother and daughter that has no equal among any other relationships. As the tears flowed freely down their cheeks, the finality of their separation finally sank in. The hands on the large clock facing the tracks in the departure hall read 21:40, twenty minutes before the train would leave for Brussels, Belgium. There was only the drone of remote people noises, the calls of train dispatchers announcing imminent departures, and the hissing of steam from the cylinders of impatient coal-fired engines waiting to push their passenger trains backward out of the station.

Carola mused to herself how Trudi was leaving her family now, having, in turn, been left behind not long ago by her new husband, David Stern. They had quietly been married some weeks earlier in a brief ceremony at the town hall. It had been a civil ceremony because rabbis of his Orthodox Frankfurt congregation were no longer legally entitled to officiate at religious weddings. Therefore, the newlyweds were anxiously awaiting the religious ceremony that was to be held at the synagogue David joined in Brussels upon his arrival. He had left quickly, having had his exit permits to Belgium ready two weeks before the wedding in order to reestablish himself in the jewelry business with the help of supportive friends.

Trudi and David each explained to Carola that their Brussels move was part of a plan of escape devised by his friends of the erstwhile Friedberger Anlage congregation, organized in the manner of an underground railroad. As each new arrival in Belgium had quickly been employed by one of the previous arrivals, one of them then gave a personal guarantee of support by demonstrating to the authorities that he or she would not be a burden to the state in return for receiving Belgian immigration papers. Both Trudi and David impressed Carola with the fact that in this way strong ties formed between old and new friends at the Brussels Jewish community. In turn, people were often given the opportunity to bring additional members of their own families into the country. They regarded the Belgian residence as a temporary respite from which they could consider further emigration moves to England, Palestine, or North or South America.

This mutual, informal aid society formed the basis of the strongest of bonds which were to last the entire lives of the Belgian émigrés as the reciprocal, often life-saving favors could never be fully repaid. The plan was also the basis of Trudi's promise to her mother to extricate her as quickly as possible from the constantly tightening noose forming around the remaining Jewish community in Frankfurt as their numbers shrank and their collective financial resources for self-help began to be taken away by the SS authorities at an ever accelerating rate.

"*Mutti*, don't cry," she said through her own tears. "It won't be long before David and I will send for you—just as soon as the paperwork is complete and we have found a small apartment in Brussels adequate for the three of us."

As they approached the gate, Carola and her daughter Trudi separated quietly. The young woman reached into her pocketbook to pull out and present her exit papers to the indifferent gatekeeper at track number fourteen near the center of the twenty-four-track departure lineup. She continued to look back at her mother as she quickly marched toward an open compartment door in the middle of the ten-car train. As she mounted the steps to a nearly empty compartment, she turned for one last time to wave to her mother, blowing her a kiss of departure that struck with such an emotional force of consolation that it dried Carola's cheeks and made her wave back with a wan smile and a look of contained courage. The doors finally closed as the conductors gave their last boarding shouts, orders, and other incomprehensible instructions and stepped on the sideboards at the end of the cars to disappear into the train's innards at the last second. The black, sooty engine came alive at last as its pistons, connected by a strong, convoluted system of rods and pinions, began to move its large load out of the station. The cold air of winter condensed and recondensed the steam emanating from seemingly everywhere, and the train disappeared quickly out from under the glass roof, which had been smudged with soot and other accumulated dirt during the many years of nonexistent cleaning and poor maintenance.

Carola Rossmann turned quickly, resolute to walk away, but was briefly stopped by involuntarily recurring bursts of tears and shudders as she began to contemplate what she was to face from this moment on. The words, "Mutti, David and I will send for you as soon as everything is prepared," rang in her head with fading power, her gut instinct telling her otherwise and doubt and disbelief taking the place of the optimism they had both pretended to themselves and to each other.

The teary goodbye she had just gone through had been preceded by a similar scene an hour and a half earlier when she and Trudi had left the apartment, embracing Trudi's grandmother and Leah Rosenthal, Esther Seidenberger's companion, for a similar last time in their old, run-down family home. The cries and wailings were louder and more unrestrained, particularly of her grandmother and more modestly those of Leah, who had essentially helped raise Trudi from her early years on. Despite promises to Grandma, which everyone knew were hollow and might never materialize, the old woman, now nearly seventy, was inconsolable and seemed in her unintelligible outbursts to recall all of the important events of their lives together that randomly occurred to her through her grief.

To make matters more painful and sad, Carola had gone through the same scene some six weeks prior to this day when her younger daughter,

Lisa, had similarly departed for America by taking a train to Hamburg for the first leg of her ocean voyage on the German liner *Bremen.* On that vessel she was able to get passage for a modest one-way ticket in a shared cabin near the steerage quarter of the ocean liner. Of course, this too had been a teary, difficult separation, although at that time in early January, her older daughter accompanied them. Trudi projected a more stoic, matter-of-fact, and accepting mien, which, when combined with the more optimistic, confident spirit (perhaps artificial and contrived) and the more jocular nature of Lisa, helped their mother overcome her grief more easily than she presently experienced it. The total sense of loss of both children that this departure represented made her whole body sag to near the point of total collapse.

Carola slowly walked back through a swinging door that suppressed noise, steam, and soot by separating the departure hall from the outer arrival area. As she went outside into the cold night, she contemplated the prospect of "and now there were three," as in the children's book *Ten Little Indians*, which she had read to her daughters in years past. In this case, it felt more like they who had to remain were worn out remnants in that there were two tired, elderly women and one whose youthfulness was fast fading into middle age.

In her own mind, she saw a picture even more pathetic. Her husband had died in 1935 of a serious kidney ailment. She was therefore a widow, well preserved but now totally abandoned by her entire small family after a life of major misfortunes without letup. Somehow, there had always been needs, poverty, silent recriminations, and a constant heaviness of life that never seemed to lift. Their mark of distinction and sorrow was that the entire family felt ever pursued by a tragic assault on their Jewishness. She was trying to imagine life while the government's campaign of hate was infecting her neighbors and all of life around them. Before the Nazi takeover, the then constant wishes, demands, emergencies, tendernesses, and fights with first innocent and then exuberant children around, had kept everyone distracted and often removed from the preoccupations of their increasingly desperate situation.

Ever since the infamous Kristallnacht of November 9, 1938, four months earlier, it had become hauntingly clear that an end to a functioning Jewish community was at hand. All evening long on that fateful night they had looked out the window from a darkened room to the police station across the street to witness the roundup of many men in the neighborhood as they were herded onto open trucks to be taken away to concentration camps. A community, now nearly eight hundred years old and an integral part of the citizenry—for better or for worse—living of late in free association with the surrounding Gentile world, had finally achieved emancipation and slowly took up residence in more distantly diverse areas from the original Jewish neighborhoods.

The community as a whole was eager to complete the process of integration in a civil, legal, and tolerant manner, striving to create a culturally advanced citizenry that could jointly build a diverse society that would shed prejudice, hatred, and the other evils of old.

Though the chancre of anti-Semitism had continued simmering beneath the surface during the past fifty-some-odd years, a number of prominent civil- and activist-minded Jews had successfully inserted themselves into the political fabric of the Frankfurt societal structure. That illusion was finally shattered, however, and the bubble of delusion under which they were now beginning to conduct their daily lives had finally burst in 1933. It was nearly impossible to accept the fact that their only recently created Frankfurt Jewish world had so suddenly and permanently changed and now appeared to be ending as the inculcated experience and environment had conditioned the Jewish population to accept its inevitable demise.

As she walked outside, Carola tucked her scarf tightly into her well-worn coat, which had not been replaced in more than ten years. She boarded the trolley car that had arrived in front of the Bahnhofplatz, trembling as much from fear as from the cold, damp weather surrounding her.

2 REFLECTIONS ON A MARRIAGE

As soon as she found a seat in the second car as far away as possible from the potentially hostile glances of tired passengers returning from their day's work, Carola lost herself in her own thoughts, delving a long way into the last twenty-some-odd years of her difficult life. It was not in a mood of self-pity but rather an intense review commingled with nostalgia, which arose with Trudi's departure.

She was totally absorbed in her own new situation. First of all, she had been left behind, after her brother and his small family made the decision to emigrate to the United States. They had gone about it, at first, with measured deliberation. Then, after a flurry of final preparations when the details had been worked out, the three of them were gone by September 1938. Her brother, Dr. Eduard Seidenberger, was three years younger than she and was sent by her parents to medical school after his graduation from the Realgymnasium in 1912. As a girl she did not continue her education because she was only an average student, and in those days only young women of unusual brilliance and academic record were admitted to advanced professional training. Her brother, on the other hand, after a prolonged study of medicine interrupted by World War I, had established a practice of gynecology and in the course of the past fifteen years had acquired an excellent reputation among his peers and patients.

Following the ascent of the Hitler government to power and the boycott of April 1933, during which two Storm Troopers parked themselves in front of his office and discouraged his patients from entering, and the subsequent loss of health insurance reimbursements by the government agencies then in place throughout Germany, he had begun to conclude that future prospects for Jewish physicians were dim. This, despite assurances that as a World War I veteran and officer in the German army he would be exempt from any ostracism, refusal of access to public hospitals, and other financial deprivations. He had, therefore, chosen to look around for countries that might have a freer environment where he and his family could reestablish themselves, and he could resume his medical practice.

His wife Eva, ten years his junior, came from an affluent merchant family in the Rhineland who assured her that she would have nothing to worry about financially, even if her own family income became less due to the new restrictive laws and covenants. They told her that there would be enough money generated by their department store business to take care of her family as well. What they did not realize was that part of Eduard's income went to the support of his own father's family. This was kept confidential so as not to make her family feel they were merely funneling funds through to people to whom they did not feel particularly close.

Toward the end of 1933, Eduard took his wife Eva on an exploratory trip to London to see if she was willing to move to England and resume a new life. He had gone to boarding school in Manchester for a year before the outbreak of World War I, had learned the language, and was in general an Anglophile, greatly admiring the ways of the British lifestyle, the jauntiness, and the matter-of-fact "stiff upper lip" manner of the British people. The trip, as it turned out, was a tactical mistake. The weather in November was miserable, and during their stay, it rained without end. It was cold and damp, which was anathema to Eva's well-being, and the darkness from three in the afternoon until nine o'clock the next morning at that time of year was very depressing to her. She therefore opposed leaving her comfortable house, and they returned without making any decisions. He subsequently explored going to America where he had an uncle, Hugo Seidenberger, who (after being expelled from the family residence in Hemsbach for a transgression that was kept a deep, dark family secret) had been sent to America where he married, raised a family, and established himself as a small businessman in the textile manufacturing business.

After many letters back and forth and interminable paperwork, by the end of 1935 Dr. Seidenberger received consent from the German government to leave the country. In turn, his uncle submitted an affidavit of support to the American government guaranteeing that his nephew would not be a charge and a burden to the public sector. Toward the latter part of 1936, he had at last been able to leave for the United States to study for his medical exams so that he could obtain a license to resume his practice of gynecology. He had taken only a very modest sum of money with him, augmented by a semivaluable stamp collection and a Leica camera to sell in case of an emergency, hoping that he could live and board with his uncle's family until his earning power was reasonably restored. Because he was unable to provide for his own family without resuming his medical practice, his wife Eva and son Stefan needed to remain behind, living in very modest circumstances to conserve sufficient funds until their own departure. This finally occurred in the late summer of 1938 and effectively removed both financial and psychological support from Eduard's mother Esther, Leah, his sister Carola, and his nieces.

Before leaving in 1936, having spent the year obtaining the necessary permits and visas and arranging his business affairs, Eduard had given Carola comfort by assuring her that he and his uncle would send for her, their mother, and Leah to help them immigrate to the United States. The entire Seidenberger/Rossmann family, young and old, could then resume a new life together in the New World. Separation was to be regarded as temporary and faced with courage and determination, as an investment toward a good life together within a short span of time.

Carola's spirits were immediately lifted by these pronouncements. At age forty-six, her life had been difficult and sad in almost every way imaginable. Many years earlier, after she had graduated from the Lyceum at age nineteen, she had worked in her father's small office answering the phone, recording orders, and doing the simple bookkeeping that was required to understand the business's profitability. She joined a young singles group at the nearby synagogue that provided a meeting place for young men and women anxious to meet prospective Jewish marriage partners. She found such contacts to be the most socially friendly way that avoided the need to mingle in a mixed, Gentile world. She smiled quietly to herself as she recalled the image of a tall, slender, dark-haired young man with an interesting, serious, and at the same time somewhat mysterious face, who (after looking over the scene for a while) came over to ask her to dance to a slow waltz. She herself was a good-looking young woman of medium height with red to strawberry blonde hair, innocent eyes, a sensuous mouth, and a well-formed figure for a person twenty-one years old. They talked at length after the dancing and thoroughly enjoyed each other's company. Carola told her new acquaintance about her family and how she enjoyed helping her father keep track of a business that seemed to be flourishing with the growth of the community.

Aaron Rossmann followed up, asking her out on subsequent dates during which they took long walks, sat at outdoor and then indoor cafés as winter approached, and engaged in long and somewhat serious conversations. After a while, greater familiarity led to flirting innuendos injected with enough rapid uptakes and banter to keep each other interested as their respective heartbeats quickened. Even though his mien was somewhat clouded and he seemed a type that was easy to anger, she was more and more attracted to him as he appeared to be seriously interested to her, and after a number of weeks of veiled expressions of intent, their mutual pursuit was in full flower.

Carola invited him to her family apartment for a Friday night dinner during which he gave her parents what amounted to a full résumé in answer to their obviously probing questions. Although he was five years her senior, he was still living at home because he worked for his father as the young marketing head of the family notions business and, with his calling on the trade, had gotten to develop a close relationship with the numerous clients that gave their business a comfortable profitability. A small showroom on the *Eckenheimer Landstrasse* held samples of the many lines of buttons, rolls of tapes, spools of thread, linings, labels, belt buckles, pins, thimbles, packages of sewing needles, spare sewing machine attachments, and the myriad of other small items required to put together a finished garment, either in a factory or at home.

As the weather improved in the late spring of 1913, their dates and time together changed from inside and family activities to excursions into the neighboring countryside. They both enjoyed the outdoors and could be together by themselves without always being under the wary eyes of their respective parents and older family members. Not being regular attendees at Shabbat morning services, they chose a Saturday or a Sunday morning to head out by trolley car, either to Oberursel with number twenty-four or to Bad Homburg via number twenty-five; go to the end of the line; and begin an excursion by choosing one of the walking paths into the adjoining woods. The trails were marked with indicated distances and signs and were also well trodden so that it was unlikely they would get lost on the way to a destination they chose. Some of the terrain was hilly and a bit challenging to the uninitiated. Therefore, before beginning on a season of these trips, they bought each other walking canes and collected little ornaments decorated with names or symbols of scenery that they nailed onto the cane after reaching a specific point of interest or village. Having walked to Koenigstein or to the top of the Feldberg and other "sub-Alpine" locations, for instance, the metal tags mounted on the front of each cane reminded them as pleasant souvenirs of the places they had enjoyed together.

Carola recalled the day she spotted an opening in the woods that was grassy and somewhat hidden from view by large trees that had collapsed years earlier. At her urging, they crawled into the hidden spot and could not be seen by other passing tourists. After resting a few minutes in this place, they spread out a tablecloth to have the lunch of hard-boiled eggs, buttered bread, and sliced tomatoes they had packed earlier. They drew closely together in the euphoria that came from the privacy and natural beauty they had found. They soon lost themselves and held on to each other while kissing rapturously.

On one of their subsequent trips, their heated passions escalated into uncontrollable lovemaking, which, however, became a little tenuous when they realized that this was their first sexual encounter. In their final haste they had used the tablecloth, originally meant for spreading out the food, as a sheet to protect themselves from the pine needles, ants, and other distractions. They could then relax and give themselves over more completely to the excitement of each other's touch with the joy and bewilderment of the first time. Their whole first experience turned out to be a bit messy as she was indeed a virgin at age twenty-three. His initial penetration was a little painful and so new and different to her that it gave her ardent desire pause to reflect on the wonderment of their now mutual state as young lovers.

As they finally separated from each other after that first time, a sense of peace and happiness overcame them both, and their quiet smiles made them hold on strongly to each other with a new knowledge that, should their acts of love repeat as they doubtlessly would in subsequent encounters, they could, at the very least, count on a life of physical happiness and contentment. This would go far to insulate them from the unpredictable adversities appearing in a newly unstable world.

It was only several weeks thereafter, on a repeat excursion crammed with all the natural, beautiful, and sexually fulfilling accoutrements of a Sunday afternoon in the country, that he declared his unconditional love and proposed marriage to her. She was the happiest of women and began planning a small, intimate wedding sometime in the fall, immediately after the Jewish High Holidays. When she returned early that evening and joyfully told her story to her parents and brother, the family excitement dominated all other activities for the next two months until the wedding date was set.

The marriage ceremony was performed by Rabbi Horovitz of the nearby Unterlindau Synagogue in the presence of their respective parents and closest family members, as well as a small coterie of friends they both had accumulated during the days and months of the singles events that had brought them together in the first place. The ceremony itself included the *Sheva Broches*, the Seven Blessings, the rabbi's remarks, and the breaking of the glass. It had all the earmarks of a Jozef Israel painting, complete with morning coats and high hats, accompanied by dignity and pomp. The loving couple, shown on canvas and in real life, exchanged rings and united under the groom's *tallit* while the rabbi pronounced them husband and wife. The ceremony was followed by a luncheon in the synagogue's social hall, which had been prepared cooperatively by the two mothers-in-law, the *machutanim*, who had begun to like each other very much once they had spent time together and gotten to know each other. Following a toast to the newlyweds was a round of fine quality *Sekt* served with a cold salmon dish poached of the best fish then available from the Rhine River with sides of cucumber and potato salads. This, in turn, was followed by homemade items on a large dessert table, holding apricot, strawberry, gooseberry, and plum tortes and other sweets. The meal was praised and enjoyed by everyone, and the entire wedding affair was pronounced a great success.

Following the wedding, the happy pair went on a brief honeymoon, to the extent they could afford a trip and time away from their duties in their businesses, by taking a train to Mainz and changing for a brief ride toward Cologne to the small wine-producing village of Ruedesheim.

Once there, they spent their time climbing among the rocks near the Lorelei and enjoyed fine food and excellent young wine along with a few guests that were still at the hotel, just before the weather turned too cool to be outside. After the day's main meal, they tended to take an afternoon's rest—not before ardent lovemaking—this time in the comfort of a bed and with a mixture of passion and familiarity that led to greater skill and an abundance of variations. This gave both of them an insight into the happiness awaiting them in the future.

When they returned after the few days of interlude to the reality of the world as they found it in the early months of 1914, they resumed their modest jobs and aspirations with the hope that their future together would lead to prosperity for them that would enable them to start a family of their own. They would soon be jarred, however, by the events of August as war erupted on the second of the month with the assassination of the Austrian crown prince in Sarajevo. The forces of Germany and Austria were now arrayed against England and France, and soon a general mobilization gave way to the massive battles and invasions that escalated and characterized World War I.

Aaron, who had a long-standing chronic kidney condition dating back to the time when he was barely nineteen years old, had the good fortune to be excused from conscription into the army and was able to stay at home to remain employed with his family business. He and Carola were able to rent a small apartment of their own in a four-story building on the *Holzhausenstrasse.* It was on the top floor of the house and required a lot of stair climbing, especially when coal needed to be carried from the bins in the basement to the stoves in each room for heating in the wintertime. The rent was somewhat below average, which they could just about afford. It was barely six blocks from her parents, the Seidenbergers, and still within walking distance from Aaron's parents. In this way she was able to divide her spare time fairly equally between both sets of the older folks. Therefore, despite the war and the terrible news of casualties as German soldiers crossed the Rhine and began invading Alsace Lorraine and the Belgian territories, both of them were able to lead fairly normal lives pursuing their same daily tasks.

In the summer of 1916 their first daughter, Trudi, was born. While she was an easy baby to care for, both parents were burdened with extra sleeplessness, diaper changing, walks with the carriage, and other newborn routines. Nonetheless, their happiness and contentment was strong, despite their modest circumstances. In the meantime, the United States had joined the Allies; troops had been sent across the ocean under General Pershing's command; and by the middle of 1917, Germany's fortunes of war had been reversed. The army and navy were demoralized; the Kaiser and his generals had made mistakes that cost them huge losses of men and matériel; and political change was rife. On November 11, 1918, the army surrendered; the Kaiser went into exile at Apeldoorn in Holland, and the noncommissioned segment of the German forces revolted against the officer corps. The war was lost. The Rhineland was occupied, and at Versailles the Allied governments began to contemplate how to punish Germany. They wanted to ensure that Germany was weakened sufficiently so that it could never start another conflagration on the monstrous scale that saw millions of soldiers die by rifle, canon, poison gas, and other recently invented horrors, leaving a landscape akin to Dante's *Inferno.*

The young Rossmann family was not directly involved in the chaos of revolution, civil strife, communist uprisings, and internal battles and was therefore relatively unaffected by the eruptions that swirled around them. In 1920 their second daughter, Lisa, was born. The notions business had been relatively strong during the war with uniforms and used clothing shortages requiring endless repair with the small items that happened to be part of Aaron and his family's business. Nevertheless, the notions industry fell off drastically in the 1920s because of the abject poverty that ultimately permitted not even modest upgrades or replacements. Both Aaron's parents and his own immediate family had to do some belt-tightening where there had not been much leeway to begin with. Although they had saved up a few thousand marks during somewhat better times, their very small nest egg began to shrink. In due course, the hyperinflation of 1923–24—with its massive bankruptcies, credit problems, and total devaluation of currency—caused the Rossmann Notions Materials business to become a shadow of its former self for the remainder of the decade. Aaron was constantly worried about his continued ability to support his family and worked longer and longer hours to obtain smaller and smaller orders at lower profit margins than he had ever experienced before. He would come home at seven, eight, or nine o'clock in the evening and would practically snap at Carola when she attempted to bolster his spirits.

"Honey, how was your day, you poor dear? After spending all those long hours, was there enough business to make it worthwhile?"

He could not respond as his guilt turned to anger and into a glowering silence, saying to himself only, "Aw, leave me alone, you don't know what I've been through and how many refusals I've had to endure from my old friends and clients." Carola did not take easily to what she misinterpreted to be a rejection of her attempt to share in Aaron's fruitless efforts, and her many unsuccessful tries began to drive a wedge between their feelings of love and tenderness.

The worsening economic situation, along with political unrest and impossibly high unemployment rates never before experienced by the hapless Weimar government, ultimately overwhelmed the political leadership. The misguided notions of excessive punishment the governments of England and France were determined to exact, regardless of the long-term political consequences, eroded the will and morale of the entire population. As these painful tensions between Carola and Aaron demonstrated, for him as the breadwinner of the family, it was a severely emasculating experience where in a household as head of the family he had been used to receiving the traditional respect to maintain his self-esteem. As not only Frankfurt's lower class and totally poverty-stricken inhabitants, but also its middle and upper-middle classes were in these desperate economic straits, their attitudes and modes of adaptation to the new stresses had a scathing effect on their lifestyles.

On the other hand, in the decade of the 1920s (where further integration into the then modern society of the city proceeded apace), the religious and cultural life of the Jewish community reached new levels of motivation and hope that slowly showed signs a freer and happier life could eventually be in the offing. This was reinforced by the fact that, despite the undercurrents of anti-Semitism stoked by the political assassinations of Carl Liebknecht, Rosa Luxemburg, and somewhat later, Germany's Foreign Minister Walter Rathenau, a burgeoning freedom of religious expression could be envisioned. Lively debates and novel philosophic writings by such Jewish intellectuals as Martin Buber, Franz Rosenzweig, and Walter Benjamin gave fresh evidence that a liberal and progressive environment might eventually evolve out of the political morass. There was also the perpetually unfulfilled hope that the revolving-door chancellorships and the legislative paralysis that resulted from excessive splintering of parties in the Reichstag and the parliamentary bodies of the states within the Federal Republic might some day be resolved.

When their second child was born in 1920, Aaron and Carola moved into a larger apartment in the same house on the Holzhausenstrasse where they had started their life together. The family income, with an occasional infusion from each of their parents, was sufficient to sustain the higher overhead, and the location once again proved desirable. It was fairly close by and about equally distant from each of their parents, as well as near the park where Carola could take the little girls, at first in their carriages and subsequently to play in the sandboxes with toys they would bring along.

3 A DECADE OF DESCENT

By the early 1930s, the family's business had taken another turn for the worse as the economy emerged from the catastrophic hyperinflation that had engulfed all of Germany during the prior decade. The Rossmann Notions customer list had been significantly shortened due to bankruptcies, defaults on payments, and brutal competition from the eastern and southern countries of Europe and Asia. The resulting depression had reduced their volume to where parents, son, and family were unable to earn a normal living from their now smaller notions company. For a while each took equal reductions in pay in a sort of polite "*après vous, Gaston*" fashion. By the early 1930s, however, and as a result of several poor investments that turned out to reduce their reserves below workable levels, Aaron's family was forced to reduce their overhead and give up the modestly comfortable apartment in which they had spent more than ten years in a fairly happy state of independent familial existence. On top of it all, Carola's father died toward the end of the 1932, worn out by failure, poverty, and age. He had aged quickly after the war, and even though he had reached seventy years, he was truly a casualty of the stresses imposed on everyone by the economic downturn of the postwar decade.

Carola remembered that crucial and traumatic day when she, Aaron, and the girls finally moved in with her mother and Esther's ex-maid and now companion, Leah. Leah Rosenthal had lived with the Seidenberger family since 1913 when she was first hired as a maid and housekeeper, who was needed for the moderately affluent couple with young children. She was also Jewish, which was somewhat unusual in those days when maids and nannies were typically from a Gentile family coming from one of the villages near the big city.

Leah originally came from Heppenheim, which had a small Jewish population of its own. After both of Leah's parents died in 1912, she no longer had a home in the village and left to be taken in by a cousin in Frankfurt. She was a single woman, forty-two years of age, who had not been able to find a husband in the country area, so she looked for a job as a domestic as soon as she arrived and found one with Esther and Abraham Seidenberger. For her, it was a pleasant new milieu of a more emancipated society that was beginning to take shape.

Carola's parents declared themselves young "German citizens of the Jewish faith." This entitled them to exercise their civil rights to be protected by the laws of the country, to have 10 percent of their income taxes allocated for the administration expenses of the Jewish community if they wanted to declare themselves as members, and, parenthetically of course, to be drafted into the army for compulsory military service. As everything deteriorated after the war, the Seidenbergers could no longer afford to pay Leah her wages as a housekeeper. In a teary session they informed her that her employment had to end. Leah broke out and cried bitterly, "What am I supposed to do? Where will I live? I have no home other than this."

The three adults sat in helpless silence trying to face an impossible situation. Abraham then spoke quietly, "Leah, we cannot have you leave without knowing that you will have a roof over your head and a family to look after. What if you stayed here as part of us but with no salary? We would include you in our own household expenses as we have done right along. Then anytime you want to leave for a regular job opportunity, you could do so. We would not stand in your way ever." Leah's face lit up immediately, "Oh, that would be so wonderful. I would be with all of you whom I've come to love as my own. I will always work hard, do my part, and never be in the way if you just let me stay."

The deal was made, and everyone agreed happily that Leah could stay as part of the family she had become. They hugged and embraced and praised Abraham's quiet wisdom and the simple solution he had found.

Now that he was gone, the apartment was a relatively spacious place that her newly widowed mother continued to occupy while she mourned her recent loss. Inserting a young family, now with teenagers who had constant needs and who had to pass on stories of their daily school lives to whoever would listen, certainly lifted the atmosphere of gloom. It also reduced some expenses for the newly contracted household and injected new life into the conversations on Shabbat afternoon when Carola's brother, his wife, and the girls' younger cousin Stefan joined the post-religious service Kaffeeklatsch or, on some weeks, the traditional chicken dinner on the preceding Friday evening.

Aaron's illness and his chronic kidney problems did not improve during the next year or so, and his mood darkened significantly as his pain increased and his health further declined. The silence and solemnity cast a quiet spell over the evening meal and made it unpleasant for Trudi and Lisa to try for a conversation of small talk with their father, as his responses became shorter and more humorless. His good looks and occasionally mysterious yet friendly smile gave way to tired, dark circles under his eyes, a more and more slouching posture, unkempt hair, and neglect of personal hygiene and cleanliness of shirts, suits, and outer clothing.

After the Nazis came to power, it became more difficult for Aaron to make his sales calls. At firms owned by Gentiles, receptionists would let him wait for an hour before telling him the owner was unavailable for the appointment previously arranged. Others told him outright, "Aaron, we're not buying from you any longer. You're a Jew, and I'm going to be getting my supplies from real German outfits. So don't come back; you'll be wasting your time from here on in. Good-bye and, by the way, Heil Hitler."

Business continued to decline, and the events during the first two years of Nazi rule with the destruction of the Weimar Republic indicated that Hitler's dictatorship was here to stay. Neighbors and friends—Gentiles now declared Aryans—turned strangers and avoided all further contact. Signs saying "Deutsches Geschaeft" not so subtly pointed out which shops were in Jewish hands. Shortly after, Eduard lost his support payments from the government health insurance by which most of his patients were covered.

Reflecting back on the last year of Aaron's life, Carola recalled that one late afternoon in early 1935, as he was about to close up shop, two

Nazi Storm Troopers marched into his showroom and proceeded to attack him, slapping him around:

"You miserable, dirty Jew; what trash are you selling to poor working Germans, who are trying to keep their clothes in good condition? How much are you cheating them, and why don't you go to Palestine where you belong?"

Arriving home, he practically limped across the foyer, trying to restrain his tears and not relate this terrible experience in front of the girls as he sat down without washing up and asked for his dinner. Midway through the meal, as he gulped it down, obviously without enjoying it, he suddenly leaned back in his chair and let out a moan of pain the likes of which no one at the table had ever heard before. The shout and scare made everyone drop their knives and forks and rush over to him in order to help relieve his agony.

"What's the matter, Aaron?" Carola cried out in fright.

"I am in terrible pain in my back," he sobbed. "I've never had such sharp jabs; I can't stand it anymore. Help me, please help me, someone, anyone, and get me to a hospital quickly before I die."

Carola ran to the phone and dialed emergency: "My husband is very ill," she shouted breathlessly. "Get him an ambulance immediately; he needs to go to the Gagernstrasse Hospital. Quickly, his life is in danger; he must get there in the next few minutes."

It was a great relief that, indeed, the ambulance arrived within the next few minutes with an experienced crew of three. They rang the doorbell and came upstairs with a stretcher and blankets. Dinner was, of course, at an end as Aaron was placed on the stretcher, wrapped in a warm blanket, and carried quickly and carefully downstairs to the waiting vehicle. Carola put on her coat and ran down the stairs. "I'll call you as soon as I know more about what's happened to him," she shouted and hopped into the waiting ambulance.

She held his hand while an attendant put cold compresses on his forehead and gave him a very small injection of morphine to ease his pain during the trip. The long distance across town to the east seemed interminable, despite the fact that with sirens blasting and cooperating traffic police they arrived within twenty minutes. As they drove up to the emergency entrance of the hospital, two other attendants rushed out and brought him into the emergency room where a physician was on duty. While other patients were waiting, the pain and now the persistent moaning gave him priority for attention in the triage system they were using so that he did not have to wait long for a doctor to examine his midsection.

His pain was now all over his front and back, and he was initially diagnosed to have kidney stones. He was X-rayed after an additional painful twenty minutes, but no stones were located on developing the pictures. Given more pain reliever, he ultimately fell asleep after both Carola and Aaron were assured that Prof. Dr. Sigmund Veilchenfeld, the hospital's chief of urology, would arrive first thing in the morning. Carola sat with Aaron for a while as he dozed off, wiping his brow to remove the sweat of his pain.

As he fell deeper into the relief of his unconsciousness, she decided to leave the room and call her mother and Leah for an update before going home. She wanted them to reassure the girls before they went to sleep so that they could go to school as unburdened as possible the next morning. In her own mind, however, she was far from convinced that this was a one-time, nonrecurring event that could readily be diagnosed and cured or at least alleviated. She walked to a trolley car stop, took two lines back, and was not excessively verbal once she got home, despite the onslaught of worrisome questions and tears on her mother's part as to the new *Schlamazel* that had now befallen them on top of everything else. Carola also quickly called her brother to inform him of what had happened. He, in turn, promised to call the hospital for an update and to meet her there first thing in the morning. As soon as she could extract herself from the questioning, she retired to her room. Once in her bedroom and under the covers, she quietly cried herself to sleep, confused, not knowing or wanting to know herself the seriousness of his illness and what would happen next. All she knew was that things would get worse, and despite her desire to concentrate on her children and remain in the role of a housewife, she would probably have to pitch in at the showroom and help out in some way with the books or other immediate needs while the remaining two employees shared the normal chores that had to be handled.

The next morning she went back to the hospital after dispatching both Lisa and Trudi to school as cheerfully as possible to see what Dr. Veilchenfeld's prognosis was. The doctor had come and gone, and the resident physician on call summarized the examination with the unhappy news that he would need an operation within the next day or two involving the removal of a diseased kidney. Her brother had joined her at the hospital and had spoken to the resident behind closed doors of a consulting room for the next fifteen minutes. He emerged with a somber expression on his face, turned to Carola, and quietly told her, "I feel confident that Aaron will make it through the operation in good shape. We've got the best surgeon possible for the procedure; he has done operations of this type many times before. Aaron is young and in good enough physical shape to withstand the trauma he will undergo."

A professional tone accompanied the comforting words, but she was less than totally convinced that the upcoming operation would restore her husband to total health. "I hope you are right, Eduard," she said, showing uncertainty in her voice. "After all, he has had this infirmity since the time I first met him, and it was the reason for his deferment from the draft into the army at the beginning of the war, now more than twenty years ago." It seemed unlikely to her that the area of his medical weakness would not have been further encroached upon over the years as a result of the stress of their difficult life together and his now middle-age.

After the next day or two of semiconsciousness, while her husband was kept in a haze of drug-induced comfort, the surgeon cancelled or postponed his prior series of engagements and undertook the operation. Carola and Eduard spent the morning and part of the afternoon in an anxious and nerve-wracking state in the large waiting room before they were finally called into the doctor's cleanup area and then into the recovery ward where Carola saw her husband slowly coming out of the anesthesia and return to a semblance of consciousness.

First, the doctor told them that from an immediate point of view the operation had proceeded successfully and that a diseased kidney had been removed. He would be able to function on his remaining kidney but would have a lengthy recovery, and his energy would likely be affected over the long term. He would therefore have to count on a reduced work schedule and guard his delicate health for the rest of his life. They had further tests to conduct on the diseased organ as well as on the biopsies taken from the surrounding areas. This would take an additional few days, but because he would need to be under intensive care in the hospital in order to ensure an uneventful recovery, time wasn't of the essence. She listened quietly and attentively, the impact of the moment not enabling her to ask further probing questions. She felt that she needed every confidence in the doctor's excellent reputation and experience, as well as her brother's expertise for backup support, and decided to place her faith in their conscientious follow-up work.

In the recovery room, Aaron looked ashen white with his oxygen mask covering half his face. Had she not had all these reassurances from the surgeon and her brother, Carola would have been convinced that he was not far from death. After she sat by his side for an hour and a half, however, some of his color came back, and he began to return to a lifelike appearance. He regained his consciousness, turned to her, and smiled wanly. He then asked the nurse for a drink of water, which she unhappily had to decline. She did, however, place a moist face towel between his lips to give him some comfort and relief.

Eduard went back to his office to finish his appointment schedule. As evening approached, Aaron quietly went to sleep, and the nurse suggested that Carola return home and come back early the next morning because he was not going to be awake for the next eight to ten hours. She reluctantly left the hospital and went home, where Eduard was already explaining some of the details to their mother, Leah, and the girls. She quietly related how she found Aaron in the recovery room and then took the modest supper she was served. She went to bed without further ado, taking a sleeping pill of which she had a small reserve that her brother had provided her in case of urgent need.

The next few days were spent by her husband's side. He slowly recuperated, although he remained in a weakened condition and needed to be fed intravenously until the surgical wounds had a chance to begin the healing process. He inquired about Trudi and Lisa, of course, and she gave him a rosy picture of their school activities, homework, and social life, mainly with their Jewish friends. Sitting in the hospital was exhausting and stressful, and it was all she could manage to do without worrying about what might be going on at the showroom.

While she was tending to Aaron, Carola left the store in the hands of their capable employees, Alfred Hempel and Elizabeth Breitenbach. They attended to day-to-day purchasing, shipping, and taking orders from the few customers that were loyal enough to call them and who paid their bills without hassle and excuses. Alfred and Elizabeth had taken good care of things since the death of Aaron's parents three years ago, one right after the other, and only some three months after the death of Carola's father. They did this not only out of apparent loyalty and conscientiousness but also out of enlightened self-interest to keep the business going so they would have continuing employment with the generous conditions that the family had given them during the many years of their association. In fact, as sales continued to erode, there were months in which the owners took less of a salary than they paid their employees, feeling the obligation of steady remuneration for them was important to maintain continuity for a better day.

After a week of all-day-long hospital visits during which Aaron seemed to make some progress, Dr. Veilchenfeld made an appointment with Carola and her brother in his office on the Kaiserstrasse. After they had both arrived at the scheduled time in midafternoon, he closed the double door to his consultation room, sat them both down, and proceeded in a frank, grave tone. It seemed that the tissues were cancerous and that a biopsy analysis had shown even the surrounding areas to be malignant with evidence that the cancer had metastasized and was probably already lodged in other parts of the body. The question was whether additional tests and biopsies should be run with affected tissues planned for excision and whether experimental medications should be tried to stave off the inevitable. The doctor could not be too optimistic about all these options, as they would undoubtedly involve pain and agony in the forthcoming months. He seemed to suggest that making the patient as comfortable as possible was preferred, a euphemistic expression for letting life come to an end while minimizing the physical torture that the disease's progress appeared to imply.

After leaving the office in tears, they sat down at a nearby café for some coffee to take time to recover from the horrendous news prior to returning to the family apartment. They faced a dilemma that, if they were frank with the older folks and the children, they would have to handle the inevitable collapse of everyone's spirit. This would probably be a heroic task, superimposed on their own misery at a time when all of this tragedy was still fresh in their minds. They sat in silence, red eyed, which would readily give away the news of the impending disaster. As they went back to the Unterlindau apartment, they decided to first have a quiet evening meal with the entire family, trying to make small talk and changing the conversation to an update on the girls' activities. When both of them had retired to their room for homework, the news was broken to the two older women. "Well," Carola told Esther and Leah, "I have to tell you both that the news is very bad. The doctor found the kidney to be cancerous, and the disease has metastasized into other parts of his body. It's a hopeless situation." Esther and Leah tried to suppress their cries and reactions of shock, but the sound of their sobs carried, and they could not avoid the girls' sharp ears. Later in the evening, the household went into general mourning.

The next day, Trudi and Lisa were taken to the hospital to see their father, which perked him up and gave some joy to a quickly deteriorating situation. Aaron was hospitalized for another four weeks but, in the end, never returned home. The surgeon had spared the family a frank assessment of how fast the cancer was conquering his body because even slower progress would not have changed the inevitability of the outcome. With ever increased doses of morphine to reduce the agony of the end, Aaron passed away almost two months after having entered the Gargernstrasse Hospital.

As is customary in the Jewish tradition, the funeral took place the following afternoon with a group of close friends attending as quickly as they could be notified by his grieving wife and family. Rabbi Horovitz conducted the dignified funeral service at the modern, dark brick funeral hall designed by the prominent architect Fritz Nathan and built some six years prior at the front of the Jewish community cemetery's new section. As he stood silhouetted against the large window wall in the austere yet elegant hall with mourners seated on plain chairs, he spoke eloquently of Aaron and his beautiful family. They had endured hardships and tribulations during the many years of World War I and the postwar turmoil that they had all faced courageously as they built their lives together in harmony. This, despite the difficult times they and everyone else had gone through these past two decades. He also referred gingerly to the terrible anti-Semitism and persecution the Jewish community was now confronting anew from the totalitarian government of Adolf Hitler and his henchmen. He offered some comfort to the family that Aaron was now at peace and did not have to face this unexpected human degradation that those surviving had to endure.

After the Kaddish and a moving rendition of the El Moleh Rachamim, the participants rose, and the gurney holding the plain pine coffin held closed by wooden pegs was slowly wheeled out the back door to the burial site. It was led by the rabbi while Carola held Trudi's and Lisa's hands as they followed the body to its final resting place. It took an interminable ten minutes to reach the spot where the gravediggers had prepared an exact hole in the ground, two meters deep by two meters long by one meter wide. The coffin was placed on straps attached to rollers, enabling the workmen to slowly lower it into the hole. Several shovels were available, stuck in the mound of dirt generated by the diggers, so that the men in attendance, led by Eduard, could begin the sad task of filling in the site. With each thud of earth falling on the modest wooden coffin, pitch and volume changing with the amount covering the casket, Carola shook slightly and shuddered as the sound of doom reached the center of her brain and left an indelible imprint of all her fears to come. The family returned in total silence via the long walk to the cars that had brought them and were taking them back to the apartment where the period of the shiva was to begin.

That evening visitors began to pay their calls, shake hands with the family, and make casual conversation with a sense of embarrassment and discomfort. All the while, Carola sat on the low *shiva* stool, shaking a few dozen hands and listening through a haze of condolence expressions, as she thought back over the twenty-two years she was married to her husband. It had been a terrible two decades in which two attractive young people, full of hope, were trying to build peaceful lives together with whatever energies had come to their union under these circumstances. It did not seem unreasonable to ask for and expect the modest happiness they had projected and talked about during the many hours they planned their future together. This was somehow not to be under circumstances that were not within their control and that managed to frustrate them at every turn.

She realized that their love and companionship was, at times, dulled by adversity, extensive familiarity, mutual stress, family intrusions, second guessing, and unreasonable expectations. She now began to experience a contrasting emptiness with the new realities that quickly piled in on her.

In addition, a sense of hopelessness became more and more evident as the entire Jewish community had for the last two years begun to suffer from abuse, ostracism, degradation, flight, and terror. She feared that loneliness and abandonment were likely to be the main events of her future. It was not a pretty picture through moments of desolation and stiff-upper-lip checks. A deep sense of gloom and depression settled over her through the remaining few days of the *shiva.*

This only worsened as the first seven days ended. Although she no longer returned to the low stool each morning, she still stayed home all day, waiting for and greeting acquaintances. They all wanted to express their condolences and their sentiments of sympathy, even after the first seven days had passed. For several more days they joined others to sit quietly on the sofas in the room and reminisce in soft tones about their memories of Aaron. They expressed how terrible they felt about the young widow of hardly forty-five years of age and her two lovely children of nineteen and fifteen left living alone in a world from here on in that was as difficult to manage as they had ever experienced and getting worse by the day.

In this bleak environment, her spirits only worsened, and she ceased to function in the household or outside as Aaron's absence, permanent and irrevocable, left her psyche shattered and in shambles. This manifested itself with silence and withdrawal to the point where her mother and Leah had to take care of the girls' needs as they pursued their social and religious activities. She stuck to her room, talked little at meal times, and slept until close to ten o'clock in the morning when everyone was already busy with the day's needed chores. She then usually proceeded into the bathroom, taking a full bath in the tub for an hour or so, daydreaming, and softly scrubbing herself over and over as if to try to remove from her whole outer being all that seemed soiled by the misfortunes and hurts she had experienced in the final months of Aaron's illness.

Finally, she realized that she had to do some basic looking after the notions business, despite the assurances of their gentile employees, Alfred and Elizabeth, that all was in good order. These two gave the business an Aryan appearance, now that ownership of many of their customers had been changed in the general Aryanization process that was taking place in every industry and business. She began to understand that without at least basic supervision and control of the money flows her modest remaining means of livelihood could well be in serious jeopardy. Therefore, she finally went to the showroom on the corner of the *Eckenheimer Landstrasse* and Marschnerstrasse and went over the books that Elizabeth had kept as the inside person while Alfred had continued his daily round of customers in the city and the adjoining region. She spent at least three afternoons a week bringing herself up-to-date, signing checks to keep payments on time and credit in good shape, and handling the tiny payroll and other miscellaneous expenses customary to maintaining a business. This also provided a necessary distraction from her own misery to lift her spirits and increase her participation within the family. In the immediate weeks and months that followed, the household, now consisting of five women, divided up the tasks so that they could better function as a cooperative unit.

Trudi was in her last year of Realgymnasium and began looking for a job for the end of the school year so that she could contribute some financial support to the family. Her boyfriend, David, had tried to get her a spot in his family's jewelry store. However, times were so hard and the atmosphere so hostile that the shop, even though it was located at the Rossmarkt in the center of town, had a shrinking clientele so that some of the existing employees had to be laid off. Lisa, who was in her fourth year of Gymnasium, would have the summer off. She was a superior field hockey player and looked forward to spending her summer in a special school tournament of the region. However, because she was Jewish, she was kicked off the team so that her teammates could participate in what was required to be a pure Aryan competition. Both of them finally applied to and ended up working over the summer at the Jewish Welfare Agency for menial wages but were at least occupied and able to contribute very modest sums toward their own living expenses.

Leah did the shopping every morning by walking to the various markets with a shopping net in hand, picking up potatoes, a vegetable or two, some canned goods, margarine, bread, and other available staples. They were only able to afford meat twice a week, one of which was the traditional Friday night chicken, and the other, if they had enough money left over, was a piece of soup meat which served two purposes—to make soup stock and, with enough horseradish to enhance its boiled-out taste, to be served on another night. With circumstances dire and funds usually insufficient to make it through the month, Eduard and Eva brought much of the additionally needed food supplies on their weekly visits for the Saturday afternoon of *Kaffee* und *Kuchen*. Eva carried up to the apartment coffee and tea, canned milk, flour, an occasional bottle of mineral water (which was Esther's treat), cold cuts from the *Neukosher* meat market, an occasional goose for the holidays, loin of veal with a pocket for stuffing with bread, some cheeses, crackers, and other relative luxuries that the women could not possibly afford to add to their food supply.

Now that everything had changed, with her brother and sister-in-law long gone, the day after Trudi's departure started with one of those mornings when Carola did not arise until 9:30 AM. It was out of a haze of reminiscing about the past and trying to return to the present that she was confused about the events of the evening before. As she shook herself more awake, her first thoughts were: Did Trudi arrive safely in Brussels and into David's arms? What do we do now, and how do I face the future together with my two elderly loved ones whose energies are fading fast under the terrible conditions we must face? After a couple of large cups of black coffee, which tasted weak because of the poor quality that had become the norm, she decided to take her bath in the tub. It was a refuge that permitted her to seek some emotional equilibrium with an orderly phaseout and retreat from reverie back to reality.

After filling the tub high with warm water and sliding in, she felt a semblance of peace returning, induced by the comforting temperature, but she soon tensed up with the problems of their ever-increasing poverty occupying her mind once again. Their basic problem, which she tried to make go away with the distracting, almost womblike conditions of the warm bath's surroundings, would not let go of her. A sense of desperation and panic set in that continued to intrude upon her fantasies. As she saw her options narrowing and the continuing responsibilities falling squarely on her shoulders, the only ray of hope came from conducting the notions business with new energy and involvement she was not accustomed to in the past. It was a frightening prospect, but the only way she could imagine getting out of their collective situation of dire need was to apply to the Jewish Welfare Agency for help with additional monthly funds to augment ever-shrinking resources.

4 DECEPTION AND BETRAYAL

After several months, Carola felt she had begun understanding some of the elements of the notions business which previously had eluded her. One afternoon, as she worked with Elizabeth on the books, payments, and inventory status, she casually walked around between the racks to see if she could make out the system that had apparently been put in place. She noted that boxes and cartons had been stacked in good order so that the merchandise could be found quickly for packing and dispatching. Before he left on his daily sales rounds, Alfred and Elizabeth had chatted amicably with her in their usual friendly fashion, even with a bit of deference that was customary for her role as the late boss's wife and member of the managing family.

After Alfred left, the two women worked together at the large desk to bring the data to a current state. After an hour or so, Carola needed to use the bathroom. As she was returning to the desk, she idly opened a closet door to remind herself of what might be stored there. She did all she could to suppress her shock and outcry as she saw the brown shirt, jodphurlike pants, armband, belt strap, gun in holster, and black boots lined up neatly, waiting to dress their owner. After letting out an "Oh my God" of desperation, she quickly turned to Elizabeth.

"Whose uniform is that?" she demanded. "I can't believe there are these awful things in our showroom." Elizabeth was obviously most embarrassed because the closet should have been locked, which she had failed to do the evening before.

"Well," she stammered, "it belongs to Alfred. He had to join, after all, in order to keep the business going, now that all his customers are also members of the SA. It was purely a business move to keep things alive."

Her lie was too obvious to absorb, and witnessing the red blotches on her face and neck, Carola turned in disgust as her eyes filled with tears.

"After all these years and the generosity with which we treated you despite the constant assault on our company ever since the Nazis came to power, I just cannot understand how you two could have deceived and betrayed us in this horrendous fashion. When Alfred comes back, we better sit down and talk about how to continue. I don't see how I can go on coming in here, looking you straight in the eye, and working with you as if we were still associates."

Her heart pounding rapidly, she pretended to examine the records in silence as they sat opposite one another at the large desk without any further conversation. The embarrassment was so profound that the thickness of the air between them could be cut with a knife. Some interminable minutes later, Elizabeth could not contain herself and tearfully confessed what she and Alfred had plotted together. While she toned down the crudest part of their conversation, Carola was able to piece it together as she listened. According to Elizabeth, after he returned from his rounds one late afternoon a few weeks ago, he said to her, "How about closing down early? She won't come in; it's too late. I'd like to talk about something with you over a cup of coffee. Let's go across the street and spend some time together."

She promptly followed his proposal, and as it was still early summer with temperatures balmy in the fading sun, they sat down outside on the terrace and ordered coffee with a small piece of cake.

"I've been thinking about the Rossmann Notions business and what's going to happen with us. My contacts at our party meetings have told me that all Jews are going to be forced to sell their assets and that all businesses will have to be Aryanized in short order. This is a tremendous opportunity for us to take over what will otherwise certainly disappear and put us both out of work. If we offer Frau Rossmann to purchase the family company, now is a good time to make that offer at a very low price that she must accept as the most desirable option and without which she will have absolutely nothing left. With my connections and your knowledge of the inside in keeping the business in good order, we can rebuild the company to where we can both benefit from the success that will be inevitable. That is impossible to achieve now under this miserable Jewish ownership. Because I have a family and will be the key to successful marketing, without which there is nothing, I would like to offer you a one-third interest so that we can be partners on a 67/33 percent basis."

Despite her limited education, Elizabeth was intelligent enough and had been observing the family's distress and Alfred's unspoken scheming. She was also aware of the financial recovery his Aryanized customers showed because they came back with increasing orders and regular delivery schedules. Not entirely surprised by his proposition, she readily agreed with it and had enough street smarts to suggest they hire an attorney to draw up a partnership agreement so that everything was down "in black and white." She also suggested they prepare a sales agreement for Carola to sign so they could begin to operate under the new aegis immediately.

They then discussed a sales price, which, although ridiculously low, had a semblance of legitimacy so it could not be challenged in a court of law but could be supported by the extremely poor condition the company was now in. They agreed on a number of four thousand Reichsmarks, including inventory, to be paid in equal installments of one hundred Reichsmarks per month beginning within ten months after change of ownership without interest on the outstanding balance. This meant that if the entire sum were ever paid, it would take more than four years from now to payoff, by which time who knew if Carola would still be in the city. The severe pressure on Jews to emigrate might make that unlikely, and because there was no interest involved on the unpaid remainder, at whatever time she left the balance could be postponed—or perhaps forgotten about altogether. They agreed to make their offer to Carola as soon as there was an opportunity to do so and to present it as the only option, giving her no chance to negotiate for better terms.

When Alfred returned, he immediately knew that whatever it was Carola had discovered totally destroyed the charade of loyalty and friendship by which they had coexisted up until this moment. He had hoped that this false state of affairs could be maintained for another three to four months before the strategy he had put in place would have its maximum effect.

Now that their plot had been discovered and spelled out, Alfred spoke to Carola in a new tone she had never heard from him before. It was clear that there was no room for negotiations in this forced sale-to-be and that perhaps she'd better think of accepting this humiliating deal. Carola tried not to show the total surprise she had received and answered both of them as calmly as she could, "All right, I will respond to you quickly, but you can imagine that I am totally shocked by the proposition of being deprived of my living by my own employees."

There was a further moment of silence during which it was hard for Alfred to suppress the smirk coming over his face. "Well, that's how it goes Frau Rossmann," he answered with the last name formality he decided to use henceforth. To buy some time she said she would like to have a lawyer look over the papers that had been prepared. Both Alfred and Elizabeth magnanimously agreed but gave her only three days to come back. They also pointed out that in the absence of this agreement, which they were not prepared to alter in any substantive fashion, they would take other steps, less desirable to her interests, to transfer the business.

She went home, totally dejected, called her brother, and sat down with him the following day to discuss any alternatives. He had no good ideas but suggested that his lawyer friend, Dr. Hans Offenbach, could look over the documents she had been given. It was a foregone conclusion that the deal had to be done. In a way, she was somewhat comforted—falsely as it turned out—that she might at least have a steady income of one hundred Reichsmarks per month, beginning in 1937, and then during the next three years.

After the meeting at which she accepted their conditions, essentially capitulating, Alfred and Elizabeth smiled at each other when she left.

"Well, that's that," Alfred said with a smirk. "Now we can really begin our work to bring the business back to where it once was. I've been asking all our customers to give me only minimal orders and to hold them for later in the year when I will let them know about the change of ownership. We're now in a position to work with both clients and suppliers on a totally Aryan basis. We've eliminated the damned Jewish middlemen, and we can proudly paste the label of

'*Deutsches Geschaeft*' on our window so that everyone knows the change when they come in. This is going to be the greatest opportunity of our lifetimes, Elizabeth, and I hope we can work closely together for our mutual benefit and also a bit of enjoyment."

He said this with a wink and a twinkle in his eye, which, she thought, she clearly understood.

"After all, we're going to have to do the books ourselves and review them together at least once a month," he continued. "That means staying late at the office, which should not only be work but also a little fun for both of us. What do you say?"

Elizabeth had worked together with Alfred ever since she started fifteen years ago when she was only twenty-three years old. She was not unattractive but had never managed to meet the right man and was therefore single at age thirty-eight. Furthermore, she was just between boyfriends—the last one having left her three months ago after a major spat only to go back to his younger, former lover and get married.

At forty-three, Alfred appeared happily married with two children and an adoring wife, living just around the corner from the shop. He seemed always to be totally submerged in the firm. The volume of beer and schnapps he had consumed through the years had begun to make him a bit rotund, and his burst blood vessels stood out on his cheeks and nose, but he was still in sufficiently decent shape to have made her think about an occasional liaison with him. She therefore smiled back with as veiled an expression as she could muster in her already decided-upon acquiescence.

"Well, maybe. Let's see what develops and how good our partnership turns out to be," she answered with a lascivious grin.

The deal between them was therefore sealed, and another layer of life had been peeled from Carola's being.

As Carola returned to moments of reality, she resumed her gentle, constant scrubbing in the soapy tub to try soothing the especially raw places and distribute the additional pain more evenly all over.

5 AN UNANTICIPATED OPPORTUNITY

After finally getting dressed and having a late cup of coffee while bringing her mother up-to-date on Trudi's departure the night before, Carola sought refuge behind the closed doors of her own room to continue her thoughts about the events of the last few months and where this had left her as of this day, March 11, 1939. It seemed that ever since her sister-in-law and nephew Stefan's departure at the same train station from which she had dispatched both her daughters, things had deteriorated very badly for the three in her family who had to stay behind. It was only four and a half months ago when, on September 23, those two took the train to Ostende in Belgium to cross the channel and visit with their relatives in London prior to taking the ship to the United States. There they would join her brother who had left a year and a half ago. She was envious but above all admired their timing, which, with hindsight and the event of Kristallnacht, was both impeccable and fortuitous. Above all, she was happy for them that they had escaped the misfortunes that had, seemingly from that fateful night of November 9, befallen the Jewish community as a whole.

A week after they left in late September 1938, the British Prime Minister Neville Chamberlain and his dubious ally French Premier Eduard Daladier had gone to their final meeting with Hitler and Benito Mussolini, acquiescing to Hitler's demand that they support the annexation of all areas outside the current German borders with Czechoslovakia, which contained more than 50 percent of the expatriate German population. This, in the face of threats of war by the Germans and Italians, on the one hand, to ensure their demands were met and, on the other hand, to guarantee a peaceful settlement for any future issues that might arise. The English and French essentially capitulated to these demands and drew up an agreement that Chamberlain waved in his hand as he got off the plane back in London and proudly proclaimed he had achieved "Peace in our Time."

The Germans promptly occupied the Sudetenland region on October 28. A little more than a month later they made other demands on territories such as Bohemia and Moravia that met the same criteria as they continued to mass their army at the newly established border. The Czech government had not been consulted in the handover of its own lands; therefore, the morale of its government and the Czech people was extremely low as they realized the distinct possibility that their future as an independent, sovereign nation was in serious jeopardy.

At the same time, measures against the Jews inside Germany were ratcheted up, and arbitrary arrests in every city were increased. As Carola learned from the headlines and lead articles in all the newspapers, on October 27, 1938, some seventeen thousand Jews who had lived in Germany for many years after settling there from Poland but had never applied for German citizenship were expelled to be sent back to the Polish border as "Polish Jews." There they were dumped and left to their own fate. Polish border authorities did not make it easy for them to return, which meant they were left to shuttle in a no man's land between the border authorities without food or shelter. Fortunately, the Jewish welfare organizations were able to make some provisions that permitted them to survive and eventually to be either absorbed back into Poland or, in some cases, to be returned to the German cities from which they had been extracted.

Frankfurt had some two thousand of these citizens, most of whom had been required to turn over their apartments to the police, who then sealed them for future use by German gentiles. Upon their return, therefore, they found their apartments locked and with the help of the Jewish Welfare Agency had to find homes or temporary rooms with Jewish families of "German pedigree." Among these was a family whose son, Herschel Grynspan, was a student now living in Paris. When he heard about the fate of his relatives, Herschel became totally enraged at what had transpired. On November 7, he went to the German Embassy and, armed with a handgun, shot one of the emissaries there: Ernst vom Rath, who eventually expired from his wounds. This signaled the

Hitler government to begin its first open pogrom against the Jewish community, which, in view of the violent circumstances, they felt would not provoke an international outcry.

The events of Kristallnacht that followed on November 9 and 10 were staged by the Nazis, all under cover of "spontaneous outrage by the citizenry." While this charade was too transparent to be believable, the international community, in a mood of appeasement and moral disarray, was unable or unwilling to respond. As a result, hundreds of Jews in Germany were murdered and thousands were arrested and sent to concentration camps, synagogues were burned down, and most Jewish shops were looted and destroyed. It was a rampage of havoc that had never before been carried out on this scale in modern times, especially in a country that claimed to be so highly civilized and humane. Further, the restrictive orders, threats, intense hatred, and open intimidation of the Jewish communities in every city and town in the country became daily occurrences. The boldness and viciousness of these well-coordinated actions were at a fever pitch.

As Carola contemplated it, she wondered was this the end, was it the beginning of the end, were more violent harassment, prisons, expulsion, murder, or other consequences in the immediate offing now? As it turned out, in retrospect four months later, the violent assault that began after November 9 proceeded apace and appeared to be part of a larger strategic plan that made it seem as if a bureaucratic control mechanism had been imposed that was more systematic in character than a continued rampage signaled. There was more afoot than met the eye, and a quick extermination of the Jews in Germany alone did not seem to be the principal item on the Nazi agenda at this time. As Carola read the incendiary articles in the papers, she feared that the atmosphere was clearly getting worse for those, like her, who had not been able to escape and who could well be trapped from here on in. For some reason, however, they were left to stay in the community, albeit under terribly restrictive conditions of suffering and deprivation. It did not seem to be the end; it could be the beginning of the end, but the glimmer of hope—false hope—and the natural spirit of survival that remains in every human being under these circumstances provided a tortured yearning for return to "the good old days" and return of their relatives who had been fortunate enough to have left. Was confusion of the spirit a deliberate tactic?

The three women who were left behind, Carola, Esther, and Leah, as well as the rest of the community, would not have long to wait. On March 15, 1939, just four days after she had seen Trudi off to Brussels, the German army marched into Czechoslovakia, occupied Prague, and took over the entire country as they had taken over Austria a year earlier. The move completed their rapacious conquest, in total disregard of the agreement signed with the English and French. "Peace in our Time" had lasted exactly 168 days, and the rest of the world now knew that the "microassault or pogrom" that had been perpetrated on the Jews of Germany was about to be perpetrated, perhaps in apocalyptic terms, against the rest of the international community.

Carola sighed in that ultimate resignation to a fate that an individual human being can only witness in a mirrorlike panorama in which she is a helpless and paralyzed bystander or participant.

She was returning from a short grocery shopping trip in the neighborhood on a Tuesday morning in mid-April when she stopped at her apartment house mail slot to open their box as she had gotten into the habit of doing. Ever since her brother's family left for America and the girls had departed, she had opened the box, not necessarily expecting to find any mail, but just to assure herself that, indeed, she had looked and verified the lack of communication. The mailbox now showed the names of those left behind as E.S. Seidenberger, C.S. Rossmann, and L.S. Rosenthal. The *S*'s were inserted in all three names because ever since the end of August 1938, Jewish women had to show the name Sara as their middle name on all documents, official and otherwise. Men, in turn, had to show their middle name as Israel, regardless of whether they had other middle names or not. These were now also shown on documents such as passports and official notices by any governmental authority. In turn, letters sent by Jewish individuals needed to be signed in that form. Further, since October 1938, passports and papers relating to police registrations had to be turned in and exchanged, having the letter *J* stamped on top in red ink. The change on the mailbox, without which mail would not be delivered, was a simple way of coding Jewish residences, in case occupants were to be arrested, evacuated, or deported.

At first glance, she was elated to find two envelopes this time, having looked inside the empty box for weeks on end. Looking back, there had of course been the perfunctory postcards from her brother, now in New York, with photographs of famous places in Manhattan on the back and a short message on the left-hand front side. These were mainly addressed to their mother to make her feel better, though he assumed that the sparse news would be shared by all three women.

He had written about their new lives in the big city. Eduard had landed a job in a city hospital for room, board, and $25 per month; his wife Eva was working as a nanny in midtown Manhattan for $30 a month; and Stefan, living with an American family, enrolled in a city school to resume his studies and a relatively normal way of life. Occasionally, he wrote a letter to the three of them, in which he tried to be cautiously optimistic about obtaining exit visas for each of them, particularly his sister. He had not been fully successful in finding someone among his family and friends to give them an unconditional affidavit of financial support, the key to obtaining U.S. immigration papers. While this was discouraging, he nevertheless left a glimmer of hope that these might be forthcoming shortly and that he could foresee their leaving Frankfurt later this year.

In an earlier letter, he described the arrival of Lisa aboard the *Bremen*, where he and his Uncle Hugo picked her up at one of the midtown piers on New York's west side. Despite the rough voyage, she had crossed in good spirits and gingerly stepped off the ship with, of all things, her field hockey stick in hand. The uncle, a somewhat dour man even when his humor was at its best, looked at her attire and greeted her saying, "I am pleased to meet you, Lisa, but what do you think? Did you come here to play hockey before you do anything else?"

Fortunately, Eduard had been in contact with the parents of one of Lisa's very good former school friends from Frankfurt who now lived in the Forest Hills section of New York City. The family agreed that they would be delighted to have Lisa live with them until she became established. They had also been kind enough to arrange for a job as a clerk and all-around helper in a bakery owned by their friends so that she was able to earn some money right away and get assimilated into the community. Therefore, after a couple of nights with Eduard's uncle and aunt, she was able to move to a more welcoming environment with her friend and the girl's parents.

He had hoped that this would show his uncle how easy it was to remove her from the support obligation he had previously provided and that he could create the proper environment for Uncle Hugo to at least give another affidavit of support for Carola. While he had not yet gotten acquiescence, he felt that the stage had been set for this to happen soon and that, without making a pain of himself, he could send her the good news soon. Lisa had also written, although in briefer form, about her initial impressions and the new life with her friend's family. She was upbeat, expressing hope that she could join her soon.

All of this, of course, motivated Carola to open the mailbox daily and have extended tolerance for the fact that it really was empty most days. Today's two letters, therefore, were a real boost to her mood, especially because one of them had a Belgian stamp on the envelope, making it obviously from Trudi. The other was postmarked in the city of Frankfurt, looked somewhat official, and had the identifying return address in the upper-left corner stating: H. and B. Notions Company, and the address on Eckenheimer Landstrasse. It was, to say the least, not a welcoming piece of communication.

Carola naturally opened the personal one first, as she wanted to read it without having her mother and Leah hanging over her immediately. She remained outside, leaning against the wall of the building to give her the privacy she needed, and carefully took the airmail-weight stationery out of the envelope as she began to read:

> Liebe Mutti,
>
> I sincerely apologize for not having written to you previously, but since my departure that ominous evening, life has been hectic and eventful so that I have hardly had the energy to gather my thoughts and write to you about all that has happened to both of us.
>
> I arrived in good shape very early in the morning following a relatively uneventful train trip. Crossing the border was somewhat uncomfortable because the train stopped for more than an hour while the officials, together with SA men, went through the train checking everyone's papers in a detailed manner, making derogatory remarks, such as: *Gut dass du raus gehst,Du schlechter*

Jud. Da haben wir Dich los. (It's good that you're leaving you miserable Jew. That way we're rid of you.) They questioned everyone who had a *J* stamped on his or her passport about their ultimate destination and looked at us with a smirk on their faces. Upon arrival, David and I fell into each other's arms, and for the first time since he left, we both had that feeling of regained security that assured us of a new life and a new beginning.

He took me to his living quarters, which consisted of a modest room, sublet in an apartment of friends who are also from Frankfurt and had arrived here about a year earlier. The wonderful thing about belonging to a congregation like the old *Friedberger Anlage*, is the warm spirit and familiarity that make people help one another to get back on their feet and a willingness to share in the network of connections they have established in the meantime. Having had practically no rest all night, I first caught up by sleeping through most of the remaining afternoon.

We shared the evening meal with our landlord's family and took a walk in the neighborhood so that I would get a feel for my surroundings. We are on the *Rue de la Regence*, number eighty-seven, right down the street from the Great Synagogue in Brussels, which is a magnificent building and is also within convenient, short distance for the men who go to early services on weekdays prior to their work. David told me that we would have a religious wedding, small but meeting all the ritual criteria, in this synagogue sometime within the next two weeks.

This indeed took place in the *Beth Midrash* with about fifteen to twenty of his friends and under a real *chuppah.* Although I did not have a wedding dress, I was fortunate enough to have taken several of my regular dresses with me. They said I looked beautiful as I circled him seven times for the *Sheva Broches.* He then took the ring he had given me and put it on my finger with the rabbi declaring us husband and wife.

In view of the modest circumstances, we had a small meal for a lunch set up outside the *Beth Midrash* consisting of the usual herring, other fish delicacies, potatoes and vegetables, schnapps, and home-baked cakes. Again, the spirit of joy and support and positive feelings in a world that seems so bleak for the Jews in Germany, Austria, and perhaps other countries in Europe was most heartening to both of us so that, together, we will be able to face all the dangers that will confront us in the future. When you write back to us, you can now address the envelope as Mr. and Mrs. David Stern; I am so proud and happy to have his name and to be together with the man I love.

He has, in the meantime, found part-time work in a diamond-cutting shop where he grades diamond qualities, a specialty in which he had become quite an expert during the past few years at the store in Frankfurt. I also hope to find work; there are some possibilities, although they are meager, but at least they should help provide us with funds to get back on our feet. I am already exploring what is necessary to get the proper papers and permits for you so that you can follow us within the next few months. As I obtain more detail, I will write to you; hopefully, both of us can then welcome you on the train platform in Brussels and take you home with us to share our new life.

Forgive me in advance if I do not write to you that often, but be assured that you are always in our hearts and our thoughts and that we will never forget what you have done for us during your own difficult life. It is now our turn to do the same for you so that we can have a happy future together. Because we are not far from "home" here in Belgium, perhaps there is hope to dream of a time when we can all return together to where we came from and live there in the way it was intended before the current unhappy events occurred. In the meantime, both David and I send you our greatest love. We hope you will share this letter with Grandma and Leah of whom we also think all the time and for whom we will try to do the same.

Yours for always, from David and me,
Your daughter, Trudi

With tears in her eyes and a happy smile on her face, Carola opened the front door and practically skipped up to the apartment on the third floor. She entered and shouted to both Esther and Leah.

"Look what I have here. Both of you, put on your glasses and start reading. This is such wonderful news. It's the best letter we've all had for months. Now that spring is here and for us there's some hope in the air, I think we should open the windows and try to get rid of all that depression and sadness in this house. Read, read, read while I look at this letter from our 'robbers' to see what's on their miserable minds."

She then opened the H&B letter, which had been addressed to Frau Carola Sara Rossmann, and read it with somber and increasing consternation.

Sehr geehrte Frau Rossmann:

We are writing to you out of necessity to let you know of important changes we need to make to the contract you signed with us, voluntarily, at the beginning of 1936 in order to transfer the former Rossmann Notions business to its now successor owners for the purpose of restoring its activities and rescuing it from certain failure.

Despite our extreme efforts to do so, which has caused us to take reductions in salary as well as working day and night at least six days a week, our hard work has to date resulted in only moderate improvement. Its future as a viable operation is, therefore, by no means assured. It seems that by the time your late husband became ill and was no longer able to fulfill his duties as general manager, sales had been run down to such an extent that it was not easy to pay for the overhead that still existed. Despite that reality, he, and then after his death you, continued to take salary and profit out of the business that reduced its working capital and forced corresponding reduction of inventories to the point where the ability to service our customers was seriously handicapped.

You were aware of these problems as a result of your weekly meetings with Miss Elizabeth Breitenbach. However, you ignored the problems in order to satisfy your personal needs at the time. Additionally, our customers whom I pursued vigorously and with whom I tried to work to restore their sales volumes month after month had either lost confidence in our ability to remain solvent or, many of them, having been in Jewish hands, were also following selfish and perhaps illegal business practices at the expense of maintaining their operations. All of this resulted in our reduced ability to furnish products for the needs of German workers and the military and to maintain the quality and quantity of garments needed at this urgent time.

In order to meet our obligations to the Third Reich and to make good on some of the damage that was done by the past Jewish ownership, we must inform you that, having paid you the purchase price in installments at the rate of one hundred Reichsmarks per month for the last twenty-seven months, we are unable to continue these payments until we have caught up on all our new obligations. Therefore, we are suspending all payments until such time as there is enough profit to resume them.

We are sorry to impart such information at this time, but we are certain that you understand the situation we are facing. We will be in touch with you from time to time to let you know our progress in this regard and hope that sometime in the future we can resume our monthly sums. If you wish to discuss that with us, please do not hesitate to contact us. However, please be advised that we will do this only in the presence of a Representative of the Office of Jewish Affairs, a branch of the Gestapo here in Frankfurt.

Hochachtungsvoll and with Heil Hitler,
Alfred Hempel and Elizabeth Breitenbach
Co-owners

Carola blanched and slumped at the table. Gone was the momentary ebullience that the letter from her daughter produced; Esther and Leah, having finished reading Trudi's letter, looked up at her in anxious expectation.

"Well, the Lord giveth, and the Lord taketh away. I have just read what the two *ganovim* (thieves) wrote me. In essence, they have shut off our last source of funds—the monthly payments they owe me from the sale of the business they forced on me. There does not seem to be any way to appeal this theft or to talk to anyone for mediation without getting into much more trouble at the same time. I don't know what to do, and I'll have to think about it during the next few days. Perhaps

I should talk to our lawyer, Mr. Offenbach, but as a Jew in our dying community, I doubt that there is any chance for restitution. Here is the letter; you read it."

Carola got up from the table, left the two elderly women with their woeful looks and shaking heads, and quietly went into her room and closed the door behind her. She lay down on the bed, staring at the ceiling, her face paralyzed. After awhile, she fell into a deep sleep for the rest of the afternoon.

Around dinnertime she got up quietly, went into the kitchen, started boiling the usual old potatoes, opened a can of peas, and cut up a little bit of Edam cheese that was left in the ice box. The two women were also just getting up after having taken a nap, following a morning of hapless discussion about where the three of them were going to go from here. The only answer for the moment was to go back to the Jewish Welfare Agency and request more support, which they knew would be a slow process, even if they were able to succeed in getting some help in the end.

After the potatoes were boiled and peeled, they were put back in the pot, covered, and shaken to break them up into a dry mealy mush—an old family or perhaps Frankfurt custom which made them taste worse. Perhaps it stemmed from the old days of making mashed potatoes when butter was still available, or perhaps it made it easier to eat after teeth had long left the elderly mouths. They couldn't even afford more than quarter of a pound of margarine per week, and the week's ration had already been used up. They ate in silence, none of them daring to ask the other if they had thought up any solutions for approaches to an apparently insoluble problem. There was no one left in the family to ask for loans, money, or other help, except perhaps Eva's mother, who was living in Düsseldorf, not having left Germany as yet, and likely in better financial shape than the three of them had been left. Carola set out to write a letter on some stationery they had left over as a long-shot hope that some temporary rescue might happen against all odds.

Ten days later, a fortuitous encounter took place which, at least in the short term, resulted in some remediation of a seemingly hopeless situation. Carola was again returning from a short shopping excursion with more of the same perpetual potatoes, a cauliflower, and some string beans in her shopping net. As she entered back into the house, opening the front door with her key, the door was pulled open, helped on the inside by someone coming out. She was surprised as she faced Frau Ingeborg Schmidt, her upstairs neighbor who smiled at her as she, in turn, was going out for her daily shopping.

"Ah, Frau Rossmann, I am so glad to see you. I have something to talk over with you that might be of interest. I wonder if you would like to join me for a cup of coffee and a piece of cake at, say, three o'clock?"

"But, of course, Frau Schmidt. I would love to do that and perhaps get caught up on some of the things that are happening around the city. Thank you for your kind invitation."

Carola could hardly wait until the appointed time. She did not tell her mother and Leah, knowing that they would take an afternoon nap, and she did not want to explain herself, going to spend some time with the *goy* upstairs. Promptly at three o'clock, she rang Frau Schmidt's bell and was led into the apartment's parlor, where she had set up a small round table with two cups, plates, and silverware. She had just been in the process of bringing in the coffee pot from the kitchen. It smelled delicious and seemed to be a much better grade than the one Carola had bought and which she knew was extended with malt and other fillers.

After pouring coffee, passing the milk and sugar, and serving her a small piece of yeast cake, Frau Schmidt got started on her view of the events that occurred the night of November 9.

"Frau Rossmann," she said in a semiconfidential, lowered voice, seemingly to exclude nonexistent people within earshot who might overhear. "I know that life for you Jews has not been easy in the past few months. The events of the Kristallnacht were simply terrible, and I don't understand how we good Germans could stand for such things that the Nazis did to you. But what can we, as ordinary citizens, do against such violence? Nothing. We have to obey and keep our mouths shut.

"I felt so terrible when I saw all the broken window panes, the men being arrested and taken away, and your synagogues burned. I am so glad that the West End synagogue right here in the area was not destroyed, even though the interior seemed to have been burned out. The neighbors on *Freiherr vom Stein, Friedrich,* and *Altkonig Strassen* would have lost their apartments if the fire department had permitted the flames to get out of control, and that would have been tragic for people who have lived on those streets for many, many years.

"I know that a number of Jewish families have emigrated from there over the past year or so. In a way, they were very fortunate to have escaped from those horrors, and besides, they were very smart to leave. But I think you would agree that it would not have been fair to their Gentile neighbors to let those apartments go up in flames."

Carola listened without comment. The self pitying hostility of Ingeborg's remarks regarding Jews having been smart to leave angered her to the point where she was ready to get up to end this travesty. Did she really know about Carola's and the others' circumstances of being trapped in Germany against their wishes?

Just then, Frau Schmidt got to the point. "Well, the reason I wanted to get together with you, Frau Rossmann, is that I wanted to tell you of an opportunity that exists for you with a good friend of mine, Ursula Schaefer, who might have some work for you and, therefore, lets you earn some pay. Ursula is the branch manager of the *Witwe Hassan* coffee store located at the Opernplatz. You have probably gone by it many times; they have the best coffee in the city because of their excellent location and the many customers that go out of their way to buy there. They are one of the few stores that still sell unground beans, which, of course, is the best way to preserve their freshness, and which I buy all the time. I'm sure that you can taste that quality in the coffee we are having right now."

"Yes, I can certainly taste the difference, Frau Schmidt. It is amazing how good this coffee tastes; it is a totally different drink, and it's like what we used to have on Saturday afternoons only in the, I might say, good old days." Carola looked at her with cold mistrust after her harangue with the anti-Semitic overtones as she was sitting in the comfort of her worn-out Biedermeier living room.

Ingeborg bore on. "I must absolutely agree with you, Frau Rossmann. Here is a chance for you; Ursula needs some more help at this time. She has one employee, and I used to work there part time to help out at the busy times during the day. She would like another full-time worker but cannot afford to pay very much. I thought of you because you might be able to take the job at a modest salary and could make an arrangement with her—a little bit under the table, as they say, so she can save the social costs for benefits to which you would not be entitled in any case.

"I know as a Jew you cannot easily find a regular position because of the new regulations since the assassination of Herr vom Rath in Paris. You do not look Jewish, you know. In fact, you look more like one of us with your blondish hair and your non-Jewish face and could easily pass as an Aryan. Take a look in the mirror over the sofa. Don't you agree?" Carola rose to look at herself. She had to agree that Frau Schmidt was right.

"If you are interested in having a position there—it is so close to this house that you can walk—I would be happy to let her know so you can meet. What do you think?"

Carola was stunned by the unexpected turn this invitation had taken, but she was also elated that this might be a chance to earn a salary. It would also get her out of the house, where the problems had become increasingly depressing as the financial pressure had become nearly unbearable.

"Well, Frau Schmidt," she said, smiling, "I would be delighted to meet with Ursula Schaefer. It would certainly help our financial situation. We are not able to leave the country, on the one hand, and not able to support ourselves on the other. So, I very much appreciate your concern and kindness in letting me know about this opportunity. Could you set up an appointment for me at an early moment?"

Frau Schmidt was obviously prepared to follow up immediately as this must all have been set up with her friend ahead of time. She turned, reached for the telephone at her side table, dialed, and called up the store.

"Ursula, I am so glad you are in. I have some good news to report to you. My friend and I have spoken about you. She and I are currently having afternoon coffee in my parlor. She is most interested in the subject of the conversation you and I have had and would like to come and meet you whenever it is convenient. Would you like Carola to come over one afternoon this week for a good visit and discussion?"

The following Thursday was suggested as a meeting, late in the afternoon, after the other employee had left. Frau Schmidt made another minute of small talk with the woman on the other end, said goodbye, and then hung up.

"Well, Frau Rossmann, I am very happy for you, and I am glad you have such a positive attitude. I think this will be good for both of you and hopefully will relieve some of the dire need in which you obviously find yourself."

After that, Frau Schmidt apparently did not want to spend much more time on matters that weren't strictly business. She stood up.

"Well, I won't hold you up anymore," she said. "So I will let you go back to your mother and her companion. Give them my best regards."

Carola shook hands quickly, went out through the front door, and entered her own apartment on the floor below. She was reviewing rapidly in her own mind the proposition she had been made and her reaction to what might be in store for her, especially with the sub-rosa conditions laid out for her as a Jew.

When she came back into their own apartment, she found Esther and Leah sitting at the dining room table, having a cup of reheated coffee to wake up from their afternoon rest. Carola sat down, somewhat flush with the excitement of the unexpected conversation she had just had with Ingeborg Schmidt. She told the older women the details of her visit and the meeting she was to have the following Thursday with the Witwe Hassan branch manager, Ursula Schaefer.

If Esther and Leah felt any excitement about the story and what was about to happen, considering the potential life-saving aspect of the support that a job might spell out, they did not show it in their faces or in any animation of the questions that were to follow. Esther's face showed both the wisdom and the wariness of old age, and her tired wrinkles and drooping eyelids reflected the many disappointments she had experienced during the past decade of non-stop *schlamazel.* She reacted with her usual, skeptical equanimity.

"Carola," she said in a weary voice, "your encounter with Frau Schmidt certainly leads to an unexpected turn of events, and for all I know, this might be good for the three of us. However, don't forget that when our friend from upstairs approaches you like that and takes an obviously well thought-out initiative, it must be to her friend's advantage in the long run. I greatly doubt that these two women are doing this out of the goodness of their hearts and that they are helping us more than themselves."

Her voice became stronger and more insistent as she proceeded. "So when you go to the store next Thursday, just beware of anything that sounds too much in your favor and not to that of Frau Schaefer. Also, please be sure that you are not getting into anything which sounds or smells as if it were illegal, no matter how little that may be.

"We really don't want to get into any trouble with the authorities and should draw as little attention to ourselves as possible because, as you know, even the slightest infraction of regulations that might exist would be treated with an extra measure of harshness when Jewish people are involved. We just can't take that chance, especially when we, or at least you, are waiting for emigration papers which would be withdrawn at the slightest suspicion involving any irregularities. Also, my dear, remember that anything under the table, in alliance with that Ursula, is bound to be unholy, and the consequences would be a lot more severe for you than they would be for her."

Leah nodded her head in strong agreement. "I completely agree with your mother. Just remember that she has been through a lot in her lifetime and that she is an excellent judge of human nature. When in doubt, trust no one except your own good instincts. Also be sure that you don't jump into anything just because it might help the three of us stave off our desperate situation. It's more important that, if indeed there is a decent opportunity here, it's good for you and that you should not sacrifice your integrity in any way for the sake of your mother and me."

"I well understand that," replied Carola with a hint of annoyance in her voice to indicate that she would rather have been encouraged and receive a boost of her morale than be warned with a bit of condescension, as if she, herself, were still an innocent child that had not had her own share of disappointments and betrayals.

"Well, we'll see what happens," she continued. "I guess there's no harm or danger in talking and then evaluating what the chances are to improve our lot once I have the whole story."

She quietly cleared the cups, taking them to the kitchen, and slowly began to look around to see what she could prepare for an early supper. She found a newspaper from the previous day, which she had picked up from a public wastebasket at the corner of the street when she walked outside earlier. She began reading it, feigning an intense interest but really trying to calm herself after what was an upsetting little episode to which she received an emotionally unsupportive response.

After she calmed down, she helped prepare the modest evening meal and afterward retired early to think about the prospect of her new opportunity. Despite her utter exhaustion, which under different circumstances would have caused her to fall asleep immediately, she was kept awake by something that Frau Schmidt had said, which resonated strongly with her as she went over and over the details of that fateful conversation. She had clearly heard this sentence and repeated it to herself over and over again. "However, you do not look Jewish, Frau Rossmann. In fact, you look more like one of us. With your blondish hair and your non-Jewish face, you could easily pass for an Aryan."

It had never occurred to her that the aspect of "passing" might have been a key to hiding "*en pleine vue*"—disappearing in broad daylight—and she began to go over in her own mind what this might mean to her in the future. She realized the great importance that the Nazi Germans assigned to appearance and the drastic steps they had taken in using facial and bodily features as one of the weapons for ostracizing, vilifying, demonizing, and thereby isolating the Jewish population from the Gentile world.

In a short period of years, they had caused a subconscious revulsion in the minds of citizens with the greatest good will and a sense of fairness they largely had prior to 1933. In just six years, they had achieved alienating the general population with the weapon of physical appearance, from the Jews among their midst who had been there for hundreds of years living among their fellow Frankfurt inhabitants. Yes, there had not been much freedom in their daily lives for the first seven hundred years of their residence in the city and the German territories.

However, in the effort to depict them as monsters by the skilled use of vicious caricatures, they had raised the Jewish physical representation to the fine art of the devil in the newspaper—*Der Stuermer*, Julius Streicher's creation. The paper's artists had honed their poisonous drawings with an evil skill since 1933. Now appearing regularly on every newsstand in Germany, not even those with the kindest of attitudes were able to ignore looking at twisted bodies, week after week after week. The caricatures focused on exaggerated large noses, ears, feet, and other extremities. It was not just the size but also the distortions, wrinkles, ugly necks, and evil-looking faces, combined with a fat body, overfed belly, and crooked bone structures that heightened revulsion of the onlooker. These were combined with a shuffling gait, a bent-over back, a sneering laugh, and an evil-looking eye to give the whole image an ugly, twisted, and bent-out-of-shape appearance. The gruesome depictions were reinforced by storylines that alternated between cheating, tax evasion, smuggling, usury, the implication of an international conspiracy by secret communication (Yiddish), false flattery, fawning, dissembling, having their hands in the till, and exploiting the poor Aryan workers and innocent maidens.

The blood libel myth—that is, the killing of an innocent child, draining him of his blood, and using that as the liquid for baking *matzoh* around Passover/Easter—made that devilish depiction into a gruesome horror story. Quotations from the long ago, well discredited forgery *Protocols of the Elders of Zion*, which proposed to have uncovered a basis for an international conspiracy of world domination by sinister Jewish powers, added to the hideous defamation. When the caricature wore a top hat, looked at an oversized gold watch, and had flashing diamonds on his fingers, he was portrayed as a rich carpetbagger, robbing the countryside as he walked from land to land committing his criminal acts. It was an ugly and disgusting continuum of publication that left its mark on everyone that viewed the cartoons as the Nazi government served to tear loose the Jewish community from the citizenry at large.

Pictorial anti-Semitism had been used before for a number of years. In fact, the famous alphabet in rhyme and cartoon by Wilhelm Busch in the late nineteenth century inculcated the younger readers as they went through each letter and finally got to the letter *Z*. The rhyme ended in: *Die Zwiebel ist des Juden's Speise* (the onion is the Jew's food). The level of viciousness of Streicher's publication, after only six years, had certainly achieved its desired effect more quickly. In fact, it was even corrosive on the Jewish community itself, who, because of these attacks, suffered from a loss of self-esteem and a sense of shame. This, along with the bad, self-deprecating jokes, led to Jewish people wanting to shrink their noses and hide other manifestations of a physically inferior appearance in the idealized Nordic sense. In one way, the community fought this by encouraging sports activities to stress physical appearance, grace, and body culture. However, it was difficult to overcome the illustrations of rape and ravishment of blond, innocent maidens with horrified faces who succumbed as victims of the sneering monsters.

Jews with any semblance of exaggerated features, therefore, wanted to hide. They did not want to rock the boat; they wore inconspicuous clothing and began to avoid even a minimum of exposure. They tried to look as much like German Gentiles as possible, covering up kinky hair with upside down flower pot hats and using other misguided attempts at modesty in an attempt to blend in with the masses. All of this, of course, was to no avail and reinforced both the timidity of those Jews that were still stuck in the country, waiting to escape, as well as the hostility with which the now post-Kristallnacht society regarded its non-Aryan remnant.

As Carola lay awake, remembering Frau Schmidt's comments about passing as an Aryan, she smiled somewhat wistfully at the thought. "Could I really walk publicly through the streets of Frankfurt, pretending to be an Aryan? Could I actually work in a public *Deutsches Geschaeft* store without raising the hackles of the most Nazified customer? Could I actually disappear *en pleine vue*? Would my Aryan appearance and unfashionable old clothing transform me into one of the Gentile masses? Could I even escape from this national prison to be free in Belgium, for example, even if just with the clothes on my back?"

But her reflections soon gave way to the reality that she had a passport with the *J* stamped all over it, that she was registered at the police station right across the street, and that she was a known member of the Jewish community registered and duly recorded in a country where records were a national bureaucratic obsession.

In other words, she was neither anonymous nor invisible. The only thing that was invisible was the leash she was on. She would not actually have the opportunity to "slide beneath the surface" and disappear because of her physical appearance. As she reviewed the core of her being during this basic stream of consciousness, she knew that although she perceived herself as, yes, perhaps having an Aryan face, she was living in a non-Aryan body, which, in turn and above all, contained a Jewish soul. This ultimate self-identification, despite the foreboding of tragic consequences it could entail, gave her a strange comfort of such fundamental value that it resolved the ambivalence she had raised in a tempting moment. It also quieted her restlessness and made her fall asleep at last.

The following Thursday she left the house at 4:30 in the afternoon, and arriving near the store fifteen to twenty minutes early, she slowly circled the opera house across the street, making sure to arrive at the front door exactly at five o'clock. Realizing the obsession most people had with punctuality as a virtue in and of itself, as well as a sign of dependability and respect, she entered with a certain cheery assertiveness and shook hands with Frau Branch Manager Ursula Schaefer. Frau Schaefer was a well groomed, tall woman at the end of her fifties, smartly dressed in business garb but careful not to exceed her customers in the quality of her outfit. The other woman clerk had indeed left for the day, and as the manager locked the front door signaling the end of business hours, she led Carola into the curtained-off back room and asked her, in a friendly manner, to have a seat at the long table. She offered Carola a cup of coffee before proceeding to matters at hand.

"Thank you so much for being on time," she said. "I must tell you, I really appreciate your punctuality; it says something about the character of a person and indicates respect for keeping one's word. As Frau Schmidt has told you, I am interested in having an additional full-time employee at the Witwe Hassan who is reliable and, while under my supervision, can also, at times, independently serve my customers to their satisfaction so that they keep coming back on a regular basis.

"As you must know, we have been here for many years and have a steady following. Because I am sometimes called away, either to the management office or for other reasons, I am looking for a mature person, rather than a young thing in her twenties who might not be quite as reliable." Looking Carola over as she spoke, she seemed to confirm the type of appearance she was seeking. "As you must also know as a housewife, coffee is neither a single item nor is it a simple product. In these days of rationing and shortages, it is no longer possible for our company to get the best coffee from all over the world. Most grades today are extended with roasted malt or other fillers. That makes the supply last longer and reduces prices to where more customers can still afford it without having to reuse the boiled grounds several times over.

"We here are one of the few stores left in the city of Frankfurt where the customer can still buy nonextended and whole coffee beans. These are now very expensive, perhaps three times the price of the extended grades and five times as expensive as the economy package. The type of clientele that can still afford to pay that amount of money is largely either well-to-do businessmen, party functionaries, or perhaps retirees with enough money so they can buy the very best."

She refilled Carola's cup as well as her own. "I know, of course, Frau Rossmann, that you are Jewish. You can imagine, I once had many Jewish customers here in the West End who have now mainly emigrated, which is too bad. Ingeborg has spoken highly of your family, and I am surprised that you are still here. You'll have to fill me in on the details of this some day, if you decide to come to work for me.

"As you also know, the new regulations state that I am not supposed to hire Jews in my establishment. Because I cannot afford to pay very much, it was my feeling that, if I bend the regulations slightly and do have a Jewish woman come to work here, her appearance has to be inconspicuous so as not to arouse any suspicions or bad feelings. I think on this point you fill the bill very nicely, Frau Rossmann." She smiled with approval and pleasure at the good judgment her friend Ingeborg had shown in this regard.

"But," she continued, "before I tell you about my conditions for your employment, I would like to hear some more about your family background and your present status." She reached over to the coffee maker. "Will you have another cup, Frau Rossmann? It's pure and unextended, you know. That's one of our fringe benefits here."

"Thank you, yes, Frau Schaefer," Carola replied. "I would very much like another cup. It is like nothing I've had in many years; so now let me tell you about myself." It was her third cup, but she could not resist the delicious brew.

"First, I am forty-nine years old, and like the Witwe Hassan, I am also a widow. My husband died of a serious kidney disease four years ago after a marriage of twenty-two years. We had two daughters who are now nineteen and twenty-three years of age and who emigrated recently, the younger one to America and the older one to Belgium, where she now lives with her husband.

"The Rossmann family owned a well-respected notions business, which my husband managed. After his death I, in turn, supervised and ran the operation. A little more than two years ago, my remaining two employees made me an offer which I could not refuse, due to the fact that as a Jewish owned company, we were being boycotted by a lot of our customers that had become Aryanized. For the time being, it has kept the three of us remaining here with our heads above water." She did not go into the fact that these payments were now discontinued in order not to lose the little bit of negotiating leverage that she felt she still had.

"Some two years ago, my brother, who is a physician, emigrated to the United States to start a new life outside Germany with his family. They left only two months before Kristallnacht and were very fortunate to have escaped the misery that has befallen the entire remaining Jewish community since then.

"You may know that in most countries which still accept any émigrés at all, it is vital that they receive assurances of support by someone in that country so that the new immigrants do not become public charges to that nation's government. The reason why almost half the prior, original Jewish population in Frankfurt is still living here is that it has been difficult for many of them, including ourselves, to obtain such assurances.

"We do have an uncle living in New York—that famous uncle in America that so many people dream about. Having given affidavits to the three members of my brother's family, as well as to my daughter, he has now run out of financial capacity to make such further commitments. My brother has assured the three of us remaining that he is working on this problem and that eventually we will be able to follow them to the United States. So you can see, we are trapped here, hopefully temporarily, but trapped nevertheless because we cannot leave.

"On the other hand, particularly after the ninth of November, the government is making every effort, now in a very brutal way, to make us emigrate. By now I am sure the entire Jewish community is trying to satisfy the regime's wish that they leave Germany as quickly as possible. Therefore, if I work for you, you must realize that the day may come when I, too, will leave. I am sure you understand." She realized that this was a lot to tell Frau Schaefer at their first meeting. However, she decided to get it all out so that there would be no surprises for her future boss.

"Frau Rossmann, I do understand completely, and I must say that I really appreciate very much how forthright you have been in telling me your unhappy story in such great detail. In the meantime, let me tell you what I have in mind and what the conditions are under which you could work with me here. First of all, I have told you that I must bend the rules somewhat because it is officially forbidden to hire Jewish persons in an establishment such as ours. Therefore, our arrangement must be confidential, and your employment should not show on any of the records I have to submit to the authorities. Officially, I do not know that you are a Jew. In fact, we must pretend that you are a distant relative of mine and have come in to help me out."

The wink in her eye made her intentions clear. "I am not prepared to pay you the normal salary for this job because that would also include social costs and other fringe benefits that would have to be recorded. I will pay you only in cash because, again, I do not wish to have any records of checks or other written material. I am offering to pay you thirty Reichsmarks per week for working here from Monday to Friday, nine o'clock in the morning to five o'clock in the afternoon with a short lunch break, varying in time at my convenience so that the front counter is covered continuously.

"There would be three of us here, including myself and a colleague whose name is Gisela Schultheiss whom you will meet when you start. She is a regular employee, a nice married woman in her thirties with a young husband who is now in the *Wehrmacht*. You must also know that discussion of these matters with her is strictly forbidden as is your background and present status. She will, of course, be very curious and wish to ask you a lot of questions, particularly when I am out of the store. However, you must devise your own way of evading her because her discovery of your Jewishness will lead to your immediate dismissal and complete denial on my part.

"This would produce a lot of difficulty for you, so please be very careful to guard our mutual little secret to the utmost. If you accept these simple conditions, I would be happy to get you started this coming

Monday morning. I will teach you the complexities of the coffee field and will introduce you to my oldest and most trustworthy customers as my second cousin. I think you have the maturity to go along with our story. I hope we fully understand each other. So, let me ask you now whether you are willing to accept these conditions and if you could start this coming week. I really don't think it is too complex to come up with a yes or a no, so tell me how you feel about the opportunity."

Carola thought for a moment, letting a quick interval of silence go by to indicate the seriousness of her contemplation on a decision she had already made before she ever walked through the door.

"Frau Schaefer," she replied, "I have thought about your proposition as quickly as I could under these difficult circumstances while you were finishing your explanations. I appreciate your offer and realize what you're trying to accomplish. In sum and substance, I will fully trust your judgment in this matter and agree to these conditions and to the confidentiality that is involved. If my appearance is satisfactory and gives both of us the cover we need against the consequences of employment violations, then you can depend on me not to give away our secret. So, if we can shake hands on our arrangement, I will now leave you to close up and be here on Monday morning."

They shook hands. Frau Schaefer seemed happy having her future employee, an obviously intelligent and mature woman, at a bargain rate. She had taken a chance, particularly with Gisela around, because she would be curious to find out as much as she could. She was, therefore, at some unnecessary risk because she really did not need to have a non-Aryan salesperson any longer for the sake of making her Jewish customers more comfortable, but Frau Schaefer never could resist a bargain.

Carola gave a wistful smile, quickly turned, and left for the walk home. She knew she had also taken a chance. There were a number of things involved that were sub-rosa and, if discovered, could lead to a lot of trouble. She also knew that her elders at home would not be too pleased but would have to accept what she had committed to. No matter how different and perhaps repulsive that might ultimately turn out to be to her, she went home at full stride bracing herself against the onslaught of *Miesmacherei* (negativism) she knew she would have to face.

As was her usual custom when she got home, Carola once again looked into the mailbox for the rare mail that would bring news, either good or bad. This time it was a letter with a postmark from Düsseldorf that, she realized, must have come from her sister-in-law's mother, Mathilde Auerbach. Without opening it outside the apartment, she briskly opened the door and called out a fairly cheerful hello. A sparse supper was already set out, and the two women had just begun to unfold their napkins.

"Well, how was everything at the Witwe Hassan?" Esther asked, smiling. "Did she give you the keys and say, 'Here is the store, make yourself a good living by selling a mountain of coffee'?"

"Well, almost," replied Carola in a quick uptake of the unexpected humor. "Let me wash up and come to the table. I'll tell you all about my meeting."

She quickly did so and began on the same humorous note as before.

"Well, let me tell you the most important part first. When I came into the store, she offered me the most wonderful cup of coffee I have had in the past five years. This and a couple of refills put me in the best of all moods, and after a thorough discussion of my background and her needs, she deigned to offer me a full-time job at the ridiculous sum of thirty Reichsmarks per week. With only minimal objection, in order not to be a spoil sport, I accepted the job because I figured that I would make up the difference in the liters of coffee I would drink every day. While the salary does not exactly solve our problem, it does take some of the desperation out of our daily needs. We talked about confidentiality, and I think that because both of us would end up in serious trouble, this arrangement should work. I am starting Monday morning."

A long silence followed. Carola used the opportunity of that thoughtful pause.

"Look what I found in the mailbox when I came in," she announced. A letter came back from Düsseldorf. It must be from Eva's mother in response to the one I sent her not too long ago. Let's see what it says."

With that, she carefully opened the envelope with the knife that was part of her table setting, and immediately read it out loud.

My dear Carola,

Thank you so much for your recent letter, which I was very glad to receive, despite all the unhappy news it contained. These must be the most difficult days that the three of you who were left behind have ever faced. However, you must never lose heart and hope as long as members of your family are working on the task of getting you the necessary documents to leave Frankfurt as quickly as possible.

My own situation has now been resolved, and I am glad that I heard from you before my departure in the next two weeks for London, where I will live with my daughter and son-in-law. I am sure it will be in better circumstances away from here in Düsseldorf. I now have my papers all in order to leave and to make the short trip to England. Because I have visited them before, I am familiar with my future living situation, and I anticipate it with great pleasure. What is not so pleasant is that I have recently completed the sale of our family business, the department store which my husband and his brothers managed during their lifetimes. Since they each passed away between 1932 and 1937, you must know that as a member of our managing board, I had been involved in the operation for some time. However, because I know little about all of these things, our general manager has been handling the day-to-day matters for me.

About six months ago, he approached me with the proposal to buy the firm, along with three other investors whom he has brought in, but he assured me that I would have to deal only with him and not with people that are unfamiliar to me. Once I started my negotiations with him, however, I learned of another, entirely different and unpleasant side of his personality, and it became both frustrating and very upsetting to meet with him time after time. The net result and final outcome, particularly in view of the current, strong Aryanization policy of the government—and then on top of all that the November 9 pogrom—was that I was forced to sell our holdings for about 5 percent of their fair value. To make matters even worse, it had to be an installment sale, wherein I will receive about 20 percent of the total amount of money every year and will not see the final, small total sum until 1944. That would be barely enough for me to live through those years considering all the expenses I have, and I am, therefore, very fortunate to be able to emigrate and enjoy the support of my children.

In the meantime, however, because I am leaving so soon, I am enclosing a postal check in the amount of five hundred Reichsmarks, hoping that this will be of some help to you, although probably not for a long period. With all the other closing expenses and additional unknown costs, I'm sorry to say that this is all I can afford at this critical time and realize that it is not much to look forward to. I hope the Jewish Community Welfare Office has some funds available for its members, as I have recently read in the newspapers, and might pick up the costs of supporting you shortly.

I will write to you once I am settled in London and hope you will have the chance to reply. Because we have the basic connection through our married children, we should keep in touch, regardless of what happens next. Perhaps things will change in the not-too-distant future so that I can return someday, and we can all resume the lives we had prior to the unhappy change in our situation. In the meantime, I bid you goodbye and hope you will live in safety, although perhaps not in the comfort you might have been used to before.

With my deep affection, I am your
Mathilde Auerbach

Carola joined Esther and Leah in silence on any response to Mathilde's letter. She was deeply engrossed in her own thoughts. First she was grateful that a life preserver had been sent to them in the form of the five hundred Reichsmarks amount. Without daring to comment, she was a little disappointed that a woman whom they perceived to be of significant wealth was able to part only with an amount that would not last longer than a few months. Nevertheless, they strongly resisted criticizing Mathilde to the others in that they realized they did not know her exact circumstances and what might have been taken from her since they last had better information.

After all, especially Carola, who had her own experience with a forced sale, knew how painful that was and how unpredictable the costs were that might have been involved. She could well imagine that the bigger the business, the worse the conditions might be that would be offered to the owner. On the other hand, she realized that with the large asset the Auerbach family originally held, the pitiful amount of 5 percent would still most likely be a six-figure value. She had no idea whether Mathilde could transfer some of it out of the country so that she had something to contribute to her daughter's household. At any rate, the answer could also have been "regretfully, no," and their misfortune could have been more immediate than the short few months this amount would give them.

Coming out of her own thoughts, Esther said to the others, "I am sure the three of us all had similar reactions to this letter as you read it to us, Carola. However, we must ultimately be grateful that we have been given a temporary reprieve from the terrible need in which we have found ourselves. I must say that even though I feel you have not adequately thought about the risk you are taking with your new job and probably have not told us about all the details, the money you will earn will certainly stave off abject poverty for a while."

Now that she reminded herself about the thirty Reichsmarks per week, Esther just shook her head in visible pain muttering under her breath, "That miserable *goy* taking such advantage of my daughter just because we are Jews and have no choice in the matter."

Carola, for her part, was relieved that a possible confrontation had been defused by the unhappy realities facing them and so the matter of starting on Monday morning had been settled.

6 COFFEE

Carola rose early on Monday in anticipation of the first full day of her new work. She was both a little nervous and excited about all the things she anticipated learning and the interactions she would have with lots of people she had never been exposed to before. In a clear "up" mood, she put on a tailored white blouse and simple blue skirt, which she regarded as a modest means of dress for a likely more fashionable clientele. She left the house after a small breakfast and with an assertive step marched rapidly to the *Opernplatz.*

Carola was in front of the Witwe Hassan window at 8:50 AM peering through the glass door whose brass frame was polished once a week to receive its affluent customers on a Monday morning. At first she thought about waiting for the others to arrive. However, as she tried the door, she realized that Ursula Schaefer had already arrived and was inside with lights on only in the back room. She, therefore, entered and greeted her cheerfully.

"I thought I would come a little early to learn my way around the new surroundings," Carola said. "I am prepared to start learning as quickly as possible so that I can be useful very soon in waiting on the customers. I hope you have had a pleasant weekend."

With that Frau Schaefer poured her a cup of coffee from the first batch of the day she had prepared only some twenty minutes earlier.

"Carola, if I may call you that, welcome. I'm so glad you did come a little early so I can show you around before my early morning regulars arrive and we get tied up. If that happens while we are talking, by the way, I would suggest that you just stick with me and observe as I fill their orders and ring up the cash register. You will see that with the number of grades and coffee types we have here it will take some time for you to familiarize yourself with what's in the different containers."

Carola was excited about entering this new world of coffee. It will be strange and different, she thought, but the prospect of acquiring a new skill would be stimulating and a great distraction from the "down" atmosphere sitting around the apartment.

As they were talking, and before Ursula could begin to get into the details of everything in the store, Gisela Schultheiss entered at precisely 9:00 AM and headed straight for the backroom. Because she had not been told anything about an imminently new employee and colleague, she was a little taken aback.

Frau Schaefer said, "Good morning, Gisela, I hope you had a pleasant and restful weekend. I would like to introduce you to your new colleague about whom, I'm sorry to say, I was unable to tell you last week. Please meet Carola Rossmann, who is starting with us today and whom I will be familiarizing with the many details of how we work here.

"Carola, this is Frau Gisela Schultheiss who has been with me for the past four years. She is a wonderful person and knows this business now practically inside and out. I am certain that the two of you will get along very well and that you, Gisela, will be an excellent teacher for you, Frau Rossmann, as you have been to others working with us here before. May I suggest that you dispense with formalities and you just make it Gisela and Carola right away so that there is no hesitancy when you two communicate with each other?"

"I am pleased to meet you, Frau—or rather, Carola—and I'm delighted to have your company and assistance in our store," Gisela replied. "It will also be a great pleasure to explain how we operate here so that we can both give our clients the fine service this establishment is known for."

Carola gave her the friendliest smile she could muster under these unaccustomed circumstances and replied in kind.

"It is a pleasure to meet you, too, Gisela. I am sure we will get to know each other well within a short time, working side-by-side. I will try to be a good student and gain by your experience as quickly as possible so I can help you serve customers and do the other tasks we have throughout the shop. Don't hesitate to correct any mistakes I might make even if it is in front of the customer. I want to do the best I can as quickly as possible."

Carola quickly sized up Gisela to be an agreeable person with a pleasant personality, which she projected in her warm voice. She was a large, good-looking woman with country features, somewhat on the coarse side, yet with a big heart and generous disposition that made her suitable for the strictly Aryan crowd. Tall and ample in chest, she had blond hair, but her dark roots gave away the fact that the light color was post-added rather than originally her own before it was smartly braided, rolled, and pinned on top of her head. This, together with a dress, suggesting but not being a dirndl creation, conveyed the appearance of a nice, Nordic woman in the idealized German mode. She didn't know whether Ursula had picked her, Carola, as the new employee in contrast to this poster child of the Nazi movement or whether she did not pay that much attention to such physical contrasts. On second thought, she felt that the branch manager paid attention to all details that her self-serving interests appeared to be pursuing at all times.

"Well, Gisela, help yourself to a cup of coffee. I would appreciate if you would hold down the 'front of the house,' so that I can begin to introduce Carola to the universe of coffee. I must tell you that she is a distant relative of mine—which means she must be smart as this runs in our family—and she has had her own business experience.

"She, of course, has enjoyed coffee a lot more out of the cup than out of the burlap sack," she said, trying a bit of forced early-morning humor.

Gisela's retort was quick as she replied in a jocular, somewhat sassy manner.

"I certainly will, Ursula, but if I get into trouble when by myself, I will call you right away."

"All right then, Carola, let's get started."

In front of either side of the counter there were several attractive metal canisters with wooden covers that could be removed by pulling at the rope handles. Inside each was a sack of coffee beans that had been slit open at the top and contained a brass scoop with rounded sides capable of holding an ample supply without easily spilling its contents over the side. Each canister was clearly marked near the top with the type of coffee it contained. On the wall, behind the salesperson and high enough so that it would not be obscured, was a chart in large letters, indicating each grade and the price per five hundred grams and two hundred fifty grams, the most frequently purchased amounts for home consumption. Grades were organized in order of descending price so that the customers could choose, either by what they could afford or by type when price was not the principal concern.

"As you can see, Carola, our coffees come from all over the world. There is *Java* from Indonesia; *Yergacheff* from Ethiopia, Eritrean, and Kenyan coffee from further south in Africa; and coffees from Latin and South American countries such as Brazil, Costa Rica, Colombia, and Guatemala. To help orient you, in the center of the wall behind you"—she turned around and pointed—"there is a map that shows where all these places are."

"That's very interesting and helpful," Carola replied, as she stared at the flattened Mercator projection of the world and found countries she had long ago forgotten about. The large map must have been issued by a coffee organization as each producing country was highlighted so that the customer could quickly identify the location and distance from Germany.

"Yes, it helps a lot, and the customers enjoy seeing from how far away these different types have to be shipped. It adds to their understanding of the high costs and gives the beans a certain mystique that adds to their value. Well, these are the pure beans we sell, as you can see by the high price, in either whole or ground form, depending on the client's request. When we sell them as they come right out of the sack, we scoop them into the weighing container and then they go into the bag the customer takes home. All our grinders are kept in the back room. So if they want the coffee in ground form, we take them out of duplicate canisters back there, scoop them into a weighing container, and grind and bag them directly."

Carola followed her new mentor through the curtained partition as Ursula continued. "We also sell extended grades that are a lot less expensive and are therefore more popular, making up the majority of our sales volume. Each type of coffee is sold according to quantity of extension, that is, with either of two different, standardized amounts of extender. The extender is kept in the backroom; it's an equal mixture of ground *Yergacheff* beans and several types of noncoffee products depending on availability. It's delivered to us by the company after blending at the central warehouse so that the extended coffee, regardless from which branch it is bought, always tastes the same.

"The extenders used, for your information, confidentially, are largely grains such as chicory, malt, barley, or other types, which are roasted together with the beans used in the mixture. That way, after grinding, it all looks like coffee, although if you were to brew them by themselves, you would not like the taste very much. After we blend this mix with the pure beans, we need to grind the whole mixture so that it is evenly dispersed and looks like a ground coffee without dilution. In these days of shortages and sometimes refusal to ship the beans from some of the countries that are not too friendly to us, these blending procedures are very important and give us flexibility of composition, which is vital to our profitability.

"Now let's go to the procedures on how to weigh in the proper quantities, depending on the customer's demand." She moved over to that part of the table containing the scale with two flat platforms large enough to hold a round container for the coffee to be weighed in. A large pointer at the center indicated the balance point "First, as you have probably noticed, we have two table scales, one on the counter out front and the other here on the long table. Each scale has a set of weights that I will explain to you how to use. Basically, in case of the pure beans, we weigh the desired amount of coffee into the metal container from which we transfer them or grind them first and then put them into the bag that the customer takes home. In order to avoid confusion, we have made the empty containers to a standard weight of twenty-five grams. So, by taking a twenty-five-gram weight from the block of the brass weights and always putting it on the side of the scale opposite the container, we achieve a balance that represents the initial or zero point before adding the coffee product. Is that clear, and does it make sense? That's something you must always bear in mind before dispensing the beans or the extender."

"Yes, Ursula, it makes sense, although I will have to get used to balancing out before I get started."

She motioned to Carola to scoop an amount of *Kenya* beans out of their barrel and shake them into their container after having put a two hundred fifty-gram and a twenty-five-gram weight on the other side.

"It's easiest when, as you get used to the volume that is typically weighed out, you tap the scoop and rotate it slightly so that small amounts can be added without overshooting your mark."

After a few practice times weighing, Carola seemed to get the idea and, with a little more practice, ended up right on the mark.

"Now, as you've probably seen on the chart up front, the pure bean types are called the premium grades. Next, the lesser extended type is called a standard grade, and a second, containing more extender, is called the economy grade. If you can concentrate some more, we will go on to the extended grades and how to handle them.

"Of course, both the standard and the economy grades come only in the ground form. The standard grade contains 20 percent of extender mix, and the economy grade contains 40 percent. Both of these are sold only in five hundred-gram and two hundred fifty-gram packages. The extender amount is weighed out first, according to the other little table I've put on the right side of each scale in this room. Having weighed out that amount, the weight is changed to the full weight of the mixture purchased, and the container is filled up to that point, with the beans selected by the customer. It is then emptied into the grinding machine, and after grinding, the final bag is filled from the outlet at the bottom of the machine." She picked up one of the bags and let Carola feel the inside of it.

"I might point out, by the way, that the bags, while paper on the outside, have an interliner of tinfoil in order to retain the full flavor of the purchased product. The client, of course, has to be told to keep that bag closed whenever not dispensing the grind into the coffee maker so as to keep it in its fresh condition.

"Well, Carola, that's a lot to absorb all at once, and when you get to actually doing the weighing operations, please don't hesitate to ask me to refresh your memory. It's a lot better than making a mistake and possibly annoying the customer."

"Thank you so much, Ursula, for showing me all of this. I'm going to study the charts next to the scales so the meaning of the numbers will become fixed correctly in my head. I do think, however, in a couple of days I will be familiar enough to do these things on my own."

"Well, let's go up front and let me show you some of the other things that people might wish to purchase when they come in."

As they returned to the front, past the curtain where Gisela was busy waiting on a customer with whom she seemed to be quite familiar, Ursula showed Carola what was on the shelves surrounding the map and framing the curtained door to the back room. While Carola had noted the items in passing, she had not focused on the displayed contents as she did now. First, there were a number of assortments of cookies, wafers, and *Lebkuchen* in decorated tins. Ursula explained that around Christmas there would also be *Stollen* and cinnamon stars on the shelves. Carola, in her own thoughts, was a little bit nostalgic about these delicacies, even though they were not in the Jewish tradition and she had only had them on occasion in earlier days. On another part of the shelves, glass coffee makers were located, boxed in colorful cartons. A sample had been unpacked for customers' inspection and demonstration by the sales person on how they worked. They were manufactured by the Jena Glass Company, were of a recent design consisting of two parts, and were said to make the best tasting finished coffee. This was because the ground coffee was ladled directly into the upper container on top of a fritted disk in the glass, and boiled water was poured into the container up to the marked volume desired. That permitted the coffee to brew while dripping slowly through the frit, enabling it to avoid the high temperature and excessive extraction of the mix to which it would be exposed if the water were at full boil while filtering through the grind. The coffee then slowly accumulated in the bottom container, and the assembly could be placed on a hot plate to keep it warm while the dripping action completed. That was how Ursula had made the wonderful coffee in the back room that the three of them could have any time they wished. If a good customer was particularly interested in this latest high-tech unit, one of them would serve a cup of that coffee from the back room for tasting. It was, of course, important that new coffee was made several times during the day because with prolonged heating even this procedure would not make it taste fresh after several hours.

As she saw after several days, it was quite amazing how many of these coffee makers were actually sold. In fact, it was rare after the customer had sampled the brew that he or she did not take a pot along, together with the coffee. Those who could afford them were very interested in having the latest way of making the best brew at home for their family and guests.

It amazed and saddened Carola how in these troubled times the affluent gentile society could admire and improve their lifestyle with such luxuries whenever new inventions were made—at which German industry was admittedly very good—while the poor remnant of Jews that were chased from pillar to post in the city without being let out were more and more impoverished and ostracized. The boiling and reboiling of coffee grounds in Esther's twenty-five-year-old pot was a very small yet visible example of that. By this time, however, Carola was caught up in her new surroundings and the determination to become useful to the business as quickly as possible. Therefore, she did not dwell on this contrast for more than an instant before applying her full energies and enthusiasm to the work at hand.

By the time five o'clock rolled around, she was almost sorry that the end of the day had come so quickly and that Ursula was beginning to close up the store. Carola helped her to sweep up because, while only a few coffee beans had spilled on the floor, walking across the floor had begun to sound somewhat crunchy. When that was done and Gisela had already left, she said goodbye to her new boss and told her how much she appreciated being taught the various tasks in and around the store. She also emphasized how much she enjoyed the interaction with the customers and becoming acquainted with all that was necessary to become an effective sales person. Her head was swimming from all the details of the different grades, the extenders and the mixing, and the blending and grinding operations. However, she eagerly anticipated the next day when she could apply what she had learned by either following Ursula around or going through the motions on her own.

As she waved good-bye and stepped outside, there was a bounce in her step for the first time in many weeks. She had a feeling of contentment at the new things she had learned throughout the entire day that left her with a newfound *joie de vivre*. Rounding the corner to the *Unterlindau*, she got out her key to the mailbox even before reaching it. After getting to the gate, she opened it quickly to see if anything was inside. Indeed, there were two letters inside—one from Belgium, and the other from the United States, both from her daughters. She smiled broadly to herself as these notes capped off one of the best days she'd had in her recent memory. She literally skipped up the steps to the apartment, unlocked the door, and called out to both Esther and Leah, who had been waiting with a mixture of anxiety and anticipation to greet her.

"*Nu*, how was your first day as a coffee maven?" Esther called out. "Are you an expert on the differences between Ethiopian coffee beans, Vienna roast, and espresso yet?"

"Well, not quite, but I learned so much today from Ursula. I met my colleague, and I was around people who seemed so unburdened and carefree as they went about their daily business that I feel more alive than I have been for many a day."

Carola also waved the letters in front of the two women and said: "Look what I have here on this great day. Judging by their handwriting, it seems that both girls have written to us and for arrival at the same time. Let's see what they say."

From Brussels, she learned that Trudi had gotten a job as a waitress in a kosher restaurant, where tips at lunch and dinner supplemented the very modest salary she received at the start. However, David was invited informally by the owner to join her for free dinners in the evening at closing time so that the fringe benefit of their food supply was significant. They had quickly made friends with other young couples that were new to the community, went to services regularly on Friday nights and Shabbat mornings, and began to settle down into a routine that felt like life was beginning over again. They were both studying French and, being exposed to it all day long, were rapidly expanding their vocabulary. On weekends they took long walks to become more familiar with the city and even began to go to the cinema once in a while for entertainment and language education. They were still working on the immigration documents but had nothing new to report. From friends, however, they had learned that this might take as long as nine months to a year, and so they were not terribly worried about any problems that would block her mother's emigration plans. In the meantime, they hoped that she, Esther, and Leah would write back so that they could learn what life was like in the place they had left.

The other letter was from Lisa, who wrote in a matter-of-fact way that her life was becoming normalized and relatively pleasant. The job at the bakery was simple but interesting; she had met many people who came into the shop, made friends with numerous customers also from Germany, and enjoyed Shabbat with a number of them. There was also a singles group in the Jewish Center near the house in Forest Hills where she was renting her room, and she had become accustomed to going to dances and other social occasions whenever they were organized. All in all, together with an occasional visit to Grand Uncle Hugo for Friday night dinner, her life had settled down. Living in New York, taking the subway into Manhattan with which she had rapidly become familiarized, and exploring the center of New York was more exciting and pleasant than she had ever imagined. She also reported that she occasionally asked Uncle Eduard to check with Hugo on what the ongoing chances of her mother's affidavit were going to be but had heard nothing definitive that was new and different. She promised her mother to keep on asking and make every effort to loosen up this apparently stagnant condition, but she really hoped that before the end of the year there would be some change in this situation. In the meantime, she also asked for letters back from the three of them. She missed them all and felt bad about their sad lives in view of the fact that she herself was on a new path which gave her a lot of hope for the future.

Esther and Leah expressed their pleasure that both girls were in such good shape and in countries where they could live in freedom. Concerns about their own emigration were secondary to having gotten the two young women out of an obviously deteriorating situation. Both elders expressed confidence that Carola, representing the next generation, would soon be on her way as well because everyone on the outside was working so diligently on her behalf.

Having read those spirited letters, the three women sat down to an early dinner that the two "retirees" had been busy preparing from five o'clock on, and Carola went into the details of all she had been exposed to the entire day. The two elders enjoyed listening quietly and smiled with some satisfaction as she related the highlights of her day with more animation than they had seen in her for a long time. She had brought home an up-to-date newspaper, the *Deutsches Volksblatt*, which Ursula apparently brought in to the store daily. This gave each of the three of them, in turn, a chance to catch up with news and, therefore, the outside world to which they had not been exposed with regularity since they could no longer afford it. After they all had read it from front to back with voracity akin to intellectual starvation, she quietly said goodnight and retired early into her own room. By nine o'clock she was asleep, resting peacefully for a change and anticipating an early rise to be fresh and in good shape for the next day's "adventure."

During the rest of the week, her coffee education proceeded smoothly. Ursula explained the roasting process, the dehydration and drying of the beans, roasting times, and temperatures in a rotating kiln. She told her about the development of the various colors from a light to a full roast with the beans turning shinier as natural oils were brought to the surface while the temperature rose. She pointed out the extent to which roasting was associated with the various grades that created the Vienna and French roasts out of beans from various locations.

Sacks were delivered from the warehouse located near the *Ostbahnhof* industrial area with the drivers bringing them in, cutting them open, emptying the beans that had remained in the old sack on top of the new beans, and taking the empty sacks back with them. After a day or two, Carola had mastered the weighing and blending process and felt sure that she was mixing the standard and economy grades in the proper proportions and with the type of coffee the customer requested. She was proud of herself at how quickly she began to fill the orders and, with the accompanying smiles of approval from Ursula, her self-esteem and confidence increased rapidly.

Judging by the acceptance and friendliness of the clientele coming into the store, she was beginning to believe what she had fantasized about previously—that is, hiding *en pleine vue* and blending in with the crowd seemed actually to be possible. The reality of her physical assimilation did not exactly produce joy. It gave her a sense of comfort, however, that her prior presumption of hostility and ostracism might have been premature. It was a whirl of new privilege that felt exhilarating and made the week go by quickly. On Friday afternoon, once again after Gisela left for the weekend, Frau Schaefer went to the cash register, pulled out thirty Reichsmarks, and handed them to her, saying "Good job, Carola. See you Monday morning." Despite the pittance of her pay, it had probably been her best week since last November before the life-altering days and nights of the Kristallnacht.

As the days grew longer in anticipation of summer, the warmth in the air pushed out the leaves on the large trees along her route to work, and spring flowers began to cover the beds that would bloom as they were carefully cultivated beside the lawns of the major villas along the way. Carola's walk was, therefore, more pleasant as the weeks passed during May. She usually arrived in front of the Witwe Hassan in good spirits with her hair somewhat blown by the spring breeze common at this time of year. She had settled into a pleasant routine with her coworkers, and after that bracing cup of coffee that by now she anticipated to give her a first jolt of energy, she was prepared to serve the shop's clients as they began to show up shortly after the door was opened.

There were even repeaters during the first few weeks—those people who were so obsessive about the absolute freshness of the beans they were buying that they purchased only two hundred fifty grams at a time so they could come back once a week for their regular refill. While the majority of customers were women on their way to do their daily shopping, a number of men were also among the regulars. She began to know their names: Frau Heckmann, Herr Goetz, Herr Wunderlich, Frau Forsterling, Frau Lochner, and quickly noted how flattered they felt when they were given name recognition on their way in the door. She felt they even added to their purchases when handled with such familiarity, as they would add an extra box of cookies or wafers to the bag of coffee and say a cheerful *Auf Wiedersehen* after completing their purchases. To her pleasant surprise, she hardly ever heard a *Heil Hitler*, and on the rare occasions she did, she did not reply, following her colleagues' leads. She fantasized that perhaps the large map on the wall gave the interior an aura of internationalism that induced clients to leave their party greeting at the door. By a month after she had started, she had adopted such a facile mode in helping the customers with whatever they asked for that the service she provided was seamless, and she no longer appeared as the new sales person in the house but worked just like an experienced old hand.

Because of her unquestioned acceptance by everyone that surrounded her, she settled in with great contentment even though news of crises constantly appeared in the discarded newspapers of the day. She knew that back at the apartment Leah had begun to take Esther out for brief walks down the street and perhaps around the corner. On a sunny day they could sit on a bench for a while before returning home. When the weather was bad, the two would not budge from the warmth and security of their living room or the dining table. There were enough friends to invite whenever they made their modest yeast cake, so they could have an occasional *Kaffeeklatsch* with whomever they asked to come over.

With Carola's new employment, their coffee at home also improved greatly, courtesy of Ursula, who gave her an occasional bag of sack bottoms to take home. Friends began to value these invitations as they enjoyed the superior cups of coffee despite the fact that the brew was made the old-fashioned way by plain boiling and leaving the grounds to settle in the chipped enamel, prewar vintage pot.

With spring and the up-and-down-the-block excursions, Leah had the extra task of getting Esther out of the apartment and up and down the stairs. Esther by now had severe arthritis, and most of her moaning as she moved about was fully justified due to the never-ending pain. She was quite bent over by this time because her spine had become weakened, and she constantly used a cane around the apartment from the kitchen stools to the dining room chairs as she navigated between them so she could sit down. By this time she even needed a stool for peeling potatoes at the sink and while preparing vegetables as they were being overcooked on the stove. The rare times she would go out now would be physical agony as she slowly walked down the stairs from the third floor of their apartment, not to say anything about the return when, on walking up, every stair step was an Alpine achievement for her and represented a challenge equivalent to climbing the *Jungfrau*.

Leah preceded her on the way down and walked up behind her on the way back, presumably to catch her or, at least, to dampen her fall in case that were to happen. At least that was the theory or Leah's intent as a precaution, although in actual practice Esther's heavy weight would have been overbearing and would have promptly tumbled both of them down the flight they were on. At any rate, even though all of this was a slow process and needed plenty of extra time, their outing into the fresh air and sunshine became more and more of a treat as the weather improved. Whenever they could spend a couple of hours out of doors, their mood would lighten up, and they would tell Carola about the people they had observed and the trolley cars they had seen pass; in other words, the minutiae of the street took on more and more significance with time. Carola, in turn, recited the highlights of the day at the dinner table, all of which made the most pleasant exchange they had had with each other for a long time.

7 EVICTION

On the way back from one of their afternoon outings in late May, Leah pulled out her postal box key before she reached the house as was her custom when she returned from a walk or shopping. She now handled that task more often, in view of the fact that Carola was no longer available at midday during her working hours. While Esther waited, she opened it and found a rather official-looking letter inside. She first tucked it into her pocket because helping Esther up the stairs was a full-time effort on which she had to concentrate without distraction. The two of them chatted with each other on the way up to the extent that their breath permitted after the exertion of the climb back to the landing on the third floor. They both wanted to make each other feel good after the stimulating effects of the fresh air and sunshine and in anticipation of the cup of coffee they were going to enjoy together.

Once inside, they quickly hung up their coats, which as elders they still needed despite the pleasant warmth that had surrounded their uncovered heads as they had slowly walked back and forth in the bright afternoon daylight. Having reheated the morning's coffee, they poured it into their cups on the dining room table and served the small leftover pieces of yeast cake whose raisins were a rare treat these days. Leah carefully opened the letter with a small knife. She was in the habit of reading the mail because even though she needed glasses, her vision was much better than Esther's whose lenses were now quite thick as she had progressed through constantly stronger magnification.

Reading silently, her face blanched, and her brow furrowed with the obvious seriousness of the letter's content as tears now rolled quietly down her cheeks.

"Leah, what is it?" Esther asked, her voice trembling. "Please let me know. It must be pretty terrible for even you to be crying with what you are reading."

"My God, will it ever stop?" sobbed Leah. "Let me read you what it says."

> Most honored Frau Seidenberger:
>
> It is with great regret that I must call your attention to the date of June 30, 1939, when the lease to your apartment expires. You have been an excellent tenant at this address for some twenty-six years now, and I believe our firm has been a satisfactory landlord, serving your needs during this time. I must inform you, however, that as per the new regulations in effect at present we cannot extend your lease for a further term. Unfortunately, we must act in accordance with the current laws prohibiting the renewal of such contracts to members of the Jewish faith. We have recently obtained this information and corresponding instructions from the authorities (i.e., the Gestapo), which indicates that you and some of the other tenants in this apartment building are verifiably Jews, indeed. Parenthetically, if this information is incorrect, you must let us know within the next fifteen days so that we may reverse these orders.
>
> If our information is accurate, however, we must ask you to vacate the premises you currently occupy by June 30, 1939, and leave the apartment in a broom-clean condition after moving out. A representative of our firm will meet with you on this last day and inspect the apartment to be sure this requirement is fully met. He will also obtain the keys from you, along with the lock on your basement bin and verify that this has been totally cleaned out as well.
>
> To help you in relocating, we suggest that you contact the Jewish Welfare Agency. The city administration office in cooperation with the Gestapo has informed us that specific houses and buildings have been made available for exclusive

occupation by Jewish tenants. In view of the current situation, we know that you will be much more comfortable in the sole presence reserved for fellow members of your Jewish community. We have also been informed that if you are older than sixty-five years of age, you are instructed to be housed in an old-age home, where rooms will be assigned to you, and you will receive your board and other basic necessities. Please contact your agency as quickly as possible so that the move can be made in a timely manner and in good order. Your cooperation is expected and needed. We must point out that in the event you are not ready by June 30, you will be promptly evicted with no consideration given to moving your belongings, which will promptly be confiscated.

Again, we sincerely regret instructing you to vacate your apartment. However, in this time of great need and a severe housing shortage, we have been informed that these premises are required for the urgent occupation by members of the National Socialist German Workers' Party (NSDAP).

We wish you the best of good fortune.

Respectfully yours,
Eckhardt Wiegand
Manager of Administration

Carola returned after work and found the two old women sitting at the dining room table red-eyed with wet handkerchiefs clutched between their hands.

"Mother, Leah," she exclaimed, "what is it, what's happened, why are you in tears, what disaster has struck now?"

"Here, Carola," Esther said in a subdued voice. "Read. It's all over; we don't know what to do any more. This is just too much!"

Carola quickly took the letter and started reading. "Oh my God," she concurred. "This is a disaster; after all these years, you can't just pick up and go someplace else that you are not familiar with. What will we do with all our belongings? Both of you are over sixty-five, so you are being pushed into an old-age home with others, probably in a very crowded condition. I am less than fifty years old. Where do I go? What happens to me?"

She was beginning to get teary herself but was able to exercise enough self-control so as not to fall apart in front of her elders. With this miserable development staring them all in the face, she now had to be the strong one and make all the inevitable arrangements. How was she going to do that and still work regular hours at the shop? She immediately decided to tell Ursula right away so that with enough understanding and sympathy on her part, she might be able to get some time off to make all of these moves. After all, they did not have enough money to hire much help and look after them as they needed to get relocated.

The three sat in silence having neither energy nor desire to prepare the evening meal. They each just had to think about what they needed to face. Tears dried and brows remained furrowed as they each contemplated the future. It was too late to contact family members outside Germany to help them out of this desperate situation; this was not a pragmatic way to look at it at any rate because a quick exodus could not possibly succeed in the required time frame of thirty days or less. The best thing now would be to contact the Jewish Welfare Agency as quickly as possible as this organization probably had the best resources to help the shrinking community.

"Well," Esther said quietly with irony and bitterness in her voice and drawing on the innermost core of her sense of humor which was fading fast, "looking at this letter, I don't really understand why they addressed me with the words 'most honored.' They couldn't honor anyone less sending me such garbage. Nor do I understand why, after threatening eviction, they could say: 'We wish you the best of good fortune.' This hypocrisy and mockery would never have been tolerated in the miserable, good old days before Hitler. In the words of all the faithful party members: '*Und das verdanken Wir unserem Fuehrer.*' (And for this we thank our Fuehrer.)"

If they could possibly imagine beyond what they saw when they looked at each other, the amount of sagging, despair, shriveling, and drooping in the two old women's faces could not have become worse. They had each added another ten years to their appearance of resignation and surrender.

Leah and Carola rose silently and went into the kitchen to prepare something to eat. Esther simply sat in the chair that her late husband of so many years had occupied, cupping her head in both hands and not moving beyond an occasional, weak shaking of her whole body. Then rising with a strenuous push of her cane, she joined the other two in foraging the icebox for something to eat. When the barley soup they found was heated and some bread was sliced to go with it, the table was quickly set, and the warmth of the food gave them some comfort.

It took a strong dose of indomitable spirit to reverse the depressed atmosphere that now prevailed. They ate quietly and cleaned up, after which Carola quickly sat down and wrote letters to Trudi, Lisa, and Eduard, informing them of what they were about to face in the months to come. There was no further request for help and speed in their efforts to get them out of the country because they knew that all was being done within the realm of possibility. As the evening progressed, they began to figure out what to do with their belongings, especially the furniture and all the little luxury items that had accumulated over a lifetime of modest acquisitions and gifts. Carola did not know how and where she was going to live and under what circumstances, so she could not predict even what modest belongings she could take. The only thing she was sure of was that she was not going to join the others. That meant it would undoubtedly take her longer to get to work and that visiting on a regular basis wherever Esther and Leah were to be housed would also be further away. She could easily imagine that her life would be lonelier from here on in. Even if there had been minor aggravations in living with the older generation, who was often not as understanding of her various problems, these would be minor by comparison to the future she now contemplated. She mused that someday she would call the present "the good old days" even though at the moment she could not imagine how they could be characterized as good.

After everything was cleaned up, there was no more discussion about their new joint problem. Everyone in her own way was trying her best to remain calm and not to give way to hysteria. Carola quickly excused herself and went to bed.

In the morning, she was dressed and on the phone to the Jewish Welfare Agency by eight o'clock. Fortunately, they were still not cut off from telephone service as a number of their friends and acquaintances had already experienced. After giving the man on the other end of the line her name, address, and the names of the other two tenants in the apartment, he seemed to be able to look up their situation on his register.

"Ah yes, Frau Rossmann," he said. "As you know, we unfortunately have to follow instructions from the authorities, but this is the information we have in your particular case. Frau Seidenberger and Fraulein Rosenthal are assigned to the Old Age Home branch at *Feuerbachstrasse* 14. This is not far from where you live now, and therefore, the neighborhood would be familiar to both of them. We think we are fortunate to have been able to find them a vacancy at that address because it is early in the program, and the designated houses are still not filled up. You, yourself are assigned to *Fuerstenbergerstrasse* 167, where you have a one-room apartment on the fourth floor. I know this is not as comfortable an accommodation as you have had, but as a single person, you must understand that we cannot provide more space. There are married couples and families with children at the same address, and we have had to make assignments on the basis of the greater needs for these people."

"Is it possible to see these facilities before we move in?" Carola asked.

"Yes, you can, subject to making prior appointments," the voice on the other end of the line said. "Of course, you must realize that we cannot change anything now or after you have seen them. It is just a matter of your determining how much of your belongings can fit into the spaces and how much you must therefore dispose of."

"The only thing I would like to request is that my mother and Miss Rosenthal could be on the first floor. Her walking is extremely poor, and if she did not have to climb stairs, she would be able to go outside into the fresh air more often."

"Yes, this has already been taken care of, and they can be assured that a room on the first floor will be shared by the two of them. Is there anything else I can do for you at this point?" He seemed to be eager to get off the line.

"You must realize that this is a very difficult time for us," a phrase which he used with great circumspection. "Many other people are in a similar position, and therefore, our phone lines are very much overloaded. As you can imagine, dealing with the authorities is not the easiest thing in the world."

"Yes, I can really understand that," Carola said in the most pleasant voice she could muster under these conditions so as not to jeopardize her ability to communicate on future questions. "I will try not to bother you too much prior to our own move. By the way, can you recommend anyone to help us make the move, because we three women cannot possibly handle schlepping our things from one location to the other by ourselves?"

"Yes, within the next few days I will send you a brief letter giving you some choices of companies to call. Remember, this will not be cheap because these people know that you have no choice about moving and may well take advantage of you under these conditions."

"Well, thank you and good-bye then, and could you tell me your name so that I can ask for you on future calls?"

"My name is Herbert Bachmann. I have been at the agency for many years so everyone knows me here in the event you call. Good-bye then, Frau Rossmann, and good luck."

Why does everyone wish me good luck, she wondered, under conditions where we have experienced nothing but bad luck? She hung up, called out a quick good-bye to her family after giving them the details of her phone conversation, and proceeded to walk the short distance to her work. She had frequently used the last few weeks since she started at the shop, as a way to distract herself from the never-ending problems which had arisen ever since the November 9 pogroms. However, she realized that with the need to move, the longer commute, the visits to the old-age home, and the inevitable greater loneliness, her own life would become increasingly burdensome and less carefree as well.

At the end of the day, she decided to walk home via a detour through the *Feuerbachstrasse* to take a look, at least at the outside of the place her mother and Leah would be living. She had not been in the neighborhood that was on the other side of the *Bockenheimer Landstrasse* for some time, and as she walked several blocks to number 14, she noticed how many houses between the apartment buildings had their outside roller shades drawn. This look, usually a sign of absence of the owner, was reinforced by the unkempt appearance of the front yard and the neglected flower beds. She assumed, therefore, that these were the homes of Jewish families that had left in a hurry and under circumstances that prevented sale of the property.

When she came to number 14, she found a large house, which, although neglected looking, showed clear signs of occupancy and habitation activity. Not much could be seen on the outside, so she would have to make the appointment that Herr Bachmann had suggested to get a better idea of what kind of accommodation her mother and Leah would have. It was useful, however, to have taken the detour she had just made in order to know how to estimate the additional distance she would have to walk in the future whenever she would visit. To her pleasant surprise, she noted that it was not more than fifteen minutes from their current apartment to the new residence and thus not far out of the way. Best of all, the two elderly women would still be familiar with the neighborhood in which they had lived for so many years. With that quick preliminary inspection, Carola turned around and went home.

Earlier—that is, during late morning—at Carola's suggestion, Esther called the other Jewish tenants she knew in the building to see if they had received similar letters. They had indeed and were feeling as confused, helpless, and despondent as she and Leah had been when they had read their own. Rather than speaking extensively on the phone, Esther invited the Friedmanns and Mannheimers for a late afternoon cup of coffee to talk about everyone's thoughts and plans during the next few weeks. Not ten minutes after Carola arrived home, Martin and Bertha Friedmann, who lived on the ground floor for as many years as the Seidenbergers had lived upstairs, rang the doorbell and with tears of disbelief came into the dining room. They had not slept or rested a wink since receiving their notice, and the dark bags under their eyes showed their state of agitation and exhaustion. They were of a similar age, at the very end of their sixties. Their children had also emigrated to the United States, and they had been left behind to an uncertain fate.

A few minutes later, the Mannheimers arrived in approximately the same state of upset and despair. Their son and his family had left some two years earlier for Palestine, where he became a chicken farmer. Although this was a dramatic career change from his profession as an attorney, he had written with optimism about their new life in

Petach Tikvah. Nevertheless, they had not yet succeeded in mustering the needed permits to bring the parents out of Germany, despite the assistance of the Palestine Bureau, which had been created for the sole purpose of moving members of the Jewish community to their new homeland. After serving somewhat watery coffee due to the large group that had to partake of the morning's reheated pot and putting out cookies that Carola had bought at a discount from her workplace, they all gave their own reactions to the earthshaking change of status that the notices from the landlord denoted. They all brainstormed in tense voices of desperation how each of the three households involved would cope with the imminent moves.

Martin Friedmann looked somewhat confused and disheveled having gotten up from his afternoon nap, which helped him escape from thinking about his feeling of entrapment for a couple of hours. He spoke up in a tentative voice: "What are we going to do with our furniture? We were going to take it with us when our papers to America came through. That's all indefinite now. We haven't heard from our children in a couple of months. They're supposed to make the arrangements. I don't know what's wrong. Will our mail be forwarded? Oh, so many problems and unknowns I just don't know where to turn next."

Because Carola was not involved in the same move as the others and had already contacted the Jewish Welfare Agency, she was very helpful reviewing for the two other couples the information she had received. Her inquiry was useful and encouraged them to make the same call the following day. Although belatedly, to their regret (they had not been close to one another during all the years they had lived in the same house together), they were determined to stick close, promising mutual help and encouragement if they ended up living in the same old-age home. They discussed the common problems of discarding furniture and other possessions that they held dear but realized during their meeting that they probably could not obtain much for what needed to be left behind because their choices were stark. Having no more friends or relatives that their excess belongings could be given to, they were aware that they were all at the mercy of secondhand furniture dealers, who would undoubtedly exploit them to the maximum. The meeting, which could not be categorized as a *Kaffeeklatsch* because of its serious and urgent nature, broke up an hour and a half later with promises to keep in close contact on any news and developments until it was time to move.

During the next two weeks, Carola made appointments to visit the inside of both residences that were now set aside exclusively for Jews. It felt like a pre-ghettoization and certainly physical separation from the gentile community, which began to move into the vacated premises as the prior tenants moved together into smaller and smaller spaces. She had made Ursula aware of what was going on shortly after receipt of the eviction notice in order to explain why she had to leave promptly at the end of the day to attend to the details prior to the end of June. Frau Schaefer was very sympathetic to her plight and graciously suggested that she take whatever time she needed to handle these critical relocations.

After making her appointment, she visited the old-age home by herself because it was too difficult for Esther and Leah to go there without taking a taxi, and they really could do nothing to change the predetermined space. At the residence, she found a number of elderly people who had moved into their modest rooms and were also upset and sad about what they had left behind. Fortunately, Herr Bachmann had been true to his word and had reserved a room on the ground floor for the two of them. It was modest, perhaps some four meters square, which, by comparison to some of the other rooms she saw on the upstairs floors, was generous. Because it was on the ground floor, there was only one other room for a private couple. The additional spaces were used for a kitchen, the dining room, and a common space where, to the extent that other residents fit in, they could socialize in between meal times.

As other people were now compelled to move out of their residences, and the house was meant to accommodate in excess of forty people as an old-age home, this seemed to make for a crowded condition. The dining room did not hold more than twenty seats with four round tables so that at the meal times people would have to eat in at least two sittings. Neither Esther and Leah nor anyone else in the house had a private bathroom; their use was, therefore, always subject to availability, and people were encouraged to wash up and do their business in the shortest possible time.

Carola quickly determined that their room could hold the two beds, a night table between them with a lamp, the wardrobe cupboard they had for many years, and possibly one or two armchairs. Because their writing desk would not fit, they would have to figure on writing their mail at a small desk in the public space, not exactly an ideal area for privacy and extensive letters. The entire house was equipped with a single phone, and none could be installed in any of the rooms for the private use of its tenants. The outside yard held some old chairs and benches that originally belonged to prior occupants who had donated them for everyone's use. The small grounds were weedy because no one had the ability to mow any longer, and no help was available for that luxurious purpose. Sitting outside was, therefore, not what it used to be in people's individual homes but still a relative pleasure when the warming sun was out. Upon returning home, she reported her findings as optimistically as she possibly could so that Esther and Leah would move there with relatively positive anticipation.

When she visited the house that was to be her new habitat in the *Fuerstenbergerstrasse*, these quarters beset her with a new reality that was most depressing. Her appointment with the superintendent of the building was made for her after working hours when it was still light during the early summer months. She walked from the Witwe Hassan to the address and determined that it would take on the order of twenty-five to thirty minutes compared to the ten or so minute walk she'd had until now.

She and the superintendent walked up the four floors, the highest below the attic floor, which in past days was used by the various tenants as maids' rooms. He quickly opened the door into a medium-sized room incorporating a modest kitchen alcove, a tiny two-burner stove, a sink, and a very small icebox. Again, there was no private bathroom but only one on the floor that was to be shared with two other occupants of separate one-room apartments, as yet not occupied. The room contained a single window and, facing north, promised not to give too much bright light for a good part of the day.

She judged it would hold her single bed, wardrobe closet, a small writing desk with chair, and perhaps one of the armchairs from their old apartment. As far as the bathroom was concerned, the days of languorous soakings in the tub were over. In fact, she now knew that the "good old days" as they related to their rundown but spacious apartment were clearly at an end. She told the superintendent when she would be moving in. He gave her a phone number where he could usually be reached—again, the number rang the only phone permitted in the house, which was located in the downstairs hallway. As she could see, he said, it would take him awhile to get to it because he lived on the floor below the street level, and she would have to have patience until he could answer it.

With disappointment and disbelief, but ultimately resolute to adapt to the new, further deterioration of her living situation, she thanked him and walked home somewhat slowly. The trend of everything, she thought, was down, down, down, yet she could not figure out what she could do about it. Ironically, her hiding in plain sight lasted for only eight out of the twenty-four hours a day when she was at work. She still considered herself fortunate knowing that she, unlike others, could have such a respite from ostracism and hostility in broad daylight.

As the end of June arrived, the three women packed their belongings, filled suitcases with clothing, and wrapped small things in crumpled old newspapers and boxes Carola had brought home every day from the store or a nearby market. They were now within a week of making the move and vacating the apartment. Despite Ursula's offer to take time off, she had left the main preparations to weekends so as not to incur obligations she might someday not be able to return.

Late afternoon on the last Sunday there someone knocked lightly on the front door. She went to open it wondering why the visitor had not used the doorbell. To her surprise, it was Ingeborg Schmidt whom, after thanking her for the introduction to Frau Ursula Schaefer, she had not seen in the interim. Ingeborg, in an almost whispering voice, said, "I hope I am not disturbing you. May I come in and talk to you for a moment, Carola?"

"Yes, of course, Ingeborg. Come in and sit in the dining room. May I get you a cup of coffee?"

"No thank you," she replied. "I wanted to tell you how sorry I was about the news that the three of you have to move out before the end of the month. You have been such good neighbors—quiet never making any trouble—but I guess the new regulations have made it impossible for Jewish people to continue living in an Aryan building. I know that you have to move to much tighter quarters and that you, Carola, will be separated from your mother and Fraulein Rosenthal, as they will go into an old age home. Well, for them, I guess that is a good solution because they will be with people of their own age range and will feel comfortable living amidst members of your Jewish community.

"I was wondering, Carola, in view of the fact that none of you can take along as much furniture as you have, whether I could buy the dining room furniture, including the large vitrine, table, chairs, and sideboard, from you. I have never had a dining room, and I would be very grateful now that I am somewhat older myself to have this additional comfort. Of course, I hope you do not feel that I am too forward, and if you have other plans for your belongings, please tell me right away. The only thing I can assure you is that if you were agreeable to selling it to me, the furniture would be very well taken care of and kept nice and clean and in good order."

"Well, Ingeborg, that is a very interesting idea because you are correct; we cannot take that along and would have to dispose of it in some fashion. I should discuss it with my mother, who at the moment is taking a rest, because it is technically hers, having bought it many years ago when my father was still alive. The vitrine used to have many nice little things in it—dishes, glasses, Chanukah menorahs, *bsomim* boxes, and porcelain figures that were collected by my parents through the years and which my brother and I always admired. These are all packed now because we plan to take them along as the last souvenirs of our past.

"However, tell me, Ingeborg. I did see your apartment recently when you invited me up to talk, and I wonder where you would put all that furniture."

"Well, Carola, let me tell you confidentially but frankly; after speaking with the landlord's representative and explaining to him my basic needs for a larger place after all these years, he agreed with my request that I could move down here and obtain a lease for your apartment after you have left." Carola looked at her, puzzled and with some consternation and surprise.

"I thought this apartment was needed for NSDAP members moving to the city and being in great need for living quarters."

"Yes, that is true," she said, "but there is the privilege of exchanging apartments with longtime tenants that have been worthy of an upgrade." Her eyes darted about with impatient glances to cut short what from her point of view amounted to an unneeded conversation.

"At any rate, this has all been agreed to already, and I just wondered if the dining room could simply be left here when you move out. I am willing to pay you forty Reichsmarks for the vitrine and fifty Reichsmarks for the table, chairs, and sideboard. Unfortunately, that is all I can afford. I know that it isn't much, certainly not compared to when it was purchased new many years ago. But it is, after all, quite old, and it would cost you money to dispose of; aside from the fact that you could certainly use the ninety Reichsmarks for living and moving expenses. Well, think about it—though not too long I hope—and knock at my door anytime when you have made a decision."

Once she had made her proposal and again had concluded her business, she quickly got up and walked to the front door. "Speak with your mother, Carola, and then let me know, hopefully in a day or two. *Auf Wiedersehn."*

Carola knew there would be an outburst of rage from Esther as soon as she passed on the outrageous offer, couched in such saccharine terms. That turned out to indeed be the case, but she was somewhat surprised at the resignation and obvious weariness with which Esther expressed her indignation. Her feistiness had gone in the course of constant assaults during the past many years. Perhaps, in the absence of alternatives, she had learned how to roll over and accede to being exploited.

"Well, let's accept her most generous offer," she said with a bitter irony. "First, what choice do we have, and secondly, the pleasure of getting to live somewhere far away from a Nazi like that is probably well worth it despite the miserable conditions that we will undoubtedly find. I wonder how she found out about all this, or perhaps, she was the one who started this whole eviction business with the authorities so that she could get our apartment at no cost on her part."

"I guess I don't care anymore," Carola said with a hint of desperation in her voice. "The worst about this whole thing is that we will no longer live together. I have gotten to accept that material things are only things after all and that our separation is much more meaningful to me after all these years. Let's take the money—we need it—and not look back. Like the story of Lot's wife leaving Sodom and Gomorrah, we can't look back except," she slowly reflected, "we can't even leave this Gomorrah."

Carola waited until Tuesday, the maximum amount of time Ingeborg had given her to respond. Her purpose was to keep her on pins and needles as long as that was possible, despite the fact that she realized showing up at her door was inevitable, and Frau Schmidt knew it as well. Ingeborg quickly pulled out the ninety Reichsmarks from her purse, handed it over, and made Carola sign a certificate of sale to make sure everything was "in good order." Again, there was a quick "thank you" and "good-bye," the door closed, and the exchange of property, along with the residence, was done. Their baggage, as it were, was lightened once again. How light would it ultimately get?

Promptly at eight o'clock the following Monday morning, the doorbell rang. When Carola opened the front door the movers, two men in workmen's coveralls with businesslike smiles, stepped in and politely announced they were to do the moves, both to the old-age home and then to the apartment in the *Fuerstenbergerstrasse*. The three women had worked as best they could through the entire weekend, making order out of odds and ends, filling a few more boxes with small belongings, and marking each of them for their destinations. All their possessions in the apartment had been consolidated into clusters of furniture and boxes ready for the move, and the rooms were essentially stripped of their lived-in atmosphere.

They had all gotten up at six o'clock, washed, dressed, and packed their respective suitcases so that once everything was carried downstairs, there would be nothing left but an empty space and the dining room furniture they had sold. The movers had brought along one of their smaller trucks because on prior inspection during the previous week, one of their men had determined that only the minimum size was needed. Herbert Bachman, the Jewish Welfare Agency representative, had kindly made the final arrangements, even organizing a taxi to take them over to the *Feuerbachstrasse* once everything was packed up and loaded.

The moving men were proficient, using their straps to carry a number of boxes at a time; dismantling the beds into headboards, mattresses, and frames and taking the armchairs stacked in ways they could never have believed possible to minimize the number of trips up and down the three flights out to the street. The most difficult tasks were the two wardrobes because they were too big and bulky to be handled by one man alone, and the two were directing each other around the tight corners of the staircase with professional and seemingly ingenious ways of using the straps to balance the load. As they carefully inched their way down the staircase, Carola and the two older women were secretly afraid that a boxy piece of furniture would slip and fall down the steps, breaking into a million pieces. However, this did not happen, and both wardrobes were strapped tightly inside the moving van so as not to sustain any damage on their way to their new destinations. Despite having chosen the lowest cost movers, it seemed that those on Bachmann's final list did their job expertly, affording their belongings a more dignified relocation than moving the owners themselves.

Because Esther was not able to move around very much or help with the final packing, she seated herself in the hallway on one of the in-transit chairs, assuming a supervisory position. Apparently, her hearing was still pretty good because she quietly called out to Carola.

"My dear, I think the jackal is stirring on the floor above to see when it's safe for her to take over."

Indeed, Ingeborg Schmidt was on her way down, walking in without knocking and seeking out Carola among everyone who was shuffling about.

"Good morning. I just wanted to tell you I spoke to the landlord, who of course knows that I will be moving downstairs after you have left. In view of that, he agreed that you do not need to leave the place broom clean as was specified in the notice, that the dining room would be left behind, and that I would take care of the cleanup both in this apartment and the one I am leaving. That will save you a little work and get me started in completing my own move.

"By the way," she again darted around trying not to look like a vulture eyeing her prey, "I wanted to ask you if you were going to need the drapes in the dining room, and if not, could you please leave them for me, which I would very much appreciate? I understand, of course, that the carpet under the dining room table will be rolled up, and you will probably use it in your new surroundings. I do have one, so that will not be a problem."

"I appreciate your talking to the landlord, Ingeborg, and any extra cleaning I do not have to do will help me very much. And, oh yes, we'll be leaving the drapes, so you're welcome to them."

Frau Schmidt and Esther only exchanged glances during all the commotion as they mutually understood that any verbal exchange would not come out too friendly or civil at this stage of the game. They each, therefore, had the good sense to part from one another without any further inanities or other pleasantries.

It took about two hours to complete packing the van. By the time loading was completed, the taxi was waiting downstairs for the relocation trip. Esther made her arduous and painful last trip down the staircase, which she had made for the past twenty-six years, first with ease and then with increasing difficulty as her arthritis took hold. She moaned and groaned, which she had gotten used to during the past three years. Carola took charge of leaving everyone's keys with her upstairs neighbor, the new tenant of the just-vacated apartment.

The three women got into the taxi with additional expressions of aches and pains. It was, in an ironic way, a bit of a special treat for them because they had not been out for such a private ride in a long time. Although it was less than a kilometer away, traversing the *Bockenheimer Landstrasse* was a momentous crossing, perhaps akin to their own personal micro-Rubicon, for it seemed unlikely, at least to Esther and Leah, that they would ever return. There was the quiet of finality inside the taxi with closely held emotions that were causing eyes to roll, heads to shake, and tears to flow.

Upon their arrival, they were pleasantly surprised that the outside of the house looked like a decent residence even if it had seen better days. Carola helped her mother out of the taxi with pains of the stiff joints she needed to use for each motion. As they slowly walked toward the entrance, they were greeted by Herr Dr. Julius Pappenheimer, an elderly retired lawyer who had been appointed the administrative head of the residence. He welcomed them and showed Esther and Leah to their room on the ground floor. Not ten minutes later, the movers arrived, and the two of them, who had marked each piece according to its final destination, began to unload.

It became clear very quickly how pitifully few belongings they had brought once they were transferred to the room they would now occupy. The two beds were set up rapidly with headboards, frames, springs, and bedding. The night table was placed between the two with a lamp on top. The big piece, the wardrobe with a clothing space on each end, a set of drawer units in between, and a mirror on top, was brought in and placed on the long wall. The worn-out rug that had been in their own bedroom was unrolled and placed in the space that was left bare at the foot of their beds. Two small armchairs taken from the living room fit across from their bed space and were placed on the opposite wall. The boxes designated for their room, to be emptied later, found space on a small piece of the same wall.

Setting up their new abode took no time at all because anything that occupied the common spaces in the residence did not need to be kept privately. They sat down in their old chairs more out of mental than physical exhaustion—after all, it was only eleven o'clock in the morning—looking about somewhat bewildered, trying to get used to their new surroundings. It was not long before their stupor was interrupted by residents who at first gingerly approached the open door and then stepped in more assertively to introduce themselves and, in turn, make their acquaintance. They commented kindly how many good things they had heard about the three of them from their neighbor on the *Unterlindau*.

Not long after a few couples had stopped by, both the Friedmanns and the Mannheimers, who had preceded them in moving, showed their faces in the doorway with quiet smiles. Their appearance lifted everyone's spirits, and the unexpected familiarity of their ex-housemates brought laughter to an otherwise pathetic situation, which soon smacked of a good reunion. It had been the custom of the house manager to let friends and people who had some connection with the newcomers show them around in order to promote friendliness and camaraderie and to alleviate the difficult changes they were all facing together. Rather than letting them brood by themselves in the barren, not as yet set up room, the Mannheimers led them out the door to show them the first floor, the bathroom they were to use, the dining room where they would take their meals, the kitchen, the living area, and the way to the small outside yard.

In the midst of all this, Carola said good-bye when she saw they were in good hands and indicated that she needed to set up her own apartment at the new location so that the movers could be discharged before the end of the afternoon. She got back into the waiting taxi and, upon arrival at her own destination, waited for the moving truck to arrive. Bringing her belongings up to the single room on the fourth floor that was to be her new home was not as friendly an entrée as the group home had been for her mother and Leah. The superintendent cooperated in leaving the front door open, giving her keys to her room as well as to the mailbox, and asking her in an offhand way if there were anything he could do to make her feel comfortable. She expressed her appreciation but declined and guided the movers upstairs to show them where the remaining furnishings would be placed as they unloaded the truck.

Again, the most difficult piece was the wardrobe, which, although being slightly smaller, had the same arrangement for hanging garments and drawer space. The movers' straps were once more manipulated in a professional way without knocking the wardrobe against the tight walls on the way up. This made the piece end up against the long wall in order to leave room for the rest of her sparse belongings. The single bed was assembled, the old carpet put down to cover the remaining wood flooring, a small table on which she was to eat her meals along with two chairs was placed not too far from the small stove, and the last comfortable armchair fit into the remaining small space. Three lamps were available, one for her night table, a floor lamp next to the armchair, and another table lamp where she was to eat and probably read. The small writing desk that had been in her room was placed at the foot of the bed so that it could fit without using extra wall space.

After tipping the men before they left—which they appreciated—she was left alone and collapsed into the armchair, lonely, solemn, and depressed. With resignation, she tried to start working to put her "house" in order but could not manage to get herself going. She was beginning to feel somewhat claustrophobic and therefore decided to go out for some basic food shopping. Thanking the superintendent for his help and asking him for the whereabouts of the nearest grocery, she quickly found the shop he had suggested three blocks down and around the corner on the *Reuterweg.* She bought some basics—milk, jam, potatoes, canned vegetables and soups, boxes of puddings, soap, and cleaning materials—all of which she brought back to the house. The distraction and new focus lifted her spirits a little, although when she got back to her room, she again wanted to escape as quickly as possible. She decided to leave everything in its packed condition and walk back to her mother's new residence to see if she could help straighten things out there first.

When she arrived after the twenty-five minute walk, it seemed that even though everyone there was elderly, the relative "crowd" of people made things more appealing, particularly on the day of their exodus from their old surroundings. Esther and Leah were pleasantly surprised at her unexpected return. They had finished their first lunch in the dining room where they were introduced to a number of other residents, all of whom were getting acclimated to their new homes. They were able to kvetch and complain about the food in a good-natured way, declaiming that, of course, it would never measure up to how it was "*bei Uns zu Haus.*" Back in their room, all three of them worked at emptying boxes and began putting things away until the older women had to lie down on their newly made up beds to take an afternoon rest.

"My dears, I will leave you now to look after my own things. I will call you every day and come back on Friday after work so we can have our Shabbos dinner together."

It was time for Carola to leave as she realized that her return had been primarily a way to mitigate another pain of the inevitable separation that their move had dictated. She stressed to them, again through a new set of tears, how fortunate it was that she had her job at the Witwe Hassan, which gave her the very modest means to maintain some independence and self support. "It will give me the chance to give you some pocket money out of my pay so you can use it for little extras that will make you more comfortable at the home."

Having said all of this in a tone of shaky reassurance, she turned and quickly left, remembering the similar scene at the railroad station not long ago. On the way back she once more avoided going up the *Unterlindau* to keep her emotions on an even keel. She would circumvent that street in the future at all costs, trying to put behind her all associations of the past and moving on with all the determination she could muster. Once back at her own room, she poured herself into straightening out her belongings, had a light supper at the end of the afternoon, and went to sleep early so as to be ready first thing the next morning to resume her job. Beyond her ability to earn a very modest support for herself, her work was infinitely valuable in creating a sense of normalcy for her and taking her mind off the slow, relentlessly methodical contraction and ongoing destruction of the entire Jewish community.

8 A NEW FACE

The next morning, Carola was out of her apartment early in the morning, taking her first trip by foot from her new home to work, a twenty-five-minute walk when unimpeded by rain. She arrived well before opening time and had expected to wait out front but found Ursula already inside. The coffee had just been set up but was not yet ready for pouring. Even so, the smell of brewing, regardless of which blend had been used, wafted into her nostrils and gave her an immediate lift. She did not realize how much she had missed this new first treat of the morning and how much it had set a positive pattern for the busy day ahead. She poured Ursula and herself the waiting cups and drank hers down quickly with a feeling of pleasure and relief.

Having gotten used to talking about the events of her day outside her hours in the shop, she related to Ursula all of the weekend's events—the packing, Ingeborg's impatient wait to move in, her mother's and Leah's resettlement in the old-age home, and her own upset and disappointment with her new, barren quarters. She had become quite dependent on discussing all of these things with her boss as a way to share her anxieties with someone she felt was a good listener and not too judgmental.

When Gisela appeared at eight-thirty, she also briefly mentioned that the reason for her absence the day before was that she was involved in a personal move without going into the details. Because her co-worker had not made reference to it, Carola had to assume that she was either not aware of her situation or that she was most discreet about it. At any rate, Gisela seemed not sufficiently curious about such detail and felt that it was better to leave well enough alone. The week went along smoothly; she made phone calls to her mother from the hallway of her new address to make sure that the two elderly women had gotten used to their new habitat within a few days. By Thursday, her mind was more at ease, and she waited on her customers the entire full day with detail and attention.

Toward the end of that afternoon as things were slowing down, an older, well-dressed man entered the shop. He appeared to be a steady customer, although Carola had not seen him since the beginning of her employment. Ursula Schaefer immediately greeted him with a familiarity that acknowledged a long-term customer relationship.

"Ah, good afternoon, Herr von Kleinhoven," she said in an energetic voice. "It's so good to see you again. It's been a long time since you paid us a visit. You must have run out of your favorite coffee beans quite a few weeks ago," she laughingly chided him.

"Well, I did, Frau Schaefer, but I have been on an extensive business trip outside the country and spent a lot of time in hotels for breakfast, lunch, and dinner. But as you well know, I always return because I am totally addicted to your wonderful coffees and sooner or later cannot do without them. So here I am back again, completely chastened," he added with a great deal of charm and totally phony contrition. "Let me look around a bit now that I'm back and see what flavor I will pick after my long absence and what else I might take along this time."

"Please take your time, Herr von Kleinhoven, and enjoy all the assortments and blends we have. There might have been some new things since you were in last, back in April."

"Thank you, Frau Schaefer. I will do exactly that," he said in a gracious, very old-world mannerism.

While it was obvious that Ursula was going to serve this important customer with whose tastes she was so familiar, Carola, standing to the far side of the counter was dumbstruck by his appearance, good looks, and personality he so strongly exuded. He was tall, erect, and broad-shouldered with a prominent, aquiline nose; his deep-set eyes with gray irises revealed a piercing look with a hint of intensity and a curiosity that would not take no for an answer that he might seek in response to a probing question. His face was angular no matter from which side one looked at him—small chin, clean-shaven, a Nordic look, strong determination, and prone to quick decisions without hesitation but with an intelligence that seemed to exclude scattered thought, lack of focus, or snap judgments. A full head of sandy-colored hair that was parted on the left side and kept relatively short inferred a habit of no-nonsense order and discipline. The charisma that he evoked was immediately obvious as he stepped into the shop and slowly ambled among other customers who had no such distinguishing characteristics. Therefore, whether one waited on him, spoke with him, or attempted to ignore him, it was impossible to forget his physicality and attractiveness.

"Frau Schaefer, I think I will take the beans from Kenya today but only half a pound, please. This way I can come back next week for beans from a different part of the world. But I will take a box of French wafers, which I enjoyed so much the last time."

"With pleasure, Herr von Kleinhoven," she said as she proceeded to weigh out and package the coffee and then bag it together with the cookie box into a smart carryout container. She rang up the change after he paid for what he had purchased.

"Thank you so much and see you next week, I hope," she said in a somewhat girlish manner. "Have a very good evening."

With that and a brief glance in Carola's direction, he turned, put his fashionable hat back on, turned, and quickly left the shop. Carola and Ursula looked at each other.

"He is such an attractive man, isn't he?" asked Ursula, leaving unspoken all the other thoughts that would embellish and round out her feelings and reactions. By the time their respective blood pressures had returned to normal, it was five o'clock, and they closed up the store. Gisela had left a little early for the day and therefore did not participate in the experience.

Once again, Carola took the now longish walk home. Back in her room, she made a modest supper for herself and then proceeded to finish putting the remainder of her belongings away, trying to figure out how to make some sense of home out of the barrenness she felt more palpably than ever. In the coming days she could not get this man out of her mind and, assuming he meant what he had said about coming back the next week, could hardly wait until Thursday or perhaps Friday would come around.

Indeed, late on that Thursday afternoon, he reappeared. This time it was her turn to wait on him because Ursula had taken off an hour earlier, and she happened to be free, not waiting on anyone else. He greeted her in a courtly manner and this time selected a South American coffee bean, again buying only half a pound together with some tea from Ceylon. He made a couple of brief remarks about the weather, summertime, and his busy schedule and, after paying, quickly left the shop. Carola replied pleasantly but did not encourage more conversation because she did not know whether this was appropriate or whether an embarrassment would result in view of the fact that she was only a new employee who perhaps should not assert herself with the same familiarity or status as Ursula.

Von Kleinhoven appeared to adhere to the Thursday afternoon schedule, setting up an expectation that seemed to be readily fulfilled. The next time he came in, Carola was serving another customer, anxious to finish up with her so that she could give her total attention to this new attraction. He, in turn, browsed among the cookies and cakes that were on the shelf opposite the counter, looked at the large map extensively, and appeared to take the cue that he should busy himself until she was free to wait on him in person. This little pirouette seemed to work well without attracting special attention of either Gisela or other customers busy with coffee selection. He chose beans from Costa Rica and a box of bonbons, which he asked her advice about. Concluding his purchase with some hesitation, she realized in retrospect, had to do with her co-worker and a customer as he moved to be out of earshot.

As she rang up to give him his change, he said, "Excuse me, I have had an extremely hectic day, and I was going across the street to have a late afternoon cup of coffee to relax a little before proceeding home. I wonder if you would do me the honor of joining me for a little while there?"

She somewhat stammered in surprise. "I was going to go straight home myself, but I would be happy to join you. I also do not have any company after work, so I am pleased to have some stimulating conversation."

"Well then, let me introduce myself. My name is Ulrich von Kleinhoven. I will proceed across the street to the other side of the *Opern Platz* where there is a small outdoor café. Please take your time; I know that you close up at five o'clock. Join me when you are finished."

She had been so flustered in this short interchange that she had forgotten to introduce herself in turn. However, when the red flush had receded from her cheeks, she realized that she would have another chance to do that. On the other hand, she would not plan on any specific subject of conversation so she could do more listening than talking and respond to whichever way he wanted to steer his thoughts.

After leaving the shop, Carola crossed over and arrived at the *Altes Opern Café* on the west side of the plaza. He was sitting off to the side and, having just been served his coffee and a small fruit tart, was beginning to enjoy the hot brew. She had crossed in back of the opera house and so was not immediately visible as she got to the other side. However, as soon as he spotted her, he rose from his chair, bowed elegantly, and showed her to her seat.

"I am so sorry," she started out to say, "but with your unexpected invitation, I totally forgot about introducing myself. I am Carola Rossmann and recently joined Frau Schaefer at the store."

Unless questioned further, she wanted to leave it at that and not volunteer the additional background that might discourage him from spending more time with her.

"I am pleased to make your acquaintance at last," he replied in the same courtly fashion that had so quickly drawn her into his charismatic orbit.

"Well, Frau Rossmann, may I tell you about myself so that you will not feel you are talking to a total stranger? But before I do that, let me order you some coffee of your own and perhaps you will join me in a small pastry."

He called over the waiter and ordered her coffee and the same delicious-looking cherry tart, which seemed to be one of the specialties of the house. The waiter brought everything promptly and deposited the tray with a flourish in front of her, pouring her coffee professionally.

"Well, Frau Rossmann, due to my extensive travel schedule, you have seen me only recently coming to your shop to buy my modest amount of coffee beans, which last me approximately a week. This way, I get new product often, which I enjoy so much in my office where my secretary brews it fresh every day." He interrupted to take a long swig showing his pleasure as the gentle bitterness restored his flagging energies.

"As for myself, I am an engineer by profession, having taken over my firm which my father started before World War I and from which he is now retired for the past few years. The name of my company is UVK Maschinenbau. Our factory, located in the outskirts of Hanau, manufactures things like tubing, pipes, and specialty high-quality boring for delicate and very exacting applications. In these days of national rearmament, we have received many orders from the government for rifle boring, machine guns, and very small cannons. So you can see, I am unfortunately involved in war materiel in preparation for a possible conflict. This is against my otherwise peaceful nature, but what can one do as a private entrepreneur but to help one's country in times of its dire need?"

He continued in an obviously studied effort to be as open and frank as he could and encouraged her to enjoy her coffee as well while it was still hot.

"In this sensitive field, I was requested some time ago to become a consultant for the Wehrmacht because over the years, I have become quite expert in rifle design and the latest weaponry for the infantry....

"But, please, let me turn to my personal life and not scare you with what could well be an intimidating subject. I am quite comfortable economically and the oldest son of an old Frankfurt family. Six years ago I built a house in the suburbs and now live in Kronberg, right outside the center of town near the top of the Feldberg." He now turned to the pastry and began to divide it into manageable pieces.

"I've been married for some thirty years," he continued, "and moved out to higher ground with my wife and family after living across the street from the *Palmengarten* for many years while the children grew up. I have two sons, now twenty-five and twenty-eight years old, who have recently joined the Wehrmacht in view of the mobilization that will soon be in full swing. I expect them to be in the Officer Corps after their training is completed as that is the tradition of our family, and they are on a well-connected path to follow in the footsteps of their forebears.

"You may wonder why, as a married man, I would feel free to introduce myself to an attractive woman that appears to be single, but my situation is as follows: my wife and I have an understanding that we can each go our own way because we no longer have any interest in normal marital relations with each other. In recent years, she goes on vacations by herself, and I no longer keep track of any outside relationships with other men that she might have developed. In turn, I feel free to do the same thing, and with this informal estrangement and separation in place, I feel quite entitled to pursue whatever interests I develop in the course of my daily life.

"Please be assured, however, that I am not a Don Juan going around seeking female conquests. I am sixty-three years old, and my time of youthful indiscretions and irresponsibility is long ago behind me. Nevertheless, when I see someone most attractive like you and closer to my own generation, perhaps having seen more of life than the shallow 'young things' that seem to preoccupy themselves completely with the fashion trends of the moment, then I am interested in joining someone in thoughtful conversation—sometimes perhaps more," he added with a twinkle, "at any rate, with a person who is a good listener and has perspectives that are more compatible with my own than most of the empty heads walking around today.

"We are living in a critical time when a lot of changes are about to happen, and when the winners and losers of this world clash in what will eventually be a cataclysm of Armageddon proportions, I want to have a front row seat, so I can contribute to the future, which I'm very curious about. But let me interrupt myself before I get too wound up in my own convoluted views and hear a little about you and what your aspirations might be for the immediate future. By the way, I hope this did not sound too much like a curriculum vitae. I thought, however, that in the interest of clarity and time, I would give you a quick overview of my past so you could better understand the reasons for my personal orientation if our conversation turns in those directions as we go along."

With this, he settled back in his seat and poured himself another cup of coffee, returning to a listening mode and away from his own thoughts. They both noted to themselves that while he was doing so, he became more animated, with an intensity and exaggerated enthusiasm as he somewhat rambled on. As he stopped, it seemed to her that he now expected a similar discourse from her. While there was no sense of pressure in his voice, his piercing eyes appeared to extract such an expectation.

"Well thank you, Herr von Kleinhoven, for giving me such a clear and well expressed view of your background," she started out. "It certainly makes it easier for me to respond. While you were talking, I was thinking of how open and frank I might be in telling you about myself after only fifteen minutes of acquaintance. Originally, I felt that I should be more discreet than I am now going to be. I have decided, however, to tell you right up front that I am Jewish, which I have even kept from Frau Schaefer. If you have any hesitation or reservation in view of the current status those of us have to live with who have not had a chance to leave Germany, we should quickly part on a friendly note without bad feelings."

"Yes," he replied with a flattish, well-knowing tone. "I must say that I find it very nice of you that you are telling me immediately what might have been a problem for me. I consider it a measure of honesty and forthrightness on your part. I must also say that you do not look Jewish at all and that, although I was born into a Catholic family, we have had many Jewish friends and acquaintances over the past years. I am, therefore, quite comfortable being with you, and despite the fact that the government is discouraging contacts between Aryans and Jews, I have no problem sitting here with you and establishing a closer rapport. I have been a repository of much personal and confidential information in my life and so anything you wish to tell me I can assure you will not go any further, including your employment status with Frau Schaefer, by the way." The hint of a twinkle rose but quickly disappeared with a knowing smile.

Feeling good about his answer and spirit of openness, she proceeded to tell him about her background as a Jew, living an assimilated lifestyle, and her current anxiety as she waited for her chance to leave Germany. She also told him that she had heard others comment on her non-Jewish appearance and that she felt this was perhaps responsible for the fact that she was able to work for Ursula without having a negative impact at the shop.

He thanked her for reciprocating with a straightforward approach to her story and, after an additional twenty minutes of pleasant, miscellaneous banter, indicated that perhaps it was time for him to go home. He had a car parked at the other end of the square with which he was going to drive to Kronberg. They parted on a most friendly note as he continued his courtly manner by kissing her hand before picking up his hat and taking leave. Carola was not put off in any way by his "correct" departure because she preferred walking alone to reflect about her feelings and reactions in this "sea" of mutual forthrightness. She realized that he was someone with a proclivity to cut through posturing and obtuseness, though she was puzzled by the rapid exposure of facts he pursued which made her respond in what may have been a careless fashion at their first meeting.

On the way home and for the rest of the evening, she reviewed every detail she could recall of the hour she had just spent with him. After her emotional reactions had somewhat receded, she was able to think of their conversation in a calmer and more analytical way. There was no question that while she was sitting there at the comfortable little table of the café's outdoors section, her attraction and the magnetism she felt sitting close to him had continued to work their magic. The intensity and piercing focus of his eyes had made it impossible to think of anything else while he was talking to her. In her present, pathetic circumstances, she could not recall the last time she had sat with someone else, let alone an attractive man close to her own generation, in such a relaxed atmosphere with little obligation of things to do or stress to overcome. She could hardly recall the last time she was in such a pleasant setting; it might have been when her husband was still alive and vital and when, perhaps, he had had a particularly good day at his work, and they could sit somewhere together with strong coffees and small pastries.

That afternoon for a short hour it had been a different world in which she had temporarily had an orchestra seat, in a gentile world from which she and everyone of her own people had been so relentlessly excluded. There were no "*Juden Sind Hier Unerwuenscht*" signs; no threatening brown shirts with black boots and leather straps; no talk of concentration camps, beatings, or knocks on the door in the middle of the night; no quick departures leaving everything behind but the clothing on their backs; no change of ownership from one day to the next; and no mysterious disappearances and deaths. This was a quiet peaceful world; it seemed like a déjà vu of the good old days, except perhaps for the newspapers hanging on the wall that screamed headlines of crisis, enemies of the state, and threats of impending doom.

What had he really told her in his résumé-like recitation of his life? That he came from an old Frankfurt family, that he was wealthy and living comfortably in the suburbs, that he owned a business benefiting from the buildup of a prewar economy that was needed by the Nazi government to pursue its warlike politics, that he had sons in privileged officer positions who would inherit the ownership of his firm some day as he had years ago. The present political tempest was inconvenient but would not affect the order of things in the long term.

He had expounded on his marriage and his relationship with his wife, which was such that he felt free to pick up women as herself, whether locally or on the business trips he seemed to be taking, to pursue his own wishes as he pleased. With the Nürnberg Laws in place for nearly four years, it did not seem to constrain his actions, particularly after she so frankly told him about being a Jew. Did he care at all, or was he of such a social—or perhaps party position—that it did not matter to him? Question after question after question arose, despite his faux frankness. Who was the real person that appeared to be hidden behind a veil of order and discipline? Only in his more animated comments on future conflict and cataclysm did she detect any hint of emotion and hidden knowledge of much more than he was letting on.

Yet her attraction to his personal magnetism and charm stopped her from pursuing her self-probing questions with more skepticism and made her wish that this pleasant interlude could be repeated. After all, he too had told her how non-Jewish she looked and how comfortable this made her, sitting there with a most gentile of gentiles, quickly losing her unease and fear of being seen by a chance acquaintance, enjoying herself in the company of someone who looked like the epitome of those that wished her people no good. Despite her self-review, she fell asleep that evening wishing he would ask her out again for such an exciting interlude in an otherwise drab life.

She spent the next two evenings after work catching up on writing to Trudi, Lisa, and Eduard to bring them up-to-date, somewhat belatedly, about their moves, giving them addresses and even telephone numbers so that the correspondence that had become somewhat sparse could at least be continued. She knew she could no longer rely on the previous practice that mail would be forwarded to a new *Judenhaus* or an old-age home. She also hoped that in the event there would be good news about affidavits or permits which would come through either from Belgium or the United States, her family outside of Germany would at least call to notify her immediately. While she had become very skeptical that such would ever materialize in the short term, she tried to keep her hopes alive so she could regard their desperately poor living conditions as a temporary station in an eventual emigration move.

It seemed that von Kleinhoven was a creature of close programming and regularity; he showed up at the shop again the following Thursday and asked her out for coffee in the same fashion. This time the hint of a twinkle in his eyes came with greater familiarity. Again, at the moment when she was at the cash register and out of earshot of Gisela and a customer, he came over and said in a low voice: "Can we repeat our little repast, Frau Rossmann? See you in a little while across the way."

She was sure that by the time she again made it across the street, the same coffee and cherry tart would be waiting for her. Indeed, she was quite right. At their second get-together, his conversation was more far ranging and jovial and less pointed as he talked about his trips to different countries and interesting cities, time spent at seashore resorts, and his love for hiking, mountaineering, and hunting trips sponsored by his business associates. She did a lot more listening this time as they were together, rather than adding to the conversation because she could by no means match his experiences of interesting places. When it came to the hunting part and his description of trophies, antlers, and the like, she thought to herself, *I belong to a people who have been part of the hunted for thousands of years. How can I possibly be interested in hunting, whether of animals or—God forbid—people?*

Her polite listening, however, only encouraged him to become more effusive in describing his lifestyle. At the end of the hour, he suggested that perhaps instead of a mere afternoon coffee, they might go out for dinner together the next time.

"Well, Frau Rossmann, it was again such a pleasure to be such a good sounding board for my ramblings. I must say that I haven't been able to 'air myself out' in a long time. It makes me feel very good. I wonder if you would have dinner with me next Thursday so we could continue our conversation together in a more leisurely fashion?"

To her own surprise, she found herself agreeing to ratchet up the extent of her dating and said she would be pleased to join him. Her sense of adventure and continued curiosity went beyond any scope she had ever expected to go in what appeared to be a building rapport.

Before they parted, von Kleinhoven had suggested that she stay a little late on the following Thursday at the Witwe Hassan and do the locking up at the end of the day after Ursula Schaefer had left. This had become an occasional practice with which her superior had begun to entrust her. In that way, he could drive up front and still keep their date somewhat less noticed. She agreed, especially because now, as it was the beginning of August, Gisela Schultheiss had gone on a three-week vacation with her husband, who had returned on a short leave from the army. They agreed on 5:30 PM for Thursday, a little early to go to dinner but not if one started with a glass of wine or two before settling down with a menu.

9 DINNER AND AN ENCORE

The following Thursday, Carola stayed late to clean up and put the shop in order for the next day. She continued to volunteer staying to clean up, which Ursula had begun to appreciate because she was anxious to leave right at the closing, especially during the summer. When she was alone, Carola took the opportunity to change into different clothes she had brought along in a small bag. She put on a different blouse in place of the plain tailored one with its business feel. The golden brown silk skirt that she exchanged for the black one was the last piece of chic clothing she owned and had hardly ever made it out of the closet during the past five years.

At exactly the arranged time Von Kleinhoven pulled up in front of the shop in a black four-door Adler sedan and waited for her to lock up. She quickly got in next to him; they smiled at each other in pleasant anticipation as he drove off, making a big circle around the back of the opera house to go in the opposite direction. He drove down via the *Rossmarkt* to the *Kaiserstrasse* and finally reached the *Kaiserkeller* restaurant, where he had made an early reservation. Parking the car across the street, he came around the other side and with an elegant motion opened her car door and took her hand to help her get out. They walked across the street and were shown to a table on the terrace at a somewhat remote location so they could talk without being disturbed. He seemed either to know the wine list from memory or knew exactly what he wanted because he quickly ordered a white Mosel wine, which came chilled perfectly. The waiter opened it with demonstrated expertise and poured some into each of their goblets.

As he raised his glass, he proposed a toast. "My dear Carola, you might feel that this is a little quick, but we have been getting along so well that I suggest we do not stand on ceremony and begin calling each other by our first names. With this *dutzen* I think we will feel much more comfortable to pursue our relationship, and so I would like to call you Carola and have you call me Ulrich, or perhaps even Uli if you wish, please."

With this, she also raised her goblet, and indicating that the deal was made, they clicked each other's glasses and both took a long, slow first drink. As they began to talk, it did not take long to finish their first glass, and by the time their first hour together had passed and the bottle was empty, they had each had some three glasses and both felt very relaxed and comfortable. In the meantime, the sun had set, and the terrace area cooled off.

The waiter appeared and showed them to their table inside in a discreet corner and away from other people that had begun to come in. The menu was presented; Ulrich did not make any suggestions before letting her make her choice, perhaps in order to see in which direction her favorite tastes lay. She tried not to show how overwhelmed she was by the array of dishes she was apparently free to choose from. It had been so long since fanciful food of this description had been an option at all. Ultimately, she chose a terrine of clear broth with mushrooms followed by a veal cutlet with sautéed potatoes and string beans as the main dish. He, in turn, chose a smoked brook trout followed by a main course of loin of venison with potato puffs and red cabbage. To remain oenologically "correct," he selected a French red wine from the Rhône region—a *Vosne Romanee*—which was brought to the table, opened, and left to "breathe."

As their courses were served, she realized how much her level of gastronomy had been raised on this evening. Perhaps he was used to eating this way when he had restaurant fare, but for her it was a most unusual and magnificent experience that, with the help of the wine, made her shed all reservations about him. The meal was finished with a light strawberry mousse and an *Eiswein* for dessert. Both of them smiled, laughed, touched on occasion, held hands briefly, and revealed a synchronous body language that held promise for further adventure. When they left at the end of their dinner, they practically skipped across the street back to his car; he again opened her car door with élan and drove off pretty much in the direction they had come.

As he was pulling away from the curb, he said, "My dear Carola, this has been such a wonderful evening for me, and I think for you as well. May I suggest that we don't conclude it as yet and spend some more time together? I have the keys to a nice apartment of friends of mine who are away on a vacation trip. We can go there undisturbed and enjoy each other's company in great comfort. Are you game?"

With fine wine of every description making her lightheaded and in the jolliest of moods, she couldn't care less and wanted nothing better than to be with him no matter where and how. As they drove back into the West End, he headed toward the *Mendelssohnstrasse* and turned, proceeding about three blocks down the street. He parked the car in front of an attractive apartment house that was completely dark, all outside shutters having been let down. A single, outside light was at the door up several steps to the entrance of the first-floor apartment, which was separate from the hallway leading to others up an inside staircase.

He quickly pulled out the key, opened the door, and firmly holding her right arm, led her inside. He did not turn on any light as he seemed to know his way around precisely, and as soon as he had locked the entrance door from the inside, he grabbed her other arm and kissed her with a passion and intensity she had never known. The wine and all of their prior evening at the restaurant had made her sufficiently malleable and euphoric so that she was not only totally compliant but, after the initial happy surprise, returned his ardor in kind. Mouths opened, tongues intertwined, hands explored, arms and legs pressed against each other, and bodies began to meld and fit without leaving any space between them.

Heavy breathing encouraged him to pull her toward where he knew the bedroom was; she seemed to follow in a dancelike step, and as soon as he reached the bed, he systematically began to remove her blouse and bra. He quickly cupped her ample yet firm breasts and, working his mouth from her lips down the nape of her neck, found all the areas that gave erotic responses of her body. As she began a pleasurable moan, first softly and then more assertively, he began to undress himself with a speed and expertise she greatly admired. Before she knew it, he had removed all of their clothes, and their mutual groping extended to the lower parts of their bodies, which they had not previously explored. Hardness and softness mixed and mingled, and as he finally entered her in what she felt had been an interminable time, they began to establish a rhythm that gave them both an epitome of pleasure. His lovemaking had an autumnal quality.

As a man in his sixties, he was still firm and strong but knew how to take his time and be sufficiently slow to coordinate the build up of their passions in reciprocal ways. His strokes and penetrations varied to arouse and calm her with enough modulation so that her desire increased along an uneven path, which made and relieved pain and pleasure in alternating waves. When he finally brought on her release after a number of minor orgasms she had along the way, she experienced a crashing relief that seemed to go on and on for a semi-eternity. His own was well coordinated, and the slow crescendo of their different moans and gentle screams came in harmonic fashion. It had been a sexual experience as perfect as either of them had ever experienced, and they both rolled back from each other in joyous exhaustion.

As a full consciousness returned from the ultra-euphoric state they had induced in each other, they moved closely together with smiles neither could see in the total darkness. After a few minutes of stillness, she finally said in the softest of tones, "Now I can finally call you Uli without self-consciousness or embarrassment!"

They lay side-by-side quietly for another twenty minutes, absorbing all the pleasure they had just experienced. There was not much else to say that could enhance the closeness they had so briefly achieved. In fact, it was not so much a feeling of love that either one of them had created within the other than a growing sense of sexual peace that now had left them spent. After a little while, Ulrich began to speak.

"Carola, my dearest, I totally forgot how quickly the time went spent in such ecstasy. It's too late now for me to drive all the way back to my home, so I am going to spend the night here in the apartment. However, you may not wish to do that, and because you have to return to your work rather early in the morning, I will drive you back to your apartment after we get dressed."

He turned on a small night table light as he broke the silence, and she quietly nodded with a wistful smile. They were both caught up in putting their clothing back on as they looked at each other, kissed quickly one more time, and moved toward the front door. As she went out into the cool breeze of the late evening, she looked back at the apartment entrance. On the doorpost, she spotted a beautiful old brass *Mezuzah* now tarnished by neglect. Showing through the slot near the top was the letter *Shin* with a small crown on its top. The rest of the first word on the scroll was hidden within—*Sh'ma*. It was hard to imagine that his "friends" were on vacation in August 1939.

They rode home in virtual silence. Though she gave him the address, he somehow seemed to know it already and headed straight for the Fuerstenbergerstrasse. As he again came around to open the door and let her out of the car, she thanked him.

"Uli, I really enjoyed this wonderful evening together with you. It was so perfect for me, and I'm so glad I acquiesced to your magnificent lovemaking. I will not forget it."

"Carola, neither will I. You are a beautiful woman with a sensitivity, passion, and understanding I have hardly ever experienced. I thank you for giving so much of yourself. By the way, let me tell you so that you will not be disappointed that I will need to be away for a few days on one of my business trips calling on clients. Therefore, I may not be back by next Thursday but will see you no later than two weeks from today. Let's have a little repeat of this evening then. I can't wait until I see you again. Goodnight, my dear." He turned quickly, got into his car, and drove off.

She took out her keys and opened the front door to her Judenhaus, walking rapidly up to the top floor to unlock the door to her miniscule apartment. With the stupor of the evening's alcohol receding and the contrast of the luxurious apartment obviously belonging to a Jewish family in comparison to her own barren quarters, it became difficult to fall asleep immediately. The adventure had ended, and although she had temporarily stepped onto the high ground of an alien world and intruded on territory she was never entitled to, the momentary taste and touch had left her with an agitation that alternated between exhilaration and sadness and from there to loneliness and confusion.

Once more she asked herself, *Who is this man from the other planet and a world far off?* She had tasted of his mind by listening and of his body by an act of sexual love. He was too different, too unfamiliar to infer much else from their rendezvous. She could not see how this could ever change. She was aware once more of the heinous racial laws that had come to mind earlier that proscribed heavy penalties for committing *Rassenschande*, the defilement of race. They had just finished with such an act; he knew the laws well. They were really written with the primary purpose in mind of punishing the evil Jewish seducer of the pure Germanic maiden. Here, was it not the other way around? Who defiled whom?

She did not feel violated and under these laws had no rights anyway. She had participated and consented willingly and was glad afterward to have joined with him. How did he feel about it in the cold light after their mutual seduction? Would they do it again? Of course they would. Would it be time after time or a one time/sometime thing? Would she eventually feel violated, having been taken advantage of or have other painful regrets? Would he become perfunctory or indifferent in future encounters? Was this the delirium of a first time that would never be reproduced? In fact, would she ever hear from him again or help him select coffee that he could purchase from any number of their competitors in the city? In face of the horrendous persecution by Nazidom that had taken over her country and her community, had she committed the ultimate sin of succumbing to the enemy? By going over to his side had she, in effect, excommunicated herself, in fact staining herself with a mark of evil that she could never remove from her soul or her psyche? For a moment she scared herself to the point of trembling and, had she not been so tired at the end of this deeply profound experience, she would have lain awake in fear and trepidation. Fortunately, as it was, she fell asleep in deep exhaustion.

The next morning she arose early, and before going off to the shop, she called her mother whom she felt she had neglected somewhat by not visiting for the past two weeks. After inquiring about things at the home, Carola told her that she would visit that evening and asked if she could have a place at the Friday night supper table with both of them. Esther and Leah were so happy to anticipate her coming that they told a number of their newly made friends about their daughter with joy and excitement. Carola felt that because Uli was going to be away for the next two weeks anyway, she should concentrate on the realities of her own world and make her family happy at the same time. She also wanted to walk in the same neighborhood where she had spent last night in luxury and pleasure to see what her own people's living conditions really looked like in daylight and by comparison.

After work, she took the short walk to Feuerbachstrasse 14 and embraced her two elders with joy. She was quickly introduced to the first half dozen housemates that were within Leah and Esther's easy reach. She inspected their room, which after the first few weeks, had now been further arranged with the various little porcelains and odds and ends that had given their old apartment charm and individuality prior to their move.

The three women then moved on to the dining room, squeezing into an extra space at the already filled table. A *Kiddush* was made by one of the men who had recently moved in followed by a *Motzi* over a single *Challah*, which was sliced and divided among the twenty people in the room. Dinner started with a thin noodle soup, followed by creamed savoy cabbage, boiled potatoes, and a small piece of chicken, not nearly as well prepared as traditionally "*bei Uns zu Haus.*" The entire meal could not have been in greater contrast to the feast she had enjoyed the previous evening.

When they had finished, everyone rose from the table and adjourned to the small living area to continue their conversations with each other or to sit with someone whom they did not have the opportunity to talk to before. Soon the contingent who had chosen to attend services by walking to the Unterlindau synagogue, where Rabbi Neuhaus now officiated, began to return and get ready for the second sitting of the Friday night meal.

As Carola ambled past other rooms, she was amazed to see how many candles were lit in plain and fancy candlesticks, among them antique sets that undoubtedly had been in the owners' families for well over one hundred years. They had been especially polished as they were once a week for the Shabbat, stubborn beacons of Jewish assertions that were maintained despite a near total deprivation of their other material possessions. Conversations were animated—those who did not go to the services by virtue of their invalided condition wanted to know what the rabbi said, how many people attended, and who was there. Despite the rundown conditions of the public space, it was abuzz and alive with bent over and stooped suffering bodies that connoted stubbornness and a determination not to surrender their spirits of hope and dignity, clearly shored up by the brightly flickering event of Shabbat. Those coming in for the second sitting promoted this vitality with the invisible mantle of their synagogue experience. In all, Carola admired what she saw and felt herself drawn back into the Jewish spirit from which she had so knowingly left out of her infatuation with Uli.

She bade her mother and Leah good-bye along with their new friends and headed for home. It was still sufficiently light to permit her to walk past the *Mendelsohnstrasse* house where Uli had taken her. The porch light was still on, or perhaps on again, and she could clearly see and verify the large bronze *Mezuzah* on the door post of the main entrance. The roller shades were down, and she speculated that she would not see them up again if she returned to this address in the future.

As she reached her own building, the depressing sight of its condition and the loneliness that had become its hallmark once again registered strongly. She walked up the stairs to her fourth-floor room and wondered which of their residences, the old-age home or her Judenhaus, was bleaker for someone whose life had been altered drastically through such abandonment, hatred, isolation, and constant restrictions of ordinary freedoms. They had taken all these so much for granted until they had been taken away with the vicious assaults on the entire community during the past six years.

As she pondered the frenetic activity in the tightly packed home, she likened it to a rabbit warren or perhaps a mouse cage in which her people, and by extension herself, were kept for accountability and the inability to escape until the Nazis figured out what to do with them. That would probably not be until such time as they had managed to reach a state of acceptance by the gentile populace as to the actions they were going to take. During that period in these holding pens, she wondered which method of scurrying around, en masse or effectively in a solitary mode, was the better way to endure her personal condition. There was so much to think about, but she couldn't pursue the answers that evening. She went to sleep quickly to avoid obsessing further about her sense of feeling trapped and in a helpless mode.

The next two weeks went by slowly, but in between dispensing coffee beans and other luxuries, she was able to think some more about her state of things. Since meeting Uli, she had done a lot of listening but had asked few questions. If they were going to sit down (or lie down perhaps) again, could she ask him about his opinion regarding the residual Jewish population in Frankfurt? Would she dare? What might happen to people like her? Would he answer truthfully? Could he help, and did he have special knowledge to which she would never be privy and give her a sense of what the future might bring? Did she really want to know? Would she have the guts to refer to his comment that she did not look Jewish and, in case worse came to worst, would this enable her to survive among the Gentile population—same question as earlier—over and over again and again and again.

On the appointed Thursday, once more around four-thirty, Uli was back in the shop. He greeted her with familiar correctness so that no one would suspect their changed relationship. However, when it was time to check out the now full-pound purchase, he leaned over and whispered, "Would you like to meet at the café, have coffee, and then go to dinner from there, say, at about six o'clock?"

Her anticipation had been so strong during his absence that she had all she could do to pretend hesitation in her answer.

"Well, I did not know whether you would be back today, but yes, that would be all right with me." She did not want to extend the conversation right then and there in order not to draw additional attention.

At the end of the day, she locked up close to six o'clock and walked across and behind the opera house. He was already there, having ordered just two coffees without pastries this time.

"I am so happy to see you, Carola. I could not wait to come back. Let's have our coffee and then go for a relaxed dinner and evening as we did two weeks ago."

They finished their coffee in short order and then got into his sedan. This time he drove her out to Bockenheim, where he stopped at a small modest-looking tavern in a working-class industrial neighborhood. They entered a rather dark dining room that had tables lit by only a single candle and a large bar running across the length of the space. He asked for the menus and ordered a local Wurttemberg wine, which came in a boxbeutel, well chilled—again the goblets, the pouring, and the toasting to their reunion. The wine was more ordinary but, nevertheless, refreshing and relaxing. For their dinner, he ordered lentil soup for each of them followed by Tafelspitz with horseradish, spinach, and potatoes. In all, they had again consumed three bottles of the wine, which created the same merriment and carefree mood.

After dinner, he did not seem to feel the need for making the same proposition as last time. It was clearly understood between them that they would be heading for a repeat of their tryst. Back to *Mendelsohnstrasse*, the same apartment; with little hesitation, the keys, the door, the kisses, the bed, the undressing, the excitement, the fusion, the climbing of the same erotic mountains and coming down the other side only to climb again, and, finally, the bursts of pleasure of which she had fantasized with such intensity over the past fourteen days.

As they once more relaxed, now with some light on and smiles visible, she was again totally transported away from the Jewish side of her brain, and the idea of asking questions about the future faded quickly. He told her a little about his business trip; he was engaged in conversations involving a joint venture with a firm located right near the Polish border and what products might be manufactured there. Beyond that, it was general conversation which dealt with the possibility of war, his concern about his sons, and his need to return for final negotiations, which would keep him away from Frankfurt this time for at least a three-week period. While she was not crazy about the prospect of being alone for that long, particularly having just come off the high ground of her pleasure together with him, she understood, accepted his explanation, and prepared herself for another period without him. He once again drove her home. After a few last ardent kisses, Uli spoke up.

"Carola, dearest, it's going to be such a long three weeks for me. I'll think of you every day and can't wait until you're back in my arms again. Good night for now." With that and a wave, he quickly drove off as she mounted the steps to her house.

10 THE DARKNESS OF WAR—THE FEAST OF LIGHTS

A few days later, on August 23, 1939, Carola picked up the paper Ursula had brought to the store and saw it trumpeted the headline that Germany's Foreign Minister Joachim von Ribbentrop had gone to Moscow and signed a mutual nonaggression pact with his counterpart Vyacheslav Molotov. The pronouncements—likely produced in a whirl of vodka—were that peace was now assured between the two countries, which both bordered on Poland. For Ribbentrop, the ex-champagne salesman, this seemed like quite a diplomatic victory. A cynical populace, reinforced by rumors from family members of many who were now under arms and stationed somewhere in the east of Germany, therefore reasoned that war was near at hand. The entire city of Frankfurt, as well as the rest of the country, had adopted a bunker mentality.

At 4:45 AM on the first of September before sunrise, the German armies stationed near the border of what had been the Polish Corridor began a powerful artillery barrage, and the Luftwaffe warplanes took off for a fierce aerial bombardment of the new enemy's towns and lines of communication. Columns of tank brigades smashed through border posts along the dividing line and, backed up by endless columns of light and heavy infantry divisions, invaded Poland with some three million men of the Wehrmacht. They rapidly advanced against a well-trained but otherwise helpless Polish army, overrunning the countryside as fast as their men and machines could travel.

Britain and France, having appeased Hitler at Munich and with the invasion of Czechoslovakia, had signed a mutual defense pact with

Poland, stating that an attack on any of them constituted a state of war between Germany and the three nations. They had finally decided against the futility of appeasement and on the fact that they had to draw a line in the sand at some point. They therefore declared war on Germany on September 3. World War II had begun, and the Nazi military machine created in full view for the world to watch was now able to show what havoc it could wreak on Europe in the near future. While Hitler had not expected a military response from the Allied forces, he remained confident that this would be a short war, and he would conquer all contiguous territories within a few months.

The Jewish community and the fourteen thousand individuals who had been left behind in Frankfurt since the ascent of the Hitler government in 1933, including Carola, remembered well his threats that in the event of a war he would exterminate all of Europe's Jews. Perhaps she was going to be motivated now to ask the questions of Uli she had been so hesitant about before.

The outbreak of the war presented the entire community with a more rapidly deteriorating situation within the city. Presumably, these changes in both tactic and strategy were the same for all Jewish communities within the confines of the original German Reich. However, what was less known to Jews living within the Old Reich borders was whether these tactics were to be employed in the newly conquered territories or whether more brutal methods would be used by the advancing Wehrmacht troops into Poland and the other invaded countries.

Within Frankfurt, a new level of fear and hopelessness was created among all Jews who had been left behind. What did Hitler's threats of total destruction mean in actuality? Would they be further deprived of everything they still owned, pitiful as that might be? Were they to be expelled and resettled in countries that had refused their entry heretofore? Were they to be physically transported and pushed across borders of, say, Switzerland, Denmark, Holland, and other countries with whom Germany was not yet at war? Would it be something like the Polish Jews who were pushed into Poland on October 28, 1938, just prior to the Kristallnacht? Would there be more killings in concentration camps, starvation, beatings, and brutalization in place? Or would there be—God forbid—actual systematic killings of all those that would not die of "natural causes" in the course of the next few years?

It was impossible for rational, peace-loving, principally elderly people to think of all the variants and horrors that could be imagined by a humane and sane people whose core beliefs and heritage—precisely those characteristics for which they were now persecuted with such viciousness and zeal by the Nazi government—had taught them to live by exactly the opposite ethical foundations. Yet, the internal debates and arguments within all the groups now living in old-age homes, *Judenhaeuser*, and identifiably segregated places continued unabated. They took on an unhappy vigor that spread the contagion of pessimism and desperation at an ever accelerating speed.

To date—that is, during the six-year period from 1933–39—the Nazis' anti-Jewish strategy had been highly successful. First, there was a propaganda campaign to turn the mindset of the populace from a neutral, perhaps selectively anti-Semitic but largely tolerant, and progressive spirit of coexistence to one of estrangement, revulsion, and disgust in an attempt to desensitize the acts of violence yet to come. Second, the city's Jews had been ostracized, constantly penalized for one reason or another, eliminated from the economy of the city, separated and segregated from its business life, and made to suffer ever expanding daily depredations. Those who had not been adequately responsive to being pushed out had been concentrated in homes, group houses, concentration camps, and other locales where the score over their existence could be more easily kept in case the government wanted to exercise its future options for elimination of some sort.

Finally, the numerous Jewish organizations that had been established, some even centuries ago, to take care of the indigent and needy, those who wanted assistance with emigration, retraining, or other pragmatic solutions to reshape their lives for survival elsewhere, were consolidated and merged into the *Reichsvereinigung der Juden*. A supervisory group for their own community was thus formed to help the Nazis plunder their resources, harass them excessively, take away their real estate holdings, and make them use their own funds to provide for the welfare of those deprived of their own means by layoffs, firings, sale and destruction of their businesses, and other forms of governmental robbery. This consolidated entity was then given the responsibility to provide for the daily lives of those trapped in the city with little means of escape. In actual practice, this was done by instructing the appointed chairman of the executive committee to show up at Gestapo headquarters every morning to receive his orders for whatever the enforcers had in mind. It was a diabolical scheme, which only a group infused with an inhuman sense of order and organization could have devised.

The relentless advance of the Wehrmacht from the borders of Pomerania in the North, across the Polish Corridor to the Free City of Danzig on the Baltic, to the Moravian areas in a straight easterly direction to Cracow in the South pushed into the territory as fast as the motorized armaments could carry them. They covered up to one hundred twenty kilometers within the first five days and advanced to the outskirts of Warsaw within the first two weeks, as the major cities such as Lodz, Lublin, Radom, and Kielce were quickly captured. On September 28, just short of a month after the onset of the invasion, the Russians moved into the remaining areas of Poland from the east, thus splitting the country in half. This had been agreed to in a separate and secret provision of the treaty that was signed during von Ribbentrop's visit to Molotov in Moscow.

The war was not started by Hitler primarily to pursue and exterminate the Jews. He obviously had more important and grandiose objectives in mind. However, whereas Germany prior to his assumption of power had some six hundred thousand Jews or 0.9 percent of the total German population, Poland had a Jewish component of three million or about 10 percent of its population of some thirty million inhabitants. As the army swept into its newly occupied territories, therefore, it surrounded another three million Jews that had not been under German domination before. Warsaw alone had a head count of 352,000 Jews out of a total population of three million, Lublin some 39,000 or 35 percent of the total city, Lodz some 203,000 Jews or 33 percent of the total, and Kraków had 56,000 or 26 percent of the total population. Together, these four cities alone had a Jewish population in excess of the number of Jews living in Germany before Hitler's seizure of power in early 1933. They had all settled there throughout the past six centuries and had become a significant part of the urban life and culture during that time. In addition, the countryside was composed of many small communities in which Jews constituted from 20 to 50 percent of the inhabitants, living primarily in peace with their gentile neighbors with the exception of occasional acts of violence disturbing that balance and driving farm and agricultural workers into the big cities.

While the German army, therefore, drove into a thicket of increasing Jewish population, the accompanying Gestapo and Einsatzgruppen could employ the strategy they had set up and practiced so well on the German Jews during the six prewar years. Moreover, they had the advantage in compressing the time frame without going through the more cumbersome preliminaries of preparing the population-at-large. They started by quickly brutalizing and driving the Jews ahead of them into the ghettos of the large cities so that they could quickly separate them from the gentile Poles and put them into controllable areas of concentration. In fact, the cities they chose had to have railroad connections throughout the country so that, when needed, Jews could be evacuated and transported to other points where annihilation and destruction could be more easily begun.

By the end of 1939, about 70 percent of Germany's original Jewish population had left the country in one way or another. In the city of Frankfurt there remained about fourteen thousand, or 50 percent of the 1931 census, who had been gathered up and trapped. This number was somewhat skewed by the fact that the countryside surrounding the city within a seventy-five-kilometer radius had been cleansed more zealously by a population that had become excessively hostile to its former neighbors.

In an effort to make villages *Judenrein*—that is, without any Jews—they had driven them out of their villages and made them move to the city. These intraprovincial "refugees" had to register with the Frankfurt police so they would not just disappear and needed to be housed with their fellow Jews in increasingly overcrowded quarters. This was evident at Carola's *Fuerstenberger* address when after a single man had vacated a similar small apartment to emigrate to America, a family of five coming in from the village of Schriesheim had to move into the tiny space. Carola was, therefore, beginning to feel more fortunate in her single room, where she could still have her privacy—except for the bathroom—and come and go as she pleased. Similarly, while her mother's and Leah's living conditions were tight and sparse, the forty people occupying the old villa were still in better circumstances than those unfortunate families who had been forced to join the Jewish community in the city at such a late date.

By the end of September, hostilities in Poland had wound down as the government surrendered, and the troops laid down their arms. They were either taken into camps as prisoners of war or escaped across the border where they were established by the occupying Russians to become guerrillas and join others in largely unsuccessful attacks against the German occupiers. Included were some 250,000 Jews who thereby escaped to Russia in the initial onslaught.

Because life in Frankfurt remained relatively normal, warfare having been totally exported to the east in the first two months, Carola's work hours remained steady and unperturbed. This gave her time to visit the home more often and remain current with the Jewish community news whose newspaper, the *Juedische Nachrichten*, became the main source of information for the house residents. Her contacts with Uli had become more infrequent and selective. While their relationship continued with dinners and trysts at three- to four-week intervals, his business journeys and a distraction she perceived when they were together began to concern her somewhat. She realized that their lovemaking had lost some of the unique edge they both experienced the first few times. However, despite his efforts to maintain a freshness and originality, she understood that these were times of war, and the pressures he was undoubtedly experiencing in his work had begun to impinge upon their mutually carefree spirit. She could sense his preoccupation and the occasional intrusiveness that began to compete with the closeness and prior focus to the exclusion of everything else that she had found so unusual and satisfying. She did, however, try to be as understanding as she could under the circumstances that seemed to cast him into the role of the civilian "warrior" and her as his captive of coincidence.

His conversation before and during dinner and other times they were together had begun to shift more toward politics and the war situation.

"I doubt that this war will last very long. We've already finished with Poland—no great surprise—and just have to clean it up and put it in good order, in good German order, that is," he added somewhat sardonically. "Then we can turn to the West, France and England, who also won't put up much of a fight. France is hopelessly corrupt, and by putting one of the old generals in charge after we defeat them on the battlefield, we can have them rule their own mess and convert them to be our breadbasket. England is tough, but our Navy can isolate them, despite any help they might receive later from America. Besides, I think there are many Englishmen who would like to make peace with a Greater Germany and work out a way of living side-by-side without getting into each other's hair." His tone assumed a self-satisfaction and conviction which she found grating on her sensibilities. It had assumed an arrogance that was new to her.

Continuing, he explained: "They will need us for manufacturing goods that we can exchange with them for agricultural products and coal. I don't think they will sustain a war against us by themselves, despite the tenacity of their Winston Churchill, who will be prime minister one of these days. Oh well, by the time all this comes to pass, we Germans will have thought out how to rule all of Europe so that we can live in the prosperity we always dreamed of for ourselves. Perhaps after that, you and I can live in peace somehow, my dear."

He tried to wink as meaningfully as he could; however, as she looked at him, he really didn't quite succeed. She wondered whether she had become involved with someone who had a solid Nazi philosophy or who saw himself as just a "good German" patriot, proud and arrogant as most Germans were, now that they were at war. She felt she was unable to judge because, aside from her clients at the Witwe Hassan, she was totally segregated from that part of the German populace in these momentous days. Perhaps her denial blinded her to the ominous and destructive events that were building up around her.

The residents of the old-age home at *Feuerbachstrasse* 14 now numbered some forty people between the ages of sixty-five and eighty-eight. Since the recent influx of the past few months, it was over its capacity, and housemates, the administrator, Dr. Pappenheimer, and the staff were all still getting used to living and operating in the cramped quarters that had become the norm. The building, originally a private villa owned by a Professor Dr. Borchhardt and his family, had spaces of generous proportions with numerous family and guest bedrooms making it at all possible to have been converted for its present needs.

Prof. Borchhardt was an archaeologist at the turn of the century, participating in a large project in Egypt. When he decided to move to Cairo with his entire family, he donated his house to the Jewish community, which always had needs for accommodating new members moving into the city. This would give them time to find affordable quarters for themselves after they had located employment, schools, and other daily amenities for a normal lifestyle. In recent months, the Gestapo, after negotiating with the Jewish Community Board in an arrogant and unpleasant manner as they had the complete upper hand, purchased the building for a pittance of its current worth and leased it back to the community at a high price for its present use. This was a simple way of extracting funds and setting up conditions in the event the elderly people would be expelled some time in the next few years. They used the same method for each of the homes that were so designated and in the course of a short period had acquired numerous such locations, which, for the time being, remained utilized by elderly residents. Many seniors had recently moved in because of lease cancellations on their residences where they had lived for many years previously.

The new occupants had much in common as they congregated in the homes. Most obviously, they were all Jewish, and as a close second, none of them really wanted to be there and longed for the locations from which they had recently been expelled. As couples, they were all crammed into single rooms, using the common areas for both and socializing, a far cry from the more or less spacious facilities they had lived in prior to their move. The oldest occupant, a retired lawyer, Dr. Julius Kahn, was well known and most respected throughout the entire community. He and his wife had owned a small villa in the *Brentanostrasse* from which he walked to his office every morning, where he still practiced estate planning and elder law, specialties in which he was a highly regarded expert after a lifetime of experience.

A further common bond of most residents was that they had families out of the country, either in France, Belgium, Holland, Palestine, the United States, or a country in South America. Their country of refuge depended upon where they had obtained their entry visa and how rapidly they could leave Germany. During the past few months, they had exchanged a lot of information on efforts their relatives were making to extract them from their situation. Dr. Kahn had also offered to help because he still had connections among his gentile professional associates, who quietly offered him to be in touch by telephone if he needed something urgently or to see what they could do to move things along. At his age, Dr. Kahn was revered by everyone and was still addressed formally by his last name. In contrast, the others in the house had quickly begun calling each other by their first names, which became commonplace in order to make one another feel comfortable.

The need for medical service by the inhabitants of all the old-age homes was important with the onset of the cold season, as well as the continued care they all needed for health maintenance. During the previous many years, most had gone to physicians of their own choosing and had established long relationships with complete records established for their entire family. Now many of these physicians had emigrated, and those remaining were no longer permitted to practice medicine except to provide care for Jews, for which they were called *Judenbehaendler.* Moreover, they had to give up the offices they had used for patients' visits during regular examinations.

The new regulations called for people in this neighborhood to go to the Unterlindau Synagogue building during office hours set up by the Jewish Welfare Agency in the *Beit Midrash* with Dr. Jakob Blumenthal. He was one of the few physicians left behind and held designated office hours for people who were able to get there for scheduled visits. For those who could no longer manage to walk the distance, the doctor would come over to the home once a week and arrange to see them between breakfast and lunch in the dining room so he could examine the elderly and invalided, write prescriptions, and continue to keep their records. Medications would have to be filled in a prescribed pharmacy where the welfare agency provided for payment because most people no longer had enough money to pay for their own prescriptions.

Anyone who needed to be taken to the hospital at the *Gagernstrasse* across town would be handled beyond routine care. In fact, several people at the house had suffered heart attacks. One was of a serious type, Herr Lothar Maier, whose wife would visit him there every other day. He had been the owner of a manufacturer of fabrics that had been purchased by his former general manager for a meager sum. The proceeds were immediately transferred to the Welfare Agency by the Gestapo and used for the Maiers' upkeep. The couple had been under tremendous stress because the proceeds from the sale were the last funds they had planned to use for emigration. These events had induced several painful angina attacks in Herr Maier, which put him into the hospital. When they had heard about his illness, his family in Amsterdam was unable to find out about the severity of his condition.

One of the strongest complaints everyone had was a paucity of mail, which they were no longer able to receive from countries at war with Germany or even from those that were still neutral, such as the United States or the South American states. From there, mail was delayed, perhaps opened and censored or held by the postal authorities.

All of these deprivations were debated and dissected at the dinner table. Discussions also included reports of new wartime conditions, primarily from the east. News from that area dealt with continued aggression against the Jewish population in Poland, although the *Juedische Nachrichten* reported only in sparse outline and rumor rather than in reliable facts. Many people, in self-denying the gravity of their own situations, felt that this war would be of limited duration and take place primarily outside of Germany and that afterward, they could leave in some fashion that would permit them to join their families who had already resettled.

The festival of Chanukah in 1939 began on December 10. Rabbi Neuhaus prevailed on everyone to take out their menorahs and such candles as they had left over from years past and light them as they had done formerly in their own homes. They would do so now in their group homes to commemorate this holiday, the miracle of the lights and of the eternal lamp, the *Ner Tamid*, which was recovered from the ruins of the Temple in Jerusalem after its destruction. This heretofore minor holiday had therefore become of major significance for the entire Jewish community.

Gone were the celebrations with family, the presents for the grandchildren, and the bad jokes about *Weinukah*, the unseemly combination of words describing the Christian and Jewish feasts. Instead, here was an important opportunity to link the destruction of the first Temple to the destruction of the temples that had occurred the previous year on the November 9 Kristallnacht. It was little past the first anniversary when many synagogues had been destroyed all throughout Germany. The commemoration might also now be thought of as the third destruction of the Jewish community's temples 2,525 years after the first.

The menorahs of this year would be a beacon of remembrance for Jews and Gentiles alike, wherever torches had been lit in front of every sanctuary, first plundered and then destroyed, in which many Torahs had been burned into ashes but not oblivion. One had to wonder whether Hitler was the contemporary equivalent of a Nebuchadnezzar of those ancient days or whether the contemporary version was a lot worse, with all the threats of things to come. After all, would those trapped here now have the chance to "weep by the waters of Babylon," or would they not even have the opportunity to sit by their own Euphrates subjected to much worse than their ancestors? They did not know. They could not know. They could only hope that their captors would not have a capacity for evil that would exceed biblical proportions.

And so, on the first night of this special commemoration, every couple in the home brought down a menorah that they had among their few remaining possessions, for which candles had somehow been found and were then placed in front of their plates at the dinner table. They were also placed on the sideboards whose surfaces were used for those who could not join dinner at the same sitting so that they could join in the lighting of the candles at the same time. On this first night, Carola joined Esther and Leah for this occasion and became caught up in the spirit of the lighting ceremony. The three joined as everyone in the room lit their first candles plus twenty *shamesses*. It made a festive sight, with the blessings including the *Shehecheyanu* that would thank God for having made it and survived until this day.

Thereafter, in the overcrowded dining room with plates of latkes, applesauce, and sour cream being served, a strong, loud chorus of *Maos Tsur* surged forth in words that dealt with the heroic action of those days.

The voices of the elderly, brought forth in strained yet powerful song, belted out the words they demanded to be heard and understood. They would send them with all the power they could still muster in dedication to their faith and within limits of their remaining strength.

11 A LETTER FROM THE EAST

Ulrich von Kleinhoven arrived at his office at 9:30 AM, somewhat later than usual, on this Wednesday morning toward the end of December. He had been out the night before with a number of business associates and customers who had arrived from out of town and settled in for the evening at the Frankfurter Hof Hotel. After a lavish dinner that Ulrich had hosted, they adjourned to the bar and spent the next two hours boisterously debating the war over a mixture of beers, cognacs, and other assorted distillates and brews until the logic of their whiskey talk became fuzzy enough to call it a night.

The seven of them had reached noisy agreement that the war on the eastern front was almost at an end and that the next four to six months in the new year 1940 would probably settle matters in the west as well. The Fuehrer had certainly proved himself to be a political genius. They had all benefited from the mobilization to date and from the war he had started three months ago. Now that it was being won with such assuredness, it was certainly propelling them all toward a new prosperity. Once hostilities ended and all of the reparations would start to flow in, they could count on rewards and business expansions greater than they had ever dreamt of before.

They finally rolled out of their deeply upholstered, caned armchairs and, with the hardiest of backslapping and handshaking, parted from one another to go upstairs to their rooms or, as in Ulrich's case, to take a cab back to the Mendelssohnstrasse apartment to spend the night sleeping off his cloud of alcohol-induced good feelings. Because the "friends" he had spoken of to Carola during their first encounter here were not ever going to return, to the best of his knowledge, he had begun to use the place frequently to avoid the otherwise long drive home to his equally lonely house in Kronberg.

His secretary had already opened his mail as usual, except for those items marked "private" to which he generally gave priority. This gave him the pleasure of cutting the envelopes open himself with his newly acquired silver letter opener that one of his suppliers had sent him as a Christmas present. He readily recognized the hand-written address and special stamp cancellation as having come from his son, who had joined the Wehrmacht some eight months ago. As he began reading with increasing fascination, he understood that it had been composed at different times during the past three months, and coming from the city of Litzmannstadt, whose name had only recently been changed from Lodz, he was fascinated by the report of events his son Werner had put together for him. It read:

Lieber Vati:

Despite the fact that this letter will reach you around Christmastime or, at the latest, toward the end of the year, I decided to send it directly to your office rather than to our house because I did not want it to be read before you personally had a chance to do so. I know that our mother is not home that much anymore since she began traveling all over the country, visiting friends, pursuing her painting, or sightseeing on her own. However, just in case she would be on a break from all the activities in her "new life," I did not want her to get into material that was subject to gossip among her friends, as the information might still be somewhat confidential.

At any rate, as you can see, I have arrived with my unit in this city of some six hundred thousand population whose name we have now changed to the German, including the name of its main street from Piotrkowska Street to Adolf Hitlerstrasse. It did not take us very long to make it here to our first targeted objective, one hundred twenty kilometers from the border, once we got going. A number of fellow officers and I quickly found comfortable quarters in an elegant villa nearby, a large house where I would be happy to stay as long as they want us to occupy this place and reorganize it for the long term.

I was unable to write to you before the war started because

we were under strict secrecy orders not to reveal our location near a small village outside of Breslau, along with seventeen other divisions scattered around the area. I must say it was an exciting event to finally cross the border, knowing what was going to happen around September 1 and after being in constant readiness and bivouacked out in the field. For two weeks we were highly camouflaged to hide our existence from the farmers and some occasional bicycle riders who strayed into what we designated forbidden territory. So when the orders finally came and we began to move just before dawn on September 1, we could hardly contain our excitement in beginning our march eastward.

Our artillery units began a tremendous barrage just before sunrise to soften up several Polish battalions that were reported to have been stationed on the other side of the border in a defensive position. This was very effective in that they immediately retreated, as they did not want to get overrun by our obviously superior forces. Despite that fact, they sustained very high casualties because our *Luftwaffe* immediately followed up from their bases to the rear and strafed both the villages and open fields in which we knew they had taken refuge.

We moved twenty kilometers on the first day alone, which was quite a feat considering all the equipment that had to be brought in after the tanks cleared the roads ahead of us. In these towns, where a large number of *Volksdeutsche* were living who were left over from the establishment of the Polish Corridor after the First World War, we were, of course, treated like liberators, the conquering heroes coming back out of the Old Reich. These good people gave us much of the intelligence information that was very helpful to us in executing our quick breakthrough in the very beginning.

What was amazing to all of us was the large number of members of the Mosaic Tribe we found among the civilian population. Our intelligence had told us that contrary to what we had in Germany within the borders of the Old Reich, the number of Jews in Poland that we would encounter would be at least 10 percent on average of the entire population and more than that within the big cities. This is mind-boggling to me. If we translated that into our German lands, it would mean that there would have been within our old borders some seven million Jews before we started pushing them out and getting them to run in every direction. Can you imagine what that would have been like in our city of Frankfurt? It would have meant that at least sixty thousand in our *Heimatstadt* alone would have been crawling all over us. I shudder to think how that would have felt, living in our beautiful city today. What's more, I understand that they moved here into Poland from the German areas beginning in the Middle Ages and continuing up to two hundred years ago so that they could leave the ghettos in which we had contained them in many of our towns within Germany. I am certainly glad we "encouraged" them to leave so that those of us alive today do not have to feel what it would have been like then.

As we move into the big city areas in Poland, I hope we can continue the work our ancestors began. We had them well contained in our own ghettos up to one hundred forty years ago where they could perform functions for us that were useful to our native population, and we did not want to do ourselves. Somehow, back in the beginning of the nineteenth century, we let them out, however—called it emancipation—and let them live freely among us to take on our lifestyle. Then our Fuehrer came to power, resolute with his announced policy of making the country *Judenrein* once and for all. The best thing we could do, therefore, is to stick them back into the ghettos, where we can control them once again, make them work for us, and otherwise maybe get rid of them altogether.

On our way to Litzmannstadt, as we moved through the small villages near the border, we realized that even in these small "nests," they comprise about 20 to 40 percent of the populations. They don't look like our farmers at home, like hard working people with practical work clothes. They wear strange, old-fashioned knickers and kaftans, have long beards and straggly hair with long curls hanging down from their sideburns, and always caps covering the rest of their heads; all in all, not a very manly appearance. They were repulsive to us, and some of our men made fun of them and slapped them around pretty well as we moved through the villages.

To gather them up so that they would be out of the way while our troops moved along the main roads, we occasionally locked them into barns so we would not have to look at them with all their wailing and incomprehensible Yiddish language. It is amazing how easily these barns go up in flames when one is not careful and sometimes lights up a cigarette in order to relax a little; you know what I mean. The regular Polish population does not seem to have much sympathy for them either, as we can best interpret their implicit approval of our actions against them. Generally being afraid of us, they, of course, try to flee to the big cities as we advance. Our planes, however, make sure that the population is reduced on its way to the east as they strafe the roads to catch them pulling their carts with the pitiful belongings they are trying to move. Well, one way or another, we will take care of them before they reach their relatives in the big city.

Once we arrived in Litzmannstadt, we began to organize the layout in order to solve this growing non-Aryan problem. Amazingly, the city had a Jewish population of more than two hundred thousand, one-third of all the people living here. What are we going to do with all these people we do not want? They just seem to increase their presence as we acquire territories now under our occupation rather than reduce their numbers. It makes me feel like we are rolling up a large rug as we keep moving along the floor of a giant house that, while being uncovered to expose the beautiful wood surface underneath, rolls up into a larger and larger mass the longer the rolling process takes. At the end we have a huge bulk that could well roll back on top of us and even crush us if we don't tie it down or take it out of the room altogether.

In the past few days we have decided to create a new ghetto in a section called Baluty, which the Jews took over when their original ghetto was taken down back in 1825, and they swarmed out of it quickly. Today it is a pretty miserable and poor part of town from which those who did not become rich merchants never left. There were, of course, quite a number who became shop keepers or began manufacturing businesses, mainly in the textile trade. They did accumulate great wealth here and built comfortable villas in the fancy Gentile section of town. By the way, it is one of these villas that we have taken over—you should see what they accumulated.

The plan is now to order them to move out of their regular in-town apartments and houses, turn over the keys and everything to the president of the police department, and move their belongings into Baluty. We will then wall it in and let them move back and forth only through a single check point. Considering those who have fled from the city and are on their way to Warsaw, there will be many apartments empty in the old section that they will take over as their new quarters. Of course, they'll live in more cramped spaces there. However, they're used to that from the old days, and besides, they better get used to it again; in times of war everyone will have to live more modestly. All of this will give us greater control and accountability. We'll make them work for us in menial but necessary jobs, like ditch digging, latrine cleaning, and street sweeping, so that they can get used to the kind of work again that the Poles themselves have had to do over the past hundred years.

It seems that the Jewish population here had been divided into four classes; first, the real rich, the owners of factories who lived off the sweat of the others after making their investments; second, the workers who were employed by them, many of whom became communists because of the oppressive conditions in their workplaces; third, a small middle class, such as teachers, carpenters, bakers, and other service people; and last, at the bottom of the pile, peddlers and beggars, that is, those who made a living from day to day off the entire Jewish population and the Poles as well. It's going to be interesting to see how they'll live with each other when all of these classes are stuck together into the ghetto. Will they fight among themselves? Will they cooperate, and how will they obey their own administrative leaders whom we will impose upon them, through which we will give them their orders?

Well, those are enough different subjects for you to consider and comment on when we get together next. I don't want to hold up mailing this letter anymore, so I'll report more soon. In the meantime, a Happy Christmas and a good and victorious New Year for 1940.

With love and Heil Hitler,
Your Son Werner

12 THE NEW YEAR 1940

Carola decided to spend New Year's Eve with her mother and Leah at the home so that she would not be sitting alone in her own room feeling depressed. She had not heard from Uli, and she didn't expect to in view of the fact that he probably had obligations to spend his evening in the company of family or friends. Because the store closed early on the last day of the year, she ambled over in midafternoon. The residents of *Feuerbachstrasse* 14 did not really look forward to this last day of 1939 because there was no reason to celebrate the incoming new year—in fact, the idea of celebrating anything in any way was unappealing to them.

The management of the home had offered to make both the dining room and living room available for those who wanted to stay up later than usual to usher in 1940, providing cups for coffee and glasses for those who had perhaps brought wine, champagne, or Sekt to the home for any toasts they wanted to make. While all of that was downright repugnant to most, they did not mind sitting together longer than they would have on most ordinary evenings and welcomed the modest arrangements. It enhanced conversation and the exchange of all the nostalgic feelings that were inevitable for this particular date.

People began to congregate between eight thirty and nine o'clock that evening, beginning conversations in a livelier mode than they were used to on ordinary weekdays. Most of them had not heard from their relatives who had emigrated. They felt a little let down and disappointed, despite their strong tendency to rationalize that silence with the fact that their families had their own difficulties in the new lands rebuilding their grossly interrupted lives. Some of this stiff-upper-lip appearance broke down after a glass of wine or two, shared by almost everybody from a few bottles that some couples had been able to bring along from their leftover supply. Reminiscences were also readily shared down to the smallest detail, as it gave them a chance to convey mental images of former homes, friends, furnishings, and the way their children and grandchildren were able to share the evening with them in the old days "before Hitler."

Martin Friedmann, Carola's family's old neighbor, recalled the set of tin castings he had bought for his grandchildren as a New Year's present that contained all kinds of shapes such as walnuts, motorcycles, flowers, houses, and trains. These would be placed on spoons provided in the set and melted down over a flame at the kitchen stove. The metal, composed of an alloy that melted down at a low temperature, would settle in the spoon as a liquid to be poured into a glass, tin cup, or sink full of cold water. This would congeal and freeze the liquefied mass instantly into weird new shapes of an entirely different nature than the original out-of-the-box form. The new shapes would then be interpreted as something that would augur good fortune for the future and would foretell important events to come. This was useful only, of course, when there were good fortunes to imagine and when days of hope were still in people's mindsets and thoughts. It was now in the realm of pure nostalgia because there weren't family, grandchildren, homes, comfort, or laughter still in the paradigm of existence for most of those assembled. It had been a terrible year for everyone here, with feelings of abandonment, entrapment, and relentless denigration forming the main preoccupations with most of the elderly residents.

In a more somber and sad demeanor, they spoke to each other about all the bad things and depredations they had to endure in this past year. There were the forced sales of their homes and businesses that came upon them without warning. For those who had lived in rented apartments for many years, there were the sudden losses of leases, forcing them to move from the comfort of decades of familiar surroundings to this home. Here, one bedroom was the most they could retreat to for the privacy that had been theirs before.

This was all happening to men and women who practiced their Judaism not so much in an assimilated manner but within the framework of an emancipated community that was eager to contribute its talents and resources to a responsible and productive Germany. As Jews, they were proud of their disproportionately large economic, cultural, artistic, scientific, and humanitarian contributions they made to the entire country. When Germany was defeated in 1918 at the end of World War I, the Jewish population felt that defeat as personally as their fellow gentile—now Aryan—citizens. They began to work as hard as their friends and neighbors to restore their democratic aspirations within the Weimar Republic so that the country could resume its responsible place within the European community. There was a sense of mission for Germany's Jews alongside their fellow citizens. They considered it their obligation, ambition, disposition, and drive. It was also their motivation for calling themselves German Jews, who wanted to be good Germans along with all the others surrounding them. Rather than wanting to be assimilated, which connoted a loss of identity, they wanted to be integrated in a free society in which others of different backgrounds, histories, and beliefs could participate as well.

Instead, this government had demonized and expelled them since 1933, chasing them out, ruining their lives, and threatening worse to come. They lost their workplaces and economic means of sustaining their place in the community. Their support now had to come from funds supplied by the Jewish Welfare Agency, which obtained them from tax revenues originating from income taxes of those individuals who had declared themselves to be Jewish. As Mr. Eberstadt asked pointedly in the discussion among those gathered on this New Year's Eve: "What happens when this money runs out—no income, no tax revenue for welfare, no support of course from the German government—how will they support us? What will they do with us? There's no doubt that this money will run out within a three-year period. Germany is at war. What happens to us after that?"

The year 1939 had seen other important restrictions and deprivations. In September all radios were confiscated from individuals, and news was spread through the home, either from government-controlled newspapers or in some fashion from a radio that was kept illegally by someone whom no one wanted to know about. Beginning in 1940, Jews were now going to be forbidden to be outdoors between 9 PM and 5 AM unless it was for emergency purposes.

Since the end of the year, Jews were restricted to purchasing food supplies in designated stores at specific, purposefully inconvenient hours. For this they needed ration cards with the letter *J* stamped on them to make sure they would not be used in the ordinary stores. They were excluded from the conventional grocery stores, meat markets, and other shops with the excuse that gentiles could not be expected to stand in line alongside them while waiting to be served. The ostracism, the contrived revulsion, and the feeling of contamination continued to be spread to alienate an Aryan people from the contaminants of their world.

Traveling on trains or streetcars and staying in hotels and inns was forbidden or restricted. More hemming in, more caging, more shackling, less emigration, and less acceptance by even the most unlikely countries around the entire world. In the face of ugly rumors from the invaded and now occupied Poland, with the construction of Jewish ghettos as a prelude to containment, detention, and extermination, the government was creating more tension, more fear, and more waiting.

Data from the city of Frankfurt indicated that some 8,500 Jews left during 1939. That meant that about 11,500 remained in the city or about 35 to 40 percent of the original count in the early 1930s. That included an influx from small towns and villages in the Hessen-Nassau area of people who were driven out from their homes as part of virulent pogroms in the countryside. Despite all that, it was not a bad record of partial escape, but was that good enough? And what was the good of statistics to those who sat around their tables that night ushering in a new year with further, predictable persecution? As the time went past ten o'clock, people began to rise in order to retire. They did not have the desire or energy to wait until midnight for a magic that was long gone. Some wished each other a Happy New Year as they had done in the past. What was there to be happy about? Some converted the wish to a Happier New Year. Was there really any conviction in their wishes? By the end of the evening, it was quite apparent that no one was left with any. They all recognized the futility of their desire to make those with whom they now lived feel any better about their future prospects.

Carola kissed her mother and Leah good night at about ten thirty and briskly walked home in the cold December air.

13 VICTORY IN POLAND

During the first few days into the New Year 1940, all the newspapers in the city began trumpeting the additional initiatives taken by the Wehrmacht in the east as it continued its brutal conquest of Polish territory on its side of the Bug River. According to the reports Carola read in newspapers left by clients in the store, this was the dividing line that had been agreed upon between Russia and Germany in their secret non-aggression pact a year earlier. Further, the former Polish lands were divided into four areas: the *Warthegau, the General Gouvernment, Greater East Prussia*, and, lastly, *Greater Danzig* and *West Prussia*.

Fighting had ceased by early October except for rear guard guerrilla action by Polish partisans as the government had surrendered at the end of September. Depending upon the degree of anti-Semitic virulence within each Frankfurt newspaper's policy, the war reporting and subsequent occupation of each town was linked to the Jews. The papers stressed the invasion in varying styles of vituperative expression deriding the enemy. It extolled the Wehrmacht's "defensive fighting" and the defeat of the Polish army with its Jewish contingent who had goaded the Polish government into "starting the aggression" against the German forces in the first place. Indeed, 10 percent of the Polish army's soldiers were Jewish, in proportion to its population. Some sixty thousand soldiers had been killed—therefore, six thousand Jews—during the initial thirty-day campaign. After that, as prisoners were collected and concentrated, a disproportionately high number of Jews were retained in prisoner of war camps, whereas a large number of Polish gentiles were sent home to resume their civilian status. The Frankfurt press maintained a euphoric and victorious tone to buoy the spirits of the general population. The Jewish community, on the other hand, worried and trembled with fear, realizing that the hatred whipped up by the media could well result in further local violence directed at those trapped in the city.

In Poland, the military drive led the Germans to push those Jewish inhabitants who were not killed outright in the smaller towns and cities further to the east but had the effect primarily of making them flee into the cities of Lodz, Warsaw, and Lublin. This was in accordance with the German strategic plan to create large ghettos in those places where their concentration and "collection" could be more easily managed for further disposal later on. Thus, for example, the town of Kalisz, which had a seven hundred-year-old Jewish population stemming from an exodus out of the Rhineland, was essentially emptied of its Jews and became one of the first occupied communities to be claimed as *Judenfrei* by the administrators of the newly established *Warthegau*. As the consolidation of the occupation proceeded further, a myriad of dictates, regulations, restrictions, and prohibitions were formulated in the conventional German manner and published in German cities as well to whip up enthusiasm for the forthcoming campaigns and drives toward France and the low countries.

In the west, the key to accomplishing a move into France and the low countries was to formulate a strategy on how to wipe out the effectiveness of the Maginot Line so named because it had been built under the supervision of André Maginot, the French defense minister. It had been designed as a series of concrete obstacles, hurdles, and traps to shield or at least delay the mechanized German forces from invading French territory until that army could muster its own defenses. The Germans were easily able to overcome those erroneous assumptions because the French concept was based on the experience of twenty-five years earlier, during World War I, and was now totally obsolete.

Once the highly mobile panzer attack began in the spring of 1940, the German High Command essentially preempted this stationary fortress approach by rapidly turning northwestward and outflanking the fortifications. At the same time, it had accomplished invading Holland, Luxembourg, and Belgium and entered France to the northeast, well past the end of the fortress that France had mistakenly created for itself giving an illusion of invincibility. Additionally, with the new capability of the *Luftwaffe*, parachute troopers, and flexible armaments that were not available a quarter of a century before, the Wehrmacht quickly out-ran and out-fought the Allied troops, who naïvely thought they could stave off the new, more powerful variety of tanks and fast-moving vehicles based on modern design. The contest appeared to get more uneven as the various invasion routes became established, and the idea that this fortification might be short lived began to take hold among the civilian population.

14 ANOTHER CUP OF COFFEE

Ulrich von Kleinhoven resumed his regular visits to the Witwe Hassan coffee store right after the new year, and it became readily apparent that the purchases of small amounts of beans he had begun during the past ten months were secondary to his primary purpose of making arrangements to resume his evenings with Carola. For reasons she could not quite understand, he would never call her at the store. She presumed he did not want his voice to be recognized. On the other hand, he also never gave her a telephone number that he could be reached at, again, presumably, so that she could not leave a message identifying herself in the event he was absent at the time she made her call.

During the first three months of the year, they did not see each other more than once a month but followed their established meeting routines in the predictable fashion. They both appeared quite comfortable with this pattern; he varied the restaurants for reasons she could only remotely guess at. Post-prandial lovemaking at the apartment with the abandoned *Mezuzah* began to have a monolithic pattern that, while still being pleasurable to her, made her feel as if there were less novelty and excitement, at least on his part.

She sensed a tension and distraction in him coursing through his entire body at what were meant to be their most intimate moments. This made her feel less connected to what was going on in his life and more excluded from the psychological and mental sharing that had seemed so novel when she was first involved. She hesitated to ask him what was going on and was glad that she had withheld feelings of curiosity and doubt when, after an evening that seemed particularly rote, he came forth with an unusual proposition.

"Carola, my dear, it would not surprise me if you had noticed my nervousness and distraction the last few times we've been together. Let me assure you that it has nothing to do with you or us. Rather, it is in consequence of my business, my traveling, and the fact that my sons are now involved in active fighting where they could easily be in harm's way. So you see, I must stress that it is really not about our relationship."

He nuzzled her cheeks with small kisses to heighten her attention. "I apologize for this and would like to make up for my lack of attentiveness to you the next time we get together. Rather than just a short evening, I suggest we spend a weekend together toward the beginning of April and drive out into the country somewhere. We can stay at a small inn, where we can take walks, enjoy the fresh air, and have the good conversations we've had on better occasions. How would you like to plan for me to pick you up in the late afternoon near your residence, say on the second Friday in April around five o'clock, and bring you back on that Sunday night so that we can both go back to work on the next Monday morning?"

"Why, Uli, what a wonderful idea," she responded. "I haven't been out of the city in years now and would really enjoy being some place with you far away and alone where we can talk freely and without any time limits. Where would you suggest we go?"

"I know of a small inn about an hour's drive from Frankfurt in the South Odenwald and not too far from Heidelberg. They serve good food and not too many of our party members find their way down there on weekends. There are also good walking trails, places to rest, well cultivated woods, and a feeling of being away from everything. I think we would both enjoy it, and I know that after another busy month of traveling which I have ahead of me, I would be more than ready for such a weekend. What do you say?"

"I think that's great. I will count the days until then," she replied happily.

Since this conversation had taken place after he had taken her back to near her building by car, they kissed lightly and bade each other good night. She practically raced up the stairs with a new infusion of anticipation and began to plan in her own mind how she could go about doing her part to expand a relationship, which she now felt was a real possibility.

15 DOUBTS, FURTHER DECEPTION, AND DIVERSION

Just before five o'clock on the appointed Friday in April, Carola stepped out the front door of her apartment house with a small suitcase in hand containing comfortable clothes, walking shoes, and her toiletries for the weekend. She looked over her right shoulder and spotted the black Adler sedan about half way down the block with motor apparently still running. She walked toward it with a spring in her step, quickly opened the passenger door, greeted Uli cheerfully, and asked him where to put her small case. He quickly popped the trunk open from the inside, motioning her to the rear. She walked around to place her case inside, next to his, and hopped in the passenger seat, giving him a light buzz on the cheek as they quickly drove off.

He turned the corner at the end of the street, down the *Oederweg*, on through the center of the city, and quickly headed for one of the bridges across the river. From there it was a matter of hooking up with one of the highways in the direction of Darmstadt and ultimately heading through smaller roads into the Odenwald. An hour later they reached their destination at the small town of Brombach. He seemed to be very familiar with the village and immediately found and pulled up at the *Waldhaus*, a small inn on a back street near the end of town. Checking in with the owner, Herr Hinkel, was perfunctory and friendly. Uli was given the key to a generously sized room on the second floor and treated with the familiarity of a frequent visitor. His host suggested they come down promptly to have some wine and sit down to dinner by seven o'clock, for which he suggested the home "harvested" venison.

Though they had not been alone together since Uli made his original proposal several weeks ago, they followed their host's suggestion, quickly looked around the spacious room with a double bed and private bath, and washed up briefly. Back downstairs they were seated in the barroom with a properly chilled bottle of *Dr. Burcklin's Qualitatswein Mit Predikat*, which they tasted with anxious anticipation and pleasure. Their first weekend away together had begun; the sun was setting slowly, and as they caught up on events from their recent separation with one bottle following another, their move into the dining room for a first rate dinner made the transition from the week's work to this hideaway in the woods seamless and practically magical.

After dinner, they went up to their room, undressed each other, and made up for lost time with an enthusiasm Carola had not felt during their recent get-togethers. Now, as they were spread out on the bed, physically satisfied, the haze of the three bottles of wine consumed before and during dinner was lifting with the energy expended during their sexual encounter. Uli rose, went to the bathroom, put on his robe, and sat down in the armchair across the bed. He lit a cigarette, a habit he seldom took up now. At the same time he handed Carola her robe, which she readily slipped on, as well as taking a cue of the seriousness she sensed in his demeanor. He interrupted the quiet, speaking thoughtfully but with a troubled tone in his voice.

"Carola, my dearest, I would like to say some important things to you about a lot that has troubled me lately as I made my rounds traveling during the past few weeks. Much of what you will hear will puzzle and perhaps upset you. But remember, they are not personally directed at you, and I do not want to debate or argue with you. You need not even respond on matters you could not possibly comprehend. But you have been such a good listener, often with just sparse yet kind and insightful responses. I feel comfortable in asking you to be a sounding board for me to unburden myself of my most confidential and innermost thoughts and to share my queries with someone I can trust.

"Let me go back to some of the things I have already told you about my past. We von Kleinhovens are from an old Frankfurt family that, to the best of my knowledge, has had its roots in the city for hundreds of years. My father never told me that much about all our ancestors; he perhaps did not have direct knowledge of our family tree or was not interested in exploring the history of the many generations that preceded us.

"We were said to have been prosperous and well-known in the past, but during my lifetime, that seemed to be no longer the case. I saw only modest middle-class circumstances when I was a child. It was somewhat later that a measure of comfort returned to our lifestyle and with it a modicum of gentility and appreciation for a cultural environment and behavior. Earlier in my youth, my father seemed more preoccupied and troubled with our immediate past and with an intense struggle to lift our family by our own bootstraps, so to speak. It was not necessarily out of poverty but more out of the need to advance, to climb within the ranks of the society in which we lived, and to achieve comfort with his advancing age and my approaching adulthood. As I told you before, we are Catholics, highly conservative, and not given to being attracted by radical movements or social experiments.

"My father was a young man during the last major depression of the nineteenth century in the 1890s, when he was just beginning to build a career for himself. He wanted somehow to establish himself in the metal field, which interested him and in which he foresaw a future. Not having a formal university education, he found a job with a reputable firm in the scrap iron industry, itself not necessarily a type of business with the highest ethical practices in its tradition.

"His employers were two partners, both Jewish, whose ownership was second-generation. Their fathers, who founded the firm not too long after Jews in the city were let out of the ghetto, had been good friends, and business opportunities had opened up to them in fields that were generally looked down upon by the gentile community at large. In other words, they were scrap dealers who came around with their wagons to residences or building sites to take away undesirable junk that they bargained for to buy at as low a price as they could possibly get away with or even cart away for free.

"They stacked their various purchases in a yard on land they had purchased in an industrial section near the railroad track out on the way to Hanau. When they had accumulated enough to fill up a flatbed railroad car, they would resell the scrap by its weight to steel mills for reprocessing. They would also sort out noniron metal objects that were worth more by weight, such as copper, lead, and zinc piping, or anything else for which they recognized premium value. It was a matter of expertise, clever bargaining, and hauling away.

"In those companies that did not feel themselves bound by honest behavior, there were practices like short weighings when buying and excess weight reporting, or adding sand or water surreptitiously, when selling. My father quickly learned that his employers, whose names were Jacobs and Krakauer, were not that kind of people and in fact were totally honest in giving fair value and selling without cheating on the weight. They told him they were both religious and good, lawful citizens, and these practices for which their trade was always regarded with suspicion and distrust were alien to their behavior. They also inculcated him with the duty and obligation never to engage in these illegal tricks himself, which he obeyed gladly and scrupulously.

"During those years of recession when many people were laid off from their jobs and unemployment again rose to astronomical levels, much economic pain was experienced all over the country. My father, however, was not only not laid off but, on the contrary, promoted to general manager of the yard with extra responsibility and pay and also with the complete trust of his supervisors and a minimum of direct oversight. This permitted him to consider his employment as stable, the beginning of a decent career, and enabled him to marry and raise a family. My brother, sister, and I were able to grow up in a cultural milieu and with a good education through the university years.

"In an effort to provide continuity in the industry in which he got started, my father urged me to study mechanical engineering and metallurgy. With such skills he felt that some day I could start a machine works and get into a sufficiently sophisticated field of metal production and tooling, including parts and shapes of great complexity. I could then build a company with expertise that could not easily be matched or competed with."

Carola sat quietly, listening and concentrating not only on the content of his words but also on the emphasis he was giving to his father's position with his Jewish employers. Was there a message here that basically tried to explain the relationship he wanted to strengthen with her? Was it to build closeness and background to remove some of the strange behavior she sometimes felt at their most intimate moments? She so hoped her assessments and instincts were right.

"I was able to accomplish these goals before World War I, and although I had to interrupt my business career because of the draft into the armed forces, as an officer I was able to serve in the planning sector of our war effort and avoid service in the front lines. My father had started the company for my benefit and continued its management while I was in the service. After the war, I immediately resumed building up our venture, and because of what we had started and our connections to the steel industry by our firm, during the hyper-inflation years of 1922–24, we did not suffer from the devastation of the kind that businesses based on mere trading had to face.

"Even before the National Socialists came to power in the early 1930s after all our revolving door chancellors, although I'd never been a strong political ideologue, I saw whatever movement was in control as an opportunity to provide growth for my company. By injecting myself at the fringes and soliciting work for my firm based on rearmament efforts for the war, I quickly realized that growth and profit by these means were grim but exciting realities. To do this I had to join the right groups within the party that was now in charge and swallow hard when there were fierce internal battles over some of the ideals I disagreed with. With hindsight, I suppose I had made a sort of Faustian bargain—simplistically put, I wanted to reap the benefits now and somehow figure out how to pay for them later.

"Some of the far-out goals, claims, and threats that I read in Hitler's *Mein Kampf* I could hardly believe as rational or real but felt they were a skewed perception of a mind full of uncontrolled rage. To that point, I must admit that by now, many years later, I underestimated the realities he created after daring to enunciate them when no one else had the brashness to do so. You can see where our government, having started the war, is following the plans outlined and executed by Hitler more closely than we had all originally believed to be possible.

"Carola, you may now or ultimately later hate me for what I have said and will continue to tell you. But I will admit that the opportunities which have opened up to me because of my adherence and cooperation with the government's policies have been large, and I am unwilling to forgo the benefits I have received so far. I'm really counting on the fact that the war will be a short one; we seem to be so well prepared and armed that we will overcome our enemies in short order. Then we will be able to establish a new order all over Europe that will benefit not only most Germans but ultimately everyone who is either ruled by us or allied with us. Our government will be run by strong and pragmatic businessmen who will sooner or later sideline the extremists and, with foresight and hard work, will provide a prosperity that has not been seen before in this world. In that way, we can prove to the Fuehrer—if he is still in power by then—how right he was, while preserving only the rational part of the vision he forced on all of us so early on."

His tone began to assume that of an academic lecturer, dispassionate in recitation, almost cold and calculating, sharply devoid of the compassion the romantic setting should have evoked. She continued to say nothing and sat quietly as he proceeded in a more animated fashion. At the same time her confidence faded and doubt arose that all these things he was getting into would be of comfort to her as a Jew.

"Let me now say something about our actions against the Jewish community to which you belong and which has admittedly gone through harder times than it has been used to," he continued. "Let me also add that, as I am now emotionally involved with you—and I'm still trying to sort out what that could mean for both you and me, especially after the war—I will try my very best for us to continue to be together and to spare you some of the hardships you have seen as they were imposed on others of your coreligionists.

"As I've said before, I was raised in the Catholic tradition. This meant that I was taught by the priests, and even through some of the occasional, disparaging comments within our family, that the Jews killed Christ and were therefore doomed to suffer the consequences living in a Christian world. We were told that this was their just fate and that, unless some day they too saw the light and converted to Christianity, their days were numbered. This is perhaps part of an anti-Semitic doctrine that creates and instills hatred in us Christians, whether consciously or subconsciously, and that leads to a will to remove Jews from our midst. We have tried to do this by encouraging them to leave Germany and emigrate to other lands, but the rest of the world has refused to accept them into their own countries or even to let them go to Palestine, their own homeland. The Evian conference in July 1938 amply proved this point. It certainly tells you that the world is not a place sprinkled with kindness, or milk and honey, as you say.

"When I still lived at home growing up, my father explained to me the conflict he had within himself because of the experience he had with his employers. He had received kind, humane, and honorable treatment from them, and they gave him a chance to build his future with them, despite the hard times. It gave him prosperity so he could bring up his family with all the advantages of economic and cultural refinement that existed within only a small segment of our German society. While he saw many of his Jewish neighbors having undesirable traits such as an unpleasant pushiness and other stereotypical habits with which his prejudices had infused him, he felt personally, that he owed them a degree of loyalty. In fairness, they were now his fellow citizens and had the right to live under the protection of the law and the benefits of equality. At this point in time, as a more pragmatic and cynical adult, I must admit that I am influenced by the current policy of segregation and eventual elimination from our society that our government is now teaching our people. I, too, have conflicts that I am trying to resolve, and that is why I am talking to you or perhaps at you, Carola, to work out what I cannot do in silence and solitude."

She looked at him in utter amazement as he continued more rapidly and with an animation closer to manic than she had ever heard from him before.

"Uli, I must say I am shocked at the thoughts behind your words. Are you sure you want to continue in this vein and disrupt our relationship? I'm so afraid at what might follow."

He ignored her state of alarm and simply went on as if he had not heard anything she said.

"I have studied the history of you Jews, especially since you were emancipated and as you lived with us in our hometown of Frankfurt. It simply astounds me that after we kept you in the ghetto for seven hundred years until the early nineteenth century, you have burgeoned forth as we let you move into all parts of the city to be our neighbors. We were often reluctant, but you adapted to our ways of life and assimilated, away from century-old habits, in only a short four generations. I find that amazing after having learned how you live in your own ways with your own strange customs.

"Until recently, you spoke your own Yiddish language in our midst, which we cannot really understand, and therefore suspect to be a secret code in which you have communicated among yourselves for the prior twenty or twenty-five generations. As soon as we permitted it, you understood our ways and quickly adapted our traditions as your own. You wanted so badly to become Germans—or as we so often say, good Germans, meaning cultured, refined, polite, indirect, obtuse—perhaps as this was our vision of ourselves and our sophistication.

"How have you done this? Some of you have converted to Christianity, although I don't believe that any of us are convinced of your long-term sincerity or loyalty. You must have studied us well from inside your ghetto looking out at us. Soon after your emancipation, you streamed into our universities to learn the subjects of science, technology, philosophy, and history—all that you wouldn't have been able to learn inside the ghetto. There you studied your Torah and your Talmud. Is that what gave you the basis for your inquiry with the skills to learn what you did as soon as you came into our secular schools? If those resources are that strong, shouldn't we be emulating you and studying them ourselves? Where have we been all this time, passing up such bases of knowledge and wisdom?"

His eyes seemed to glaze over with a rush of excitement Carola had never seen in him before.

"When you arrived in our medical schools, you not only learned from us, but because of your long tradition as healers, you turned around and taught us medicine. You copied our fraternity system we used in our German medical schools, wore the same uniforms we did, learned to guzzle beer in the same enormous quantities, learned to get drunk and bleary eyed, and then cut up each others' faces and carry scars of honor for a lifetime, just as we had done for hundreds of years ourselves in that ridiculous Junker tradition. Separate but equal through wisdom and stupidity. You not only quickly became students but soon teachers as well in all the other subjects too. Is that the secret of your religion and your heritage?

"You joined our army, although we would not let you become part of our Senior Officer Corps. I don't imagine you've seen the famous etching of Jewish soldiers wearing steel helmets with spikes on top instead of skull caps while conducting a High Holiday service in Alsace Lorraine. It was near the city of Metz during the Franco-American war in 1870–71 and an act of implied loyalty to the German army in the face of your traditional observance of Jewish customs, thousands of years old.

"Again, in World War I, you joined our infantry, artillery, our medical corps, and our airship bombardiers. You contributed to chemical warfare; you sacrificed, as we all did, in the name of one thing: to be accepted, for wanting to be good Germans. *Zum Krieg Fuer's Vaterland*—Land of our fathers. What a strange concept for a people whose fathers were Abraham, Isaac, and Jacob and whose greatest leader was Moses. Not fifteen years ago, one of yours, Ludwig Landmann, even became the lord mayor of our city of Frankfurt—absolutely astonishing and, in a way, incomprehensible.

"Ever since the establishment of the Nobel Prize, you Jews have won some twenty of them, while you were only 0.8 percent of our population. Of these twenty prizes, eleven went to German Jews, winning them not only for yourselves but also for the Fatherland. Adolf Hitler regards all this as evidence of infiltration, penetration, and the corroding of the Germanic spirit. He wishes to build a pure Germany for racially pure Germans. He has announced this goal often: the removal of all Jews from the *Altreich*, our original nation.

"I can tell you in the highest of confidence that I have not only been calling on my customers throughout Germany in my travels but have also participated in organizational meetings in Berlin, among an elite group that has debated these issues on their merits. Some of us have taken the position: Why are we expelling the Jews when they have demonstrated their desire to contribute their talents to give us what we Germans want and need? What if we did not try to get rid of them but used them to help us win this war and establish a different but new order? Would they oppose us or would they support us? They've done it before. Would they not be an asset we could use with which to conquer our enemies?

"As I just said before, I have never been able to figure out the source of your intellectual and spiritual power and drive for inquiry, for study, for your reasoning and the willpower to absorb unlimited suffering while sticking to your heritage. What is it within you Jews that makes you so stubborn and impervious to misery? What is it with us Germans? Do we hate you, or do we really love you and are outrageously jealous to see you compete with us? Do we think ourselves incapable of competition, and is our self-confidence and arrogance really out of fear that we will break down and expose ourselves as a people of less than perfection? Did we let the genie out of our bottle when we let you out of the ghetto, and do we really feel we cannot contain or integrate your talents?

"In proclaiming our superiority and the need to eliminate you, are we really admitting the opposite, that is, our own inferiority without you in our midst? Can we not tolerate the competition inside Germany or outside in the rest of the world? We did not rearm and put five million men in the Wehrmacht in order to eliminate five hundred thousand Jews in our own country or even the poor miserable millions more we will inherit as we conquer others. No, we rearmed to recover justice and honor for ourselves and to obtain revenge for the horrible treatment we received at Versailles. Do we really see you Jews behind the powers of every nation arrayed against us and behind every tree in the forest surrounding us? I can't believe that our paranoia is that immense; in the long run, it would consume us. Perhaps this is what I am really afraid of. This is what I have held within me despite my outward successes. And this is what I am confessing to you despite the fact that you are my lover and not my priest and did not necessarily come here with me to hear my innermost, troubled thoughts."

By now, the level of his voice was raised another couple of notches, and a fury, blended with anger and pleading, had settled into his tone. He was covered with perspiration and seemed close to tears, although he was trying to retain a near-shouting volume to project a strange strength that had probably left him some time ago during his convoluted and contorted monologue.

Her eyes were open wide as she had listened in silence, comprehending some but not all of what he had said and wishing the romantic atmosphere of denial was still there between them and that this political philosophic monster had not been raised in such an unexpected manner. Finally, she could no longer contain herself in the silence and restraint she had managed over the last half hour.

"Uli, I must interrupt; after listening to you so diligently, I cannot contain myself any longer. You have said many things that obviously come out of your innermost self and that you have never told me before. I am flattered that you are sharing these thoughts with me, and

I promise they will stay between us and not go any further. On the one hand, there has been frankness and, I hope, honesty that have opened up an entirely new and intimate relationship between us. You have begun to explain to me the background of your attitudes and readily confessed to me the roots of your opportunistic view of things.

"However, when you began to speak to me about matters concerning my people—that is the Jewish community—I clearly began to hear a hostile tone and a separation you wished to infer, such as when you repeatedly used the term 'you Jews.' What I kept hearing, not with my ears, but in my head was, 'You dirty Jews, you miserable Jews, you filthy Jews, and, perhaps even, you subhuman Jews,' and it leaves me in fear and tremors. Here I am with a man in the greatest of intimacy who appears to me as a gentle, refined person, who has treated me with kindness and respect since I have known him for the past ten months, who is obviously a member of the Nazi party, and who has a high enough standing to disregard every paragraph of the Nürnberg Laws that at this very moment we are both violating with such impunity. Why is that? Why 'confess' to me?

"The consequences of being caught would be much greater for me than for you. If we were caught, I doubt that I would survive. Why do I put myself into that position? Do I love you? Do I need you? Do I think of you as my life preserver? Do I think of you as the enabler of my denial, as the helpmate for my survival in my dependence—now that I am trapped in Germany and cannot escape any longer—and also having disappeared 'in plain view' until such time I can reappear in a different Germany at a different time?

"You have cited some of our Jewish history to me, particularly as you say you have studied our history of the last hundred years. You must realize, however, that I am a plain woman and don't have this knowledge with my limited education. I went to a Lyceum studying only what my gentile friends also learned. I was also brought up mainly among Christians with whom I played and socialized and among whom I lived freely. In our religious school I began learning some things about my heritage, our Jewish heroes, and the meaning of our religious services during the holidays that many of us observe.

"I did not know how we evolved out of the ghetto or much about our history as we lived in Germany over the past eight hundred years.

I did not know the difficult struggles under which we came to live among you, our neighbors. I played with my friends as a young girl and as a teenager. Then my family and I were consumed with difficult times during the war and afterward because we were Germans of the Jewish faith. And we suffered, like all our neighbors around us. My brother was an army doctor who helped save lives at the front in France and Belgium. They were not Jewish lives or Christian lives; they were just lives because those are the ground rules laid down by Hippocrates, by which he studied medicine.

"After the war, he opened a medical office and treated the entire community, not one part or the other. He practiced his Judaism, though with a secular, sometimes even cynical and self-deprecating approach, probably in a spirit of modernism and the liberalism of assimilation. At all times, however, he respected those who were more observant than he was and always thought and acted in a spirit that would raise the welfare of our entire society. The Hitler government took away his political liberties and his economic freedom and drove him out. He was fortunate to emigrate to America, where such freedom is nurtured and protected, as he writes to me and my mother in his letters. I was not fortunate enough to escape, to be let out of here and to go somewhere else in the world so that I could feel sure of my own survival. Since I met you I have regained a sliver of hope that I could perhaps survive and be with my family once again someday, although the picture you have painted is a very different one from what I, as a Jew, have learned during this past year."

She stretched in her chair and partially turned away from him to hide her changing expression. A mixture of disappointment, fear, and disgust overcame her whole being involuntarily and uncontrollably.

"Uli, forgive me if I am confused; I am puzzled, and to be very frank, I don't quite trust what I have heard, although, again, I respect your confidence and your trust in me. You must understand that what I have heard does upset me. So perhaps we should end this conversation for the time being, until I can regain my equilibrium, and we can perhaps enjoy the remainder of our weekend without these heavy, very troublesome thoughts."

She stopped abruptly, breaking down into a quiet sobbing that she hoped he would hear. Of course it was impossible for him not to be affected by her tears and quiet sounds of despair. Why had she ever agreed to go out into the country with him? Did hope override reality so completely?

"Carola, my dear, forgive me for having caused such upset," he continued, "but in my intense desire to unburden myself to someone I love and respect, I forgot that I might have just shifted that burden on to you. Before we leave these unhappy subjects, and so that we do not spoil tomorrow's good times as well, let me outline to you briefly things I have learned that may give you additional understanding as to the future of the Jewish community here in Frankfurt and about which I have had discussions with people of influence. I know that you don't want to hear much about this anymore, as it is late and you are already in a state of agitation. However, let me tell you what the thinking is in places of power."

Despite her desperate wish to turn off the conversation, he seemed impelled to ride roughshod over her feelings and to continue what he appeared to have prepared in advance to talk about. It seemed almost like an involuntary disgorging of facts he was unable to hold in any longer, and she decided to give in to his irrepressible urge.

"Our government believes that the war will be over by the end of the year. At that time, all countries on the continent from Portugal in the west to Poland in the east will have been defeated or will be allied with us through treaties of neutrality. Scandinavia will have been conquered, and England will be isolated and ready for a mutual nonaggression treaty. We do not believe they will have the continuing willpower to maintain the war with us and will sue for some kind of accommodation. We do not know what will be with Russia, who will continue to be a threat. However, judging by their performance in Finland, we don't think they will pose any great military danger to us.

"At any rate, we can address that problem later now that we have an alliance with them regarding Poland, which gives us plenty of additional time. At that point, the Jewish community will have been reduced by at least half the population of five hundred thousand, which we had prior to the war, and the 'Jewish threat' will have been largely dissipated. As we defeat all our neighbors, who had other significant Jewish populations, we will find the means to have those countries develop accommodations different from our own; perhaps it will depend on the numbers and percentages, which are different in each case. For example, there is no point worrying about the seven thousand Jews in Norway or the nine thousand in Estonia.

"Here in Germany, the old folks remaining will be permitted to live out their natural lifespan, further reducing population count and strength. The Nürnberg Laws will not disappear, but the authorities will be allowed to look the other way. Therefore, the number of mixed marriages, continued emigration, and integration, say, by conversions, will continue to reduce the middle-aged population and further lower the count. This is the category in which you and I can think and perhaps find a good solution for ourselves.

"Younger people who have not by that time been accepted by other countries in the world will be sent to worker colonies—that is, small cities outside the *Altreich* located near production facilities in which they can live and find work in factories where they can make a living, be useful, and eventually adapt to their new surroundings. They will become natives of these regions as they have in times past, living relatively free and unencumbered and being permitted later on to leave or to establish new home communities with their own places of culture and customs.

"In this way, we can be technically *Judenrein* but will also have caused a shift of population, which will be satisfactory to all concerned. The details of exactly where and how this will be accomplished have not been laid down. But the principle has been discussed, and I think it can form the basis for some sort of peaceful coexistence. I know, my dear Carola, this is once more a very upsetting, surprising, and very unorthodox thought. But I am again sharing with you things I have listened to that should give the two of us some hope for a quiet life together after the war. I am sure you are as exhausted now as I am after unburdening myself of all these ideas. Let's go to sleep, and if we want to pursue this discussion despite its seriousness, we can do so in the morning."

With that, he slid under the covers, and she could not tell whether he just lay there quietly or quickly went to sleep.

On her part, the agitation and disturbance he had caused her, particularly with the latter part of what he said about worker colonies and letting people die natural deaths just increased her fears more and more. A million questions raced through her mind. Why had he told her all of this? Did it help him to get it off his chest, or was there a deeper purpose? Was keeping all of this confidential really a signal to leak it out to her community, increase fear, and boost the efforts of relatives outside the country to send for their loved ones with greater speed and desperation? He had used the word love and implied living together after the war; what did all this mean? He had never spoken of divorcing his wife, of proposing marriage to her, of directly expressing his love with sufficient ardor to make such changes in his life, exposing himself to such risk. Was he teasing her, and what was the sense of raising her expectations? She was only a single individual, attractive in a mature way, but neither glamorous nor stunning. She could offer nothing except her own tenderness and sensitivity in what would otherwise have been only a pedestrian relationship. It would not have the context of glamour a man of his stature would obviously enjoy. Is this a good man who has sincere longings or a devious man with evil motives who has things in mind she could not remotely understand or calculate with her limited life experiences?

As she lay there with more and more confused messages coursing through her brain, the extent of her agitation became nearly unbearable. She finally turned to him.

"Uli, I am sorry to disturb you, but I am terribly agitated and cannot fall asleep. Can you help me, talk to me, or settle me down in some way?"

He sat up, having indeed been asleep for a little while, got out of bed, and walked over to the bathroom. He quickly came back with a bottle of medication and a glass of water. He gave her a single pill and handed her the glass.

"Again, Carola, I am so sorry to have done this to you, but here is a pill that will quiet you down quickly and give you a good night's sleep. Give it a try, and we will both wake up cheerfully in the morning."

She stared at him, still somewhat distrustful, yet she took the pill, swallowed it, and asked him what it was.

"Oh, it's a common remedy, Veronal," he said, "which many people take to get a good night's rest. I will hold on to you for a while, and you'll see how quickly you will become quiet."

"Well thank you, Uli, and good night. It's been quite an evening."

She was asleep quickly as he held on to her shoulder; he stared at the ceiling before nodding off himself.

With sunlight shining through the many windows, Carola slowly awoke the following morning around seven thirty feeling well rested and at peace with herself. She was amazed that the one pill Uli had given her seemed to have done the trick quickly and that her state of intense agitation had apparently gone away in a matter of minutes. As she rose to wash in the bathroom, she heard him getting up as well, wish her "good morning," and in gentle and tender language asked her whether she had a good sleep during the night. They quickly got dressed and because they had decided to go for a long walk in the adjacent woods, they put on their boots and sweaters to provide for some insulation in the early morning air.

They went downstairs, had their breakfast in a practically empty dining room, put on their jackets, and went off on a path behind the garden area with which Uli seemed quite familiar. Both of them walked together in silence for a while without making reference to the highly animated and upsetting conversation in their room last night. Uli made a conscious effort to be polite and perhaps even affectionate in the words he used when he began to speak.

"Carola, my dear, I want to tell you again how sorry I was to agitate you in such a crude fashion last night, but there were things I have held in for so long that I just had to get out and, in a way, reduce the severe pressure under which I've labored for a while. I do have more to say on the subjects I was trying to cover, but I will be sure to do that in a more sensitive and considered way. So today, as long as we can, let's just enjoy ourselves in the fresh air and the wonderful isolation of these woods that I find so rejuvenating."

"I appreciate that, Uli. It's just that I was so completely surprised at what you spoke about in such a vehement and forceful way. I, of course, still think about everything you said, but I am trying to understand it, especially from your point of view, so I can better absorb your thoughts without thinking of them in an anti-Jewish way. You must realize that we, as Jews, have been under such psychological hammering and persecution that each of us takes any seemingly hostile remarks with the greatest fear and suspicion. It is becoming more and more difficult to live among our once friendly German neighbors when things have changed over such a short time, and we have essentially been expelled from participating in anything we were part of before 1933."

He simply nodded and marched slightly ahead of her so that he was able to take himself out of a physical position to continue the conversation in the direction it appeared to be drifting. The path widened, and as the wooded area surrounding it became more dense, the trees had obviously been replaced with second- and third-growth evergreens that were beginning to touch each other, having been planted now some many years earlier. They were lined up in straight rows along two dimensions and gave the appearance of green battalions ready to guard the pedestrians contained within them. An occasional deer bolted out ahead of them, sometimes a singular animal and at other times a female at the head of her small family of recently born offspring. They apparently had good information on the dates of the hunting season because they did not seem to be afraid of encountering humans in the early spring when this two-legged species had made rules prohibiting shooting, trapping, or other means of reducing their innocent population.

After a two-hour walk on level ground, the density of the trees was reduced, and they came upon clearings followed by fields that implied a village ahead. Indeed, within ten minutes they came out at the back of some farm houses, leading to a main road with a few shops and a small inn with a restaurant through a side entrance. Uli beckoned Carola to enter, and while it was a little early, he suggested they have lunch before more customers came in and the kitchen became busy.

He ordered a draft beer, and Carola followed, even though she was not used to having an alcoholic drink at the noon hour. They looked over the menu and decided on the fresh asparagus that had just been harvested for the first time in the season accompanied by small boiled potatoes and a house-prepared fillet of herring. All of this seemed adequate, and after finishing their meal and making inconsequential small talk, they were off on the second leg of their excursion, winding their way back to Brombach via a different route on a walk that adjoined a good size, rapidly flowing brook.

Flowers were breaking out of the ground on its gentle banks, and ferns were beginning to rise in fiddlehead fashion as they did every spring around this time. All in all, having returned by about four o'clock in the afternoon, they both agreed they had a wonderful day in the fresh air, peaceful without raising problems or having them raised by each other or outsiders, and they went upstairs for a rest. It seemed that Uli was quite worn out and went to sleep immediately.

At six o'clock they once again got up, dressed for the evening, informally but more appropriately for indoors, and found themselves a remote table in the bar area. A small space was set up for a band, which was the Saturday night entertainment at the inn. After again chatting about casual matters, Uli reverted to his own thoughts, which took off from the night before.

"You know, Carola, how much I am counting on the end of this war happening in short order. Having admittedly taken advantage of our war economy, my business has now been built up sufficiently so that I feel my two sons Werner and Klaus can come into the operation with me as soon as they are deactivated from army service and take over the day-to-day business activities. That will relieve me from my heavy travel schedule and permit more time to stay in the city.

"Again, I see a distinct post-Hitler period after which our Fuehrer, who has accomplished so much within a short time to restore Germany to its world leadership position, can rule over the new European order with greater benevolence and a less harsh manner. After all, we Germans cannot occupy all the other countries we are in now forever but must sooner or later provide more autonomy to those we have conquered. We will have all the advantages accruing to the victor, but a structure of peace must be devised. Perhaps then," he said with a twinkle in his eyes, "there will even be a restoration of relationships between non-Aryans and ourselves."

Carola quickly interjected, "Uli, may I suggest that we don't pursue this subject too much since I will misunderstand, and there are so many ways in which you and I can enjoy one another's company without getting into future politics that mean nothing to me."

"All right, Carola, I fully understand, and I don't want to shake things up again. The band has already begun to play, so let's have a dance now that we've had our first glass of wine." As it turned out, they were both quite adept at dancing, and the strains of *O Donna Clara, Ich hab Dich tanzen geseh'n (O Donna Clara I Saw You Dancing Last Night)* seemed like a fitting piece to restore the floating feeling that kept out any problems between them.

After a light evening meal, they did not come back to the dance floor but went to their room and quickly slid into bed. They held on to each other closely for a while and dozed off. The next morning, after a leisurely breakfast, it was time to pack because Uli had suggested they take a little tour through the *Odenwald* on the way home to sightsee and enjoy the pleasant scenery. While they were getting their things together, Carola raised a delicate subject she had been wanting to ask for some time now:

"Uli, let me ask you something I have been embarrassed to ask before this. Whenever we part from one another, I am in a position where I am unable to reach you in case of, say, an emergency. I wonder if you can give me a telephone number at your place of work so I have some way of contacting you, only when it is absolutely necessary, of course. I promise I would not abuse this privilege, but I do want to be able to contact you as a last resort. Do you think this would be possible?"

He thought, somewhat puzzled by her remark and perhaps slightly annoyed, but tried not to show his concern.

"Carola, I know this could be important to you, and I have tried to avoid your contacting me because I wanted to keep our relationship completely confidential. However, in thinking about it, here is what I would suggest. I will give you a number to a phone that is completely private in my office and that you are not to use, except for the most urgent of needs. One of my secretaries will answer and say: 'Number 27—von Kleinhoven—private.' You can then give her a code name which we can agree upon now, and she will either call me to the phone or, if I am out, leave me a message that she will forward to me in short order. Let's agree on a code name so that you do not have to expose your real name to her. I suggest we make it Frau Brombach, the name of this town, of which no one will be aware, except you. If she asks more, so as not to raise her suspicions, you can answer that you are calling about my latest order of coffee and when would I be in a position to pick it up. That will be all you need to tell her, and I will then get back to you as quickly as I can. How does that sound?"

"That's a good idea, Uli, so let me put the number down in my little calendar so I don't forget it."

"Fine, it's 47980."

"Thanks, my dear."

"And by the way," he added in an casual, offhand manner, "while we are both packing, let me give you this vial of Veronal I had among my things and which I can readily replace for myself. You slept so well the other night that nothing woke you after I gave you the one pill. In case you need it again sometime, it would be good for you to have some on hand."

"Thanks, that's very kind of you. I have never had such a fine sleep before, and I might need to one of these days."

With that, they completed packing; von Kleinhoven took their baggage downstairs to the car, checked out with Herr Hinkel, and they drove off.

As soon as he had wound his way through the back streets of Brombach and found the secondary road which, after a short distance turned north, von Kleinhoven turned onto a small but picturesque highway that led straight into a continuing northerly direction. While this was not the most direct route to return to the city, he told Carola that he wanted to give her a little tour through the eastern part of the *Odenwald* to show her some of the villages where he had spent time with his parents on their summer vacations together many years ago.

They found their way through the villages of Beerfelden and Erbach and soon arrived at the town of Bad Koenig that seemed to be one of his planned destinations. He soon turned off the main road into farm country as they drove past quaint old barns and farmhouses with exposed beams. Behind enclosed barnyards one could hear roosters crow and the occasional mooing sound of cows slowly moving from one place to another. He explained to Carola with a certain nostalgic tone in his voice how he and his parents had boarded with several of these farmers many years ago before the turn of the century. They had taken walks to and from town through the fields and newly planted woods in the quiet, peaceful settings of those days. One of the attractions in the town that otherwise was of modest interest but made a deep impression on him as a teenager was a pottery owned privately by two families that made a living selling their wares in the area all the way to Heidelberg, Mannheim, and beyond.

"I used to walk from where we stayed to the workroom by myself in the morning after breakfast and just watch the potters at their wheels. I was fascinated by their skill of turning the lower disk of the wheel with their feet at what I thought were unbelievable speeds as they threw a wet pile of clay on top of the plate directly in the center. As the blob was spinning around, they would insert their fingers or hands in such a way that the clay would rise evenly in a circular fashion, building into a primitive cup, vase, or bowl, depending on subtle changes in their finger positions.

"After shaping the spinning object according to what they had planned for the final piece, they would begin to remove excess clay with a spatula or knifelike tool. They then wet the clay another time by dipping their hands into a small tub filled with water and smoothing out the rough sides created by the first shaping step. After repeating these operations one or more times, depending upon the degree of smoothness or refinement they wanted to achieve, they would slow down the wheel for trimming the object and then remove it onto a table once the wheel came to a complete stop. The semifinished piece, depending on size and the amount of clay used to produce it, would end up either as a cup, goblet, vase, or small pot.

"I even saw them make small egg cups, which they would turn out quickly and by the dozens. They seemed to be a popular item because they were inexpensive and readily purchased by visitors who stopped by to shop. The whole process was exciting to watch, and I spent hours there by myself, occasionally talking with one or more of the people operating the wheel.

"I developed a secret passion for becoming a potter myself because it seemed like a very satisfying craft to produce such elegant shapes with my hands and the spinning clay. I also carefully watched their procedures as they put the finished but wet clay pieces into the kilns, first to dry them out carefully so they did not develop any holes or cracks and then to fire them up in the hotter ovens to harden and cure. Putting handles on cups or teapots and painting the plain fired shapes was the next exciting step. It transformed the products from the unfinished, monochromatic vessels to the vibrant ones I could see in the showroom.

"The whole operation made me wish to learn the craft, and I discussed the possibility with my parents to spend a summer or two here at the pottery in an apprenticeship so I could someday become a potter myself. However, by the end of the summer, I had to come back to reality as I resumed my studies that were more in line with what my father had planned for me in the engineering profession. The potter's craft was therefore only the summer fantasy of a teenager which quickly faded once I was back in the big city school."

Carola listened in silence and hoped that the pottery of forty or fifty years ago was still there so they could visit what Uli had so vividly described. However, after searching over familiar ground in the village, he concluded that the shop was gone, and what he had described had been replaced by a less romantic factory of the present day. Because the noon hour was close at hand, they stopped by a small tavern, had a fast lunch, and took off toward Frankfurt. It seemed that this was the main attraction von Kleinhoven wanted to show her because they soon turned onto a larger road toward the west and headed more directly back, driving through *Offenbach* before entering Frankfurt at its east end.

They had a pleasant, inconsequential conversation during the remainder of the trip, not touching on any of the controversial subjects he had raised over the weekend, and returned to her *Judenhaus* on Fuerstenbergerstrasse in the late afternoon. When he dropped her off, they parted with the now familiar peck of a kiss as he told her he would be in touch within two or three weeks. He also added that he was off on a business trip, which she by now anticipated as a standard, if not necessarily truthful, excuse for the long intervals until their next get-together.

As she went up the stairs and opened the door to her room, she was struck by the musty odor compared to what she was exposed to over the weekend. On the one hand, she was happy with the pleasant if somewhat upsetting time she had had with him over the past two and a half days. On the other, the enigma of his disappearance began to gnaw at her. While it did not negate the pleasure she had felt and the comforting anonymity she had enjoyed in Brombach, totally occupied by the "Aryans," she did begin to be disturbed by the diametrically opposed societies with which her room confronted her and to which he transported her only to disappear shortly after. It was a good thing she was too tired to dwell upon this strange dichotomy as she quickly fell asleep.

16 A DIFFERENT NIGHT—THE SEDER OF THE REMNANTS

The Passover holiday of 1940 began on the evening of April 22 with the night of the first Seder. It was also the first year that the residents of the home at *Feuerbachstrasse* 14 would celebrate this significant holiday together. Most of the couples, singles, and widowed people had moved in during the prior year after the Passover of 1939. In view of their confined lives with regulations, restrictions, and other forms of ostracism now all around them, celebrating Jewish events had become more important to them, regardless of their prior degree of secularization or other aspects of their formerly assimilated lifestyle.

Because they came from varying backgrounds of observances, everyone wanted to be sure that a joint celebration of the Seder would contain enough compromises and blended material from the Haggadahs they were used to using, permitted a fair amount of participation, and inclusiveness that was appropriately felt by all participants of the evening. To this end they had decided to appoint a committee of respected and learned residents to work out the details of such a composite conduct of the text that was more or less satisfactory to all. Therefore, at one of the meetings arranged for this specific purpose a month before the Passover date, they nominated three of the men, one from each denomination, to form a Religious Affairs Committee. Although the cynics in the group called the committee the "three wise men," the residents had confidence that they would arrive at satisfactory proceedings. The group of three, composed of Dr. Julius Kahn, Dr. Herbert Rosenfeld, and Mr. Jakob Semmelmann, got together every third day to go over in good detail all the issues that needed to be agreed upon.

Thus, for example, they decided to alternate the readings between the three of them from Haggadahs that were familiar to each, as they might have been to other participants of the same respective denominations and as they would have used the same texts in their own traditions over the years. This meant, however, that others had to adjust and find equivalent places in their own books, which each reader would point out with patience and delicacy so that there would be no irritation about having to flip pages, lose places, or deal with other distractions.

They each decided to wear the traditional kittel and yarmulke as some had done in the past, despite the fact that in their own former homes they might not necessarily have worn one. This was to demonstrate solidarity as a singular Jewish community, celebrating a common Passover holiday and eliminating any possible idiosyncrasies of the past. Furthermore, they agreed that whoever still owned a Seder plate would bring it to the large U-shaped table. This table configuration was the only seating arrangement that would make everyone fit into the dining room at the same time and allow each to have an arrangement that their respective families were used to, even though they might not all look alike or conform to each other.

It was also agreed that the kitchen could be used by each different family remnant to prepare their own charoset, hard-boiled eggs, roasted shank bone, salt water, and greens, such as parsley. They would be encouraged to bring their individual or homemade matzoh covers so that each family could display the decorative items they had used within their families in the past. The men also decided to choose their own melodies as those had been familiar to them and read in German instead of Hebrew if that was the way the liberal group had been used to proceeding.

Perhaps of most importance, they decided that they would freely pause to have interruptions for questions, comments, and discussions, even though this would digress from and lengthen the total service, at least prior to the meal. It was more important to give everyone a chance to voice their views and reactions individually, particularly on this first service, wherein their other loved ones who had been around the table in their houses or apartments were no longer present. In other words, everything was to be an easy transition to participation with strangers. It was going to be painful enough to think of those members of their families who were celebrating the same holiday a far distance away from themselves, and they did not wish in any way to exacerbate this loss and create more sadness than what was unavoidable.

Because the dinner part of the evening needed to be all of one menu, a subcommittee of ladies known for their skills in Jewish cooking—with emphasis on matzoh balls and chopped liver—was nominated by everyone to arrange the menu and see to it that all the products needed remained available, despite shortages or the inability to obtain them in view of the new restrictions. They agreed that relatives still living within the city could be invited on a first-come first-served basis with a total of fifteen extra seats available, representing the limits of the room. All of these details and significant points were presented to a last-minute assembly of everyone two days before the beginning of the holiday and consented to, with compliments for the sensitivity with which the committee had addressed every issue which could be thought of.

One point had been left open at this last meeting prior to the event—that is, whether the *mah nishtana* (the four questions) were to be read by the youngest of the assembly, as was traditional, or whether by someone special in view of the fact that no youngster was left. Samuel Speyer proposed—no one could gauge whether seriously or in jest—that perhaps this year the oldest among them should recite the important four questions. However, because that person would be the highly respected Dr. Kahn, one of the principal readers and at eighty-eight clearly the senior resident, it was not considered to work out as it did not provide the important intergenerational link to the youngest participant. Therefore, after a quick review and discussion, the youngest of the oldsters, Adam Hirschberg, age sixty-five, was selected for this particular assignment.

With everything consented to, each family unit went about its preparations and, despite the realization that this Seder was going to be different from one that each had ever held, a joyful anticipation overcame everyone with all the issues now resolved. The Seder was to begin promptly at 6:00 PM so as to have enough time to reach the *Shulchan Orech* (the meal) at a reasonable time, including possible discussions and digressions that made use of the various Haggadahs' texts on such a special night.

The following evening, all assembled punctually at 6:00 PM. They came dressed in whatever finery was left among their possessions and took their seats at the inside or outside of the long horseshoe-shaped table, pillows for themselves or their spouses in hand, with which they could lean to the left side imitating the customs of the noble class of old in response to one of the four questions. As had been announced, the leaders of the three denominations, Julius Kahn, Herbert Rosenfeld, and Jakob Semmelmann, entered the room in silent dignity, dressed in their white kittels and yarmulkes, the traditional garb not only of celebration but ultimately of burial as well.

Now, as they followed one another and took their places at the narrow end of the horseshoe so as to be facing everyone, their common dress was a defiantly appropriate symbol of unity of the Jewish community that remained. There was no more room for worshipping as different denominations, neither here nor in the synagogues that no longer existed. All had equally been destroyed by the Pharaoh's minions eighteen months earlier.

When the participants were seated next to their spouses or with such friends as they might have had as guests in their former homes to share the evening, Dr. Kahn rose and brought the group to attention. The room became totally quiet, permitting him to speak in a normal tone.

"Good evening, my friends, our guests, and such of our fellow Jews who have not been with us before. Tonight is a very important occasion for us. It is indeed a night that is different from all other nights and that is all so different from what other nights of this holiday of Passover have been for each of us in the past. It is a night that we celebrate collectively in each other's company for the first time—an evening at our new home and the first away from our old homes, where we lived for most of our lives—once upon a time.

"This morning some of us spent our time searching and collecting for the disposal of *chometz* throughout the house so that we could cleanse and purify our residence for the Passover. As you know, for the past thirty days, three of us have been putting our heads together to plan on how to conduct our Seder so that all of us, coming from different customs, traditions, and observances, could feel comfortable and acquainted with what each of us had been doing in our own former homes. I, therefore, welcome my colleagues Herbert Rosenfeld and Jakob Semmelmann who are going to join me in an alternate reading from their respective Haggadahs this evening. My own tradition is conservative, as my family and I attended the Boerneplatz Synagogue regularly and faithfully for all the many years we lived as natives to our city until it was destroyed by fire on the unforgettable night of November 9. Similarly, Jakob Semmelmann's congregation, the Friedberger Anlage Synagogue, was destroyed on the same night, depriving him and his family forever of their place of worship for the past thirty-three years. Lastly, Herbert Rosenfeld's religious home, the Freiherr vom Stein or West End Synagogue, had its interior totally burned out on the same night by the Nazi perpetrators, ending his faithful attendance of prayer and devotion and that of his family to which they were committed in a lifetime of tradition.

"Because this gathering is a blend of all these backgrounds and possibly includes other houses of worship that people were used to attending and supporting, the three of us have decided, as leaders of our prayers this evening, to wear the traditional centuries-old garb of a kittel and white yarmulke so that we could represent a united image in solidarity, as it were, regardless of the variants in our modes of worship. We will use the Haggadahs of our individual traditions—the story is the same from one to the other. We ask your forbearance as we switch and alternate readings from our different sources, and we ask for your patience in finding your place, perhaps sharing your texts, as we continue our reading in Hebrew or German, again depending upon our various *minhaggim*—our customs.

"Our holiday of Passover is indeed a feast of freedom and liberation from slavery. Never before have any of us experienced its motif in a more personal way than today. This by unhappy coincidence is exactly the way our sages have asked us to experience this evening—personal slavery, personal liberation, and personal freedom. At the beginning of our text we say the prayer of *Shehecheyanu*, the prayer in which we all thank God for having reached this day. Never before has that prayer had as much meaning to all of us personally, as many of our family members and friends have not been able to survive to this day. I'm sure the widows and widowers among us are thinking of their personal tragedies at this very moment, of spouses and companions killed by the brown-shirted minions of our Pharaoh in recent years, and we console them with our friendship.

"The story we will tell tonight in many different facets speaks about our Exodus, our expulsion, and our wanderings after leaving Egypt some thirty-five hundred years ago. However, in the broader context of Exodus, we are indeed a people who are acquainted with wandering from one place to another across the many parts of our globe. The father of our people, Abraham, left the city of Ur because he could no longer tolerate and believe in the clay gods of his father, Terach, which broke and disillusioned his customers. And so he made his Exodus from Mesopotamia, headed to the sea, and then went south. His grandson, Jacob, was the first to enter Egypt with his tribe of seventy members after the family migrated across what is now Palestine. After four hundred thirty years of living there in good times and bad, our people, by then six hundred thousand strong, were expelled from that land where they had lived as strangers among the native peoples.

"Perhaps this can be compared to our period of eight hundred years right here in Germany, where a few hundred Jewish settlers, also now multiplied to near six hundred thousand, as we are once again expelled. In the interim, our people who settled in Israel and lived at the pinnacle of our existence under the kingdom of David were expelled and taken back to Mesopotamia with the destruction of our first Temple in 586 BCE. They lived there in exile and returned some seventy years later for another six hundred years of various kingdoms—some better, some worse—until the Romans once again took us out in the year 70 CE. From there we wandered along the Mediterranean rim and into Europe, establishing ourselves here and in surrounding countries to be welcomed but ultimately persecuted depending upon the whim of the ruler of the day.

"In the fourteenth century, many Jews from our lands migrated to what is today Poland and Russia at the invitation of King Casimir III, who extended his friendship to the Jews and welcomed us onto his lands. That is the origin of our brethren to the east, who are today once more being killed or penned up in ghettos until their captors decide by what means to get rid of them. Our prayers go out to them tonight, as they perhaps have their last night that is different from all other nights.

"In the west, the Catholic king and queen of Spain, in partnership with the Roman Church, again expelled us through the Inquisition and with death and torture in 1492. So, my friends, we are familiar with slavery and the absence of freedom. We are familiar with our passionate wish for liberation, and we are familiar with deprivation, ostracism, torture, and death, despite our yearnings and wishes. Today, in 1940, we have our own Pharaoh who wants us out but does not let us out! And there are many governments around the world that won't let us in; we can't even go to our own homeland, the land that took us forty years of wandering through the desert to reach after we left Egypt. Can you imagine that? Fortunately, half our people have been let go, but unfortunately, we, the remnants of our families, have not been released. After all, when you try to make an Exodus—that is, to leave one place—you must also find another to go to. Where are we to go? Where are we to go?"

At his age, he knew the answer to his rhetorical question all too well—as did the others in the room.

"Well, my friends, I think this has been enough of my sermonizing. However, I feel I wanted to express my thoughts so that, together, we could all relate tonight's Seder to the circumstances in which we find ourselves as we celebrate together. Perhaps the word celebrate is an oxymoron under these conditions, but let us begin and draw comfort from the words we will say at the end of the evening.

"*L'shanah haba'ah b'yerushalayim*—next year in Jerusalem. I wish we could predict that we could all sit together on the 15 of Nissan in the year 1941 of the Common Era in a reunion of this evening.

"And with that, may I ask Jakob Semmelmann to continue?"

Everyone had listened intently to Julius Kahn and, with tears in their eyes and a sad smile of concurrence and identification with the words he had just spoken, they each opened their own Haggadah, ready to start.

Esther Seidenberger, Leah Rosenthal, and Carola Rossmann, the latter practically a quasi-resident of the home by now, sat midway down the left leg of the horseshoe where Esther and Leah could still hear the readers. Their closest friends, the Friedmanns and the Blumenthals, were seated across the table from them and between the seven of them shared three Seder plates and two matzoh stacks as they had previously agreed upon. They had all taken along the old Haggadahs they had in their possessions, and as the evening progressed, despite the fact that other books were read from, it turned out amazingly easy to keep up with the proceedings. The story was the same, after all, as Dr. Kahn had said somewhat wistfully, and their ability to find their places readily encouraged them to pay rapt attention.

For Carola, it was a more difficult evening than she had expected. First of all, the generational difference between her and her mother's friends gave her a sense of once again being a child at the table, participating with perhaps forty of her imagined parents, aunts, uncles, and cousins, which she didn't actually have, but who were always there when they had been invited to other peoples' homes in the past. Her father's deafness and depression rendered him totally incapable of running a Seder himself, and her brother was not sufficiently schooled in religious subjects to enable him to conduct the readings, having traded in Hebrew for medical studies.

The other great distraction to her attention span was the absorbing extent to which she operated within the gentile world between her job dealing with non-Jewish customers all day and seeing Uli perhaps every two weeks, and coming more and more under the influence of his thought processes and the ideas he conveyed. She found herself living outside her Judenhaus, in a totally abnormal, "normalized" gentile environment. Her Aryan appearance once again was making a major difference in her individual life, and although living by herself in almost social isolation, it seemed to give her the constant option of disappearing *en pleine vue*, in full view, or joining the remnant of the Jewish community for a powerful event such as tonight that would bring out the elements of her Jewish heritage and her loyalty to it.

This conflict was building steadily within her, especially on a holiday like this, as she was more and more affected by her deepening emotional involvement with Uli, the ultimate Aryan, who was (in many ways) the antithesis of her entire past environment. As the holiday this year had fallen late in the month and after her weekend outing with him, she was particularly troubled to be here on this "different night." It certainly could not have been more different than the nights spent with him in both physical pleasure and sexual fulfillment, especially considering Uli's own apparent conflicts that he expressed to her toward the Jews. She likened it—with some desperation and shame—to eating a piece of matzoh with butter and a slice of ham on top. It was a revolting thought she needed to bury deep within her tortured conscience as she sat among these faithfully committed, elderly Jews who were trying to practice the joys and obligations of their heritage as long as their cruel masters would still permit.

At the end of Julius Kahn's introduction, Jakob Semmelmann asked each of the women present to light their candles and pour the wine in the cups in front of them, including, of course, their spouses', so that they would be ready for blessing the first of four cups of the evening. Following this, each of the participants who wished to wash his or her hands rose to go to a sink in the kitchen to do so. He then asked each household to bless the children in absentia as there was no child—at least of a young age—in the room. He then proceeded to dipping the parsley into salt water and encouraged everyone to eat the hard-boiled egg located on top of their plates to hold them over during the lengthy reading. This was followed by breaking the middle matzoh in their stack of three, and because there was no place to hide the afikomen, no children to find them, and no prize to hand out, he suggested that they be stacked beneath the often beautifully embroidered envelopes that each family had brought to their place at the table.

The Seder then continued with *Ha Lachma Anya*, the story of the bread of poverty and persecution.

Let all who are hungry, come and eat.
Let all who are in need, come and share the Pesach meal.
This year we are still here,
Next year in the land of Israel.
This year we are still slaves—
Next year, free people.

Adam Hirschberg then rose and recited the *Mah Nishtanah* using the melody that had been the tradition in his family for many years.

How is this night different from all other nights?

On all other nights we eat either leavened bread or matzoh,

but on this night we eat only matzoh.

On all other nights we eat other kinds of vegetables,
but on this night we eat maror (bitter herbs).

On all other nights we need not dip our vegetables even once,
but on this night we dip twice.

On all other nights we eat either sitting upright or reclining,
but on this night we all recline.

When he was finished, he spoke of the answers that had been discussed in his home among his family in the years past and added his own ideas as he went along.

"There is no time when any of us can think of how different this night is from all other nights in the past in all of our experience of years back. We were in our homes then with our families, secure that we could live as Jews in freedom, as citizens of Germany protected by the law, and in equality with our gentile neighbors. How different this night and, for that matter, all other nights have become for us all!

"On this night we eat only matzoh to demonstrate our insecurity in perhaps having to leave our country at any moment, or in our wish to do so at any instant. It is also our bread of affliction, a state of existence that we have been in increasingly over the past seven years.

"When we taste our maror this year, we do not even feel that it is so bitter. We have become used to bitterness and rancor, living in this state of daily uncertainty and danger. It's easy to eat our bitter herbs now,

"We dip vegetables twice as we used to do when enjoying social events, the hospitality of our friends, and gatherings of happy celebration. Let us dip twice on this evening, either under the illusion or with the determination to regain these joys of our normal lives someday.

"On all other nights we have eaten our meals in haste and with dispatch. Let us recline on this night in symbolic remembrance now that our comfort, luxury, and leisure are gone, seemingly forever.

"Those are one set of answers to the questions I have recited. They are only those that come to mind for the moment, but there are many others, and I expect that those in your minds are more profound and deeply thought out than my own. We would all like to share your thoughts to give us an insight into the mystery of the seemingly simplistic questions that have found their way into our hearts. Why are they there, and is this night perhaps different from all other nights because on all other nights we do not ask them in the first place?"

As no one else spoke up, the story continued with the *Avodim hajinu*. "When in time to come, your children ask you: 'what is the meaning of the decrees, laws, and rules that the Lord our God has enjoined upon you?' you shall say to your children, 'we were slaves to Pharaoh in Egypt (we were slaves to Hitler in Germany), and the Lord freed us from Germany with a mighty hand and an outstretched arm…."

This was followed by the all-night discussion of the five rabbis of B'nai B'rak, ending in: "the more one expands and embellishes the story, the more commendable it is."

"Well, with that, let me turn the reading over to my colleague Herbert Rosenfeld, who will continue with the allegory of the four children."

Everyone turned in their Haggadah to the passages, many of which were easily recognizable by the accompanying drawings.

"Thank you, Jakob. As we read the story, it alludes to the four children: one wise, one wicked, one simple, and one who does not know how to ask. We have all read this story over many years in the past with our families. It would not surprise me that as one of us reads it, others look around the table thinking of their own children that are not with them any longer and saying to themselves silently: 'How do you suppose I would characterize my own son or daughter? Is he or she wise?'

"'Yes, of course.' That would be my own first and almost knee-jerk characterization. We all like to think that our children are wise and smart. After all, they inherited our own traits.

"Is he or she wicked? No, we would immediately deny that to ourselves—he's a good boy; besides, he's cut out of my own template and so he is obviously not wicked, as I am not.

"Is he simple? I don't think so because there are many times I can't figure him out, and he doesn't really tell me what he wants or what he is angry about. He's not simple; on the contrary, many times he is so complex that I can't understand him. And who is closer to him in spirit and in thought process than I?

"Does he not know how to ask? That's not him. On the contrary, most of the time he asks too many questions, and occasionally, when I lose my patience, I have to ask him to stop."

He continued with the animation that was typical of the professional he used to be."So why do I have to make up different answers to these four different personalities that I don't see in my own family and my own experience? My own answer to this puzzle is that, despite our self-denial of undesirable characteristics in those most beloved and closest to us, there is a portion of these traits in each one of us, either in a blended composite or with a different degree of dominance at different moments of our lives. I have searched myself to test this proposition and have confirmed—albeit reluctantly—that this is true, even of my own disposition. As you know, I am a retired psychologist and so I have had long years of experience, speaking with and treating peoples' ills and problems. Again, I can confirm the validity of those concurrent traits in everyone.

"But to relate the allegory to our current condition as virtual captives of our own government, it can be said that when the wicked around us is proclaimed as the good, when hate against us Jews is glorified as great, and when the most despicable crimes are clothed in some kind of ritual and rationale of purification, then a nation of millions can be subverted to the wickedness of immorality, violence, crime, and the breakdown of our civilized norms. We are the victims of all this at this moment, and others, at other times will share in our tragedy."

Although it was originally contemplated that there be a discussion on this important part of the text, Herbert Rosenfeld's comments, not only as a leader but also as a professional expert, led to much quiet acceptance of his ideas without debate or dissent.

Rosenfeld, therefore, went on to *V'hi She'amda.* "This promise has stood for our parents and for us in good stead ... but in every generation there have been those who stood up against us to wipe us out. Yet the Holy One, blessed be He, keeps on saving us from their hands."

There was not a participant around the table who either questioned the concept quietly or who did not digress within his own mind, in silent prayer that this might actually come about.

With that, he turned the reading back to Julius Kahn, who continued with that portion of the text, tracing the history of the Jews from a small tribe wandering into Egypt and growing to a numerous nation. He reviewed, as the times changed, to where the text read: "The Egyptians treated us badly; they persecuted us and imposed hard labor on us."

"Familiar?" he invoked. "How history repeats itself, even over thousands of years when the illusion has been raised in the most recent generation that 'those bad old days' cannot recur since civilization has made such immense progress, and authors, philosophers, rulers, and politicians have articulated these advances in such elaborate and seductive terms."

He then proceeded to the episode of the ten plagues and went around the table asking a member of each family unit sitting together to proclaim one of the plagues that persuaded the Egyptians to let the Israelites go out of Egypt. The last and most severe punishment, which finally proved effective, was the event of slaying the firstborn in each Egyptian household, the *Makat B'chorot.*

This, by seemingly preordained coincidence, fell upon Else Birnbaum, who sat together with her friend and roommate, Lore Zinsheimer, as they shouted the plague with conviction and defiance. Dr. Kahn was about to continue when Else interjected.

"Excuse me for interrupting everyone, but there is something on my mind and in my heart that has been there for a long time and that I now wish to share with you. It is not only to relieve my own sorrow but also to make known to all here and ideally to the entire Jewish community all over the world what I have seen and what I have endured over the past eighteen months since Kristallnacht. I refer once again to the night of November 9 at which my first experience with *Makat B'chorot* took place. As others of you may also have witnessed, I saw my own husband and oldest son go out from our home to look at the Boerneplatz Synagogue as it was burning to see if anything could be done to save the Torahs or other sacred implements. I warned them not to go, but they insisted because we lived close by, and they could not tolerate doing nothing under such terrible circumstances.

"I looked out the window of our third-floor apartment to watch them go. After about an hour, they did in fact return, but as they reached within twenty meters of the entrance of our apartment house, a truck of SA men, dressed in brown shirts and black boots with revolvers drawn, jumped out, grabbed them, hit them hard and brutally, and loaded them into their truck. The beatings continued as a trail of blood followed the truck, and they snatched others coming back to their homes, not having been able to do anything to stop the inferno. I called the police station immediately but was unable to get any answers on the whereabouts of my son and husband. A few days later I was told that they were sent directly to Buchenwald for the crime of violating the edict not to be out on the street. I never heard from my son and my husband again until I received a notice in the mail that, due to their defective hearts and weak physical condition, each of them had suffered a heart attack and died four weeks later. I could collect their ashes at our police station if I made prior arrangements for prompt burial. That my friends, was my own *Makat B'chorot*."

The group sat in shocked silence as she continued.

"As if that were not enough, when I saw them being dragged off, I put my warm coat on, wrapped a shawl around my head, and went outside. Without thinking and following only my instincts, I went the short distance from our home to the synagogue. This walk, my husband and I, or sometimes the three of us, took every Saturday morning, and having a regular seat in the first row right behind the beautiful grill work of the women's section upstairs, I prayed and occasionally proudly watched them both as they also prayed without distraction, wearing their *tallesim* and moving in their customary *shokeling* rhythm. As I came close to the burning building, I found myself a spot to watch, to witness what was happening without being noticed by the Storm Troopers and the indolent firemen who were standing around. The huge windows on each side were beginning to crack and finally fall out. I had positioned myself nearest the window that, in turn, was closest to the Holy Ark, and I was able to see in from afar and witness the extinction of the *Ner Tamid*, the eternal light. It was a frightening sight as the beautiful lamp that I had always considered to be truly eternal—forever—went out.

"As I looked at this scene in disbelief and horror, the situation grew worse. The next thing that happened was that the first Torah was thrown out of a vacant window and landed crashing to the ground in front of me. Its ornaments, cover, pointer, and binder were gone. In its flight through the air with flames all around, it opened and unrolled, its *Etz Chaim* posts flailing helplessly in the air as the arms or legs of a human being might look being tossed onto a scrap heap.

"The unrolling exposed a section of the text which, of course, I could not read during its fiery descent. What I could see between the columns, words, and sentences were the scratches for all the lines a scribe had made to keep his writing straight and neat and to let him define the spaces within the lines as he copied the text. Have you ever seen the skin of an animal burning? It is different from paper, you know, which goes up quickly in flames as its charred pieces tend to fly through the air. The goat or calfskin of the Torah slowly turns yellow, then orange and brown, and then dark, as it curls, weaves, stretches, twists, and writhes in the agony of its slow destruction. I suppose human skin does the same, not that I ever wish to see that in front of my eyes. As the gradual discoloration proceeded in front of me, the letters of the text slowly seemed to curl and wobble and recede into the darkening background of its substrate.

"Soon the lines were blurred into undecipherable, bleeding dark blobs for the better part of a column, then a total column, and after that, several, with the parchment colored, former spaces merging and melding into one another. I was thinking of the writing and the fact that the Torah is written in consonants only. The reader has to understand the words as if vowels were also on the page or section of the parchment. He has to augment the reading with the trope he was taught so he can articulate the whole word when he reads them as the *parsha,* the designated portion of the day.

"I was glad that there were no vowels in the text because vowels are the evocation of sound and all emotion. As the sounds are made by the Torah's reader and the emotion of its fiery destruction are undoubtedly the most horrid experience of its existence, the sounds that the vowels would release in the final agony of its auto-da-fe would be such that no civilized human being could withstand them. The wisdom of him or of all those who wrote these texts in silence is, therefore, beyond any commentary of our sages.

"Despite my understanding that we, as Jews, should not rejoice in the tragedies of our enemies, even as they seek to destroy us, I cannot help wondering whether in the war that Germany is for the moment winning, the parents of those five million men under arms who are now traipsing across Europe, destroying, raping, burning, and slaughtering not only our people but all those they consider their enemies, will also someday experience the *Makat B'chorot* in many of their own families. Will it all have been worthwhile, or will it collapse into a heap of ashes? Will the vowels of their script be heard as their agonies echo to the consonants of their plans for the destruction of our people and of their world as well? Who will then conduct the Seders of the future? Who will then retell the stories we have heard tonight?

"Thank you for listening to me tonight. You have all helped me so much, and my love goes out to you."

As she stopped, she wept silently, and again, all were silent in the spirit of identification, sympathy, and sadness that prevailed in the room.

Julius Kahn quietly responded. "Thank you, Else, for the most beautiful and poetic description of your pain and sadness. We are glad that the story of the plagues which we continue to tell makes it possible for someone with your tragic experience to find solace in the words and phrases of our Haggadah and the wonders and miracles we can all still experience together."

The heaviness and melancholy that Else's story had cast over the entire room did not lift easily. At last, Julius Kahn made an assertive effort to continue with the *Dayenu* in the text, breaking the silence that had fallen over the entire room and interrupted only by discreet, if embarrassed clearing of throats, coughing, and blowing quietly into handkerchiefs to dry tears evoked by her poignant remarks.

He then went on to explain that they had come to the hymn of gratitude, where each paragraph of thanks for God's protective deeds ended in the refrain, "It would have been enough." When they sang the melody accompanying the stanzas that were familiar to every resident, everyone's spirits lifted as they reviewed the biblical experiences of escaping from their pursuers, of being fed manna, of receiving the Torah at Mount Sinai, and of entering their new homeland—*Eretz Yisrael.*

It was only in Esther's mind that a new verse of her own gave her pause to stop her own rhythm and think.

If only my son Eduard and his little family were able to escape to America and Carola, Leah, and I had to stay behind and not be saved, would it have been enough? What did staying behind mean; why couldn't Carola also escape and be saved far away from this godforsaken land? Why could we old women, Leah and myself, not be the only ones that were left behind? This might not have been enough, but certainly it would have been better, more enough, than the three of us trapped in this hopeless situation. If we could just sit here next year to celebrate another Passover without our condition having gotten worse and our lives not deteriorated further—which I really don't believe to be a reality—wouldn't it then have been enough? She was unable to continue singing as she was unable to answer these questions in her mind as to what would have been or how little more could have been enough. Would all gathered here have been grateful, even without a *Dayenu* in the refrain?

As the storytelling part of the reading neared an end and they reviewed Rabbi Gamliel's checklists on the essential foods, Jakob Semmelmann took over once more and reviewed the reasons for eating each of these essentials, the matzoh, the maror, the horseradish, and the charoset, the sweet mixture of apple, honey, and walnuts. However, most important was the reading, which now became the prime, pertinent paragraphs for each of them to absorb.

"In every generation one is obligated to see oneself as having personally gone out from Egypt, just as it says. And you shall tell your child of this very day, it is because of this that God did for me when I went out from Egypt." What children were there left behind to tell that to?

After the *Halleluyah,* the blessing and drinking of the second cup of wine, the readings finally wound down to where the meal could begin. All participants now relaxed as the first course was served and soon—as everyone engaged in conversation with someone sitting next to or opposite them and between the matzoh ball soup, the chopped chicken livers, and the modest if well prepared roasted chicken—the spirits that had been so dampened by Else's poignant recitation came back to a greater degree of animation. There was real gratitude for being able to sit together in a calmer atmosphere, temporarily sheltered from the unhappy, adverse circumstances outside that all of the family remnants gathered here on this night would experience together.

The readings following the meal suffered somewhat from the inability of many around the table to maintain their attention span, having been well fed and the hour becoming late. Therefore, there was a tendency to rush through the remainder of the service: the blessings over the food, for Jerusalem, and for divine goodness; the prayer for Elijah and the opening of the door to welcome him to the table; the Great Hallel; and the final cup of wine blessed first and then imbibed. By the time of the final blessing of hope to be in Jerusalem next year, the late hour had taken its toll on the elderly residents of the house and most of their guests, and there was not much singing to follow. Everyone slowly rose to bid each other good night and retire.

Carola hugged and kissed her mother and Leah, said goodnight to Dr. Kahn and the others to express her gratitude at having been included in the wonderful Seder, put on her coat, and quickly headed home. In reality, she was quite shook up, disturbed, and bewildered as she walked rapidly through the darkness to her Judenhaus on Fuerstenbergerstrasse.

When she finally entered her own room after having mounted the stairs quickly and unlocked her door, she tossed her coat across her armchair, threw herself onto the bed, and dissolved into uncontrollable sobs that seemingly had no end. The confusion, guilt, regret, loneliness, and inability to find her mental compass in all of the events that had spun around her own world had created a near vacuum and a choking, monotonous sorrow. She finally found some realization that she had so obstinately pursued her baser needs with a totally unrealistic new lifestyle. She wondered how this could continue and whether there was another route of escape from what would become an increasingly unbearable way of life.

The spectrum had widened. Her psychological oscillations were becoming increasingly difficult to sort out—at one end, she enjoyed a comforting anonymity, while at the other end, she was part of the Jewish remnant, now hopelessly trapped. What was worse, she was a child of the elderly at age fifty. How was she going to handle this increasing dichotomy? It felt as if she were being pulled across a rack of torture she did not know how to tolerate in the long run. Questions and agonies were at the end of a very traditional evening on the one hand, and on the other, there was a somber, collective celebration that was new and strange to all the participants of the 1940 Seder.

It had indeed been a different night, different from any she had experienced in her whole life. The four (and many more) questions were just beginning.

17 1940—THE WAR NEARLY OVER?

As late spring arrived in May and slowly turned into early summer, the German Wehrmacht, which had been planning its offensive during the preceding winter, sprang into action and began its *Blitzkrieg* (lightning war). The main strategy was to overrun the Maginot Line the French had constructed and to neutralize what France had regarded as its principal deterrent in the event of war.

The line was built mainly along the border between the two countries within the Alsace province. It was built to a depth of about twenty-five kilometers in various layers of defensive obstacles to halt or at least slow down a German attack if it were mounted in an unanticipated manner or as a surprise move. It consisted of various fortresses known as *ouvrages*, each of which was built of heavy concrete, camouflaged in the countryside, and armed with many artillery weapons of various sizes and range. In addition, there were steel post obstacles by the thousands, anchored deep into the ground as deterrents against tanks and backed up by miles of barbed wire to block large infantry movements behind the armored vehicles. The problem with this "line" concept was that it was steeped in the experiences of the French army during World War I and, therefore, did not take into account radical improvements made in the more than twenty years since the previous armistice was signed in 1918.

With the line concept came the mentality of the French military leadership as these armaments represented a new degree of perceived invincibility that would protect France against an invasion by the German Army and would give them a chance to counter and defeat any German attack. The fallacy of this obsolete strategic planning lay in the fact that the German *Panzer Korps* now had tank-type weapons with guns and treads that were much more sophisticated than those existing at the end of World War I. These vehicles could move much faster and had the power to ride through more irregular territory and knock over barriers that were thought to be impenetrable twenty years earlier.

Further, the Germans employed strategies that rendered the Maginot Line impotent once an attack started. The first was that instead of attacking the French army head-on, the *Panzer Korps* outflanked the enemy by moving through the Ardennes Forest in Belgium and then, turning southwestward, invaded France at points where the fortifications had ended. Second, the French fortifications did not take into account the then revolutionary developments by the German *Luftwaffe* that changed the balance of power totally in favor of the new aerial attack mode. They had, in essence, been tested during the Spanish Civil War, including the infamous air raid on the civilian population of Guernica, and were also confirmed by the Italian forces in their uneven contest against the Ethiopians. In addition, parachute units were a new entry into military operations, as German battalions of these forces could be dropped behind French lines to capture territory and cut off the French infantry from the rear. The results of these new *Blitzkrieg* tactics were spectacular and from the first attack had incredible success. The total strategy created a giant domino effect.

Beginning on May 10, the Belgian Army surrendered and then the Dutch forces, despite the fact that they had flooded the below sea level portions of their country so that the German tanks were obstructed from rolling through the low-lying countryside. Both King Leopold of Belgium and Queen Juliana of Holland fled to London to set up governments-in-exile as Great Britain became the last refuge for the defeated governments of Europe and an ultimate assembly point for European resistance movements once they were able to form. The French forces were also in prompt retreat as their British allies, having been backed up to the beach at Dunkirk, were evacuated by many rescue vessels assembled there so they could quickly escape across the English Channel to their home isle.

On June 22 the French government surrendered and signed an armistice in the Compiegne Forest, mirroring the German surrender there in November 1918. Meanwhile, the German army had advanced on Paris, which was occupied a week earlier and was made ready for a visit by Adolf Hitler. All of the newspapers in Frankfurt, and for that matter all over Germany, proclaimed these events with great pride and banner headlines as they showed the Fuehrer doing his famous hip-hop of joy in front of the Eiffel Tower with a broad, smiling face with which he was seldom shown publicly.

The score was now two to one in Germany's favor, one in 1871 that formed the German *Kaiserreich* in the first place and after the defeat of World War I now again in 1940. Hitler's thoughts were undoubtedly that this was the last time and that France was now defeated for good. He had achieved in Western Europe what he had plotted and planned ever since his move to power and could now declare victory for much of his closely held objectives. The lone holdout was Great Britain and, with Winston Churchill's recent assumption of the prime minister's post, only he continued to be the challenge and obstacle to total victory.

Summer came and went; von Kleinhoven's trysts with Carola were now confined to dinners at small restaurants all over town and evenings in the Mendelssohnstrasse apartment at three to four week intervals. There was a regularity about all of this that took some of the spontaneity out of Carola's anticipation. In addition, half the conversation dealt with an update of the war and information that Uli was in a position to get beyond what was published in the papers every day. He began to be regularly critical of the fact that the government did not pursue a policy of armistice in victory that would permit the army either to occupy recently won territory or to send home many of the soldiers for a return to civilian life. He really could not understand why their expansion objectives had not been totally met, even without the conquest of the British Isles. Underlying his personal rationale, of course, was the return of his sons Werner and Klaus, so they could resume taking over his business, and he could relax and enjoy the fruits of his labor and prior collaboration with the Nazi party.

The Jewish High Holidays began with Rosh Hashanah on the evening of October 3. Those residents at the *Feuerbachstrasse* home who could still walk the distance to the Unterlindau Synagogue attended services there because it reminded them of former days, met their religious needs, and gave them a chance to meet with other members of the Jewish community who either still lived in *Judenhaeusern* or in other old-age homes. It also gave them a chance to exchange information that was harder and harder to come by with the isolation they experienced during most weeks at the home. The synagogue, having been totally wrecked on the inside but not burned down during Kristallnacht because of the way it was squeezed in between the regular apartment houses, had been primitively restored to some semblance of utility by repairing furniture as best as possible and by refurbishing—albeit sparsely—with decorative items that individual members still had within their households.

The holidays following, such as Sukkot and Simchat Torah, were celebrated quietly because there was only one Torah left after the vandalism and destruction on the night of November 9. The service, therefore, was very carefully conducted so as not to draw attention to the authorities, who had at least one SA man in uniform stationed outside whenever there was a service planned or in progress. Rolling back the precious remaining scroll to its beginning text—*B'reshit*—was done silently, and the new beginning of the reading, which in the past was accompanied by melodies of joy in celebration of the perennial, repetitive cycle, were knowingly eliminated. It was read without any special emphasis, again not to cause anyone to look in as to what was going on. There was no sukkah built in the yard outside as had been done in the past, but rather modest decorations of leaves and fruit were hung on the walls in honor of the festival. Rabbi Neuhaus carefully explained in his sermon that these were the circumstances under which the congregation had to "celebrate" but that this had happened many times before during the lives of Jewish communities under siege and that everyone needed to be grateful for the modest extent to which the meaning of these holidays could still be emphasized.

At the home, Chanukah was also celebrated in a more inconspicuous manner than it had been a year ago when there was still a Maccabean spirit of defiance in lighting the many menorahs. During the past year, a few members had died and their rooms occupied by new arrivals, mainly from small village and country communities. These people came largely with only the clothes on their backs and nothing else and were given furniture that was stored at the agency from people who, in turn, had to leave the country from one day to the next. The newcomers did not integrate as easily into the existing core group because they were strangers to the city and could not reminisce with the old-timers as to what had gone on in their various congregations in the past. The lighting ceremonies were more sparse and subdued with candles also scarcer by this time and only available from the very limited inventory that individual households still happened to have.

18 MORE PERSECUTION

New Year's Eve ushering in 1941 passed quietly without an iota of celebration or reminiscence. The word "happy" had been eliminated from everyone's vocabulary, and hardly anyone stayed up in the public rooms past the dinner hour. All in all, with mail deliveries shrinking by the day, newspapers predictably reporting military victories, and isolation increasing as time went by, the occasional humor and animation in what had become an almost comfortable conviviality even under these pitiful circumstances was now practically gone, and the long period of waiting—waiting for more misery—took hold of everyone's spirit in tension, fear, and resignation. When—when, if ever—would it be over?

As the pages of the calendar turned to 1941, German dominance and the continued victories of its Wehrmacht proceeded at full speed. Western Europe extending to the south of France and the diplomatically arranged neutrality of the Iberian Peninsula ensured largely pacified territories. Marshal Petain had been installed as head of the French government, and his collaboration with the Nazi establishment was being worked out by constant communication between the two capitals with orders flowing from Berlin.

The French had initially withdrawn from Paris after signing the Compiegne armistice in June of the prior year. They had at first established their seat of government in Tours before moving to Vichy from where Petain, joined by his Prime Minister Pierre Laval, could administer the unoccupied part of the country. The Germans quickly began to establish rules and procedures for the transfer of goods and agricultural products to the homeland so that the shortages, which had long begun to make their effects felt on the population, were somewhat relieved. This reinforced support for the war by the general public because its citizens saw tangible benefits flowing in their direction within a short time after their victory over the French. With peace at their back—albeit subject to constant harassment by French partisans and the underground network that arose quickly throughout the more remote areas still under German occupation—the Wehrmacht was able to concentrate on its plans for the upcoming invasion of England.

While the German forces had expanded their offensive into North Africa under the command of General Erwin Rommel, the key to ultimate victory was still the United Kingdom. There was some urgency not to let the battle for Britain drag out too long because the United States, led by a recently reelected President Franklin D. Roosevelt, began to form effective military supply lines to the nearly isolated British Isle. This support, although frequently interdicted by submarine attacks on supply ships, could not be stopped or slowed down significantly. Both leaders, Churchill and Roosevelt, had established a close working relationship with each other that served the war effort well and began to build popular support within the United States against Germany and the concept of an evil dictatorship. Reinforcing such support were the terribly destructive air raids over British towns such as Swansea, which was totally obliterated by a German air raid campaign in February 1941. In the United States, a lend-lease program had been initiated by the U.S. Congress giving England, China, and other Allied nations the privilege of purchasing military equipment with greatly delayed payment schedules.

Meanwhile, the Germans turned in a southeasterly direction and went on with their conquest of Yugoslavia. With the help of the Italians, they defeated Greece so that sooner or later all of Europe, with the exception of the Soviet Union, was under their control. A psychological setback occurred as Rudolf Hess, second in command after Adolf Hitler, fled in May on a solo flight to Scotland, where he bailed out of his plane by parachute and surrendered to the British government. The strategic effect of this desertion, however, was minor. Bombing of London and other parts of England continued to wreak significant destruction by the *Luftwaffe*. The Royal Air Force was not without retaliation, however, even before the full participation of the United States began the following year.

In the city of Frankfurt, the gathering of Jews from the surrounding village communities continued, and the de facto ghettoization was an accomplished fact with the remaining eleven thousand Jewish citizens when the trickle of emigration roughly matched the inflow from the outlying areas. Jews were being "cleansed" with particular diligence and speed in anticipation of achieving an exclusively Aryanized *Judenrein* population in the province of Hessen-Nassau.

At *Feuerbachstrasse* 14, a relatively quiet, if increasingly restrictive, lifestyle became the norm, and with food supplies more and more limited, the dietary constraints began to have their effect on the residents' health. The roster at the house was at first reduced by at least six, who, having been in a delicate condition for a while in the first place and reaching their mid-seventies, became sick and were taken to the Gagernstrasse Hospital from which they never returned. Their spaces were quickly filled by new arrivals from the villages, assigned by Herbert Bachman to the vacated rooms.

One morning in mid-April, moans were heard from the room of Julius Kahn on the second floor of the house. As Herbert Rosenfeld heard these pitiful noises, he knocked on the door, which was not far from his own, and entered the room quickly. Dr. Kahn, who could hardly respond in an audible way, was writhing in pain and pointing to the area where a physician would suspect a gallbladder, pancreas, or spleen might be located. He could hardly speak in a comprehensible manner, whereupon Rosenfeld ran downstairs and called the ambulance service after quickly consulting with Dr. Pappenheimer, the house manager.

The emergency vehicle came within ten minutes, and with Rosenfeld accompanying him, they were off to the Gagernstrasse emergency room across town. Esther and Leah stepped out of their room to which they had returned a little while earlier and just caught a glimpse of the stretcher on which he was taken out the door. Remembering her son-in-law Aaron Rossmann's rapid departure six years earlier, Esther commented sadly. "At his age, I doubt we will see him again. He is such a wonderful man; I hope he won't suffer too much."

When Carola visited them in the evening after her work, her mother brought her up-to-date on Dr. Kahn's sudden attack. She, too, said little; her feelings of empathy and sadness left her subdued for the evening.

When Herbert Rosenfeld returned several hours later, after having spent the entire day with his suffering elderly friend, he shook his head in despair and quietly indicated the hopelessness with which Dr. Kahn was taken in to be cared for. Morphine was the standard palliative medication for people who could only be made more comfortable as their disease progressed to its final stages. Three days later, a call received from the hospital confirmed that Julius Kahn had quietly expired during the night and that burial at the New Jewish Cemetery would take place the following morning at ten o'clock.

The news quickly spread throughout the house, and there was a strong desire by all those who could still walk to attend the funeral. Although she was not a resident, Carola had come to appreciate the eminence of Dr. Kahn and wanted to join those who went to the funeral. She quietly asked Ursula at an appropriate moment, receiving her quick consent. Arrangements were made to share taxis, despite the high costs, in order to avoid the now unpleasant rides on the trolley cars with numerous changes to be made, long waits, hostile glances, and nasty comments made by gentiles who happened to share that transportation. Some fifteen residents who were able to get around without assistance, among them Else Birnbaum and Lore Zinsheimer, decided to share five cabs that took them to the gates of the cemetery and agreed to wait for them for the ride back.

All who went felt strongly about being together with him during perhaps their own limited time "above ground" to bid him farewell. They were met at the funeral hall by Rabbi Neuhaus, who gave an extraordinary eulogy. In addition to his fellow residents, a number of gentile friends had the stamina and courage to participate in the service, despite the presence of an SA man at the rear of the hall. The rabbi's eulogy was composed of a brief summary of Dr. Kahn's long life, stating the fact that so many of a man's good deeds could not be summarized in a mere few minutes but that he should rather be characterized as a true *tzaddik*, a righteous man in the finest of Jewish traditions. Many in the audience quietly shed tears, often remembering how his many kindnesses affected their lives, their families, and their acquaintances.

There was no oblique reference to the Nazi regime and the in-place persecution of the Jewish community, not only because of the presence of the brown shirt but also because of the general feeling that he had lived a full life, if not a painless one with the special tragedies of these terrible, recent days. Every one of the seventy or eighty participants in the service who came from other old-age homes as well as the population at large, accompanied the coffin on its gurney to the gravesite, and the men all participated in shoveling the dirt back into its grave. Cantor Nathan Saretski sang a particularly moving rendition of the *El Mole Rachamim*, and everyone of the assembled congregation recited the *Kaddish* as a whole because they all considered themselves part of his family.

As Else Birnbaum and her friend Lore Zinsheimer slowly walked back to the waiting taxi, she was joined by Carola, who had developed a particular fondness for both of them after Else's eloquent plaint at the Seder evening. Carola's impression of the pain Else had described was indelible. The whole association with Julius Kahn's regal conduct of the Passover proceedings had reinforced the strength of her Jewish soul in the midst of the conflicts with which she was beset in her difficult situation.

Along with the other residents going back to the house, Else turned to her companions. "You know, Lore and Carola, I have been thinking about Julius and how much we all revered him. He was indeed our leader as we could regard no other in our community. While the rabbi was giving his eulogy, I kept on thinking about the greatest leaders in our history, and to me, he evoked the memory of the four Moseses of our people. There was of course the first—Moses Rabbenu, who took us out of Egypt and received the Ten Commandments nearly five thousand years ago. Then there was Moses Maimonides, about eight hundred years ago in Spain, who gave us our *Guide for the Perplexed* and many other extraordinary scholarly treatises—at about the time when the first Jews came to our city of Frankfurt. Our own Moses Mendelssohn, the third Moses and advisor to King Frederick, was perhaps responsible for making him Frederick the Great. The fourth —Moses Montefiore—was the nineteenth-century Englishman who lived to be one hundred and one years old. He was a great leader and philanthropist within the Jewish community, not only in England but also all over Europe, the Middle East, and North Africa."

She had obviously studied the subject of the Moseses in history and wanted to tell both her companions all she had retained.

"But, you know, I can't help thinking of Julius Kahn as the fifth Moses in our history. Perhaps he won't achieve the same reputation as the others, and perhaps there are not the same accomplishments as those attributable to the others. But for me, he was such a person nevertheless; for me, his greatness made him our Frankfurter Moses."

All three women were quiet thereafter as they had been after her eloquent outburst during the past Seder. They were awed by her thoughts and her praise and quietly agreed that this had been a eulogy of which Julius Kahn had indeed been truly worthy.

19 THE EASTERN FRONT IGNITES

On Monday morning June 23, 1941, the citizens of Frankfurt, and for that matter of the entire Reich, woke up to newspaper headlines that loudly proclaimed, "Wehrmacht Begins Invasion of Soviet Union—End of Bolshevik Enemy is in Sight."

Carola picked up the paper Ursula had brought in and quietly shook her head as she read the news in a remote corner of the shop. Reaction throughout the city was mixed after the first flash of euphoria had worn off. By this time, almost two years into the war, everyone had a relative—husband, father, or son—in one of the armed services who would somehow be participating and would, therefore, be exposed to the new hostilities. Germany was practically the master of most of Europe, and its move into the East would seem to assure dominance over the remainder. There were quiet debates, however, in the privacy of many homes between people who felt they could trust one another as to whether this additional guarantee of the war's extension would be worth the risks and dangers of putting millions of men in harm's way for perhaps an additional two to three years. On balance, the discussions came out on the positive side because the Wehrmacht and *Luftwaffe* had performed so well. The Soviets were felt to be undisciplined, ill-equipped, and composed of many different ethnic groups. It was difficult to see how they could continue to be united when their differences, ranging from East Europeans to Mongolians with different histories, lifestyles, and interests, had been hard to understand by the parochial German mind in the first place.

Initial reports had the usual *Blitzkrieg* character, showing different army units along an extended front making rapid advances into the

Soviet territories from north to south. The Red Army was ceding large tracts of land by their rapid retreat, despite the Soviet dictator Joseph Stalin's announcement of a scorched-earth policy that was designed not to let the Germans have any benefits from the land they were conquering. Because it was the middle of summer, there was no speculation of what might happen with the advancing seasons and the winters that were known to be very cold and brutal. There was no room in the media for pessimism or idle speculation because, who would know, this Eastern front might be conquered by the time the elements became a problem.

For Carola, the news, despite its momentous nature, came on just another day at work, though her coworker Gisela's husband was known to be stationed somewhere on the Eastern front. She knew, therefore, to behave with great circumspection, keeping her comments general and devoid of any alarm. During the past two years, despite constant German advances into other territories, the Witwe Hassan's coffee supply chain had become more restricted, with the amount of inventory and types available from far away becoming reduced and of poorer quality. It seemed to Carola that there were fewer clients purchasing the pure beans, either because fewer could afford the ever-increasing premium prices or because a certain reticence had evolved against buying luxury foods while most of the population was making more basic sacrifices.

Despite the constant tightening of the noose around the remaining Jewish community and the reduction of the "cage" sizes in which they were kept, Aryans took over their apartments and houses as they moved into the city for war-induced work opportunities. Carola's employment seemed unaffected, with Ursula closely watching over their mutual secret—the fact that she was a Jew and actually lived in one of these designated "cages." To avoid any potential interference with her employment, Carola kept the extreme paradox in her daily, otherwise drab life absolutely confidential—on the one hand, she had her regular visits to the old-age home, and on the other hand, she had her continued liaisons with Uli. After all, the very meager living she earned had kept her going independently as a single, if totally isolated, individual just doing her ordinary routine thing from day to day.

Shortly after the Soviet invasion was announced with such fanfare and press reports were still glorifying the new offensive, something strange happened to Carola as she reached near the end of her workday around four o'clock. The phone rang, and Ursula answered it with a somewhat quizzical reaction. She turned to Carola, who was not waiting on any customers at the time and had moved to the back room for a last cup of coffee, calling out to her: "Carola, this call is for you. Please take it where you are so that you'll have more privacy, and customers won't be involved."

Carola was shocked and amazed, as she had never received a call at the shop since she began to work there. She hoped that it was not her mother or Leah with some kind of bad news about either of them, which was the first thing that came to her mind. She picked up the receiver with great trepidation, fearing the worst. Totally to her surprise it was Uli on the other end of the line speaking in a tone of voice she had never heard before, shaky and tentative.

"Carola, I am terribly sorry to bother you during your work, but I wonder if you could come over to the apartment on Mendelssohnstrasse. It is terribly important to me that I talk with you and that you can keep me some company for a while."

She thought she was hearing a very quiet sobbing in the halting manner of his voice, but because this was something completely new to her, she did not want to speculate what might be wrong. What was so important to him that he would violate his own rule to never to call her when his voice might be recognized by Ursula or even her colleague Gisela? Recognition would, after all, expose their relationship, which neither of them had wanted to do and which might endanger its continuity. Nevertheless, she quickly answered.

"Of course, Uli. I will be there about twenty minutes after I leave here for the day. That is how long it will take me to walk over."

"Yes, Carola. Even though it will still be daylight, I'll leave the outside light on so that you are absolutely sure not to miss the house. I so look forward to seeing you. I can hardly wait, my dear."

For the balance of the afternoon, before it was time to leave, she could not remotely figure out what the problem might be or what might be so important for him to have her company. However, the natural loyalty that was instilled in her for as long as she could remember made her stop questioning herself, and she just continued with her work until five o'clock came around. Rather than staying past the formal end of the day, she quickly said good-bye to Ursula and assured her she would be back first thing in the morning.

As she left, she rapidly walked across the front of the opera house and continued on *Bockenheimer Landstrasse* until the beginning of *Mendelssohnstrasse* to her left. The light at the house was totally redundant because she had walked past it several times before to case out where he had taken her that first evening. She quickly walked up the steps and rang the doorbell. When he opened the door, she was shocked by what she saw.

Contrary to his neat, somewhat Nordic appearance, clean-shaven and a model of self-disciplined facial features, the color had drained out of his face. He was unkempt and unshaven; his eyes were unfocused, and his whole manner was one of desperation and grief. He also held a glass of whiskey in his hand and, as he approached her, gave her a light, distinctly nonsensuous kiss. She was repelled by his breath, which smelled strongly of alcohol. It was obvious he had been drinking the whiskey undiluted for a number of hours because as he led her inside into the living room, he staggered and reeled, hardly able to find a chair to fall into. From the table in front of him, he groped to recover two folded letters, which he pushed at her after she had sat down opposite him. He handed them to her and in a gravelly, alcoholic voice said, "Here, read these, and you'll understand."

While she looked at him still perplexed, she unfolded the first letter and began reading. It was from Lt. Klaus von Kleinhoven and was postmarked with a stamp from a French town totally unfamiliar to her. It read as follows:

> *Lieber Vati*,
>
> I have been even more derelict in writing to you than my brother Werner from whom you would undoubtedly have heard from the Eastern front. However, I was angry for a long time, especially with my mother, because she essentially left you in order to gallivant around, pursuing whatever she seemed to feel like at the moment and with whomever she found attractive, other than yourself. With all the family obligations you always instilled in us, I felt she had essentially broken up

your relationship but without clearly and cleanly calling an end to it.

Because I did not wish my letters to fall into her hands, I simply decided to stop communicating and do my own thing in the armed service. Your work address, if I ever had it, I had lost, so that I could not have avoided sending any communication to our home in Kronberg. At any rate, that's all water over the dam, but I wanted you to know that I have thought much about you and how you must wish for the end of the war so that we can all work together and go about our business in peace.

As you may know, as a lieutenant in the infantry, I am in charge of a platoon of men with whom I have been fighting on the French front with much success, contributing to the defeat of our enemy. When our offensive began last year, we were attached to a *Panzer Korps* division and followed the tanks to mop up French infantry groups that were left behind. As our vehicles and artillery units moved on through Belgium, across the Oise, and finally on our way to Paris, French defeat came quickly. Their troops were demoralized and did not put up a very good fight. We inflicted many casualties on them, and I came close to feeling sorry for the way they surrendered in droves without much effort on our part. Nevertheless, I was very glad that we finished them off so quickly. We were all very excited to enter Paris within three months, marching down the Champs Elysees and enjoying the city, the food, the wine, and the girls. It certainly has its benefits to be victorious.

Now that the country has been pacified and disarmed, I am glad to tell you that we have taken up occupation duties in Normandy, near the town of Dinan in a manor house in the midst of a beautiful countryside, again with wonderful food, good billeting, and enjoyable "company"—if you know what I mean. Our only military duties are to search out pockets of partisans that have formed around here and continue to harass us and occasionally inflict casualties on our squads out in the field. I wonder how long we will be here—I suppose it will be sometime until we invade England and bring this damned war to a final conclusion.

In the meantime, I want you to know that I think of you often despite the fact that I have not written before, and hope that when we are all together again, the three of us will enjoy working in our company that our grandfather built for us with such skill and knowledge many years ago.

With a hearty Heil Hitler from your loving son,
Klaus

Carola put down the letter, somewhat puzzled because despite its somewhat arrogant tone, she did not see what could have been so upsetting to Klaus' father. As she picked up the other letter, however, she quickly understood. It was from headquarters of the War Department, the official document addressed to him:

Most Honored Mr. von Kleinhoven:

It is with great regret that we inform you of the death of your son, Lt. Klaus von Kleinhoven, while on a patrolling mission in the province of Normandy, outside the city of Dinan. Lt. von Kleinhoven was personally leading two squads of his platoon searching for French partisans who were known to operate in the area and were receiving guns and ammunition dropped by parachute from British aircraft during the night.

It has been extremely important for us to interdict these weapon drops so that our troops could occupy the sparsely populated areas in safety and good order. However, the population in these parts is still highly inimical to us as they do not yet understand that our occupation is permanent and that they will sooner or later have to work and produce goods for our benefit.

In view of the fact that he and others of our troops were killed in an unfortunate ambush, a large number of partisans were captured shortly afterward. Some twenty-five of them have so far been executed in retribution for this heinous crime. I hope that this is of some small consolation to you, although the loss of a son is never easy to accept. We are returning his decorations to you with this letter under the assumption you will want them for safekeeping as a memento of his short life.

With a wish for the rapid conclusion to this war in victory and for a long-lasting peace we greet you with a sincere Heil Hitler.

For the General Staff of the Wehrmacht:
Colonel Richard Graf Elfenburg

Now Carola understood, and for the first time, she was able to see an instance of personal tragedy from which her Aryan friend was not excluded. He had lost half his offspring, and with his older son Werner still in harm's way some two thousand kilometers to the east, there was no guarantee that his suffering had ended. They both rose from their chairs, and with glass still in hand, Uli embraced her, holding on tightly, and sobbed without restraint.

This was not like when Trudi bade goodbye to her at the railroad station more than two years ago. Despite his clutching and clinging to her, holding a glass that was now beginning to spill its contents on her dress, she held him "correctly" but without emotion or passion. That would have been reserved for tragedies of her own people. While her compassion had not completely died, she was unable to muster a palpable empathy. After all, he had none of his own compassion for her community, despite the fact that he was her lover. Could he feel that, or was he so shaken that as long as he was held in someone's embrace, he was able to unload some of his grief?

He loosened his hold on her and sat down, slowly and carefully so that he would not fall with his balance impaired. He stared ahead quietly, put his glass down, and tried to find some semblance of order within his brain. Was this part of his payback to the devil? He was sure it was—the beginning of a punishment of which, he suspected, there might be more to come.

There really was not much more to say on Carola's part because she could not manage to get out words of sympathy on behalf of one of Hitler's soldiers when her own people seemed to get nothing but contempt and hatred from anyone around them. In light of the fact that Uli did not want to go out and be seen in his miserable state, he asked her if she would go to a nearby shop to bring in food for a cold supper that they might share in the apartment. She was in no mood to do that. So, she made a lame excuse, saying that she had to visit her mother, which he quietly understood as he asked himself why he had called her in the first place—a Jewish woman, ostracized, unable to flee, caged in, and held for disposal—to console him and comfort him at a moment of the greatest grief he had ever experienced. What was this all about? His world was beginning to look a lot less rosy than it had been before he had received these letters.

After another few words of inconsequential talk, Carola decided to take her leave. As she proceeded toward her Judenhaus to eat whatever was available in her own room, she shook her head in a sense of disbelief that she had just witnessed a sorry spectacle happening to someone who was beginning to feel like the "other side."

20 THE YELLOW STAR—THE ULTIMATE DECEPTION

On a Thursday morning toward the end of August when the main activity at the old-age home had been reduced to reading newspapers with the greatest of detail given to scanning and interpreting each article on every page, the residents quickly discovered a new bulletin prominently displayed next to their mail slots in the hallway. The notice came from their central organization, the *Reichsvereinigung der Juden* in *Deutschland*, and was signed as usual by its representatives Alfred Weil and Arthur Kauffmann.

> As per notification from the authorities (Gestapo) received by us along with the appropriate instructions, all Jewish persons above six years of age are henceforth required to wear a yellow star badge of recognition on their outer garment whenever they go outside of their homes for any reason whatsoever. The stars will be issued to the Jewish community central offices in every city and town throughout the greater Reich and must be distributed to every Jew at a cost of ten *pfennigs* a piece. The person receiving them must confirm their receipt and must commit to treat the badge with care and to maintain it in good order. Each star must be affixed to the outer garment worn at the time on the left side of the person's body at approximately the location of his heart. If more than one outer garment is used at different times when leaving his residence, then that person is entitled to purchase a sufficient quantity of stars to permit multiple usages without transferring it from one garment to another each time he leaves his residence.

Wearing of the badge is absolutely mandatory, and anyone caught violating this order will be arrested immediately and subjected to the penalties and punishments outlined in the laws promulgated on this matter by the Interior Ministry and the *Reichssicherheitshauptamt* (RSHA). In order to permit time for the delivery of the yellow stars, this regulation will take effect as of September 19, 1941. It is your responsibility to look out for the arrival of the insignia supplies and to complete the purchase immediately upon availability at your location. Those living in individual houses, where delivery cannot be made separately for practical reasons, it is your obligation to inquire about availability of the stars at your synagogue or community main office so that you can obtain them in time for your compliance with the law. There will be no excuses allowed for not having obtained the yellow stars by September 19, and as stated above, harsh consequences will result from noncompliance after this date.

Signed: Alfred Weil and Arthur Kauffmann
on behalf of the Jewish community

As soon as every resident had read the new notice, with heads shaking, tears rolling down their cheeks, and signs of hopeless resignation proliferating, an atmosphere of noose-tightening with new, sinister, and ominous restrictions on their movements on the outside, took hold of everyone. Esther and Leah shook their heads in helpless quiet and sadness, commiserating with Carola on her next visit to the home. There was not much to discuss, and frankly, it concerned both of them less than those others in the home who were still more mobile and therefore able to take walks in public for occasional shopping or just plain exercise purposes.

"As if we Jews were not sufficiently marked for exclusion, avoidance, chicanery, hateful comments, and racial attacks," Esther said. "Now our long noses and bent bodies will have the Jewish star in bright yellow attached to them so they can walk across the street to get away from us, curse us to our faces, and tell us to leave, get out of their way, and go someplace to die so they are rid of us.

"What is the point? Are any of these *goyim* so stupid that they need a yellow star to recognize that we are the hateful ones? Can't they tell the difference between us Jews—broken down, sick, and unphysical from themselves, the Aryan athletes—without this yellow sign of condemnation? They seem to have perfectly adequate eyes. Are they so nearsighted that it takes a bright yellow spot on a black coat to tell a Jew from a Gentile? Well, what's next?" Carola shook her head in quiet agreement and wondered to herself how she was going to handle her own situation as she walked to and from her forbidden work.

Two weeks later, on September 12, a box was dropped off and left in the front hall. It was marked "Jewish Stars" and delivered from Geitel and Company, a manufacturer of flags in Berlin. An old blue *Keren Kayemet* box was left next to it with a notice: "Please put ten *pfennigs* into this box for each star you take—you are on the honor system. Please sign for its receipt, and your pledge to treat it carefully on the sheet next to the box."

Again Esther's comments to whoever of her residence's companions was within hearing distance: "Hah, a blue box of the *Keren Kayemet* to collect pittance money for the latest sign of denigration. If this is not the ultimate indignity, it has not been invented yet. But," she added with a biting certainty, "I'm sure it will be before they're through. And what if every star is paid for by every Jew remaining in Germany? This will give them a few thousand Reichsmarks more than they had before. I don't think that will run a single tank from Berlin to Moscow, but it could certainly pay for quite a few more Friday night chicken dinners in a lot of old-age homes throughout the country."

Both women took two stars each from the cardboard container, deposited a total of forty *pfennigs* into the box, signed the sheet, and took them to their room in order to sew them onto their garments. Leah did the sewing because Esther's arthritis no longer permitted her to wield a needle in a careful manner. Instead, she directed her friend with great detail and care to affix the star in exactly the right spot. All through the house this important sewing activity took place in every room so that the garments had their infamous signs of recognition properly attached long before the September 19 deadline. Even though they were all now ostracized and segregated Jews, hated by their Aryan ex-compatriots, they were German enough in their makeup to have completed their self-destructive tasks in adequate time and "in good order." The ingrained habit was a sign of assimilation into this society of which they could not rid themselves, even though that society was in the process of ridding itself of them.

When the job was done, Esther sat and looked at the garment with its star in her face for a long time and in silence. She seemed to examine it in a cold and abject analytical fashion to see if she could form an insightful opinion about what she was looking at. She finally turned to Leah.

"Leah, take a look at this. I've been staring at it for many minutes now, trying to make up my mind how I feel about walking around with the star. My first reaction is that, despite the hateful intent these people have toward us and how it is designed to hurt and humiliate us, perhaps subject us to more violence, I must say my first reaction is that I am proud of it. I have come all the way from having been a secular Jew to this ultimate identification so everyone can recognize who I am.

"Do you remember in the Jewish history books, and I think in one of our Haggadahs, how the Jews in the Middle Ages were made to wear Jew hats, the flat hat with the handles up on top that made them immediately recognizable for who they were. I don't know how they felt at the time and how they were treated as a result, but I do know that they were clearly recognized. Well, I feel the same way now; in fact, I am tempted to go out as much as I can still walk and shout to the world, 'Here I am, my friends. I am a Jew for all to recognize from near to far so there is no mistake. I am a Jew who is in your cage, whom you will not let out, and with whom you will do as you wish, whenever you wish. Doesn't that make you feel as good as it makes me feel proud? I don't need to survive any longer, but I do need my identification.'

"If they bury me in a shroud, I would like this Jewish star sewed on it. They don't need to know who I am, but I want them to know what I am or what I was when they could see my face which was to go with my star. Look how they made this star, Leah. This must have been Goebbels' design; it looks like his work. The star's points are round, and they are worn. It looks like they're on their way to melting down; not like the gentile Christmas stars made with cookie cutters that are crisp and sharp before they go into the oven. They also have their edges rounded with the heat in which they are baked. These points are wilting under the Nazi atrocities.

"The lines of the two intersecting triangles look like they're drawn with a shaky freehand rather than in crisp, accurately measured strokes making equally sided triangles with accurate 60-degree angles in the true German manner of absolutes. The yellow color is really gold. We've used that color on our Torah covers for hundreds of years, and again, we can be proud of it as signifying value, worth, and honor. I'm even proud looking at the word *Jude* written in Hebraized German letters. Look how the *J* looks like a *yod* with an extension on it, the *U* looks partly like a *shin*, and the *D* is somewhat like a *samech*. And look how I can all of a sudden remember Hebrew letters that I haven't used for decades; look what memories it extracts from my innards, memories that neither I nor anyone else realized I still retained. Yes, a sign of indignity and hateful intent makes me feel proud, and I will wear it gladly to wherever they will ultimately take us, and until my last breath."

With that, she leaned back in her chair and smiled to herself, not caring whether Leah or anyone else for that matter was still listening. She was satisfied that she had once more fooled the Nazis, bested them in their evil intent, and given her a temporary peace of mind. That must have been the last thing the authorities would ever have thought to have been the reaction to the mark of condemnation they had so quickly designed and delivered.

At 167 *Fuerstenbergerstrasse*, a smaller box containing the stars with the accompanying *Keren Kayemet* box and instructions for depositing the coins was left on an old chair in the hallway. Even though the number of yellow stars was less, they were counted out so that each resident could purchase two of them. For Carola, this was very upsetting, although it seemed inevitable because upon visiting her mother and Leah, she had already known about the distribution of the badges.

Her distress was, of course, caused by what to do about complying with the order and wearing it despite the fact that she was still employed in an Aryan shop. She was obviously not supposed to be there, to say nothing of waiting on customers with many of whom she was by now on very familiar terms and who basically enjoyed the friendly banter and her expert recommendations when they came in to buy coffee.

With rationing and restrictions having serious effects on quality and taste, her suggestions were largely followed. She was frequently complimented on her good judgment in recommending mixtures that had maintained their taste despite the limitations of grades the war had imposed on the coffee supply. Most of it now came from Ethiopia via Italy because the Italian army had kept the supply lines open, one of the few successes they continued to maintain after their brutal invasion of that largely primitive country.

When Carola came in somewhat early the next morning following the yellow star delivery, she immediately asked to have a private talk with Ursula about this very troubling subject. Ursula's reaction and response were totally predictable.

"Well, Carola, you have been doing a wonderful job here. Every client I have spoken to is very happy with the service you are giving them and the courtesy and cheerfulness with which you wait on them, despite all the shortages and reduction of our inventory since the beginning of the war. But, of course, it is totally impossible that you wear the yellow star when doing your job here in our shop. Can you imagine how shocked our customers would be if they came in for their next purchase to be waited on by a Jew and how Gisela would react if she knew she had been working right next to a Jewish woman for more than two years now?

"Not only you but also I would be in serious trouble and likely to be arrested immediately for violating our laws, despite the fact that I would strongly deny ever having known you were Jewish. They just wouldn't believe me, and of course, you'd be gone on the next deportation train to the East. No, it is not possible that you comply with this nonsensical order. If you do take a star from the supply in your house, you must somehow hide it whenever you're on your way to and from our store and during the time you are here. Somehow you will have to work this out yourself. Let me know what your decision is because it will affect your employment immediately, and I would have to look for another person to take your place."

Carola expected no other answer but now had to figure out how she would handle the star question and whether she could leave it off her garments for good or find some way to put it on and remove it, depending on where she was. For example, whenever she visited her mother at the old-age home, she felt she would have to wear it, at least inside the house, so that she would not be regarded as a traitor and lawbreaker by all the other people there who did everything to comply with the regulations. The problem was also that she would have to remember very clearly where she was at a given moment and never forget to either put it on or take it off depending upon her location. She could not afford to make a mistake and leave it on. Supposing she was walking somewhere in the West End or on her way home and met a customer while wearing her badge? That would be an equal or greater shock and would also be the end of her employment.

By the time she had mulled over this dilemma during the rest of the day and was walking home to that "box in the hall," she had decided to buy two stars, leave one of them in her chest of drawers and put the other at the bottom of her pocketbook, hidden underneath a handkerchief and other bulk she had accumulated. She figured that by this time she had violated three laws that had been promulgated by the Nazi government against Jews over the past few years. First, if she did not wear the star, she was in violation of the latest regulation; second, she was working in an Aryan establishment, which was totally against the law and had been for a long time now; and third, she was maintaining a relationship, sexual at that, with a Aryan man who would immediately deny having ever laid eyes—or hands for that matter—on her, regardless of the actual facts.

The next time she was with Uli, she mentioned her dilemma and the decision she had made. He quickly told her that she had done the right thing and made light of the fact that she was not compliant with the law on these three counts. Above all, with his absentmindedness of late, he was not really very interested in pursuing this. He seemed to have other, larger issues on his mind that he did not share with her. She could sense they were a major distraction in his communication with her once again.

As to wearing the star whenever she visited at *Feuerbachstrasse*, she developed a subtle way of pinning it on whenever she was there so that Esther, Leah, and the other residents whose eyes were not exactly perfect anymore could not easily detect the temporary nature of the attachment. As time passed, she became inured to the double standard with which she now ran her life and rationalized her ambivalence, the fence-sitting, and a constant re-identification she was faced with, depending on what day it was or in what company she found herself at the moment. It was difficult. It took alertness and attention at all times, but it was worth it for the sake of self-preservation and survival. It had now been more than two years that Ingeborg Schmidt and Ursula Schaefer had both told her how Aryan she looked and how they had referred to it a number of times. Was this not a low price to pay for that "compliment"? She had long ago decided that this was her lot in life and perhaps her small, good fortune in a lifetime that had held nothing but worry and misfortune for the better part of her fifty-one years on this earth.

Several weeks later, in early October, the residents learned that the Nazi authorities had given an order to the Jewish Central Office to prepare a card catalog for them in triplicate, giving detailed information on all the Jewish members of the community still remaining residents in the city of Frankfurt. This was demanded quickly during the period of the High Holidays and set off quiet but frenzied rumors within the office staff that perhaps it would be used for deportation purposes. The rumors, of course, spread outside the staff and rapidly diffused into the rest of the community, producing fear and unrest among many, particularly those living in the old-age homes.

In mid-October, Alfred Weil and Arthur Kauffmann were summoned to the SS office and told they had heard about these rumors. The *Oberscharfuehrer* who was in charge of conveying orders to them every time they appeared at his small window at the head of the stairs, gave them the instructions to convey to Rabbi Neuhaus. He was told, under threat of penalty, to include in his sermon at the Friday night service in the Unterlindau Synagogue on October 17, that he had heard about these vicious rumors and that there was absolutely no basis for linking the preparation of a card file with any idea about deportation. The message was conveyed that an SS man would be attending the service in back of the sanctuary to listen closely to make sure that the subject was properly addressed. If it were not, the service would be discontinued henceforth, and the rabbi would be arrested and sent to a concentration camp.

Weil and Kauffmann quickly left and conveyed the ominous threat to the rabbi, who assured them he would include a calming note in that portion of his sermon. When Friday night arrived, Neuhaus did an excellent job reassuring the attendees that the rumors were unfounded and the community should not draw conclusions from actions by the authorities with whose context they were not familiar. He suggested that everyone concentrate on spiritual reflection of the good things they still had in their lives, that many of their families and relatives were safe and sound outside Germany in their newly adopted homelands, and that everyone should adopt an attitude of "sticking it out" until this difficult war was at an end. It was inferred that when the war was over, the fate of the remaining Jews in Germany would improve and that they would either be permitted to leave then or a mitigation of the campaign of persecution intensified in these days would be put in place.

As it turned out, the rabbi's credibility was not enhanced with his sermon. Two days later, on the following Sunday morning at 6 AM, two SS men knocked at the door of each apartment or house of those Jewish families whose card files were selected, apparently at random in the West End of the city. The families were woken up quickly and told they had two hours to pack their baggage. They were given orders as to forms to be filled out by the head of household, told to bring provisions for three days of food, had their apartments inspected and searched, and were told to surrender their keys, whereupon they were instructed to wait outside for further directions.

With the same SS men as guards, they were marched in the direction of the Hauptbahnhof and along a designated route on the Main River Quays to the Great Market Hall for assembly and collection. The confusion, panic, shock, and fear that were instilled in both deportees and those remaining behind were incredible to witness. Everyone recognized that this had been the ultimate deception, and no one held Rabbi Neuhaus accountable for essentially telling an unintended lie from the pulpit. It was the beginning of a new turn in the persecution of the Jews in Frankfurt, which augured poorly for their future and removed a layer of denial that expulsion from the city was the ultimate aim of the Nazi government.

At the same time, a few days later an order was promulgated that prohibited further emigration to anywhere and under any circumstances with no exceptions to be granted. The size of the cage had been relentlessly reduced during the past two years, and now the door was irrevocably shut and locked. It seemed that the key had been thrown away. The thousand or so Jewish persons who had been assembled in the Market Hall were loaded onto a train that left the following day. They were sent off "to the East" and never heard from again.

The whole Jewish community was slow to get over the lies it had been told by its own leadership as ordered by the SS authorities. The first mass deportation had taken place from the city of Frankfurt. Despite the fact that they had heard about such evacuations from other parts of the country and that it had occurred under false and surreptitious conditions, everyone was still hoping that, for some reason, it wouldn't happen to them. A train with more than a thousand suffering passengers, taken out so suddenly and under such brutal conditions, dispelled all these notions of personal security and made everyone feel that one of these days it would be their turn.

They did not have long to wait as on November 8 the next notices with the "generous" time period of three days, was disseminated. The names, apparently random but on closer analysis having been chosen from the more affluent segment of the Jewish population, concentrated on those West End residents and families from homes with the maximum residual bank balances and other properties that could still be confiscated. There seemed to be a method to this state-sponsored madness; no element of speculation could be discounted anymore among those that were at this time not caught in the SS net of deportation, no matter how wild and far out.

When contacting the main office, Herbert Bachman was unable to deny any of the theories that were now floating around. He knew nothing; he had to follow orders and simply transmit everything he was instructed to do. As it turned out, the shock of these evacuations had a quick ripple effect because the next train and the collection of another thousand-some-odd persons was now scheduled for November 22. The fear and quaking, the turning of stomachs, the panic, the thoughts of suicide, and the psychological head banging against walls or bars of the cage they were all in were now widespread and did not wane readily. They no longer discussed and debated heatedly. They just looked at each other with sad, drooping, pitiful eyes and shook their heads knowingly and helplessly; they no longer used the word *if* but more often the word *when*.

When these trains left "for the East," they just made people disappear never to be heard from again except for preprinted postcards from Lodz, Minsk, Lvov, or other towns known to have ghettos but about which most Frankfurters had known nothing during their whole lives. The postcards, signed to indicate life, said the deportees were well; they had employment, and they sent their best regards. Most recipients knew otherwise. They did not buy the preprinted messages, not with the lies and prevarications they had experienced ever since Rabbi Neuhaus's now-famous sermon demanded by the SS had been delivered on October 17. In fact, attendance at the Unterlindau Synagogue for the Friday night services had been more sparsely attended ever since, even though some could walk there, badges and all. They did not want to be exposed to more lies in a house of worship even though they realized that the poor rabbi had been forced into telling them from the pulpit.

At the home, people got together in small groups, frequently ignoring the requirement for minyan, the need for ten men together in prayer. They weighed their choices and came down on the side of prayer together, regardless how few—both men and women—assembled at any one time. Even Esther and Leah joined in, which they had not done for some years. They wanted to be with their people rather than to be alone in the abject sterility of their isolation. To be segregated from their old, mixed society was more easily overcome when they appreciated that they were part of their fellow Jews, even though their "crowd" was small, old, and dejected.

The spirit that now developed in the home became sad and very subdued. There was the occasional chess game between those who knew how to play and were still challenged by the strategic approaches that were required. An occasional skat game was organized by those who had a tradition of playing it regularly in the past. Solitaire was for those who wanted to be left alone but who, by themselves, were able to focus on the challenge of winning a hand.

In all of these pastimes—and that's exactly what they were, the need to pass the time to take one's mind off the denials and the inevitable—the element of competition was practically removed. One did not want to win anymore, to best one's neighbor, to beat him or her at anything. Neither did one want to be left alone to fight the now ever-present depressions that had become more contagious than the common cold, or ultimately to help one's fellow Jew overcome the paralysis of being inside the cage. The isolation; the prohibition against further emigration; the removal of all communication via radio or telephone; the inability to get around the city by trolley car; the requirement of sitting on benches painted yellow for identification purposes of people who already wore yellow stars in the first place; and the prohibition against other places of rest such as cafés, parks, and lawns, took down their spirits relentlessly. Chanukah was minimized, and the New Year was ignored as the calendar once again turned; the war ground on, and their condition deteriorated on every front and in every way.

In the meantime, that was true not only of every Jew remaining in the city but also of the general state of things inside the Reich, despite the constant drumbeat of so-called good news and military successes wherever the Wehrmacht expanded its operations. Reading the newspapers, now the major remaining contact the residents of *Feuerbachstrasse* and every other old-age home and Judenhaus had with the outside world, the invasion of the Soviet Union proceeded deeper and deeper into that endless territory, even though the Russian winter had set in, and the temperatures were dropping precipitously by mid-November. The army had achieved a penetration to near Moscow with temperatures dropping far below freezing, and reports of bitter cold and frostbitten German troops came back even though they did not hit the front pages. At the same time, the reports spoke of the Allied forces' counter-offensives in North Africa with tanks racing through the desert in Libya and Tunisia, attacking Axis troops in the sand, and fighting over territory neither of them owned in the first place.

By the beginning of December, rumors were rife of forthcoming conflicts in the Pacific. On December 7, 1941, Japan, Germany's bellicose Axis partner, launched an aerial attack on Pearl Harbor in Oahu, Hawaii, destroying the many ships at anchor there and killing thousands of people. President Roosevelt and the U.S. Congress declared war on Japan the following day, and in accordance with the alliances previously arranged, Germany and Italy, in turn, declared war on the United States on December 11. The United Kingdom declared war on Finland, Hungary, and Romania and joined the Netherlands in declaring war on Japan.

The world was now in total conflagration as war spread to all parts of the globe: China officially declared war on Japan. The United States and England declared war on Romania and Bulgaria. India declared war on Japan. Hungary declared war on the United States and the United Kingdom. The Japanese invaded Borneo, Hong Kong, the Philippines, Malaysia, and Burma. War was everywhere, and Europe's Jews were Germany's largest aggregation of its prisoners of war, despite the fact that no Jew under its domination had weapons to retaliate or could attack it from within. They could not even hide because the yellow star did not make good camouflage material. Rather, it made the Nazis' favorite target more readily visible.

On one of their evenings together, which now took place at the Mendelssohnstrasse apartment after a quick dinner in a tavern near town, von Kleinhoven rambled on in his preoccupation with the ongoing hostilities.

"I just don't understand what our Fuehrer is doing. First of all, he just made himself commander in chief of the German Army. What does he know about military operations? Why doesn't he leave these matters to the professional staff? Doesn't he trust them any longer? He's got enough to do running the country and all of the occupied territories we now have to administer.

"Why are we all over North Africa with our weaponry pounding desert sand when we don't have any strategic objectives I can see there except to confront the enemy wherever he may be? That's wasting ammunition and precious raw materials we use for conducting a war in the east and occupying the west and southeast, which we have already accomplished. In the Soviet Union, the Russians are just sucking us in more and more as the weather gets colder, and our troops are freezing their asses off. Napoleon couldn't do it and was defeated. What makes us think we can conquer them so easily, and even if we can remotely accomplish that, what do we have then with scorched-earth policy all around us and a population of well over a hundred million people our perpetual enemy? Where is our strategic thinking? Why can't we concentrate on the British? Is it too late now that the United States has joined them and is feeding them arms and provisions that will ultimately come back to the European continent? Why can't we bomb the British into submission with our new rockets?

"The combined air forces, once the Americans are established in England, are a formidable threat to us and might destroy many of our cities if they get a chance to retaliate our attacks there. I don't understand any longer. I have been loyal to the party, worked hard for them looking for benefits and rewards, but I can no longer see what we are doing and how we are to accomplish our new four-year plan."

Carola listened quietly because she had nothing to contribute; she knew that no answers were required or possible and that the questions were rhetorical anyway. They were probably the frustrations of someone not informed in the grander scheme of things. She tried to divert him with questions about the Jews right here in Frankfurt, although she did not want to agitate him into remarks she might ultimately not wish to hear. In the newspaper there had been oblique references on one of the inside pages of a conference to take place at the Berlin-Wannsee in early January on "the Jewish question." Did he know of it? What might that be all about? And did it provide for some relief to the suppression and misery of the Jewish community? He confirmed that he was remotely aware of it but did not or would not elaborate. It was more of an administrative matter, he said, and indicated that it involved employing the Jewish workforce in the East so they could contribute better to the overall war effort.

Shortly after this question was disposed of, he quickly took her home. He seemed to have enough fuel to run his car back and forth, despite the intense rationing the rest of the population had to endure. She remained puzzled—many questions, no answers, obfuscating statements, and puzzling behavior. What was she doing, and how could she stop her continuing relationship? How could she ask for reassurance that he would take care of her, that he would save her and hide her someplace so that—perhaps together—they could survive this terrible time? Was a mixed marriage or other arrangement within the realm of possibility after the war? Was she fantasizing or monumentally naïve in her idle speculations? Who only knew?

21 THE END OF AN IMAGINED DYNASTY

While the shock of the three deportations in October and November did not wear off within the Jewish community or the *Feuerbachstrasse* home, the knowledge of what was suspected to be inevitable dulled the senses of the residents. It was simply impossible to maintain the level of tension created and at the same time survive on a day-to-day basis. Life continued on a basis that was least complex, even if it was dull and stupefying.

Holidays were no longer formally recognized. Voices in conversations were lowered, even though there was no one present to overhear any of the subjects, let alone be critical or suspicious. Shuffling about quietly and doing everything in a subdued manner became the operating norm, and an atmosphere of awaiting doom became the common mindset in everyone's waking hours. On her regular visits Carola was struck by the lethargy and lack of energy the occupants projected. Their lives were now empty of content and communication. Mail from relatives had essentially stopped.

A new theory of denial began to develop among the participants of their favorite card game, skat, that succeeded in breathing some new life into everyone. The curious speculation, derived from an optimism that refused to die, lifted the extreme heaviness of the air all around the interior, which in view of the cold January weather, was where most of the elderly people spent their entire day.

Moses Oppenheimer, Meyer Levy, Georg Samson, and Solomon Oestreicher were four of the housemates who spent the greatest amount of time together playing cards on a rolling basis almost around the clock. Because their only other activity was a thorough reading of the day's newspaper to keep up with some semblance of the outside world and they no longer had any of their former business or professional activities to absorb their energies, their conversations and debates took up the many intervals between shuffling and holding their cards, developing their strategies, and keeping their perpetual scores. In reviewing what they learned bit by bit about the recent deportations of their unfortunate fellow Jews, they concluded that despite the fact that more than three thousand members of the community had now been shipped to unknown destinations in the East, none of the old-age homes, whose residents totaled six to seven hundred men and women in excess of sixty-five years of age, had been emptied during the last two months.

"Could this mean," Meyer Levy speculated, "that people our age were not worth moving out of Frankfurt? Perhaps the Nazis feel that because we are not going to live that much longer anyway, it is not worth the expense or logistical problems to move us out. Perhaps it is simply cheaper to let us die here and bury us in the cemetery nearby so that they will get rid of us by normal attrition while at the same time getting some points for treating the elderly with kindness and consideration."

"But why would they do that?" argued Georg Samson. "With us out of the way they could transfer at least another thousand *goyim* coming in from outside the city who would work in the armaments factories around the area and replace us with productive people in this time of war."

"Yes," replied Moses Oppenheimer, "but aside from the space we occupy, we are low-maintenance people here in town whose remaining financial resources go to pay for our own upkeep as they systematically rob our bank accounts."

"Yes, but they'll do that anyway," suggested Salomon Oestreicher. "Every time a group has been ordered to be deported they've had their savings and other assets taken away from them as they were loaded onto the trains. I've heard terrible things occurring at the last minute when people had to sign away all of their belongings. Why shouldn't they just get rid of us physically so that when we are out of sight, we are also out of mind, and the mindless, cowardly citizenry that line the streets as they watch us go can feel relieved of any guilt or burden that might remain in their heads?"

The discussion and its pros and cons went back and forth between the four men in between shuffling the cards and dealing the new hands, conjuring up new arguments for both sides of the question. They also lost track of the hypothetical and speculative nature of their argument as they became serious advocates of one position or the other. This went on for at least two days after which those who proposed the "dying in place" theory won out as they wore down their deportation advocates who finally threw in the towel with everyone feeling better about the denial that had been put in place in a rational manner. With everyone in the skat group keeping their spouses current on the discussion, the result was quickly disseminated throughout the house and became the official mantra. After the last holdouts had been convinced, this finally reduced tensions, and to some degree, the extreme fear that had built up in everyone as a modicum of comfort was slowly reestablished.

The downside of their speculative fate and future was of course fed by the daily reports in the newspaper, which now became somewhat more realistic and less heraldic in the articles about the war's progress. The press realized that they had to report in public what was often sent back privately from the millions of letters that were received by the families of soldiers at the front lines in Russia, the Ukraine, and other parts of the Soviet Union. Despite official censorship, these clearly indicated that it was going to be a long, hard, and primary battlefront. Soldiers returning on leave for short periods of rest and then another tour of duty told of the impossibly freezing conditions, ice, snow, and mud they had to overcome.

Military and populace began to realize that this was not going to be a short expedition with the kind of victory they had experienced in the West. Rather, the territory they were invading was immense, supply lines became ever longer, and despite military victory after victory, it was difficult to see an end in sight. The Soviets were extremely tough; they had been through invasions century after century. The fate of Napoleon some one hundred thirty years ago had been studied by every German schoolchild and was not lost on the calculations and attitude of every German adult. Their faith in the Fuehrer was still intact, but questions of how he was going to pull a victory out of this quagmire began to creep slowly and timidly into the tenor of the reports.

The Nazi press published its stories and opinions in a walking-on-eggs fashion, never abandoning the Germanic tendency for accuracy, exactitude, and compartmentalization beyond the call of duty. It became clear after several more months of this strange, increasingly ambivalent reporting that there would be endless casualties in the Wehrmacht and that the armies moving ever deeper into enemy territory would be decimated if these massive battles continued for months and even years. It then followed within the Jewish community, which had by now dwindled to seven thousand persons in the city of Frankfurt, that there was no ready postwar period to look forward to during which the fate of the remnants caught in the trap of the German dominated territory were going to be remediated. At the home this weakened the denial theory, and with early spring approaching, tensions were heightened once again.

Carola was kept well informed of the attitudes at the home through her periodic visits with Esther and Leah, particularly for the Friday night dinners, which, although sparse and poor, had now become a regular habit by which she could stay in contact with her remaining family. This did not conflict with what had become regular Thursday evening trysts with Uli every three weeks or so. His relentless regularity and predictability had taken on a pedestrian and frankly somewhat boring character. The dinners around town and subsequent times spent at Mendelssohnstrasse were still in place with discussions about the war, second-guessing of Hitler's leadership, and some vague references to his work remaining the regular pattern of how their time, outside their now perfunctory lovemaking sessions, was spent until he took her home. There had been no outing of any sort such as the Brombach weekend in the spring of last year, but Carola really did not expect a skiing weekend in the midst of a serious war.

As Uli explained, the Soviet invasion and strategy was now led by Hitler himself, and routes the Wehrmacht took in their fight to capture Eastern territories were composed of three parts. In the center, the armies were headed directly to Moscow and were now practically at its gates. Destruction of the government was expected to conclude the war, analogous to what had happened in France. A southern route, invading the Ukraine, which was the traditional Russian breadbasket region, continued in a straight line to Kiev, then to Kharkov, and finally to Stalingrad. It would serve to ensure capture of the food-producing areas of the Soviet Union and also ensnare an important industrial sector that was keeping the enemy's military reasonably well supplied. As German supply lines became longer and, consequently, Russian defensive capabilities became stronger, the Wehrmacht was counted upon to supply the knockout blow on this front by its military superiority and better planning capability. In the northern sector, the drive was toward St. Petersburg, now called Leningrad. The city became the national and cultural target that would be most demoralizing to the Russian people, as it was at the heart of its national will, character, and historically unifying strength. In view of the vast territories involved, this would take millions of men. Included in the strategic planning was the use of local militia in the service of the German Army to help control and perhaps subdue local resistance groups that would spring up to the rear of the invaders.

Occasionally, Uli would worry aloud about his son Werner. "I have not heard from Werner in a long time," he told Carola, "and I don't even know if he is still in his position of occupying Litzmannstadt and keeping things in order there. It may be that he has moved on, in which case I hope that he is not at the immediate front where casualties are heavy. I do travel to Poland occasionally, but I have not been able to come near enough to where he was stationed when I last heard from him, so I could not contact him in any way. My business is nearer to the south, closer to Kraków, which is quite a way from Litzmannstadt, and in these days of rationed fuel, I am not able to take any detours from my primary destination."

These updates became regular during their get-togethers. She understood little of the war's progress when he first started to tell her about his ongoing analysis and was somewhat bored as he droned on. She listened politely, however, nodded occasionally, and asked questions that continued the conversation to give him a chance to vent or share problems that she'd gleaned he wanted to air with someone. She had really wanted to become interested and to better understand this gigantic upheaval in all of Europe. It seemed to her this would greatly affect his continued interest in her and even their future together in a post-war world. She understood his loneliness as he missed his sons, especially after the death of Klaus and because he hadn't heard from or seen Werner in the longest time. His wife was apparently gone altogether, and by the desperation now apparent in his voice, the style of his conversation appeared to beg for response and unloading of burdens she did not comprehend.

Toward the end of March, she received another phone call from him while working at the Witwe Hassan as she had in the summer of the previous year. Again in a flat tone he said only, "Carola, please come after your work." It was terse as if no answer was required, and he hung up after a few seconds. It seemed to be a déjà vu of his call when the letter about Klaus' death had come from the War Department, and she hoped that this was not a similar event. The loyalty she had developed to him for reasons she had not properly analyzed herself made her walk over to the apartment without questioning only trying to subdue her curiosity as to what again seemed to be an urgent call for help. As she mounted the steps of the house, she quickly stared at the *mezuzah* that always jarred her consciousness when going there. She once more found the door ajar and, knocking perfunctorily, walked right in.

As she spotted him again sitting in his armchair at the table, she was taken aback by what she saw. This time there was no alcoholic dissipation; he was not red-eyed and dissolved in tears. What she saw was a changed man. Somehow, he had shrunk; he was smaller in every dimension. There was no more gallantry and charm exuding and no smile acknowledging her presence. He was not disheveled or showing any signs of not having slept or being confused.

He sat up reasonably straight, staring at her without animation. His eyes were slightly dilated, and his face no longer had its usual tautness of skin and aura of discipline by which she had come to characterize him, sometimes feeling guilty and ashamed of herself that she admired such a Nordic appearance. In fact, there was now a flabbiness in his pale and blotchy cheeks that she had never noticed before. His nose, which she had considered aquiline connoting a certain nobility, was now hawklike and had the appearance of a small beak that was ready to carry off its prey after plunging from a circling altitude to its unsuspecting victim on the ground. There was a rapid tapping of his foot from a leg he could not keep still, with his right hand providing a contrapuntal motion and his fingers drumming away on the table. She imagined if he had been wearing his chic fedora as he was the time she had originally met him, it would now be much too large on the top of his head and would rest on his ears in a ridiculous, unattractive fashion.

Once more, a folded letter was lying in front of him. He half threw it at Carola as she seated herself in front of him, saying, "Read," without another word of amplification. It was a frightening appearance but no longer intimidating. He had become a small man with a set jaw and teeth clenched in a bitter, vengeful mode. Without saying anything, she picked up the letter and began to read. Again, it was from the War Department, Official Notice.

> Most honorable Herr von Kleinhoven:
>
> It is again our sad duty to inform you of the death of your son, Captain Werner von Kleinhoven, who fell on the shores of the Donets River during the battle for control of the city of Kharkov. Captain von Kleinhoven was in charge of a battery of howitzers that was pounding targets in the center of the city and was making great progress in enabling the infantry to proceed with its final charge. Unfortunately, his command post was hit by a large artillery shell from the responding enemy, and he and several of his lieutenant subordinates were killed immediately.
>
> In a way, his death was merciful because, unfortunately, the Russian counter attack was later successful, resulting in the capture of several hundred courageous German troops, who were led away by the enemy under indescribably brutal conditions. Many of the prisoners did not survive the initial onslaught as the Russians were in total disregard of the Conventions of War that our armed forces so scrupulously observed on other occasions.
>
> Captain von Kleinhoven conducted himself heroically and had the admiration of all under his command as well as his superiors in the way he exerted his strong leadership. Even though his loss will be a tragic event for you, your family, and the Fatherland, you can be proud of how he conducted himself as a true soldier of the Third Reich throughout his all too short life. We are sending back his decorations for your safekeeping.

With All Due Respect,
Colonel General von Breitenstahl

Carola was genuinely shook up after reading the letter.

"Oh, Uli, again I am so sorry; you must feel totally destroyed having lost both your sons, which were your future and your first love—I am so sorry."

She got up and began to walk over to him when he held up his hand to stop her from embracing him in any way that was to indicate comfort and sympathy.

"Yes, Carola, I am destroyed. My life has lost its meaning. Everything I've done, all I've worked for, is now gone. I feel castrated, my legs cut off, my manhood, my future—my family has been destroyed. What am I doing? What difference does it all make? Is this my punishment? What have I done wrong; have I done anything wrong? Why is it not enough to follow orders, to believe in the Third Reich, to believe in the superiority of our cause, to believe that we are better than the rest, that we are destined to lead and that we are entitled to dominate? We are entitled to purify, to get rid of dissension in this world, to cull out the weak ones, the questioning ones, the obsessive, the lazy, the leeches, and the uncooperative, those who don't enjoy victory, who don't enjoy command, who don't strive for self-improvement and discipline, who don't work for order and preciseness." He trailed off and seemed to forget that she was still sitting in front of him.

This time she did not respond or try to stimulate the conversation. She was in her own thoughts and did not want to encourage debate or dissent. She was thinking instead about the irony of his position that, in an absurd way, mirrored hers. Here he was, having lost his progeny, his two sons, and seeing the war he supported with such enthusiasm and the dynasty he was trying to create destroyed.

She was exactly in a reverse mode. She was probably not going to survive the war in this city, her former home, because apparently there was no room for her in any other place in this world that she could have reached or could still remotely do so by some sort of daring, dangerous escape. On the other hand, she had sent her progeny, her two daughters, out of the country—one within Europe and one to the New World. They were alive, able to have families to ensure their perpetuation even though she, as their root, might not survive. She had not heard from either of them in a long time—all mail had stopped, and perhaps Trudi and David in Belgium were in danger themselves. What an absurd, implausible counterpoint—injustice in every other way; what clarity it evoked in the notion that she and Herr Ulrich von Kleinhoven could never have a relationship other than this thrice-forbidden one.

He just sat, teeth still clenched, upright, staring straight ahead in the vengeful sullenness of a Mephistopheles who had lost this round but was not about to lose the next.

At *Feuerbachstrasse* 14, as the month of May approached, the theory of deportation denial that had gained a moderate credibility for "dying in place" was rudely dispelled with letters to selected groups of the remnant Jewish community. They ordered a trainload of Jews for transportation out of the city on May 8, May 24, and June 11, 1942. These were now the fourth, fifth, and sixth deportation trains sent out, which reduced the remaining population to three thousand Jews. The inevitability of the cleansing process of non-Aryans was proceeding apace, and no one doubted any longer that their day would come. Not that they could do anything about it anyway—except to wait and let it happen to them as well.

22 1942—THE OTHER SHOE DROPS

At 6:30 AM on August 15, which was a Sabbath morning, Max and Paula Binswanger came down from their room at the home and picked up the *Frankfurter Zeitung* newspaper to share in reading it. For some benign reason, it was still being delivered to the house at least an hour earlier. This way they could do so without competition, usually induced by an anxious person next in line who would place himself in close proximity to the current reader. In this way, the waiting intruder could produce a certain discomfort so as to move the one in possession along more quickly than would have been warranted had the reader been sitting in his own living room without anyone directing powerful beams through the printed sheet with piercing eyes.

The dining room doors did not open until 7 AM with the now cursory breakfast put out for self-service between that time and 9 AM. This two-hour interval was to accommodate those who did not rise as early as the Binswangers. They both, therefore, had to read sitting on a bench in the hallway to wait for the anxiously anticipated moment when the doors would finally open, and they could spread out over one of the tables.

This morning, when they sat down, however, it appeared strange to them gazing around the corner to the mail rack mounted on the wall and divided into slots with the requisite room numbers at the bottom of each cubby, that these were already all uniformly filled with what appeared to be the same envelope. Max, as soon as he spotted the apparently uniform delivery, rose immediately to go over to his number and withdrew the letter addressed to Max Israel Binswanger and Paula Sara Binswanger. He carefully tore open the envelope and withdrew the multipage contents, which was apparently written as a form notice from the Jewish Welfare Agency. He read slowly as he could not believe its contents and had to overcome his ability to absorb what appeared in front of him and what he had conditioned himself to deny over the past three years. The impossible had arrived, not only for him and his wife but also for all the residents at *Feuerbachstrasse* 14. It read as follows:

> Sir or Madam,
>
> Based on orders of the authorities, we are apprising you of the fact that as of Tuesday, August 18, 1942, at 8:00 AM you are to remain in your apartment/residence in readiness for your deportation. We hand you herewith the Declaration of Assets form you must fill out prior to your departure.
>
> With the submission of your Declaration of Assets, the entire amount of these assets is considered confiscated. Accordingly, you are directed to withhold any disposition of the same; particularly, you are strictly prohibited from giving away items in your possession, selling them, or asking others to hold them in safekeeping for you. The asset declaration is to be filled out by the eighteenth of the month at 8:00 AM by following the exact instructions on the first page of this notice; be sure to fill it out with the utmost care and to keep it in readiness in your apartment. Underlying and supporting documents and contracts (lease agreements, e.g.) are to be furnished with this declaration.
>
> In case of violation of the prohibition against prior disposition, as well as false or insufficient filling out of the asset declaration, you are forewarned of strict measures that will be taken against you by the state police.
>
> According to orders of the authorities, accompanying the preparation of the declaration of assets, you must furnish a special payment to the branch office of the *Reichsvereinigung der Juden in Deutschland* representing at least 25 percent of your cash assets—that is, available cash or cash deposits with banks or savings institutions (for example, unrestricted assets in free accounts, fixed money accounts, and savings deposits) but not including securities or other assets. For this purpose,

you must fill out the form letter, Attachment One, and hold it in readiness for collection by one of the representatives of our organization to be picked up at the latest on Monday the seventeenth of the month at 2:00 PM. Whoever does not possess more than fifty Reichsmarks as cash or cash deposits per person, is exempted from the payment of this special charge but has to give handwritten notice thereof.

For those persons who have to make additional payments to the *Juedische Kultusvereinigung*, or the Jewish community in Frankfurt/Main, an Attachment Two has to be filled out, and the corresponding payment requests must be included. The reconciliation of the requested amounts has to be followed by the preprinted transmission request to the bank (back page of payment request) in filled out form and be kept in readiness for pickup by our representative as of the seventeenth of the month at 2 PM. If you do not possess more than fifty Reichsmarks as cash or cash deposit per person, you are exempted from the payment of the special charge but have to give special written notice thereof.

In the event you wish to make the required payments from your savings deposit, you will have to hold your savings account book in readiness so that we can collect it and present it to the bank for withdrawal of the amount; you will be provided a receipt. Each person is limited to take along no more than fifty Reichsmarks. Taking along larger amounts is strictly forbidden. Violations will incur the strongest measures by the Gestapo. There is no objection if more fortunate participants in the deportation advance you the amount by which your own account is deficient up to fifty Reichsmarks. For persons who cannot come up with fifty Reichsmarks, the amount will be made available through community funds of the deportation leadership.

Taking along foreign currency, securities, savings account books, or other valuables, particularly items of gold or silver of any kind, is strictly forbidden. However, each married person is permitted to take along a wedding ring. All items that are not permitted to be taken along are to be put into a folder or small bag, accompanied by a list of contents, and be left in the apartment.

Taking along warm clothes and shoes in good conditions is strongly recommended. For baggage, you may take along a small hand-carried suitcase or backpack, which should contain only what is absolutely necessary. Taking large luggage is prohibited. A separate handbag of food sufficient for three days should be taken for the trip, as well as tableware, a spoon, and a drinking cup; however, knives are not permitted. Do not put food supplies into the handbag.

The bed covers to be taken along for each person should include a warm blanket or quilt and are to be held in readiness in an unwrapped state to be collected by us Tuesday the eighteenth of the month in the morning at 8 AM. You may attach a name to your cover-all blanket. Featherbeds cannot be taken. In case you own more than one cover, we ask that you make excess covers available to those participants in the transport who lack sufficient blankets of their own.

Every transport participant is free to send flatware, including knives, by collective shipment to the designated destination. These items can be marked with your name but must be held unpacked for collection by Tuesday the eighteenth of the month at 8 AM. We can also accept razors and blades or straight razors for general collection and shipment to the designated destination. It is permitted for each transport participant to take along one set of flatware, with knife, to be made available for collective shipment to the destination.

If you still have in your possession bicycles, typewriters, cameras, or field glasses, you must deliver them, but only at 29 Friedrich Strasse, by Monday the seventeenth of the month at noon. If for compelling reasons you are not in a position to deliver a bicycle at the designated address, you have to notify the undersigned of the *Juedische Kultusvereinigung* by Tuesday the eighteenth of the month at 2 PM so that the bicycle can be collected by 8 AM of the following day. The items that have to be turned over are not to be included in the declaration of your personal assets.

The food purchase cards in your possession are to be taken along with you when you leave your residence and will be collected later on demand.

Signed,
Alfred Weil and Arthur Kauffmann

As he quietly passed on each page to his wife without comment, she finally, after finishing the initial three paragraphs, let out an enormous moanful cry, practically shouting, "Oh my God—this is the end. I never thought this day would arrive!"

At this, she broke down sobbing and collapsed on her husband, who held her tightly and silently. The volume of all this was loud enough to be heard through most of the house, and within seconds, doors opened, and others shouted. "What's happening, what's going on, who shouted, what's wrong?"

Within a short few minutes, others came hurrying down the stairs and corridors in their bathrobes, half dressed, in partial disarray, and with worried frowns. Max said nothing and pointed to the wall with all the filled mailboxes. As each couple arrived, they immediately understood the discovery in their own box, pulled out the letter addressed to them, and opened it quickly. As they read, the shouts of "Oh my God" were repeated over and over again.

When the dining room doors were opened, people rushed in, sat down, and broke out crying, holding their heads in their hands and staring incredulously at what they had received. As they shook their heads, wringing their hands and holding them over their hearts as if trying to ward off a physical attack, the noise level in the house rose to where everyone had finally come down, quickly extracted the letter from their box, and collapsed into a chair with the same reaction again and again.

Because of their inability to move quickly to at least put on their bathrobes, Esther and Leah were two of the last residents to come out of their room. By that time they could guess from the broken phrases that were flying through the air what the content of the letter might be. After Leah quickly pulled theirs from the slot, she tore it open, and both of them read the horrible news together. Over the years, the element of denial had developed such strong roots at the idea of reporting for a march or transport away from their dilapidated sanctuary at the Feuerbachstrasse in three days time that the shock could not be absorbed quickly. There had been six other deportations from the city of Frankfurt beginning on October 19, 1941, some ten months earlier. Residents in the various old-age homes all over the city had rationalized after each deportation that this was either the only or the last one and that from here on in they were personally safe. As each subsequent deportation took place, the credibility of these rationales rapidly diminished, of course; nevertheless, it was impossible to accept that the next one would come directly to where the affected group of residents was located.

Here it was, however; for them, the day of infamy had arrived. The entire world was now once again engulfed in a war that isolated Germany from every country to where Jews could have escaped. Letters to and from America were sent through the Red Cross, taking months to arrive and became useless when they dealt with urgent appeals for help on part of the trapped remnants.

The residents now began to discuss among each other and think to themselves about the details of the orders they had received—whether they had the right clothing, blankets, and food to take along and where they might possibly be going after leaving their lifelong home city. Rumors had spread that many had gone to Theresienstadt, a small town in Czechoslovakia that had housed Austro-Hungarian garrisons for many years and that had been designated as a place where Jews from Germany would be kept during the war. Not much else was known about it because few had received letters from those who were deported there. Those who did receive letters quickly recognized the extensive censorship that warped communication of real facts beyond discernible ones. Optimists and pessimists among the residents, therefore, interpreted the information according to their dispositions, yet no one actually knew how to separate reality from speculation.

Within a half-hour the one phone in the house was being put to constant use. Residents contacted their relatives and friends to tell them what was about to happen to them. They asked for visits from friends still in a position to comfort those who now felt doomed. After talking it over with Esther, Leah decided to call Carola, tell her what had just transpired, and ask her to come over immediately. She reached Carola at the Witwe Hassan and told her about the letter.

Carola blanched, sat down next to the business phone in the back room, and called out to Ursula when she hung up.

"I have just had some very bad news, and I'm afraid I'll have to leave the shop for a few hours. My mother and her companion Leah got a letter from the authorities telling them they are being deported on August 18. Frankly, I don't know where to turn to help them, but I must go to comfort them as best as I can and find out what can be done."

"Well I'm very sorry to hear that," said Ursula, raising her eyebrows but averting her eyes so as not to look directly at Carola's pleading glance. "But certainly, I understand completely; so you go ahead and see what you can do to make them more comfortable. It must be quite a shock to get used to moving like that, although in recent months it seems to have taken place in different parts of the city. Gisela and I will take care of things around here while you're gone. Let me know what is going to happen—and how this may even affect you," she said somewhat knowingly, "so that we can make plans together accordingly."

Carola rushed out, breezing by Gisela with a quick "I'll see you later" and then, in a half running gait, made it over to the home in less than ten minutes.

There, in addition to the milling, excited crowd, she found the two old women in total despair, holding their heads in their hands, leaning on a dining room table with their elbows, and sometimes reaching out for each other's hands to find some magical flow of consolation in what appeared to be a totally hopeless situation. She gave them both long and strong hugs, trying to reinforce their courage, but their sobs shook them to the core now, and she found herself quietly weeping, trying not to collapse into the same sadness that had spread around the rooms. She read the letter, shaking her head, tears streaming.

Esther asked Carola, "Did you get a similar letter at your house?"

"No," said Carola, "not that I know of. Of course, I haven't been home since early this morning so who knows whether I, too, have such notification." Indeed, she wondered to herself what might be in her mailbox when she came home.

Esther continued timidly, "I wonder if you'll be going with us to the same place; at least we could keep each other company and take care of each other."

There was an unreal tone in her voice, knowing that anything that had been impossible was now not only possible but probable. The manager, Dr. Pappenheimer, had in the meantime come down among the small crowd, trying to console everyone in the dining room and around the halls. He asked to have a free telephone line for a few minutes so he could call Herbert Bachman, who might come over to explain some of the details and perhaps what they could expect. After all, he probably had more direct knowledge of what had gone on at the other houses during previous evacuations.

Within the hour, Herbert Bachman arrived to answer questions as best he could, knowing on the one hand what was inevitable and on the other hand what he could not possibly answer as he could not see beyond the immediate stage of getting the group ready to leave. When he entered the dining room, he was immediately besieged with questions, requests, pleas, and other expressions of desperation without regard to the needs and frustrations of those who also needed to relieve their stress from the surprise they had just experienced. He quickly placed himself at a table where he could see the whole room and in an assertive voice asked everyone to calm down so he could proceed with giving out information and answering questions. After a while, the shouts and protests lessened, and the assembled residents were ready to listen. Herbert Bachman then spoke.

"Ladies and gentlemen, first let me read to you the notice in this morning's *Frankfurter Zeitung*, which you may have failed to see in the excitement and tumult you have all just gone through."

In the confusion that followed the receipt of the letters and with only a single copy of the day's morning newspaper in the house, no one had focused on the inconspicuous article placed at the bottom of page two, which was a notice from the Gauleiter's office reading as follows:

> In continuation of the *Entjudungspolitik* (*de-Jewification policy—expulsion of the Jews*), which was decided upon in principle by our government when it first came to power, we are putting the general public on notice herewith that another evacuation and resettlement of approximately one thousand

persons will take place on Wednesday, August 19, 1942. It is planned that those Jews living in old-age homes around the city will be evacuated on Tuesday, August 18, from the houses in which they currently live. In view of the lengthy process of documentation, verification of their local possessions that they are required to leave in the city, and procedures to ensure that they have complied with travel readiness according to the notices they have received, they will be required to leave their current residences and spend the night housed in temporary places before boarding the trains the following morning.

Those residents in excess of sixty-five years of age who have been living in various designated homes will be transported to the large home at the *Rechneigrabenstrasse 18–20* and will proceed the next morning to the Ostbahnhof, the Eastside Railroad Station, for boarding of trains that will be ready for them. Those younger than sixty-five years of age will be accompanied from their homes after it has been verified that they left their residences clean and in good order. They will then march along designated routes carrying light suitcases and necessary belongings to the Great Market Hall for their stay overnight and final exit examination. Those Jews arriving from surrounding towns and suburbs at the Hauptbahnhof will assemble there, check in with SA personnel, and similarly be accompanied along the same route to the same overnight location.

In view of the large number of the evacuees to be transferred, we have designated a route along the Main River so as not to interrupt and interfere with traffic running through the center of the city. This route goes from the Hauptbahnhof to its final destination via *Wiesenhuettenstrasse, Hermann Goering Ufer, Mainkai, Schoene Aussicht*, and *Mainluststrasse to Rechneigrabenstrasse*. In view of the general unimportance of this resettlement, we request that citizens do not congregate along the route causing further traffic congestion. Because there is plenty of time on August 18 and the roads to their destination are well out of the center of the city, partial groups of the evacuees will be moved along over several hours during the day, and too many spectators would only produce undesirable crowded sidewalks and distractions that are completely unwanted at this time.

We can announce that the resettlement for the evacuees will have as its destination the town of Theresienstadt, located in Czechoslovakia, very near the German border and some thirty kilometers south of Dresden in a pleasant countryside area. This town is a historic old garrison village that has been especially set aside for its new population after a long history within the former Austro-Hungarian Empire. There are many apartment buildings located within the town, and such public facilities as a soccer field, several public parks, a bandstand, and a shell for music performances are situated in the center. It is planned that the living spaces will be completely dedicated to Jews so that they can be among themselves and finally totally separated from the area where our Aryan population lives.

Nine years after a New Order under our National Socialist Regime was established, we are certain that the removal of these undesirable people will provide great relief and satisfaction to our citizens so that they will no longer be troubled and aggravated by their presence around our public facilities and in our shops. It is our plan to continue this work and to resettle the Jews until we have accomplished an orderly and pure Aryan environment. I salute you in anxious anticipation of our work and trust as our cleansing process continues that we will find additional motivation and energy to be victorious in the war against our enemies in which we are currently so diligently engaged.

Heil Hitler,
Jakob Sprenger
Gauleiter, Region Hessen Nassau

Bachmann then continued.

"I know what a horrible shock and surprise you have just experienced and how confused you must feel, not knowing exactly what to do next and where to turn. I can only tell you that I was very glad to be able to come over as quickly as I could, even though it is Shabbat today, and the only reason I was in the office was that I expected your call and those of the other homes after seeing your letter myself only late at night yesterday. I must tell you in all candor, however, that this is not the first time I have seen such a letter and that other groups were resettled several months ago and other times before that. They had the same experience, and it has been extremely difficult to get our people used to such misfortune, as none of us has ever experienced anything like this before in our whole lives.

"As you can imagine, these orders come from the authorities, that is the SS, and we, at our agency or at any of the other remaining Jewish community organizations, are absolutely powerless to do anything but to follow the instructions we get. It has become a standard way for them to communicate, and we are currently under constant threat that if we don't obey serious and harsh measures will be taken. In plain German that means that people like myself would be removed from my job, deported, and someone else more obedient than myself would be placed in charge. So I look at myself as the lesser of two or more evils, and I must tell you that the responsibility and the impossible tasks of coordination that I have had to undertake are so terrible for me personally that I don't know how much longer I can tolerate doing my job.

"At any rate, to be perfectly blunt about it, none of you, none of us, has any choice. Please read and reread the instructions contained in this miserable document and prepare yourselves as best you can to fill out the forms. These will be reviewed by the SS men who will examine them on Tuesday. So please be sure you do not commit any infractions that will harm you or otherwise be of great disadvantage to you. Please take along warm clothing and blankets that you can protect yourself with a minimum of weight and carrying problems. You should have food along for the trip, which the house will provide for you.

"I suggest that you write to your relatives outside the country who've been fortunate not to have to go through this terrible experience and explain to them what is happening. Whether those letters will arrive at their destination is of course not certain, and it is unreasonable to expect a response because you will not have a forwarding address any longer. However, it's the responsible thing to do, and you will be much more at peace with yourself if you can handle such a letter, even though you must realize that it might be the last one sent out of the country from Frankfurt.

"From other houses I have learned that in a crisis situation like this people get to know each other as they never have before. Please tell each other what you might need that you don't have and share with each other if you have excess and someone else does not have enough. This is the time to be as selfless as possible because you don't know what you will need; you will probably not need anything beyond what you are permitted to take, and therefore, those who don't have enough of these small things should now be able to receive from those of you who have too much. I would suggest that in the next two days, before you all leave here, you figure out how to help the others and how you can be as cheerful and polite as you can possibly manage. You will need all the support and all the positive spirit you have ever mustered. It will be of enormous comfort and will help you survive to get to your new destination.

"On Tuesday, probably sometime in the morning, you will be taken to a much larger old-age home at the *Rechneigrabenstrasse* 18–20. Because most of you cannot walk or carry your suitcases, the only good thing I can tell you is that there will be trucks here on which you will ride to your overnight stop. The suitcases will be brought along on a separate vehicle, and you will retrieve them at the overnight location. As to Theresienstadt, I only know what I have heard, but I must tell you that I have not spoken to anyone personally that has been there. It is said to be better than any of the other places I have heard about, such as Lublin, Lodz, or Riga, all of which have ghettos, not very pleasant places to live in. At least this is a town in the country with a small river and probably fresh country air. I just don't know; I have heard that they have arranged for cultural activities, and hopefully, that will make your life more bearable, but I just don't know, I just don't know."

He realized just how hollow his little speech was, how it did not really say anything, and how much it hurt him to pretend matter-of-factness from his words and a stiff-upper-lip attitude that was fake to its core. With that, he broke out in tears and could not continue speaking. He could not even ask if there were any questions.

Everyone was sympathetic and respectful and, consequently, did not bombard Bachmann with questions he could not possibly have answered. He thought to himself, *What can I possibly tell them that has any meaning, and when will the day come that I will be on one of these deportation trains myself? When will it come? It's only a matter of time.*

By the time he had finished, the room was completely silent, and everyone had the courtesy to remain so because all appreciated their helpless situation—they were aware that they were all in the same boat and that it was probably rapidly sinking. Questions were, therefore, withheld as self-reflection among all began to take place. Finally, as Bachmann quickly left, husbands, wives, and roommates began to talk in the lowest of voices to figure out the details of folding their tents as it were, leaving their sanctuary of the past three years, and facing the reality of a new life that could, indeed, be the end for many of them.

A few minutes after Bachmann had left and the emotions of empathy and respect that had created the silence and withholding of questions had begun to fade, the volume of unanswered issues began to rise once again, and people remaining in the dining room tried to answer one another, using either self-generated logic or nonexistent experience to calm down their housemates. Esther, Leah, and Carola, however, continued to sit in silence, each trying to assimilate what they had heard and the contents of the letter they had read without increasing their puzzlement manifold and without asking each other an additional bundle of questions that would add to the confusion. After a little while, as the hubbub continued and the noise level once again became somewhat overwhelming, Esther, who had sat quietly, staring straight ahead as if she were in another world, finally spoke to the remainder of her family.

"Let's go to our room and close the door behind us so we can have some quiet and share our thoughts and plans for the next two days to see what we have to do to get ourselves ready."

She pushed down on her wooden cane, and with all the strength she could muster, she slowly rose into as upright a position as her ravaged and contorted body could still manage and, step by step, shuffled back to her bedroom. She was deeply bent over, but that did not prevent her from moving ahead with the utmost determination to get away from the crowd whose agitated behavior she found understandable but also disturbing and upsetting. The two women followed her respectfully until she was seated in her armchair; then Leah closed the door behind them. The noise had faded, and Esther, now leaning on her cane even as she sat, resumed her blank stare in an infinite, distant gaze. Both Carola and Leah sat on the beds so that all three could look at one another to figure out what had come to each one's mind as they tried to expand on the consequences of all they had heard in the past few minutes.

Leah, wishing to break the oppressive silence and to digress into more inconsequential thoughts, said, "You know, when we leave with nothing but our suitcases filled with our clothing and toiletries, I'm going to miss the little decorative pieces we brought with us when we gave up our apartment and that were our most cherished luxuries."

She was looking around at the few items from their vitrine at the *Unterlindau* that they had placed on top of the chest of drawers in between their armoire sections on the inside wall of their room. First and most important to Esther were six small teacups, some totally gilded on the inside and with intricate designs on the outside, others with oval portraits of wigged nobility next to the fancy handles. Then there were three Meissen figurines dressed in eighteenth-century fashions. Next to them stood two menorahs, one of conventional design with four concentric semicircles, and the other with eight little oil containers lined up in a row to be guarded by a larger, taller oil can standing to the right that served as the shammes. Looked at objectively, it was a pitiful little remnant that had survived the move to the home, but to the three women, it was a way of clinging to their lives of now long-forgotten normalcy remembered only in terms of "once upon a time."

"Yes, Leah," said Esther, coming out of the stupor of staring at these remaining objects. "I also am going to miss my teacups terribly. They were the last pretty things in my life. Despite our poverty, they made me smile and feel that I was special. As you remember, Abraham bought them for me, one at a time, when he could still afford to do so. They were either for my birthday or just as a way to tell me he loved me. They were my precious and tender belongings that gave me pleasure in my otherwise harsh life.

"But let's remember that these are only things—things, frills, and objects of vanity that none of us need when we are stripped down to the bare essentials of our existence, as is now the case. We will leave all that behind; they will not fit into our suitcases, and if they did, they would be broken upon arrival at our foreign destination. Both of us—forgive me Leah—are now old and haggard. I am almost seventy-five years old, and you, Leah, will be seventy-two right after the first of the year. I am crippled and weak, and there is not much life left in my body. I don't even know whether I will survive this trip—to somewhere into the wild *Welt herein*.

"However, we both still have our minds, our souls, and our spirits. They cannot take that away from us unless they kill us outright. But even if they do, we both have, in a way, already bested them; we have lived beyond the biblical age of seventy, so we owe them and ourselves nothing. In a way, they owe us, and they can't take away from us our lives that we've already lived. So let's get on with it."

Having said that, Esther's demeanor seemed to change, and her far away, diffuse manner receded in favor of a sharper focus that concentrated on the details she wanted to discuss. She had revived to reassume her dignity and her role as the head of her family. First, she turned to her daughter.

"Carola, we've sat here for nearly four years hoping to emigrate from this hell as Eduard and his little family were able to do, as well as your daughters Trudi and Lisa. After all this time, with the letters that have gone back and forth, the promises that came to naught, and the expectations and disappointments the three of us have undergone, I have been left without hope that we two weak, old women would ever leave. After all, why should those countries accept us useless old people, who can't possibly support ourselves anymore and whose children are just getting on their own feet themselves?

"However, I can't understand why you, a fifty-two-year-old of good mind and body, were not able to be sponsored by our relatives or somebody to go somewhere and start a new life of your own, reunited with the girls. I just don't understand it, and now, all the good intentions of everyone have been wiped out by the war in which we Jews have been trapped as a special category of prisoner and hostage, forced to wear a yellow star.

"Everyone has always said in our family, that you, Carola, looked the least Jewish and could easily pass for a *goy* walking down the street. Undoubtedly, when you work at the Witwe Hassan, you can't be wearing your star, and your customers must accept you as an Aryan.

Otherwise, your manager would not be employing you any longer. Is there not a way by which you could escape on your own, tuck away the star, take a train, and walk across the border somewhere to become a Belgian, a Dutchman, a Dane, or a Swiss and disappear into the blue horizon? You've got to save yourself now that we old women will be moved out of what is no longer our homeland, to which we will probably never return."

Carola, sitting in sadness, spoke quietly.

"Mutti, I must admit I have thought about this very idea for many months, particularly after I stopped hearing from Trudi and her efforts to bring me to Brussels, which must have failed. But you know, the Nazis have this all figured out, and the trap they've created for us is shut securely. My passport has a *J* stamped all over it, so anyone demanding to look at it would immediately see that I have violated the law by not wearing the badge, even if I tuck it in my pocket. I live in a Judenhaus so that my address would give away my religion. I would be imprisoned, and my employer would probably be fired and thrown in jail as well. She really couldn't claim that she did not know after all this time. Not that she is a lover of our tribe, but she has had a large advantage in her shop, hiring me far below the normal wage and possibly pocketing the difference or somehow getting a benefit from having an unregistered employee working in the establishment.

"I really don't expect this to go on for much longer, and then I won't know what to do. So while I have not had the infamous letter that you received this morning, I cannot say that I would be surprised if I were also deported soon. I must tell you, the one possibility of some help is an acquaintance I have made who periodically comes into the store. I am going to ask him what he might be able to do for both of you and to provide a place of hiding for me until the war is at an end. This person has good enough connections with the SA or SS to be able to do something. I'm just not sure, but I'm going to try."

She did not want to elaborate on this relationship anymore, and both Esther and Leah had the good grace not to question her beyond what she had volunteered.

"Well, Carola, I just thought I should mention the obvious and that you should not be constrained by the fact that we are still living here, especially now that this will no longer be the case."

Leah interjected at this point in order to change the subject. "It's a good thing we saved our suitcases, Esther. Shall we see which ones are the lightest that can hold enough of our clothes and what we might want to take along?"

But Esther's stream of thought would not be diverted. "Well, I think we can leave our ballroom gowns behind and take only a couple of dresses, skirts, and blouses, shoes, sweaters, underwear, toilet articles, and our coats to stay warm. I think it's a good idea to see if all this fits into the cases we have that somebody can carry. Otherwise, they'll leave it behind, and we will have nothing.

"However, before we get to that, I would like to tell you what else I would like to do before leaving. Leah, tell me, how much money do we have left between us?"

Leah got up, went to the bottom drawer, where all the sweaters were kept, and opened it fully. At the back and on the left side she had stashed a small pocketbook in which their money was kept. She opened it and counted. "It looks like we have two hundred fifty Reichsmarks left between us, Esther."

"Well, that means that after the fifty Reichsmarks each of us can take along, there will be one hundred fifty Reichsmarks left. We will give you the excess, Carola. However, here is what I want to do. I want to visit the cemetery and Abraham's grave in order to say good-bye to him. I know that we can take various trolley cars, assuming I could get to a stop in the first place. However, as this final gesture, I would like to go in style and take a taxi, have the driver wait for us, perhaps an hour or so, and then bring us back here. I know this is expensive and luxurious. It will probably cost fifty to seventy-five Reichsmarks, but I can't think of a better way to spend some of our leftover money that is as important to me as this final visit to my husband's grave.

"Let's go tomorrow morning. I will also need a wheelchair because I cannot walk from the taxi to the gravesite, which, I remember, is fairly far inside the cemetery. Carola, could you call the office there and see if they have such a chair available? I imagine this is a fairly frequent request. Ask them to reserve one for us when we arrive, say, around ten o'clock in the morning."

"Yes, Mutti," replied Carola. "None of us have been there for a long time, and I think it is a wonderful thing to do. I'll make the call first thing in the morning because they are closed on Shabbat, and right now I'll order a taxi for 9:30 tomorrow morning. In the meantime and from now on, I'll stay with you and not go back to my work until after you have left here on Tuesday."

At this point, their energies were flagging, and their focus was exhausted by the stress of the subject at hand and all the details to be thought of. After Carola had made the call, the three women just sat quietly and reviewed in silence all the ground they had covered with each other. After a while, Carola opened the door and silently led her elderly charges into the dining room to have lunch and regain their strength somewhat with the food that was being served. Oddly enough, yet not unexpected, was that the conversations around the room had changed and were not about this morning's notification of their collective deportations and all the worry of preparations everyone had to make. Instead the room was filled with a general effort at digression, courtesy, and pleasantness that took over the exchanges around the tables. There was a heightened sensitivity that had taken hold of all the residents to lower the level of anxiety they all had gone through earlier that morning, so as to make the last days and hours together as pleasant as each one was able to manage.

After lunch, they went outside into the small garden space and sat together on one of the benches, catching the strong rays of the early afternoon sun warming their bodies with its mid-August strength. When they tired of this pleasant interlude, they finally returned to their room and, at Carola's urging, sat down and jointly wrote the letters recommended by Herbert Bachmann. For the sake of clarity and ease of reading, Carola was made the scribe for all three, and the joint effort of composition, while it slowed down the spontaneity had only one of them been the author, created three brief works of unique pathos of which they could each be proud.

While there was no guarantee that this would be a final letter or that each of the notes would ever reach their destinations, the presumptive spirit with which they were written and the gentle tone of forgiveness used in referring to the recipients' failure to extract them from their horrendous future gave their words a noble quality and expressed the strongest familial bonds. These would undoubtedly be a lifelong reminder to those family members who had actually attained refugee status. Each letter had been written in a different idiom that would fit the different degrees of sophistication and personality for each person. Carola was assigned to take them to the post office for dispatch, mailing two of them off to the United States and one to a now uncertain address in Belgium.

The rest of the afternoon they spent together resting and in relative silence, recognizing that they just wished to be with each other as they might have in former days at their apartment, doing their own thing or having visitors over for coffee and cake on a quiet Saturday afternoon. At the end of the day, Carola went home to sleep at her house after anxiously checking in her mailbox to see if she had received a similar deportation notice. In fact, she had not, and so, for the moment, she was safe—albeit, who only knew for how long.

23 GOODBYE, MY HUSBAND

Carola made the arrangements for Sunday morning regarding the visit to the cemetery, having ordered a taxi the previous day to be at *Feuerbachstrasse* 14 at 9:30 AM. She also called the administration office at the cemetery before they left and inquired about the availability of a wheelchair. This was confirmed by the person on duty; she reserved the chair in the name of Esther Seidenberger.

After she arrived at Esther and Leah's room, she again joined them in their meals. Because this was their last Sunday there, the chef made a special effort, starting with breakfast, to prepare the best he could with the food that was still available. Before it was time to leave, they reviewed the state of their suitcases and selected two of small to medium size that would not be too heavy when filled up with the most needed belongings and could be carried by someone assumed not to be too strong. Both women's clothes were pulled out of the closet and, where judged to be impractical to take, replaced in favor of more necessary items. Because neither of them had purchased any new things over the past five years, these became easy decisions, and items that were either repaired many times or thought of as luxury or decorative pieces were left behind. The selections were made in a careful and deliberate manner to act more as a distraction and take up the available waiting time rather than stuff things into the suitcases in a hurry. Many of the households throughout the city had to just pile their clothes in quickly when they were given a mere two hours to pack up instead of the "luxurious" notice that the Feuerbach residents had to work with.

"Everything is relative, including the priority of miseries," Esther said wistfully. "I suppose we should be thankful now with only the smallest things in life remaining to us and say to ourselves, *it could be worse*." She did not realize how prophetic her words were to become.

The next morning the three busied themselves until the taxi arrived, including scanning the precious, sole copy of the newspaper for ten minutes while other residents waited their turn. Fortunately, they did not discern any fresh calamities, and when the taxi arrived at precisely 9:29 AM, driving up with the pride and zest of Teutonic punctuality, the three were ready to get in promptly. The driver had agreed on a fare of fifty Reichsmarks, which, under the circumstances, was a fairly decent arrangement. Technically, he could have charged an outrageous amount without having found much resistance on the part of three Jewish women who wanted to pay one last visit to a beloved family member's resting place before at least two of them would be deported from the city, presumably forever.

The driver was knowledgeable enough to take shortcuts through the smaller streets of the West End so that they arrived at the gate of the New Cemetery sometime around ten minutes to ten that morning. The taxi man assured them he would wait until they returned, which they felt might be between forty-five minutes to one hour. A little farther to the left and on the way to the main hall, a funeral was in progress. Esther, with her gallows humor still intact, remarked:

"Well, ladies, as you can see, their reduction of our population is still in full swing and seemingly successful. The Nazis must regret it is one at a time only, and they're probably sorry that some of the attendees will—for the moment—go back to their homes. Oh well, let us proceed."

Carola went into the office, picked up the wheelchair she had reserved, and got the directions to the gravesite of Abraham Seidenberger. She and Leah transferred Esther into the chair with further help from the taxi driver and her cane. As they proceeded down the center lane before making the proscribed right turn, they took note of the freshly dug graves which corresponded on their fresh little wooden markers within a day of the last deportation date. Without saying anything to each other, they noted to themselves that these were likely individuals that had chosen *Freitod* (suicide) so that they would not have to face the worst of their anticipated depredations and dehumanization as they were being deported.

After a few minutes of rounding corners at various intersections according to the instructions Carola had received, they arrived at a rudimentary gravestone with Abraham's name and the dates of his birth and death inscribed on it. It was made of cast concrete and undoubtedly the least costly stone to be purchased at the time. While Esther did not remember why it was made that way or who had ordered it back in 1933, a year after her husband's death, she presumed that their poor economic circumstances had made it necessary to opt for the cheapest marker of remembrance available.

Carola wheeled her right up to the stone, and with the greatest of agonies holding on to the top of it and leaning heavily on her cane, she managed to stand on the sparse ivy bed beneath her feet. Bent over, in a gesture of deep reverence, she stood there, obviously in pain but quietly, and remained silent for a few minutes. Only her lips moved as if she were reciting the *Kaddish*, which she had likely forgotten over the years. With Carola and Leah standing slightly behind and to the left and right of her, supporting her under her arms so as to lighten the load of her own weight beneath her, she quietly began to speak.

"Abraham, my beloved husband—my husband, Abraham. I have come to visit you in your peace. Although I have not been here for a long time, this visit is probably my most important one. It is likely to be my last one in my upright position of life because I will be leaving our home the day after tomorrow. As it has turned out, it was fortunate for you to leave me, now some ten years ago, back in 1932. When you died as a sad, broken man with many years of misfortune behind you that was not of your own doing, none of us were able to predict the harder times to come.

"As you were never to know, a year after you passed away, the Nazis came to power at a time of unparalleled political turmoil, greater than anything we ever experienced when we lived together. With the Nazis, a policy of anti-Semitism—the most horrible Jew hatred—unfolded. Unfortunately, very few of us Jews, or even our gentile neighbors, believed what Hitler had openly written as his goal: to drive out all Jews living in Germany. And so now we Jews from all over Europe, not just Germany, are being eradicated by this monster of the twentieth century. Half the Jews of Frankfurt have been able to escape to other countries, but those that are left will be deported. Carola, who so far didn't make it out, Leah, who is now like a sister to me, and I have been trapped here, and Leah and I will be taken from our old-age home to a town called Theresienstadt somewhere in Czechoslovakia from which we will never return.

"At my age of seventy-five, I will probably die soon and join you wherever you are. I hope they will send me back in a box of some sort and bury me next to you with my name next to yours on the stone. If they respect our tradition—which I doubt they will—they will send my body back in a box to fit. If they cremate me, then perhaps a small box will contain my ashes, which could also be buried right here. Knowing them and their cruelties, they might take anybody's ashes from a mass grave far away, put it in a box, send it back here, and charge one of our survivors with collecting it and putting it here into the ground. They might also never send anything anywhere under some bureaucratic pretense.

"That's the kind of people they are, and the rest of our fellow citizens do nothing these days but follow orders in a spineless, self-serving way that, they hope, will protect them from harm. I doubt that it ultimately will. Well, I will be gone myself soon. I am glad to go somewhere else to pass away out of the goyims' own harm's way which, I'm sure, will come to them soon.

"As you can see, Abraham, I have become a bitter old woman, despite my old sense of humor and good-natured disposition, which I think I had when you were alive. We had a good life, Abraham. We were not observant Jews, but we were Jews to the core, and we lived in a Jewish community that had its pride, its history, and its traditions over its eight hundred years. We were happy with each other, had decent children, and lovely grandchildren. We were not a large family, but we were a cohesive one, and we loved each other even though we sometimes kvetched about the little things that aggravated us during the difficult years after World War I. We fell into poverty because of your good nature and the help you gave to your friends and customers in the 1920s. In the last years of your life, this put you into a deep depression, and my heart cried for you, but there was nothing I could do as you lost your will to live.

"I hope that those of our family who will survive can look back with love and pride on us, their ancestors, who gave them a sense of justice and obligation and a sensitivity, stubbornness, and tenacity whereby we have always landed on our feet, and then some."

She trailed off but remained bent over, stroking the rough surface of the stone with her tired hand. Finally, she motioned to Carola to bring her and Leah a couple of small rocks so she could honor the custom of leaving them on top of the gravestone as witness to their visit. Carola obliged, taking them from a wire basket on the path nearby, and each of them placed a small stone on top of the grave marker. Leaning heavily on her cane and supported by the other two, Esther backed off from where she had stood and let herself drop back into the wheelchair. Both women could see that her face was wet even though they had not heard her sobs. Going back to the waiting taxi, she did not look up off the ground and after being helped in said nothing on the way home. She had said her good-bye, and there was nothing else to add. Upon their return to their room, she settled back into her armchair and remained silent for the rest of the morning and all through a lunch of thick soup with hard bread that with her few remaining teeth and soft gums she could hardly chew.

The afternoon was dedicated to finalizing the belongings to be taken; the suitcases were packed, and the three women sat quietly, each one internalizing her grief, not knowing really what to do next but wait. Every once in a while they could hear Esther mumbling to herself.

"It is you, Abraham, I am going to miss the most, and then—my teacups. Goodbye, my beloved husband."

24 PREPARING TO LEAVE

Early in the morning of the following day, Monday, August 17, Carola went down to the hallway of her house where the building's single remaining phone was located. It was the first time she would be using the confidential number that Uli had given her more than two years ago. She wanted to be sure that she was going to handle the call in as efficient a manner as she could project with a sound of self-confidence that would shorten the conversation as much as possible with whoever answered on the other end of the line. As she dialed the fateful five numbers, she once again silently prayed to herself that for some reason and by some magic Uli could in some way intervene. Would he have connections to keep her mother and Leah from being deported and dragged off to the unknown, far away Theresienstadt from which they would never return? Of course, she had not thought through—that is, even if he were able to perform such a miracle—where the two elderly women would stay after the old-age home was shut down. Was there a consolidation planned to take care of the remnant of the remnants at the Gagernstrasse Hospital? Would other homes still stay open somewhere in the city that would take in the remaining few? She was quickly distracted from these thoughts of such far-out consequential contingencies when her phone call was answered. An officious sounding, low register female voice answered in a clipped and impatient tone.

"Heil Hitler—number 27—Von Kleinhoven—private."

"Yes, is Herr von Kleinhoven available, and may I talk to him?" Carola responded.

"I am sorry, but Herr von Kleinhoven is not in his office. He is away on a business trip and is not expected back for several days."

"Will he be back by tomorrow?" she pressed on, despite the fact that she knew the answer in advance.

"No, as I said to you, he will be back at the earliest by the end of this week and perhaps not for several days thereafter. It is quite indefinite." The impatience of the voice increased. "And who is calling please?"

"Well, no, by then it will be too late."

She quickly hung up so as not to get into the Brombach code name and the coffee routine they had agreed upon. She really wanted to save that for a time when there might be another emergency, even though she could not think of anything more urgent. Carola slumped against the wall in despair, not knowing where to turn next. It seemed as if her sole lifeline, however threadlike, was unavailable when she needed it most. Perhaps it was even nonexistent. She slowly opened the front door and walked away from her house, going on to the *Feuerbachstrasse*, where her elders were awaiting her. With the saddest of expressions, she shook her head and embraced Esther and Leah quietly.

"I was not successful to where I thought I could turn."

The two understood. They spent the rest of the day together in a tender closeness that had seldom been as palpable as this day in its finality. Esther wrapped several of the ceramics into leftover newspaper and loaded them into a bag for Carola to take home. She included the teacups, wrapping them with extra care in layers of the paper to ensure their safe transport. It was as if she had willed these precious mementos that were still in perfect condition to the next generation and was performing an important ceremony of transition to denote and guarantee continuity within the rapidly disintegrating pillars of her family traditions. After that, there was nothing else to pass on.

They had counted out the few remaining Reichsmarks stashed in back of the bottom drawer, Esther and Leah keeping what they were permitted to take along, which would be taken from them as soon as they were forced to pay for their own transportation. Carola kept the rest to increase her few scant reserves for purchases of extra food for her own use. After that, they just ambled up and down the street—Esther in constant pain, even with the support of her cane—to and from the backyard, in and out of the dining room, waiting, waiting for the next day's departure to arrive.

Because the evening meal was their last one, the dining room was once again rearranged for a single sitting. The horseshoe configuration that had been used for the Seder in the past gave every one an opportunity to again confirm arrangements with one another, to talk about meeting whenever they got to whatever their destination would be, and to shore up each other's courage against impossible odds. Just before a final meal was to begin, the room was entered by three men, only one of whom, Herbert Bachmann, was known to everyone there. The other two, each of whom had a particularly grave mien, were introduced by Bachmann.

"These two gentlemen are with us tonight because each wanted to speak with you seriously and individually. I would like to introduce to you Mr. Alfred Weil and Dr. Arthur Kauffmann, who were the joint signatories of the terrible letter you received last Saturday. I will let them speak for themselves."

The three had seated themselves at the head section of the long U-shaped table, but now Alfred Weil rose to speak, with head bowed, and he began in a low voice.

"Ladies and gentlemen, I am here as co-president, together with Dr. Kaufmann, and as a representative of the *Reichsvereinigung der Juden* and a signatory to the horrible letter each one of you received, as did the residents of all the other old-age homes in our community of Frankfurt. As you must know, those letters were not written by us, but rather by the Gestapo; we were merely forced to sign them. I cannot tell you with what pain and soul-searching both of us followed these inhuman orders. Yet, in the end, we had no choice, under threat of grave punishment, but to obey.

"In fact, I want to describe to you the daily agony we have undergone since we were appointed to head the agency we were once able to administer independently. Every day, Dr. Kaufmann and I have had to report to our masters at their headquarters, climb up a long flight of stairs, knock at the small reception window, and speak to an official at the desk in an audible voice, 'I am the Jew Alfred Israel Weil. I am here to obtain my orders for the day.' Dr. Kaufmannn had to do the same. Thereupon, we received our orders for whatever large and small matters they wanted us to take care of. We then had to go back to our office, and whether by letter, by phone, or by personally going to one place or another directly, we had to pass on what these Nazis ordered us to do. We are here, both of us, to apologize to you, our fellow Jews, for sending you this letter for your evacuation. Soon I expect we will receive our own letter.

"In about a month, we will have our highest of holidays, Yom Kippur. If I survive until then, I will remember this night—tonight—when I had come before you to forgive me, and I will also ask the Lord, my God, in his mercy to do so. For the rest of my life I will not only think daily of you and ask your forgiveness, but at every anniversary of this day I will do so. And now I will ask Arthur Kaufmann to give you his thoughts."

With that, he sat down, slumping uncomfortably into his seat.

"This is the blackest week of my life," Kaufmann began. "Alfred Weil has expressed himself eloquently, and I will echo his sentiments completely. I, too, have lived with the agony of carrying out the daily orders of these fiendish Nazis against my will and conscience. I also don't know if I will make it much further along, but I ask you now as well to forgive me for what I have done, something which I will promise never to do again."

He looked at everyone around the table and then looked down and quietly said, "I hope the day will come when we, the old Jewish community of Frankfurt, can come back together again in celebration of the end of this persecution and destruction of the human spirit. We are a people of strength, of long and endless suffering, and of eternal faith. But even our hearty resilience and toughness has its limits. I, too, will pray on Yom Kippur to our Lord God for forgiveness, and I ask all of you to let me see mercy in your eyes so I can survive until I too am finally taken away."

Any response would have been too humiliating to these men who had followed the instructions they received so brutally and had to carry them out in order to survive. There was a stony silence at the end of these pitiful mea culpas. At the end of the meal, the residents rose and formed two queues automatically, lining up to shake hands with each man. There was no need for comment, as a sense of futility flowed from one hand to the other, and forgiveness was exchanged from eye to teary eye. There was also a final, silent sense of gratitude for the sanctuary that the residents had long come to understand, along with the realization that tomorrow morning, as they were to mount the trucks or to commence their march, the doors of that sanctuary would, at long last, close behind them forevermore.

25 LEAVING THE SANCTUARY

None of the residents of the home caught much sleep when they went to bed on that Monday night. After lingering in the public spaces, they tried to make arrangements to live together in whatever buildings they would be placed at their destination and said tentative good-byes in the event that it would not work out. It became a pathetic but sincere effort to cling to one another against all odds. A number of them, when returning to their rooms, did not even get undressed, because they wanted to take along a maximum of clothing, even what was on their backs. They did not want to leave anything behind by mistake in the morning confusion when bathrooms were tied up, and they hoped to avoid the mix-ups that might occur if their single suitcases were rearranged or partially unpacked. Besides, the couples in each room shared with each other their fears and speculations, consoled each other with encouragement they often did not believe in themselves and, at times, tried to buoy each other's spirits with optimism bordering on transparent unreality. Only exhaustion and clinging to the last shred of denial finally gave some of them about three hours of rest before it was time to get up and face this day with the final and most painful departure of their lives.

By 6 AM, most of the residents were downstairs in the dining room, which had been set up earlier than usual to accommodate everyone before the men in charge of their transfer would arrive. They all, therefore, heard the two sedans arrive at 6:30 AM with four men from each car getting out and approaching the front door. According to their differing uniforms, they recognized one car holding officials from the SA and the other car containing men dressed in the black uniforms of the SS. The group entered briskly and shouted a hearty "Heil Hitler," moving among the small crowd concentrated in the dining room, most of who were in the process of finishing their breakfasts.

One of the SS men, with more elaborate decorations on his collar and sleeve, obviously denoting a higher rank and looking like the man in charge, addressed the residents in a curt, commandeering voice.

"We got here early to get started on the examination of your papers, which, we assume, you have filled out properly as those were your instructions. If we do this now, we will all save ourselves a lot of time later so that all who are part of this evacuation will not have to stand in line at the end of the day or tomorrow before boarding the train. Some of the Jews who will join you will be coming from towns outside of Frankfurt and will have to be examined separately tomorrow at the Great Market Hall before proceeding to the Ostbahnhof, from where you will depart. However, because we can finish the work with you this morning, you will be able to get to sleep earlier tonight when you have reached today's destination at the *Rechneigrabenstrasse*. We expect your strict cooperation and the answers to all the questions we will have so that we can get done within two to three hours with four of us doing the work. We, therefore, instruct you to line up in four columns in front of the tables we will arrange shortly.

"Anyone whose documents are not fully satisfactory will have to go to the back of the line and start over again. Therefore, do yourselves a favor, and let's do it correctly the first time. Before you get on line, however, we want you to bring down your suitcases and blankets, all properly labeled. Our colleagues from the SA will load them on a truck that will be here shortly and will transport your belongings to the *Rechneigrabenstrasse.* Make sure that everything is labeled as per our instructions. If anything gets lost, remember we are not responsible for it, and it will probably be your fault if it does not arrive in good shape at the home tonight. So go back to your room now, get the baggage ready, bring it into the front hall, and then get in one of four lines that we will set up in the dining room in the meantime."

By now, everyone within earshot and sight had tensed up because most of them had not ever come in such close proximity to these brown and black uniforms. As blood pressures rose throughout the house, they all shuffled obediently back to their rooms, quickly finished their packing and labeling, got into little arguments with each other with their different interpretations of how to do it correctly, and hand carried their last belongings, some with great difficulty, into the front hall. As soon as they let go, one of the brown shirts immediately picked up each suitcase and blanket, taking their belongings outside on the walkway in front of the house.

When the owner looked after his suitcase nervously, the SA man said to him in a mocking and contemptuous manner, "Don't worry, Israel, it won't get lost. We'll take good care of it because we want you out of here with every last bit of your things."

Those couples and roommates who were finished with their first task either sat down in front of one of the black shirts or lined up, remaining standing in back of one of those persons who was already sitting at the table in front of an examiner. In most cases, they quietly answered the questions or confirmed what they had written down in anxious voices, sometimes stammering, clearing their throats, or hesitating, revealing their anxiousness.

After about ten couples had been processed, Jakob and Inge Wertheim sat down in front of the tall SS man working the second table. This examination took longer, as the two of them had a greater net worth than most. They had apparently been fairly wealthy, owned a larger home, and had many belongings they were forced to leave behind and business interests that had been taken over by Aryans in purchases at a small fraction of their value. Jakob Wertheim began to get more and more agitated as he was reminded of everything he was leaving behind and the statement he was about to sign, confiscating everything and handing it over to the government authorities. As his tolerance dwindled, he could not contain himself any longer and quietly turned to his wife, saying to her in a stage whisper, "Now they've taken everything, these state robbers."

The examiner perked up and said in a sharp voice, "You dirty Jew, what did you say?"

"I said, 'State robbers.' You've just taken everything from me I worked for my entire life, and now you're sending me out of the city in which I have lived and where I earned all I just signed over to you."

He knew right then that it had been a mistake to say these things, but he had completely lost his ability to keep it inside himself, feeling if he did, something would just burst within him. At that, the SS man got up and slapped him across the face with a force that threw him off the chair on which he was sitting. The act gave his wife and all those who were standing nearby a fright that seemed like it could be a prelude to produce a number of heart attacks in this group of elderly people. A couple of friends helped Jakob, who winced and moaned quietly, to get up off the floor. His nose was bleeding profusely, and one of them helped him tilt his head back and press the bridge of his nose, hoping it would stop soon.

"All right, Israel and Sara Wertheim." He gave them their papers back. "You will go to the back of the line and stand there until I'm finished with the others. If I hear another word out of you, you Jewish pig, I'll finish you off right here as an example to the rest of them. Then we won't have to fill out these documents, which is a big pain at any rate, and we'll take you to your cemetery directly. If I hear another word other than straight answers out of any you, there'll be a lot of bloody noses around this room."

With this, the room became even more deadly quiet than it had been before, all present realizing that only more pain and harm could come from any comment outside of answering their demands, reasonable or otherwise. The level of fright also increased greatly at this point because they realized that this was the first time they had experienced the physical brutality of the Nazi henchmen. Ironically, it was on the last day at what they had not realized was their sanctuary—their "home"—where civility had set the tone of their lifestyle. It had been a relatively safe haven from a pitiless and cruel world outside that they—fortunately, in a way—no longer recognized as their once familiar home city. All this was now over. What they had just witnessed made the last bit of denial as to what was going to happen with them from here on in, vanish into the recesses of their minds. The images of mourning *By the Waters of Babylon* took over at that very instant.

The documentation process took about two and a half hours to complete. Esther and Leah's check out took only ten minutes because they had very little left to be confiscated and because none of it made any difference to either of them anyway. Carola, who had come over to witness the procedure, stood way in the back, practically out of sight; she was not involved in the process and did not want to be noticed as one of the occupants of the home. When everyone had gone through this first examination, the man in charge spoke in a stern and sharp tone.

"It looks like most of you can't walk to your overnight location," the man in charge snapped. "That doesn't surprise me since you Jews are weak from sitting around most of your lives, not like us Germans, who believe in physical culture to keep ourselves strong. We will have two trucks here in short order to transport you on your evacuation. That will be a slow process, however, because the trucks will be driven behind those marching to pick up anyone who can't make it. Get yourselves ready now, including using the bathrooms, collect your food for the trip in shopping nets from the kitchen, and report to one of the *Unterscharfuehrer* outside on the sidewalk in fifteen minutes."

With that, he turned sharply and left the room. His disappearance lifted some of the worst anxiety, but much remained. There were the quick bathroom calls, the poignant good-byes in case they would lose track of one another, the uncontrolled weeping, and the quiet resignations. Carola went over to Esther and Leah and held each one in turn with the strongest, seemingly endless, embrace: "Mutti, Mutti, I will follow you to Theresienstadt and find you there, I am sure. I love you for always and forever!"

"Carola, my dearest child, please take care of yourself as we discussed on Sunday. You must … you must survive and tell your family and all the others what happened. Please listen to your old mother and do your best."

"I will try, Mutti, but I don't have much hope."

"You must have hope, my child. That's the only thing that will keep you alive—and you must stay alive, you must."

With that, they let go of each other, and Esther dissolved into quiet, unending tears and sobs once again. Now it was Leah's turn. Carola hugged her firmly and lovingly. "Leah, I love you forever. You raised me and my brother from the time we were born. We're as much your children as we are Esther's offspring. You have always taken care of us. Now I ask you to take care of yourself since I can't take care of you in your old age as I would have liked to. Both of you are like sisters as you have been for a long time. Take care of each other so that no further harm will come your way. I will find both of you—I will."

"Carola, I will take care of your mother until my last breath. I've always loved her, and it has been my life's purpose, but listen to her and fight for your own survival—as she told you, you must."

"I'll try, Leah, I'll try," she answered softly and unconvincingly. Now Leah, who had always been the strong and stoic one, also became teary as she slowly turned toward the door, taking Esther's arm on the other side of her cane. Her eyelids were lowered, infinitely weary, and the large bags under her eyes were a deep brown, darker than they had ever been before.

Just then, the SA man at the door yelled in his hoarse, loud voice, "Come on now, everybody, let's get going. *All' Ihr' Judde', 'raus!*"

As they stepped outside and slowly went to the curb of the sidewalk at the continued beckoning of the Nazi official, they approached the two large trucks that had pulled up in the meantime. Both vehicles were old and beat up army trucks, open all around, without top and with loosely stacked rails on both sides. In the center were fixed benches across, six rows of them, having been affixed to the floor so that six persons per row could be seated firmly without slipping off during a trip over rough terrain. It seemed as if there were enough seats for a platoon of thirty-six men being driven on the way to the front, ready to hop off quickly on arrival. To transport the elderly people who were now to be passengers to the deportation assembly point, an open, foldable staircaselike mount had been rolled against the back and then firmly attached to the truck bed.

Two brown shirts stood halfway up the stairs, one on each side, to help each elderly person climb up with as much assistance as he or she might need. In Esther's case, where she was totally unable to do any climbing under her own power, two of the SA men took her under the arms and effectively lifted her halfway up the stairs, while the two men on the stairs lifted her the rest of the way. She felt as if she were handled by a crane but said nothing. She managed to hold on to her cane and, once standing firmly on the truck floor, worked her way to a spot on the third bench near the left side with the assistance of her friends, who had already settled on their own seats. She also managed to cling firmly to the shopping net with its food supply, and once she arranged her dress and moved herself back and forth on the hard board, she stayed put and stared ahead, expressionless and in stolid silence.

Leah had followed her up the stairs closely, needing less help from the officials than Esther with her somewhat better remaining mobility. She came right over to where Esther was sitting, moved close to her, and took her hand.

Despite their silence between them, the two women held each other's hands tightly and, in a way, communicated all their emotions and thoughts to each other in this "digital" manner. There was no attempt to make conversation with others or to do any final socializing for the purpose of mutual distraction from what was about to happen. All the now-former occupants of *Feuerbachstrasse* 14 recognized the gravity of the short trip they were about to take, their total helplessness, the finality of this journey along the Main, and their last look at the river that had been like a beautiful waistband running through the middle of their city, in apparent perpetuity. Everyone's baggage had been loaded into the vacant area behind the benches so that there was at least some assurance these would arrive together with the passengers at the same time.

When all residents were loaded into the two trucks with room to spare, they slowly drove away, first making a U-turn in the direction of the Hauptbahnhof and then proceeding via the West End Platz to the front of the main railroad station. To the left of its front was a special parking area, ordinarily reserved for buses and tours. The trucks pulled up into the spaces, parking alongside three others that were already standing there. In addition, there were also a number of Jewish men and women who had arrived sometime in the morning from outlying towns by special commuter trains and were apparently waiting for other arrivals designated to join the final evacuation march. They were all on their way to the *Rechneigrabenstrasse,* the Great Market Hall, or the East End Railroad Station, any of which they had been assigned to, to spend the night before boarding the train the following morning.

Those assembled and waiting for others were largely elderly people, looking haggard and exhausted, clothed in extra things they wanted to take outside the one suitcase they were permitted to have with them. With their baggage placed in a heap, it all began to look very much alike. The pile assumed the appearance of a uniform mix—badly worn, scuffed, scratched, partially covered with travel stickers from past vacations and pleasure trips, old-fashioned, twenty to thirty years old, and very heavy for their size. Some of the deportees—from Wiesbaden to the north, Bad Homburg to the northwest, Mainz to the west, Darmstadt to the south, and many small villages in between—had gotten there earlier in the morning and waited patiently for more than two hours already. All waited in silence, some sitting on their suitcases to take the load off their feet, others having climbed into the additional trucks to sit on the same benches as the Frankfurters. Everybody was waiting, waiting for the one-way voyage to begin.

Promptly at ten minutes after twelve o'clock, trains having arrived at the noon hour and passengers taking ten minutes to disembark and walk to the meeting place designated for the Jews, another group of about eighty joined those who were assembled around the trucks. A selection was made by the attending Storm Troopers as to who was eligible for a ride because of their inability to walk, and these "lucky ones" were helped on board. Thereafter, those who had to walk were lined up in columns of five abreast, flanked by the SA men. The march began.

The trucks followed slowly as this motley group, tired and discouraged to the core, headed down the *Wiesenhuettenstrasse* toward the Main. There they turned left proceeding up to the *Hermann Goering Ufer*, parallel to the river. While a group of curiosity seekers had assembled near the deportees at the railroad station, they remained at a distance on orders from the officials. A group of spectators who wanted to watch this evacuation also gathered at the river and grew on the sidewalk along the *Ufer*, its continuation, the *Mainkai*, and ultimately the *Schoene Aussicht.*

Because the traffic bed had been blocked off by the police as of early that morning in order to proceed unimpeded with the march, the five-person columns of Jews took up the normal vehicle path of the streets, while the gentile population, who were out to witness the operation, stood two to three deep on the sidewalk. As the column slowly approached each area where a large a number of spectators had congregated, the low buzz of conversation and apparent debate in some of the spots ceased, and the local crowd became totally silent. The contrast between the Jews marching, shuffling down the street with their yellow Star of David badges, and the witnesses dressed in their clean summer garb was stark, like a yellow pointer underlining the direction of the deportation route.

As the column of marchers and trucks reached the *Mainlust* cross street, the extension of the *Weserstrasse,* a group of twenty Hitler Youth boys between the ages of twelve and sixteen who had been assembled by their leader, shouted repeatedly at the top of their voices, "*Juda Verrecke, Juda Verrecke.*" (Jews, you should croak.)

Their words landed like the lashes of a whip on the backs of the deportees who cringed at this final insult but pretended not to hear. With the procession moving along the Main, they were to hear this pejorative chorus at practically every block along the river. These young adolescents, who were receiving their Nazi brainwashing continuously through regular training and who were ultimately slated to be drafted into the military when their age was right, were heaping their final abuse on the ex-citizens of the cities and towns in which they had grown up and whose cultures they had assumed as their own. The Jews, unable to escape previously, were now stripped of their final dignity as their expulsion became complete.

26 *DIE ANSTAENDIGEN* (THE DECENT ONES)

Inge Bauer and Charlotte Goetz were the best of friends. They were the same age, each having been born in 1877, the first decade of a united Germany ruled by Wilhelm I as the first kaiser. It was the victory over France that had united the prior German principalities and states after the Franco-Prussian war of 1870–71. Inge was the only daughter of Gerhard and Hilde Hoefler. The Hoeflers had bought a fine house with the proceeds of a sizable inheritance after the death of Hilde's widowed mother in the late 1870s, a beautiful villa on *Forsthaus Strasse*, about three blocks from the Forsthaus Platz. This made it an easy commute for Gerhard, as there was a trolley car stop near the bridge leading into the center of the city's commercial district.

He was a young, successful lawyer, respected by his fellow legal practitioners in the city, and had built up a sizeable practice from the social networks he had established during the first few years. His office was located on the *Taunus Anlage*, and as a little girl, Inge frequently visited there after shopping excursions with her mother to say hello to the receptionist and to spend a few minutes with their father and husband in between office appointments with his clients. With his now prestigious reputation, he followed in his father's footsteps in his practice of real estate law, estate planning, and wills, as well as other personal and private needs of his clientele. He made a generous living because his ample fees were never questioned by people who could well afford them to obtain first-rate legal advice and service.

Inge particularly enjoyed visiting her father. The office building had the latest, most recently invented technology in elevators to take them to the third floor where his rooms were located. The elevators, called *Paternosters* after the prayer beads many Catholics used in their private worship, consisted of open cabins arranged in a chainlike fashion with an open side facing the floor on which a given group of offices were located. They were to be stepped into quickly at exactly the right point when they were level with the waiting area. Occasionally, there were accidents when people slipped and fell either in or out. However, these were mostly attributed to the carelessness of the user, as the movement of the chain of boxes was slow, and it was presumed that anyone with a decent sense of timing could manage to do this rather daring feat. Inge had always wondered what would happen if one went to the very top and whether the elevator box at the top of the shaft would turn upside down or was pushed across so that anyone who went down the other side could do so in complete safety. She constantly nagged her mother to take her for a ride across the top and was not satisfied until mother finally relented to have her see the mechanical device—the big wheel with a motor that turned the whole contraption.

At home, Inge frequently went to the neighbor's house, lived in by Leopold and Hannah Flegenheimer, who happened to be Jewish. They were always pleased to have her come over for a piece of cake and milk or lemonade to spend time with them even though they had no children of their own she could play with. Instead, as a very bright child and a highly curious nine-year-old, she would ask the two grownups all the questions she had on her mind at the moment. Hannah told Frau Hoefler that Inge had a fine sense of inquiry, and with a self-deprecating sense of humor, she said she made them almost feel part of their family as she seemed like a little Jewish girl in her persistent questioning.

On the other side of the Hoefler family house, a new set of neighbors, Juergen and Hedwig Boehm, moved in from their old apartment on *Textor Strasse*. By sheer coincidence, they had a young daughter Charlotte, or Lotte for short, who was born the same year as Inge. For Inge, this was, of course, a stroke of very good luck as she developed a friendship with Lotte, which was to last for the remainder of their lives.

Juergen was an insurance broker by profession and had an office not too far from Gerhard's location; therefore, they frequently commuted together by taking the same trolley car. His business dealt with homeowner, travel, small business, and other liability insurance categories, also for an elite clientele. He generated and cultivated his business in social settings so that much of his time was spent participating in meetings of clubs he had joined, charitable organizations, veterans and political groups, as well as cultural affairs.

As their friendship grew, Juergen and Gerhard not only referred each other professionally to their respective clients whenever they had needs served by one or the other, but they began to take some of their vacations together, taking their families by train to the Black Forest region, Switzerland, or other first-rate scenic spots. One August they would go together to *Baden-Baden*, for example, and spend their time at the *Buehler Hoehe*, one of the hotels nearby in the hills above the city. Another year, they visited *Luzern* in Switzerland and stayed at the *Buergenstock* above the end of the lake. From there, they had a fine view back to the city and an endless selection of walking paths on which to enjoy the fresh air and remote countryside.

Another year, they took a trip to *Venice*, crossing the Alps in a Trans-Alpine Express train to a point just outside the city. From there, they took a water taxi to the hotel *Cipriani*, where they had made hard-to-get reservations many months in advance. Everyone, including the two girls, now at age twelve, had a magnificent experience exploring the endless little streets and canals, sometimes playing hide-and-seek among the columns in front of the shops at the *Piazza San Marco* while the four parents sipped cups of espresso on the square, relaxing and watching the crowds as well as the pigeons.

Back home in the fall, they resumed school together, and as years went by and they became teenagers, they both attended the Lyceum, always in the same grade. Both mothers were on the Board of the *Staedel* Museum near their homes. They, therefore, spent much time at the museum doing volunteer work and accepting fundraising assignments but also took their daughters at times when new exhibits were featured for a month or two running. That gave them the chance to go repeatedly for in-depth visits and study of the major European artists. Similarly, both parents had subscriptions to the opera to which Inge and Lotte were taken along, albeit to different operas depending upon the taste of their elders. Inge saw productions of *Martha, Haensel and Gretel, The Barber of Seville, Figaro's Wedding,* and other works her mother felt were beneficial from a cultural point of view without turning her off in her teenage years to the length of a Wagnerian *Nibelungen Ring* performance. Both families felt privileged to live in the City of Frankfurt am Main, where an acute sense of history pervaded the life of an affluent family, and one had the ability to be exposed to the benefits of music and the visual arts.

More locally, however, it was important to them that they were true *Sachsenhauseners*, as were so many of their neighbors and fellow inhabitants of the suburban area. The families visited the Ebbelwoi Stub'n when the cider season called for the presses to work at full speed, and many visitors sat on weekends sipping the intoxicating brew. When early evening came around at the end of a Sunday afternoon and a quick supper was called for, they would order the local cheese in the form of a particularly obnoxious smelling, opaque orange patty in which lots of caraway seeds were embedded, called *Handkaes*. A hearty couple slices of rye bread with some butter toned down the sharp taste—although not too much—and after a while of acquiring a taste for this "delicacy," it was a pleasure for everybody to conclude the day with such a smelly morsel. The cheese was often associated with the phrase "*Handkaes mit Musik,*" which referred not to a band playing nearby but to the heavy flatulence that guests of the taverns experienced after eating the native food. This was the reason why many people ate outside at a picnic table under a trellis, so as not to pollute the air in an enclosed space and make it unpleasant for all the others who were sitting close to one another.

All in all, their first years of youth, up to near the turn of the century, were a pleasant time in which the young women grew up in trouble-free households. With such closeness and friendship between parents and daughters, their upbringing and early experiences were figuratively "joined at the hip." Theirs was a life of relative affluence and a feeling of security, both economic and cultural, in a Germany where the mantra was that "everything was in good order." Such an idyllic existence, however, was not to last for the next forty years to follow, and the changes they witnessed from the Wilhelmine period through the Third Reich were to be grotesque, unimaginable, and ultimately too horrible to predict.

Following completion of their Lyceum examinations, both young women expressed the wish to continue their education at the Frankfurt

University. Inge selected art history as her principal field of interest because of her extensive exposure at the Staedel Museum during her years of adolescence. She had developed a proclivity in this direction, particularly because of her mother's active participation there and her many visits when new exhibits were opened. For the next four years, 1896–1900, she concentrated on the history of Renaissance painting in the various countries of Western Continental Europe—that is, Germany, France, Italy, and Holland—while also studying ancient to contemporary political history of the European continent and the development of the North American countries in the nineteenth and twentieth centuries.

While enrolled at the university, she met an interesting and attractive young man who was studying law, with whom she developed first a very comfortable Platonic and then a romantic relationship. Ludwig Bauer, whom she quickly called by his nickname, Lutz, was a frequent guest at the Hoefler house and, with Inge's father in the same field, had much to discuss with and learn from Gerhard during dinner and weekend times at their home. When they both graduated from the university at the same time, Lutz proposed marriage to Inge, who readily accepted his offer.

As Lutz' family also lived in Sachsenhausen, following their wedding, the young couple rented a modest apartment on *Thorvaldsenstrasse* so that they, too, could be close to their respective parents. To make their lives even more comfortable, Gerhard offered Lutz, now his son-in-law, a job at his law firm as a junior associate, having, of course, partnership potential if his performance merited it.

In 1904, a daughter was born to them, who they named Erika. She was to be their only child in view of the fact that the political environment all over Europe was slowly, but with some certainty, deteriorating. Following the next three years as a homemaker and mother of a young child, Inge and her husband were able to afford a full-time nanny and housekeeper, which permitted the young mother to look for a position outside the home so she could pursue her own profession.

Through her family's connections, she was employed first as a docent and then promoted to an assistant curator at the Staedel Museum, a position she held until her retirement in 1937. As World War I broke out in 1914 and her father became a partner emeritus at his firm, he promoted his son-in-law to full and managing partner, running the day-to-day operations at the firm. Lutz had proven himself to be a very capable attorney and was highly respected by his peers that had been hired over the years by his father-in-law as the firm expanded.

By 1916, the war had left all of Europe in a terrible state of conflagration. That year, Gerhard suffered a massive heart attack and passed away within a short time at age seventy. One of his colleagues in Frankfurt, with whom he had frequently cooperated and worked together and who visited to pay his sincere respects, was Julius Kahn. The whole family went into deep mourning, and Dr. Kahn's gentle words of consolation were most meaningful to Hilde, Inge, and Lutz as they struggled to accept his death.

Hilde, however, remained inconsolable about her loss after a marriage of nearly fifty years. She never fully recovered and died in 1920 at the relatively young age of sixty-seven. Consequently, the Bauers took over her parents' home and lived there another ten years, until 1930 when Germany was in a deep depression, unemployment was rampant, and the political situation became more and more unstable. Fortunately, the Hoefler-Bauer firm had an elite class of clients that was minimally affected by all of these events and was comprised largely of retired executives concerned primarily with protecting their wealth by shifting funds into safe assets outside the country.

In 1930, with Lutz now age fifty-eight, he began to show signs of an illness that was promptly identified as lung cancer, probably caused by the fact that he had been a persistent smoker for the past thirty years. He, too, passed away within a few months. Inge went through another period of deep and intense mourning, this time along with her daughter Erika, who had remained single up to this point and had never moved out of the parental home. Erika maintained a modest job as a secretary in the family law firm, and in subsequent years, the two women lived quietly, spending their spare time with the few friends they had been close to throughout their lives and careers.

Inge also continued her particularly close friendship with Lotte, long past the university years, when they needed each other for reinforcement to combat the prejudices to which they were exposed as female students, comprising a very small minority of the student body. Lotte had been more scientifically inclined and had considered medical studies, but when she was rejected for that field, she opted for an education and training in biochemistry. She turned out to be an excellent student, achieving high grades and a large measure of respect from both faculty and her largely male peers. At the university, she met an attractive fellow student who was enrolled in the school of architecture, with whom she fell in love and became engaged following her graduation. They were married two years later in 1902.

By then, Helmut Goetz, her new husband, had landed a job at a prominent Frankfurt firm and felt secure enough to assume his responsibilities as a married man. Helmut became a good practicing architect, innovative in his skills and specializing in office buildings, many of which were built in the sandstone style that was so popular throughout the city and the region. Meanwhile, Lotte became an assistant in the laboratory of Paul Ehrlich, who was working on a cure via chemical means for the terrible disease of syphilis, which was so rampant throughout Europe in the nineteenth and first part of the twentieth century. Prof. Ehrlich was to receive the Nobel Prize for Medicine in 1908 for his trailblazing work.

Unfortunately, as he was approaching the most productive years of his career in his early forties, Helmut was drafted into the German Army with the advent of the war in 1914. He became an artillery officer, commanding a battery of howitzers as the Germans invaded France via the northwestern route through Belgium. In the spring of 1916, Lotte received a notice from the War Department, one that had been sent to hundreds of thousands of soldiers' families that, much to their great regret, Lt. Goetz had been killed in a particularly fierce battle on the banks of the Marne River, wherein he showed great heroism in saving a platoon of his men from many casualties and preserving much of their equipment from utter destruction. Posthumously, he had been awarded the *Pour Le Merite* decoration—enclosed herewith. Lotte was devastated by her loss and was now all alone as the marriage, despite her closeness to her husband throughout the fourteen years they had been together, had been childless and left her with an irreplaceable void. Her best friends, the Bauers, tried to be as supportive as they could under the circumstances, and the three of them spent much time together, even repeating the pattern of joint vacations in the summers that their parents had started so successfully. Lotte submerged herself in her lab assistant job with the Ehrlich Group, despite the taint the laboratory came under with industry-induced anti-Semitic agitation. She later transferred to a better paying position with Chemische Werke Hoechst, one of the major chemical companies located in the nearby suburb of the same name.

When in 1930 her friend Inge's husband passed away, the two young widows became inseparable and spent practically their entire free time together in each other's company. They both decided by 1937, when their work environments became unpleasant and they had earned comfortable pension rights, to retire at age sixty so they could spend some of their time traveling together and enjoying the cultural aspects of their background and education, which they had had less time to do previously. It was their hope that, in this way, they could remove themselves as much as possible from what to them had become a thoroughly repugnant political atmosphere throughout Germany.

They could live their lives uninvolved in the internal and external turmoil the Hitler regime was constantly promoting as it became warlike and threatening to their mostly democratic neighboring regimes who were engaged in their own internal struggles for survival. The Spanish Civil War, the invasion of Ethiopia by Italian forces, and the devastation of large parts of China by an aggressive Japanese military campaign had created much destabilization worldwide. It seemed that the totalitarian governments around the globe were in the ascendancy at the expense of republics that were constantly assailed from the extreme political right and left parties within their own countries. Inge and Lotte wanted to get away from all that and spend their time with gentle people such as themselves, a wish they found more and more difficult to fulfill.

As their parents before them, they both had established friendships with Jewish individuals and families in what had become "normal" as the assimilation of the Jews into the mainstream of German society proceeded at an ever-increasing pace. Within the Weimar Republic, centrist and democratically liberal parties made strong efforts, ultimately in vain, to survive the constant political erosion instigated by forces of both left and right. The Nazi Party and the Hitler government subverted and reversed all that when it came to power in 1933, as its anti-Semitic policies, actions, and persecutions segregating and eliminating Jewish citizens with its diabolically contrived "Aryanization" policy, pursued the active expulsion of its Jewish population from the mainstream of society.

When, in November 1938, Kristallnacht occurred and the populace was able to view the damage caused on the night of the ninth and visible the following day in terms of destroyed synagogues, smashed windows of Jewish owned stores, looting, and other criminal activities, both women were shocked and disgusted to the point of outrage. However, they could not figure out how to demonstrate solidarity with their Jewish friends.

Following their retirements, Inge and Lotte met almost daily, either for lunch or for an afternoon coffee and pastries at one of Frankfurt's many cafés. From their now downsized residences in Sachsenhausen, they would meet near one of the bridges crossing the Main River to take their daily walks into the center of the city. Their destinations were either the Cafés Kranzler, Rothschild, Falk, or Café Fuerst, where they joined with the many familiar faces of other steady patrons at what became very pleasant discussions and people-watching activities for those who could afford not to work during conventional business hours. Other times, during the summer months, they would meet at an early evening hour, have a no-frills supper together in one of the small restaurants in the *Altstadt* and see an outdoor performance of one of the German classics—perhaps Goethe's *Goetz von Berlichingen*—at the Roemerplatz.

Their feelings of helplessness and frustration were exacerbated by the phone calls they each received separately from a number of acquaintances pleading for help in freeing their husbands who had been arrested and practically kidnapped to concentration camps during the night. Others had ended up in hospitals after having been brutally beaten by the Storm Troopers and their cohorts. Inge made a number of calls to the various attorneys at her family's law firm to see what they could do. However, several of the younger attorneys had been persuaded not to get involved and were threatened to work with party members or lose some of the benefits the firm was receiving from local government business. They were, therefore, unwilling to make what could have been key phone calls and what her father and husband would have done without hesitation to help their Jewish friends. It was simply too late.

This humanitarian paralysis and the refusal to hear pleas for help had been induced by an overwhelming need, which was conditioned over the past five years, to protect self-interest at the expense of championing justice instead, parsing information, and compartmentalizing the urge that had once been an integral part of their cultural foundation to "do the right thing." Unfortunately, "this does not concern me" had become the mantra of the day, and both women were "shut down," as it were. As the years went by and the aging process overwhelmed their activist emotions, they outwardly became more passive spectators of the increasing injustice. They would amble together through the city, helplessly viewing the deteriorating circumstances and instances of violence and hatred that were now going on in broad daylight and in full view, no longer escaping the general citizenry's perceptions.

27 THE WITNESSES

On August 15, Inge and Lotte read the public notice piece issued by Gauleiter Sprenger about the upcoming evacuation of approximately one thousand Jews to take place on August 18–19, 1942. They knew this was not the first time for such a deportation. In fact, there had been six since the previous October when the first surreptitious exodus began. As they got more agitated about these movements, the two women finally wanted to witness one of them to understand the cruelty and heartlessness with which the Nazi party brutally expelled the mostly older people who were trapped in Frankfurt and who had exhausted all options to escape their continued persecution.

Therefore, at 11 AM on that Tuesday, August 18, they joined up at their usual meeting point at the corner of the Staedel Museum where the *Duererstrasse* ran into the *Schaumainkai*. At that location, there was a bench on which the first one to arrive could sit down in the event the other was delayed for whatever reason. It was a warm, sunny, late summer day, so they began their trek together a short block up the river to the Old Bridge leading across into the center. This extended right into the *Neue Mainzerstrasse* from where they had a large choice of small restaurants for lunch. They picked the Garten Café, one of their regular places because during the summer one could sit outside, either on the sidewalk of the Taunus Anlage or by walking through to the back into a small, trellis-covered garden area with a group of tables where it was shady and somewhat quieter.

As they were early, despite their mere ambling pace, they had their pick of tables and opted for a quiet rear spot. Their midday meal was still of high quality, despite the fact that the ongoing war economy had begun to place ever more stringent constraints on everything from food to other supplies previously imported from surrounding countries and overseas. Of course, while Germany was continuing to win the war, at least in the West, and territory was occupied with control taken away from the native population, agricultural products were still in sufficient supply. Goods would simply be shipped back into the *Altreich* at the expense of the local populace.

After finishing their meal, the two women slowly walked back through a different set of streets, window shopping at stores that, by now, had more sparsely decorated store fronts, and arrived back at the corner of the Old Main Bridge and the *Mainkai*. They were just in time to witness the arrival of the first section of Jews who were slowly making their way, five abreast, carrying their small suitcases. They were flanked by brown-shirted SA men, marching along as if they were guarding this group to prevent their escape. It was a pitiful and ironic sight to see these older civilians struggling to keep up with a bunch of Storm Troopers, who were between twenty and forty years old and in prime physical shape, having been trained in a paramilitary fashion. The suitcases imposed additional difficulties to their march and seemed very heavy and cumbersome for most of them. Interspersed between the segments of walking groups, old, requisitioned military trucks were moving slowly with elderly and obviously invalided people sitting on benches, some six across, with luggage piled up in random fashion behind them.

In the first truck, seated in the third row all the way to the left nearest the sidewalk, was Esther Seidenberger and, next to her, Leah Rosenthal. Esther sat perfectly still, as upright as she could manage, though still hunched, leaning on the handle of her wooden cane and staring straight ahead with the midday sun pouring down on her head and those of all the others in the march. By now, her face and arms, the only parts of her body exposed from the drab, gray dress she was wearing, were close to ashen white, giving the appearance of someone who was neither fully alive nor completely dead. Her totally white hair, now very thin and straggly, blew in the light breeze with the slightly rocking motion of the vehicle. Her hair had a random, unkempt and matted quality that connoted a short remaining lifespan and a limp finality after a long struggle to defy the force of gravity for the seventy-plus years it had been on this German earth. Her eyes, tired unto death yet fully cognizant of their obligation to see, stare, gaze, and take in this final, miserable tableau, pierced the crowd, the faces that rolled along continuously, but were silent when she passed them, showing neither respect nor mocking disdain. In her mind, she was trying to discern any expressions of guilt and remorse on the part of the onlookers but found none. There was a clueless curiosity and a vulgar expressionless demeanor with pained indifference and nonexistent emotions in most of their faces. It was a fitting way to say good-bye to a populace she had lived amongst but who showed not an iota of empathy as their Jewish ex-neighbors and perhaps ex-friends departed, most likely going to their doom.

Esther's bulbous nose pierced the warm air and was pointed as high as her otherwise drooping head could still manage. Her near-toothless mouth was closed to maintain an aura of dignity, making her prominently protruding, yet small chin point ahead of her in a mode of ultimate defiance of what was happening to her. The very visible wart on her chin had a bouquet of long, loose white hair growing from it and gave testimony to her pride in the imperfection she had always maintained. Her face, similarly, was deeply etched and fluted, with brow and cheeks furrowed into a series of folds that, had she been familiar with them, emulated the hills of Montserrat.

As they saw the procession go by, Inge and Lotte covered their mouths in shock and watched wide-eyed and horrified. Inge could not contain herself and finally spoke in a tone of total dismay.

"I can't believe it. How can we as citizens of Frankfurt tolerate such brutal eviction of all those who were once our neighbors and to whom we were willing to give equal rights and protection under our laws? How will we ever be able to live with ourselves having seen what we are doing to these others?"

She caught herself briefly and lowered her voice to make sure that someone with a solid Nazi indoctrination did not overhear them and perhaps report them to the authorities. It was not quite clear how a stranger would do that in the absence of knowing their names, but these days you never knew whether a Storm Trooper or a Gestapo man in civilian clothes from their Secret Operations Division could be called over to interrogate them. You never knew in these days, you never knew; be careful, just be careful!

Inge continued to speak in a normal voice. She did not seem to worry about being overheard, and she needed to get these things out.

"Lotte, remember when, in the Lyceum where we studied English literature, we read the book: *A Tale of Two Cities* by Charles Dickens? There was this scene that impressed me most and that I remember to this day. It was after the trials by the tribunals that condemned the royalty and many of their estate to death by the guillotine. That instrument was considered to be a humane form of execution, invented by the 'compassionate' Dr. Guillotine. The carts in which Louis the Sixteenth, Marie Antoinette, and others were hauled to their final destination were called tumbrels in English, and I have never ceased to visualize what they might have looked like from Dickens' description.

"Well, I think of the trucks passing in front of us with these poor people who, I am sure, had to be lifted into them judging by their physical state and old age, as the tumbrels of our day. They are motorized with engines and have steering wheels, and the people inside them are dulled by what they must realize is their final voyage of condemnation. Is there a guillotine rigged up someplace that they're being dragged to, out of our sight and, they think, out of our minds? How can they perform this final act after what they've done to our Jewish citizens for the past nine years? Do they think they've gotten us used to this treatment? Is this our de-Jewification policy? When will their heads roll? I already feel like Madame Defarge, knitting away while one after the other head goes into the basket or is held up to the masses for applause and approval. How can they do this, and how can thousands of people witness this horrible march, some of whom, a few of whom at least, must be decent Germans in the sense of our parents and the values with which we were brought up and just stand there in silence and indifference?"

With this and other thoughts coming out in random phrases and words, Inge began to cry softly into her handkerchief as she continued to watch the seemingly never-ending column of these wretched individuals passing by. Lotte, who had been listening in amazement and was beginning to picture the tumbrels and the guillotine images with sympathy and horror, responded in a lowered voice:

"Inge, my dear friend, I certainly agree and feel with you the pain that these people are experiencing and that the two of us feel for them as well. But remember, we are just two single women who have known different days in better times. What can we do about all of this now? We can't just stand here and cry out, 'This is wrong, this is criminal, this should be forbidden. Go home, everybody; go home and take all our Jewish friends back to live with us in harmony.'"

"We would be arrested so quickly, we wouldn't know what had happened to us. We don't know if those standing next to us, surrounding us, feel the same way. We don't know whether they would join us and cry out as well or whether they would look at us askance with hostility and would say, 'Shut up, you two. If you don't like what you see, just go home and leave us alone. We just want to see that the Jews have gone, so we don't have to listen to this problem and read about it in our newspapers on a daily basis. In principle this does not concern us. We are just bystanders who want to be left alone, so we are just here to see that they have finally solved the problem and our city has been purified.' So please, my dear Inge, be quiet. Control yourself so that nothing happens to the both of us and our pleasant life, despite the war and despite these things that are going on right in front of our eyes."

Most of the people surrounding where they stood were too involved in the scene to have overheard them and said nothing, or perhaps, it was because they shared some feeling about what the two women had said between them. No one realized, therefore, that one of the individuals standing some two rows behind them, dressed in plain gray summer garb to remain as inconspicuous as possible, was Carola Rossmann, who, after her most painful separation from her mother and Leah, had walked down to the river where she knew the trucks were to pass. As her mother appeared, staring absently at the onlookers, Carola suddenly had the overwhelming urge to wave, blow a last kiss, and yell out, "Mutti, again, good-bye. I love you."

However, she managed to bring out only the first *M*, which sounded like a loud hum before she caught herself and did not shout out the rest. She had obviously removed the yellow star badge from her dress so that she would not be pushed aside by the rest of the crowd and arrested right on the spot for this violation. She, therefore, remained anonymous, an Aryan onlooker like the dozens of others surrounding her. It was an intense struggle and took all the willpower at her command to restrain herself for this last time, knowing that she would not see her mother again, perhaps ever. She once more realized that she could not be her Jewish mother's Jewish daughter on the one hand, and on the other, her very Aryan friend Uli's mistress and perhaps future wife in an ethnically undistinguishable society of the future.

The bargain had been made with the devil, and the chips were being called in at this very moment. She had just become rudely aware of the fact that her payment had been settled, and in a way, she had made a choice that was against everything she thought she believed. She moved to the back of the crowd and leaned against the building behind her in near collapse. It was over. She was on their side, on his side. She was in; they were out. Her mother and Leah and the hundreds of others who would join the train of a thousand leaving in the morning for expulsion, exile, and certain death, were gone. She was alive and could be alive if she chose to play out the scene. But could she take it? Could she handle it, surrounded by a hostile, insensitive, and brutal crowd that, yes, did not know who she was but, in principle, was rid of the problem that others handled for them? "It doesn't concern us. We just want to see how they do it and be sure it gets done. We are, after all, only onlookers."

Was there really a yellow star in her small pocketbook? Would it burn a hole through its bottom with the heat of guilt it contained? What if it fell out onto the street and all the bystanders saw it? Would they pick her up and throw her onto the last truck? Would she go with the others? Would she also go to her death? Would she be so lucky?

Having revived slightly from the total drain of energy she had just experienced, Carola quickly walked away from the river and retreated to her Judenhaus in the *Fuerstenbergerstrasse.*

As the pitiful procession of Jews moved along, slowly now, tired unto death after covering a distance most of them had not walked in many years, some of them carrying their suitcases that became heavier the longer they were on their march, the column finally reached the *Schoene Aussicht* part of thc roadway adjacent to the river. The trucks were moving slower as those on foot could not keep up their original pace, and even the files of Storm Troopers covering both sides of the column began to slow down with the hours-long trek.

Onlookers who had been three to four deep on each side of the column along the *Hermann Goering Ufer*, closer to the areas near the center of the city, now thinned out somewhat as it was getting to be time for them to head home, prepare their evening meals and be together with their families. The shouts and howling by the Hitler youth platoons had ended and the pain of these curses felt by each of those sitting on the trucks was reduced somewhat on the one hand, while their discomfort from the hard benches increased, on the other. Esther and Leah were almost to a final point of exhaustion and hoped they would reach their night's destination in short order. Some of the marching columns now kept going straight ahead in the direction of the Great Market Hall, while the trucks made a left turn up to the *Rechneigrabenstrasse*. After another two blocks and a further left turn they were in front of a very dilapidated old building which was one of the old-age homes that had been put to use in the East End of the city. As the trucks halted, those on their wooden seats hoped that they would be helped down on some kind of stairs in order to enter the building under their own power. There seemed to be an endless wait without help forthcoming as the storm troopers were gathering opposite the trucks, the street now having been blocked off completely to normal traffic. At a signal, they all broke out into song, shouting at the top of their voices the Nazi party anthem, the *Horst Wessel Lied*. All of the evacuees were familiar with its tune which they had heard many times over the last nine years. Every time it had made them cringe in fear and disgust and by association with all the acts of violence against the Jews that had often accompanied it. To have to hear the raw and harsh lyrics added final insult to injury.

Our banner high, our columns tightly closed

S.A.'s on march, with strong and quiet stride

Our comrades whom the Reds and the Reaction murdered

They march in spirit with us in our ranks.*

(non-literal translation to conform with melody)

Again, the words were like lashes on their tired backs as they waited for some assistance in being helped off the trucks. They badly wanted to proceed and go into the building to feel temporarily sheltered from whatever the outside still held for them by way of attacks and physical or psychological torture. When the Storm Troopers had finished the hateful stanzas of their song, they finally came back to the trucks, mounted the portable stairs that had been stashed with the suitcases in back of the passengers, and began to remove people by walking them off and releasing them on the street. Some could still walk down the steps, being held by their arms to retain their balance. Others had to be literally lifted, as they could not handle the steps by themselves. Leah preceded Esther because she was still one of those that could manage almost by herself. However, when it came to Esther's turn, there was no way she could descend with even the slightest degree of independence. Therefore, two of the troopers grabbed her roughly under her armpits, holding her slightly above the level of the stairs, and swung her quickly on to the pavement. She nearly passed out from the process. Only by willing herself to "survive" on the way down through the air did she land on her totally unsteady feet. It seemed that, at last, she understood what a sack full of coffee beans felt like that Carola had told her about, as it was being delivered to the Witwe Hassan shop over all these years. Perhaps this was the job these Storm Troopers held when they were not swinging Jews on and off old army trucks.

"There you go, Grandma, I bet you never had such a good ride from any member of your family. You Jews aren't strong enough to help each other that way. Now go on into the building with your old cane. I hope I'll never see you again."

The Storm Trooper walked away quietly. Esther tried diligently to ignore him and pushed hard against her cane to make it over to Leah who would help her up the few steps into the building. On her way to the entrance, she spotted part of the Dom spire, the cathedral's top that had been the place where kings and emperors were crowned before their procession to inauguration festivities at the Roemerberg, a few blocks away. This was now hundreds of years ago and was her last glimpse of the city's eminence as the place for bestowing the consent of the governed upon the person of ultimate authority. It seemed the ultimate irony to be "parked" here overnight prior to being stripped of her civil rights and human dignity before finally being sent into exile and ultimate doom. It was indeed her last view of the city before leaving in the morning in a covered truck to the Ostbahnhof for departure.

28 FINAL BLOWS—AN ILL-TIMED ENCOUNTER

As soon as she saw her mother's hunched figure and straggly flowing white hair disappear in the distance, Carola stepped out of the row where she had placed herself, stretching to see the lines of the march. She realized that this might have been the last glimpse she would catch of her mother and Leah, unless she ultimately ended up wherever their destination turned out to be. She was in a state of total revulsion to have watched this ultimate degradation of her family and her community, both from a physical point of view and the psychological trauma that their final journey through the city along its river banks caused them to suffer. Their route was lined with only a passive sea of spectators and a hostile crowd.

In turning her back to the river and moving away in the direction back to her house, Carola felt as if she'd been trapped in a large spider web whose slimy strands were rubbing against her face and hands and whose stringy, elastic bands she could not break through and escape. She walked faster and faster in desperation trying to rid herself of the horror of this scene, which would remain as a lasting impression on her brain. As she reached the front door of the Judenhaus, she quickly opened it and practically ran up the stairs to the top floor and her ultimate, dilapidated refuge. Closing the door behind her, she opened the window to let some overly warm but fresh air in from the end of the summer day and flung herself onto the bed sobbing uncontrollably.

She was all alone now, not even able to express her last sentiment of love to what had remained of her small family because at the moment of public declaration, she had, whether she fully realized it or not, declared for the Aryan world in which she was so effectively hiding.

Here had been the trade-off—the comfort and anonymity her outward appearance had given her in this mass of her fellow inhabitants in the city of her birth. Yet it had deprived her of that freedom of expression and the basic emotion to which she had given her love and the closest ties of a lifetime, previously a given and an entitlement. It seemed that this concept had totally disappeared in the course of the isolation from human behavior that especially she and her community were undergoing. She was now by herself and no longer able to assess the value and power of hiding, and she did not really know its reason other than what was in her fantasies and the recesses of her intense wish fulfillment.

As she had done in the distant past after her husband Aaron's death, she totally undressed, changed into her robe, quickly moved into the bathroom hoping that no one would need to use it, ran the tub, and practically submerged herself trying to scrub the nonexistent spider web off her body. She could not even succeed in doing that. Though it wasn't really there, it did not come off; it stuck and clung, and its sliminess would not disappear, even with the strongest of soaps. She was tempted to submerge herself completely in the water and not even come up when her breath ran out. In view of the nonprivate nature of the common bathroom, she did not linger excessively in the tub, stepped out, dried herself thoroughly, slipped her robe back on, and quickly marched back to her room. She hoped there would be no encounter with any of her fellow roomers in the hallway. Indeed, she snuck back incognito and unnoticed, and after gulping down some cold leftover potatoes and vegetables, she quickly got under the covers and willed herself to sleep. Her last thought was of Esther and Leah, and she hoped that these two loved ones would also have a decent resting place for their final day before their departure.

In the morning, she arose early and quickly walked to the Witwe Hassan. She had been given the key so that she could open the front door, make coffee, and get started even before Ursula and certainly before Gisela would arrive. She made the coffee and had her first cup to revive her sensibilities by the time Ursula came in. She told her manager of the horrible scene she had to witness and the pain she had to experience in watching her mother and companion disappear in the distance. Ursula listened with polite interest and feigned sympathy but seemed a little too eager to get away from the subject and back to her daily preoccupations.

The day went quickly despite the fact that Carola was really not able to concentrate on her work and even made several mistakes in serving the usual mix of customers. Fortunately, they were on the side of packaging excessive weight and undercharging in several instances so there was no complaint from the client, but rather her employer would sustain a small loss on the transactions she completed. Following Friday, the last workday of the week, she spent a quiet weekend at home, though restless and at loose ends, not knowing where to turn next. She walked over to the Holzhausen Park and, in view of the warm weather and sunshine, spent hours sitting on different benches at and near the small pond, daydreaming absentmindedly and, in more lucid moments, reminiscing about her two daughters playing in the sandbox when they were little. In those days, the girls were riding their tricycles on the paths, scooting in snakelike patterns to avoid grownups who were making inconvenient inroads into their unpredictable paths, and chasing each other on the lawns while she and Aaron looked on smiling, occasionally calling them back so they would not get lost. Both days went quickly, as she willfully and obstinately sat on the benches from which Jews were excluded, feeling at once proud, embarrassed, and guilty that her yellow star was with her but hiding at the bottom of the pocketbook to which she was holding on tightly.

Returning to work on Monday, she felt a change in the atmosphere surrounding her. There was a strangeness and vibrations of hostility emanating from her fellow workers, which she had never felt before. By Thursday, three days later, she received the answers to her puzzlement. At the end of the day as soon as Gisela had left and the front door was locked, Ursula called for her.

"Carola, come into the back room with me and join me in a cup of coffee. I need to discuss something important with you now."

Carola quickly put down the glass coffee makers she was rearranging on the display shelf and joined her superior.

"I have something very sad to tell you, Carola," Ursula began. "You have been here now for more than three years, and it has been a pleasure to have you work for me. All our customers, part of who are your personal clients, come in time and again waiting for you just to be served to their complete personal satisfaction. They have consistently spoken well of you and how pleasant you have been at all times. None of them knew, of course, that you are Jewish, especially since none in the Jewish community who might at one time have recognized you have come in for a long time as their entry was really forbidden—even though the sign at the door only said that they were not wanted.

"It seems in recent days somebody did discover that you were a Jew; perhaps it was Gisela. I don't know, and I don't want to ask her because this would tip my hand. At any rate, I had a visitor from the SS Office Confidential Branch, a man in civilian clothing, who came in the other day while you were out to tell me that he had learned you were a Jew. Had you been here, he might have arrested you immediately so that your absence was, in fact, a blessing. I pretended complete surprise and told him I would never have believed that because of your totally Aryan appearance and because I had never asked for your papers. He made me commit, and I promised to do so quickly, that I would immediately terminate your employment and sever all my connections with you. I did so because I really had no choice without jeopardizing my own position with my employers and, in fact, could also have been subject to arrest had I not vehemently denied what I have really known all along.

"I am, therefore, forced to let you go immediately, which I'm doing with great regret and remorse. Because it is only Thursday today, I will nevertheless pay you for the entire week and hope that you have some reserves to get along on your own for a while. In the meantime, I don't know how you could really keep in touch with me since calling here is hazardous to both of us. I certainly wish you the best and hope you will remain in Frankfurt and survive the war—and this regime—so that we might someday in the future resume our relationship. So, good luck and realize that I will miss you a whole lot."

With that, she pulled her away from the open doorway and gave her a strong hug, which expressed an undeniable sincerity. Despite the powerful embrace, Carola was totally shocked as yet another blow had struck her within the last few days.

"And then there was one," she murmured silently to herself She took the thirty Reichsmarks Ursula had given her as a final payment, which did not add much to her existing reserves, but at this point she had to reckon with the notion of one day at a time. She left quietly, not quite knowing what to say, except for a short expression of thanks for the pleasant time she had working in the store and what a help it had been not only economically but also from the point of view of keeping her spirits and sanity intact throughout these horrid times.

As she went out the door to walk home, she subconsciously crossed the rear of the opera house where she had gone to the café to meet Uli for the first and subsequent times. Without paying any attention to her suddenly changed circumstances, she sat down at the outdoor table that had become their familiar and often recurring meeting spot and ordered another cup of coffee and the pastry he had introduced her to at their first meeting. Somehow, there was an overwhelming need for her to reconstruct a déjà vu situation that placed her at the beginning of the unreal period in the life she had lived during the past three years, and which had now so abruptly come to an end. She, therefore, did not even mind paying for these luxuries out of part of the thirty Reichsmarks she had just received, reducing her reserves by a significant percentage. She sat there by herself, many thoughts racing through her mind, until the sun went down and she noted the air cooling off. Finally paying her bill, she walked home and sat in her chair in the room staring mindlessly at the branches of a tree outside her window. There was a sense of "end," which she did not want to accept but knew instinctively that she had to. She just could not figure out how to get her arms around the concept and, if she ever could, how to get to the next one and call it "a beginning."

The next morning she was going to go to the park again and spend the rest of the day trying to figure out what she could possibly do next. On the way down through the hallway, there were ominous white envelopes in all of the mail slots. She had no doubt what they were all about and quickly opened hers. It was an exact replica to the form letter her mother had received less than two weeks earlier—the deportation notice with all the forms and regulations verbatim and a date of departure designated for September 1, 1942. She quickly stuffed it into her pocketbook and stepped out the front door. The reminiscing or daydreaming mode was gone in an instant, supplanted now by a near panic and confusion in view of the deadline mentality that had taken its place. There was an open-ended certainty that, despite its unhappy prospects, did connote the finality of what was now sure to happen.

As of early Monday morning, her life in the city was over. There was the rousing by the SS men first thing in the morning, the terse, unpleasant interview and collection of all the forms, the orders on where to line up and wait with suitcase in hand, and the march to the Ostbahnhof for departure to the east, wherever that was going to be. At best, she would end up in the same place as Esther and Leah, and there would be the very modest joy of a reunion—perhaps Theresienstadt as the rumors had it for the earlier deportation train. At worst, some place further east where rumors had it about a ghetto in some Polish town and even further transports into murderous unknowns.

She walked to the park at a fast pace, as if by doing so she could escape the expulsion that was about to happen. When she got there, she, of course, did not feel like she had gotten away from anything and continued at a tempo around the perimeter paths as if she were running away. But away from what, which way, where to, and in what direction? Gentile mothers with their babies in carriages or young children in hand glanced at her quickly, not being able to figure out what was troubling this lone woman racing around the pond to nowhere, troubled, with furrowed brow seeing nothing around her, glancing straight ahead but apparently without focus or destination in mind.

After a half an hour of this escape fantasy, she came back to herself realizing she was practically running in circles, getting nowhere and accomplishing nothing. Somewhat self-consciously, she took hold of herself and slowly returned to the house. Her only salvation now was to call Uli to see if somehow he could save her from being shipped away within the next three days. This was the moment when he could really snatch her from exile and certain death and prove his love or at least fondness. He could validate his loyalty to their friendship of the past three years, which they had experienced together, talked about, listened to one another, and felt a closeness of spirit—at least on her part—despite their grossly divergent pasts and objectives for the future. Was this not a moment of proof that indeed a bond had been created over all the periods of trysts or time spent otherwise whenever he called her, once every three weeks between his alleged business trips.

As soon as she got back into the hallway and to the house phone, she called up the number he had given her for an emergency. Well, this was an emergency; this was one of the last times she could contact him on the spur of the moment to beg for help. Quickly dialing 49870, she heard the phone ring, and after two intervals, the familiar voice of the private secretary answered.

"Number 27. Who's calling please?"

"Is Herr von Kleinhoven available? This is Frau Brombach. I need to speak with him very promptly. It is terribly important."

"I am very sorry, but he still has not returned from his last trip. He is expected back either tomorrow afternoon or at the very latest on Monday. I will tell him you called, Frau Brombach. Does he know where to reach you so that I can have him call you directly from out of town in case he calls in before actually returning to the office?"

"Unfortunately, that will no longer be easy to do as I am not at the last number I had given him anymore. On the other hand, can you give me his number where I can reach him directly so that no time is lost in my contacting him?"

"Frau Brombach, as you must well know, I cannot do that. In fact, I don't have that number myself. On his trips he moves around a lot. So let me hope that he will, in fact, call in yet this afternoon at which time I will tell him of the urgent nature of your call. Until then, I'm afraid you're going to have to be patient and hope that he connects with you. Is there anything else I can do for you at this time? You understand with all that is going on, I am now very busy and cannot stay on the phone any longer. Good-bye, then."

Desperate and at loose ends, Carola quickly retreated to her room feeling helpless, as if she were losing her equilibrium and a chair was being pulled out from under her. What if she could not reach him tomorrow? The last opportunity to talk to him would again result in failure. What was this business anyway that she was calling, this number 27? Was it a street address and office number, a code of some sorts? Sooner or later, she had to cut through the mystery that had continued after all these months when he had finally broken down and given her a way to contact him—with the repeated admonition that it be used only in a real emergency. While this was one indeed, if she were not able to reach him tomorrow or perhaps Sunday at the latest, assuming the office were open at off hours, it would be too late. She would be gone by Monday morning, and her last chance to be rescued would be lost.

Now what? She went into her room, locked the door, pulled out the smaller of two suitcases she still had with her, and began to open the drawers to see what she might take in the event she had to face eviction from the house and march to the railroad station. She really did not have enough clothing to fill a suitcase to overflowing but managed a pro forma packing trial, fitting all her necessary things into the suitcase. Perhaps the only thing that filled it up completely was the old worn overcoat, which she would need in a new location. She also wrapped a lone teacup, her mother's final souvenir of the past that her father had given his wife as a present. There was such agony in all this. She realized that when you pack someone else's possessions as she had done when her mother had to get ready, it was different and less emotional than when they are your own things, threadbare and worn-out, yet your own that need to be taken along.

By evening, with items in her possession, juggling them around, she tried subconsciously yet purposefully not to make any decisions so that she would not have to close the suitcase and call the packing job done. No, it was too early. It was not time yet, and ultimately, after having rearranged her modest possessions time and time again, she quickly put them all back into the drawers as she could not face a departure of her own. It had gotten dark. She was again near panic not knowing how to fill her remaining time, although time was precious now since there was an ordained end to it, courtesy of the deportation letter. As she was looking around for perhaps the tenth time, there was a gentle knock on her door. She quickly opened it to see who it might be because there were undoubtedly other people in the house in the same state of shock if they had read their letter and knew what was in store for them.

A man was standing in front of her, almost the height of the door frame, with black hair, a face with wrinkles that seemed premature for his age, which she judged to be at the end of his forties, well-built with piercing eyes, a large nose that could be characterized as "Jewish" by any measure and shape, large hands, and a good build. At the same time, he appeared gentle, perhaps lacking a certain amount of self-esteem and confidence.

"Excuse me, I hope I am not disturbing you, but I have just gone downstairs to pick up my mail. I am still in shock after reading the letter in my mailbox. I noticed that your letter was missing so I figured that perhaps you had read yours and were in the same state I am in now. Somehow we have never met, but I also live in a room down the hall from you, the one closest to the bathroom. I've been in the habit of going in there only after I hear from inside my room that the last neighbor on my floor has used it. I am very sensitive to disturbing other people while they do their chores in there because I, in turn, really like to be able to take my time without feeling interrupted or that I might hold up someone else here on the floor. It is perhaps one of my idiosyncrasies, but that's how I am, and it's too late for me to change my habits. I hope you understand," he said in a clipped, frenetic manner as someone perpetually embarrassed and unsure of himself. He finally smiled a bit, hoping he would find a sympathetic reaction in her face to his attempt to make conversation.

"Certainly, please come in. In these bad times it is so difficult to be alone, not knowing what to do next, only realizing that these could well be our final days in the city that has become so terrible for all of us who are Jewish."

As she spoke, he took one step inside, still standing politely, now on the other side of the doorway.

"Thank you so much. Let me introduce myself. My name is Simon Rosenstiehl. I am really not from Frankfurt but have just moved here in the past few months from my native city of Fulda, where I lived all my life and where my family is still located. Could I stay awhile and just talk and relax with you? I am in such a panic now that I know I am going to be deported on Monday morning and probably never see any of this city or my parents and family again. By the way, one of the few things I left in my room are some bottles of wine, which I always enjoyed greatly, especially when I needed something to calm me down. Would you like to join me in some as well? If so, I will just go down quickly and get them."

"Well," Carola said, "I enjoy wine myself, especially for good conversation." She thought back of her numerous times with Uli and the ability for both of them to speak more frankly of things that without the "lubrication" would have been more difficult to approach. Simon quickly went to his own room mumbling "it will only take me a minute" and was back before she could finish locating the two glasses still in her possession that would seem to suit the occasion.

He had also brought back with him a corkscrew, which he expertly applied to the first of the bottles of Burgundy red wine he had brought back with him. He poured the wine quickly after taking a sip to make sure it was still drinkable and had not turned with the hot weather and time since he had brought them from his home.

"*Prosit,*" he said as he clinked her glass. "Let's both enjoy this in the short time we have left until they come for us. We'll probably each have to go our own way to wherever they have in mind.

"Well, let me tell you a little bit about myself". Simon continued in a somewhat urgent voice. "My family has lived in Fulda for many years. As you may know, even though it is a small town compared to Frankfurt, Jews have been there since the thirteenth century, almost as long as they have lived here. Having visited the cemetery with my parents every year at the *Yahrzeit* of their parents, I have seen the tombstones of our ancestors for quite a few past generations.

"My parents are very observant; they kept a kosher home and attended our synagogue until it was burned down during Kristallnacht. My father owned an electrical supply business, where he sold lamps, chandeliers, fixtures, and all kinds of switches and other small appliances. He started his shop and built it into successful operation over the past decade. Fortunately, he had officially sold it before 1938 to a friendly Aryan neighbor, who promised to keep it as a surrogate owner until after the Hitler time. This man is a decent German, and up to now has kept his word, paying my father surreptitiously in installments on the price they had officially agreed on. My parents were, therefore, able to continue meeting their living expenses, contrary to the shops owned by our Jewish neighbors that were destroyed on November 9 four years ago.

"After going to high school," he continued somewhat breathlessly, as if he needed to get it all out before an internal "time is up" feeling, "I attended the University in Düsseldorf and studied electrical engineering since my interest was always in that direction after being exposed to the subject in our family business. When I had graduated, I came back to Fulda and shortly after married my high school sweetheart. Unfortunately, and much to my family's regret, she was not Jewish. In fact, her parents were on the unfriendly side and remained very cold and distant to my parents as well.

"Elise and I were, of course, not too happy with this difficult state of affairs. She was constantly conflicted and had a difficult time staying in touch with her parents in normal fashion. This was especially true after our daughter was born in 1933. Her father joined the NASDP, which helped him when he was promoted from teacher to principal of our local high school. From then on his hostility toward me and agitation toward my wife increased sharply, and he urged her to get rid of me so that there would not be a mixed marriage in his family that could become an impediment to him rising through the Nazi ranks.

"By 1935 when the Nürnberg Laws were passed, his insistence that she divorce me became unbearable, and with much regret and remorse she finally obeyed her father and went through with a legal separation. Even though I had visitation rights, I have been totally by myself, and my former wife is now engaged to a good Nazi, who will make a suitable son-in-law for her father. I guess this is my penalty for having stepped out of my own community to try achieving personal happiness in the environment in which I was raised. In a way, I felt it served me right for disregarding what I now realize was a transgression but at the time felt more like assimilation into the mainstream."

He now went on in a somewhat more relaxed fashion. "For a while, I thought of emigrating to Palestine and starting life over again in what seemed to be a promising homeland for our people. In view of the fact that the friend who took over our business secretly employed me in our warehouse to keep control of our inventory, I procrastinated, never making the move to leave my parents. I've just sort of existed on a day-to-day basis, but now over all the years by myself I've been lonely and depressed. My few friends have left the country, and to be perfectly frank, I have taken to drinking a lot of wine to dull my senses and make my general unhappiness more bearable."

Carola took it all in with rapt attention but thought to herself, *Here is another man living in loneliness and with problems that I'm listening to so he can find some comfort. How many thousands of men, Jewish or gentile, Simon or Uli, are living in despair in this land or perhaps all over the world when they could search for a better way to live their lives?*

What is it about me that makes them wish to bare their souls and share their misery? Am I the receptacle, the vehicle of their pain that makes them feel better when they have shared it with me rather than with a thousand other women or even men? Is this my role in life, even if I cannot look beyond the next two days? How different might things have been if I had met this Jewish man, Simon, instead of Uli, my super Aryan? And yet, if I can reach Uli in time, he could be my potential savior. Is my yearning for personal survival so great that it ignores the conflict with which I would have to live the rest of my life?

She had no ready answer for herself as she took a long sip of the wine he had continued to pour her and himself while he was talking and reviewing his own sad life.

"What made you come here to Frankfurt?" Carola asked. "After all, even though you had an unhappy life being by yourself now for many years, you were able to live with your parents, have their company, and live in a Jewish way."

"I did have the support of my family and was not totally alone. Well, I did not tell you that I have a younger sister who married within our faith, had two children, and lived with a very nice husband in an apartment above our own. Fortunately for them, they were able to emigrate to Palestine and start a new life in a small town near Tel Aviv some two years ago. As you know, it was still possible then; in fact, the Nazis encouraged it. They were unable to bring my parents with them; otherwise, I might have come along.

"Last year, my father suggested I leave for Frankfurt and 'disappear' from full view so that my ex-father-in-law, who had vaguely threatened to turn me over to the SS authorities for reasons I could not figure out, could not easily entrap me. For once, I heeded his advice and came here only to be directed right away to this Judenhaus because my passport quickly identified me as a Jew. Now I will be deported, not even knowing that perhaps my own parents are in the same unhappy position. I have not been able to call them because I was afraid the call might be traced and my father-in-law would have me tracked down by the local SS."

After that orderly recitation of his life and background, even though it was not lengthy, she responded with her own background and why she, too, was here as a single and lone survivor. She did not tell him about Uli, as this might have been so repellent to him that he would have left her room quickly, perhaps feeling a sense of contamination, despite having been entangled with the Aryan world himself.

They were now engaging in an animated repartee and felt comfortable as fellow Jews with the things they had in common, particularly with respect to the horizon they were now both looking at. The final weekend in the city was staring both of them in the face.

The second bottle of Burgundy was near empty, and Simon quickly went to his room and brought in two more, indicating they were the last among his worldly possessions. The pace of their drinking reduced suppression of the total emptiness that was immediately ahead of them. Their conversation had its pauses, and the intervals of silence increased as their exchanges slowed with one topic or another now exhausted. Simon became somewhat quiet, staring at her intensely with a strange smile as she was responding without words, drawn by a certain magnetism of his gaze and the wine's soothing effect. He interrupted one of these silences gently and tenderly with real hesitation.

"Carola, I have looked at you so intensely, not just now but for quite a while from afar or whenever you did not notice. You are a beautiful and attractive woman with an enormous reservoir of empathy, compassion, and, I believe, real passion as well. I hope this will not offend you; I'd like to ask you a strange, yet forward question. I have been alone for so long, and after Monday, I don't even know whether I will still be alive. Perhaps your thoughts are similar to mine. I wonder if you would do me the honor and give me the privilege to make love to you so that we can both take with us a recent memory of what is now fading fast from times long ago. Wouldn't that be a wonderful way to spend what might be our last hours, accompanied by harmony with a few moments of happiness that we will not ever experience again. What do you think about my proposition, and what do you say?"

She was taken aback but not offended by what he said. The specter of Uli appeared and faded in front of her. A sense of her loyalty somewhat blocked out her temptation to acquiesce. She certainly understood Simon's fate and dilemma and realized her remote attraction to him, despite the fact that she had only known him for the past two to three hours. She noted to herself his somewhat similar features to her husband Aaron, now gone for seven years, and the fact that the only man she had given herself to at her own peril of the Nürnberg Laws violations, was this Aryan man who over the past few months had been thoroughly deflated in her attraction to him despite their association now more than three years old.

"Simon, I certainly understand your proposal, and I am not in the least put off by it. Despite this atmosphere of desperation we both feel with our forthcoming, extremely dark future, it is difficult for me to respond so quickly to your attraction, which I also feel. In one sense it seems so right, in another so difficult, for me at least. I have never lived in an environment of courtship where things happen so fast and suddenly without the ability to count on something beyond a sexual act. Therefore, it's difficult for me to respond, and I don't quite know what to say without seeming cruel and crude."

As she paused with both a feeling of slight embarrassment and awkwardness, he stood up, pulled her out of her seat, and began to kiss her passionately without letup. Again, she was surprised and neither resisted nor encouraged him. In the small room, he gently but firmly pushed her onto the bed and began to grope under her clothing to excite her and have her respond. Uli's image continued to stand in the way, and while she was unable to muster reciprocal stimulation and excitement, she appreciated his.

"Simon, please, please give me time."

"Carola, we don't have time. It's too late, and it's too late for me to stop and interrupt myself. Please let me come to you and give me the satisfaction of having made love one last time before life swallows me up and there is nothing, nothing."

With that, he rapidly opened his pants and hoped to penetrate her. She grabbed his member quickly, both to stimulate him as well as to prevent him from entering her without further preparation on her part. As she did so, his release came quickly and massively with a loud and extended moan that would have been heard along the top floor if other residents were in their rooms. It seemed interminable as he shook and trembled, coming over but not into her and slowly began to recede and relax. As he rolled over, he remained with his back to her and sobbed quietly.

"Carola, thank you. I'm so sorry; I know I intruded on you, but I got to the point where I could not control myself anymore. I so appreciated your compassion and hope that somehow there will be enough time for both of us to make love again and reciprocate each other's feelings. I am so embarrassed and don't know what to say. I am sober now. Will you forgive me?"

"Yes, Simon. I totally understand, although I could not respond for reasons we'll perhaps discuss another day—or perhaps not at all. I think it is best you go to your room now so I can be alone with my own thoughts. I really appreciate sharing your wine, but for now, let's call it a night."

He left the room not looking back and, once down the hall, closed the door firmly behind him. The hours spent with him, the unsatisfactory lovemaking, the mutual embarrassment, and the awkward ending all felt as if they had been compressed into a short moment before final disaster would strike. Carola locked her door and went to sleep without further hesitation.

29 WHY?

The following morning she woke up, suddenly realizing it was Saturday— Shabbat, the day of rest in another life and another time. This was the last chance to call Uli's office, even though it was not a regular workday. The secretary had hinted that she might be available on the phone. After a quick cup of coffee, Carola went downstairs into the hallway and dialed the five fateful numerals with a final deliberateness. She could feel her heart beat with a hope that she knew would be her last within the next few moments if she did not succeed in making contact.

The officious voice with which she had by now gathered some familiarity answered, again with the mysterious "number 27, who is calling please?"

"I'm sorry to keep bothering you, but is Herr von Kleinhoven available this morning? This is Frau Brombach calling once again."

"Frau Brombach, I realize you have been trying to call von Kleinhoven repeatedly, so it must be very important to you, but I do have to tell you that he is not available. He is back in the city but not in the office. He's had to go to numerous meetings that are being held on a last-minute basis."

There was something about her voice and the way she framed the answer that did not seem genuine or truthful to her, and she wondered if, in fact, the secretary really did not know or perhaps he had not wanted to talk to her over the past few days.

"Frau Brombach, you must really know Herr von Kleinhoven extremely well because, after all, he's given you his private number, one he only gives out to a very few of his closest confidants. I must admit that he has told me about you in a very special way—I suppose in a weak moment."

Obviously, he had left out a few salient facts. She spoke as if she was letting her guard down but with a certain expression of studied carelessness. Then she continued in a somewhat more gossipy, perhaps mischievous way that indicated she had no reticence in telling her something highly confidential she was sure they were both aware of.

"Frau Brombach, he must have told you, of course, that 27 refers to our confidential headquarters at number 27 Lindenstrasse of which he is in charge. He does not like to use his title because of the secret nature of his work, but," she continued with some pride, "he is the *Obersturmbannfuehrer* of the SS here in Frankfurt, and so he exercises a great deal of his power with discretion. I cannot even give you my name, even though by now I feel I know your voice very well. Perhaps another time we can get more acquainted."

"I don't know who you are, but what … did … you … say? He … is what?" She reeled and sat in the chair that was near the telephone, feeling as if she had been struck on the back of her head with a heavy instrument.

"He is in charge here, I said, and as *Obersturmbannfuehrer* is very influential. He is a prominent member of the SS and on the same level as Gauleiter Sprenger with whom he works very closely. You can also guess that he is now terribly busy executing the *Entjudungspolitik* that was resumed in the spring and that will only be concluded when," she said with a certain self-possessed pride, "the last Jew is gone from our beautiful city of Frankfurt.

"His travels to the east, to Theresienstadt and Auschwitz, have taken up all his time lately, as these Jews disappear but, for some reason, don't become fewer. So you must really excuse his absence, as the good friend you apparently are. The time will come when his work is complete, and he will be able to go back to his own business more often and have more time with you. I hope that gives you a better explanation and—I also hope I have not spoken out of turn and revealed any confidences I should not have. Well, good-bye, Frau Brombach, until next week then, when I hope we can return your call."

They both hung up, and as Carola staggered up the stairs, tripping occasionally, seeing nothing, yet all of a sudden seeing everything, she groped for her door, locked it behind her, and collapsed into her chair. Her brain, heart, and all pulses were pounding as she tried to absorb the unabsorbable with which she now felt irrevocably besotted.

"Oh my God—my God—what have I done?" she moaned loudly to herself over and over again. She could not stop; as interminable minutes went by, she continued sitting in the chair, burying her head into her pillow to drown out the sound, the screeching she heard that would not go away.

"I cannot go on; I am forever besmirched. What's left of me? Am I that Jew with an Aryan face, or am I an Aryan with a Jewish face? Why don't I wear my star with pride instead of hiding it at the bottom of my pocketbook? That *J* on my passport, my Judenhaus, my residence where I now proudly live with my fellow Jews who are slated to take a long train ride on Monday morning that was arranged by Herr *Obersturmbannfuehrer* von Kleinhoven.

"Thank you, Herr Uli, for arranging our escape from your city of hostility, out of the cage you've kept us in, and for sending us to the 'East,' to those wonderful cities you described to me in such glowing terms, those workers' paradises where we will work or go to Palestine or to our destruction even further away from here. That way, we will not only be out of your mind and out of your sight but perhaps also out of our life. Did you arrange that as well, Uli, while you were taking me to dinner, charming me, using me, making love to me to satisfy your own carnal desires, and throwing me away now that the time has come?

"Why, Uli, why? Why me, a Jewish woman in her fifties? Why not—despite what you told me—a long-legged, lively, sexy Aryan blonde whether sincere or not, someone willing to give in order to get, to make you forget that you've lost all your family, that you've lost your two sons who—you said—meant everything to you. According to you, you really have nothing left, so why not start over with a young thing and procreate more in your image—if you can still do that and are not sterile and impotent by now.

"Do you have a woman in every city that you travel to 'on business,' perhaps on the business of death? When you undress is it out of your uniform there rather than your civilian clothes, and is she awed by the clusters of oak leaves on your shoulders which connote the power you have over so many others? Will she fantasize that she is the only one who, in turn, has power over you—the Aryan of her dreams?

"Why, then, a middle-aged Jew like me? Is it that you are rebelling against your father whom you have told me about, who felt as a young man that he owed his Jewish employers everything for the chance they gave him to make something of himself? Were you angry that he was weak enough to have needed them to elevate him above where he was going on his own and that there was not some grand mystical organization with a demigod that permitted him to make it on his own? Was he not strong enough to build for himself the bourgeois background he never had? Were you angry with him and looked down on him for this failing? Did you want to make sure this never happened to you?

"Were you furious with Jacobs and Krakauer, who tried to pull him up to their level of values, of culture, and of decency that he then acquired, but you could never tolerate being exposed to by his kindness and humility? By rebelling and ranting against him, did you succeed in pulling down what he had built, but in secrecy and by surreptitious means so that no one could tell? Will your ambition and greed be successful in shaping your future, or did you have to make your bargain, your deal with the devil after all?

"What was it about me that started you at the café behind the opera house at that table outside with the pastry and the seduction of civilized pretense? Having your liaison in secret, you could throw me away at any time as you are doing now that you have satisfied yourself without giving away your illicit dalliance and avoid being discovered. Are you too cheap to put yourself in a position of blackmail with that blond young thing who might interfere with your career as she whispered your indiscretions to another with even more power? Was power over a woman like me, helpless and naïve in the ways of the Aryan superworld, more important to you than living on the edge of a politically dangerous plan?

"Monster that you are, this way you could wipe out your crimes at will. But are you really a traitor not only to me, but to your country and to your party? You violate your own laws with cavalier indifference. You sleep with Jews before discarding them; you rob them of their houses, their apartments, and their property; you take them to country inns, hotels where they are forbidden to stay on their own—Brombach is the euphemism of all your hypocrisy.

"Why are you immoral to the core, unscrupulous, and false in every emotion? Did you look me up in your card file of the Jewish community and vet me for my employment at the Witwe Hassan so you could take me on and then have me fired on time and on schedule? Why do you have so much hate and even more after your sons were killed in the war you started? Why more desire to kill, in turn more dominance and enslavement of people all over Europe and perhaps all over the world, all in the service of your party?

"How did I not recognize a beast as it was smiling at me, as I sympathized and mentally supported you? As I hoped—God forbid—to even marry you someday, to live with you in peace afterward, after what? But when you'll finally marry one of your Nordic goddesses after the war—as you surely will—you'll produce your Aryan post-war offspring without thinking back on your previous life. Then your newborns will be swaddled in brown shirts and diapers so you can't tell their excrement from their garb? As they would grow up to be monsters, masters over all the world, to live in glory, how? Why did you choose me to accompany you for even a moment, a minute, or an hour? Why did you take advantage of my nature, the way I was educated in your society with the illusion that I was a part of that which had accepted me and in which I had rights of my own? Were there really ever any good old days, or were we deluded by the hypocritical beasts lying in the bushes, waiting for the right moment to pounce on us and destroy us? We strayed; every one strays from his own standards and expectations and ideals, but did we deserve this? Is our punishment in just proportion? I think not."

She went over all of these calamitous thoughts and the variations thereof again and again. She rambled in her mind through the expansive scenarios that led her through a labyrinth of guilt, revulsion, and exhaustion from her inability to understand, to find answers for the hellish world of grief she had created for herself. She realized that she wanted to see no one again, not Simon whom she had just met, not anyone in the house, none of her former associates, though they were now on the other side of the fence, as it were. Not anyone at the Welfare Agency, at the old-age home as it had been emptied a few days before, not anyone in her distant past, no one in her family that she might meet up with again, if for some miraculous reason she would ever escape this hell.

Her state of agitation grew as she became more tired and worn-out from self-recriminations and confusion. All of this went on for hours. Sometimes she tried to rest without success; sometimes she paced the room not daring to go out of it. She clutched at the pillows, the chair, the wallpaper, at nothing as she could no longer tolerate being with herself, let alone anyone else.

As she kept going into the early hours of the morning, she became irrational and could no longer figure out how to shed her demons. In one of her pauses and calmer moments, she thought back to the pleasant weekend at the inn at Brombach, which was probably the moment of her greatest pleasure and hope in the past three years. She recalled von Kleinhoven's rant and her responses, which at the time were still spirited and had left her in such a state of agitation. She remembered that he had given her a sleeping pill so she could get some peace in the middle of her restless state. He had called it Veronal and had given her a vial of them "in case you need it to calm you down sometime in the future."

This was such a moment. She searched and found the vial among her toiletries. She rose and quickly opened it, took a pill, and with a few gulps of water swallowed the white round disc. Within minutes, calm set in and much reduced the rage and fear she had undergone for the past several hours. Yet the shaking did not subside; after another fifteen minutes, it began to well up all over again as the horrid deception and betrayal, as well as her naïve denials, came to the fore once again. She took another pill quickly to avoid the panic that was beginning to build up around her and could not be suppressed.

The pill continued to slow down the process as she had hoped, yet the internal shaking and panic were not erased. It seemed that the medication was becoming no longer effective and that the Veronal itself created a new type of fear that would not go away. She was almost asleep, and the edge of the horrors she had experienced were deep-seated as her head began to swirl. She was afraid that in this state she would not be able to help herself in case the panic returned and her demons would no longer go away. With the last bit of energy and fading consciousness, she took the vial, and in her now raging mind, decided to increase her dosage for good measure by swallowing its entire contents. It was for protection, for insulation, as armor against an overwhelming revulsion, and a fortress of peace in which she could take refuge against the outside world she could no longer hold off in its efforts to destroy her.

As a sense of ultimate calm overtook her mind, she lay down on her bed covering herself with the light blanket she normally used and quietly stared straight ahead up at the ceiling. The harsh light dimmed at last; the sounds and drumbeats faded into the distance, and finally all intrusions disappeared. The battle against her continued rage and grief had at last receded and had seen its day.

30 VERSCHOLLEN (VANISHED)

At five minutes to seven on the morning of September 1, 1942, a small *Kraftlastwagen* truck drove up in front of the Judenhaus at 167 *Fuerstenbergerstrasse*. The driver turned off the motor as he and his passenger stepped out. *Unterscharfuehrer* Johann "Hannes" Mueller and Franz Schrade bounded up the steps to the front door. They had been there the night before to collect the skeleton key from the superintendent. Their assignment this morning was to examine and review the documents which were to have been made out with complete accuracy by the residents in each of the apartment units, to check over their belongings that were to stay behind, to officially confiscate them by list, and to issue a receipt. They then had to check each resident who was to be prepared for deportation on the personal items they were to carry with them in accordance with the instructions received. Following that, the two were to receive the keys to the apartment and the bin located in the basement, seal the door with strong tape, and instruct the occupants to go downstairs and wait in front of the door. From there, the assembled group was to walk to the gate of the *Palmengarten* to meet the same truck that had pulled up at the front of the house, and on which they had been instructed to place their entire luggage. Alternately, they could also carry their own luggage to the meeting point if they did not care to leave their bundles on the truck.

Mueller and Schrade decided, as they had in the past, to start from the top of the house and work their way down. At fifteen minutes on average per apartment, that would take them roughly two and a half hours before departing, according to their time schedule. They, therefore, told each of the families that the official departure time was 9:30 AM.

As they had done in other houses, they began knocking on the door of the apartment all the way over to the left of the corridor. On proceeding, they merely experienced the usual moaning and wailing with the first two families who had been prepared for their upcoming ordeal by the notice they had received three days earlier from the *Reichsvereinigung der Juden*. They then proceeded to unit number three, which they presumed to be a one-room studio apartment as per a layout of the house they had been given earlier by their office. They knocked at the door several times and then called out, first in a normal voice, followed by increasing their volume to a near shout. "Come on, my dear Frau Rossmann, this is not the morning to oversleep; you've got to get ready for your nice trip out of the city."

With neither a reply nor a rustling sound indicating some reaction, after consulting with each other, they finally decided to use the skeleton key and enter on their own so as not to lose valuable time in finishing their job.

As they half opened the door, they began to detect a slight odor that was unhappily familiar to them. On the bed near the window, they spotted a woman ostensibly fast asleep. She seemed relaxed with her right arm hanging down over the bed but otherwise totally motionless. Mueller moved quickly to the bed detecting no breathing motion or any other sign of life as he looked at her closely. Her eyes were closed, and as he opened one lid, he saw the total dilation of lifelessness. Her skin was completely devoid of any color, a porcelainlike translucency pervading the visible areas, below which were veins in a soft blue that seemed rapidly in the process of disappearing. Her mouth was partly open, indicating that her last breath was taken through it before she had finally expired. Both men looked at each other with extreme discomfort even though it was not the first time they had seen what they were looking at now.

Mueller spoke quietly, "You go down to the hallway and call Von Kleinhoven. Tell him what we found and ask him what we should do with the body."

Schrade followed his instructions, going rapidly down the four flights to make this embarrassing call.

"Heil Hitler and good morning, Herr Obersturmbannfuehrer," he said as soon as he heard a voice on the other end. "This is Schrade. I am sorry to disturb you so early in the morning, but I must tell you that we just found another Jew who likes it so much in Frankfurt that she decided she did not want to leave. We want to have instructions as to what to do with her."

"Tell me, where are you?" the voice on the other side of the phone asked.

"We are on the Furstenberger Strasse working on our first Judenhaus."

There seemed to be a rustling motion on the other side. "What number?"

"Number 167."

"What is the name of the occupant in the apartment?"

"According to the records the superintendent gave us last night, she must be a Carola Rossmann."

"*Ach Du …*" he sighed, which was followed by a silence with further strange noises from von Kleinhoven's receiver. After a long pause and clearing of his throat several times, he finally replied in a slow and uncertain voice.

"If you found her in the bed, wrap her in her sheets completely like in a shroud, immediately carry her down to your truck, and bring her back here. Then put her in our small panel truck that is in our garage behind the office over here. Close the door and go back to the house to finish your job getting the rest of the Jews over to the *Palmengarten*.

"Don't worry about being late; they can damn well wait. It doesn't matter; their train isn't leaving until tomorrow morning anyway. Hurry, so that as few people as possible see you move your unpleasant piece of baggage. Report to me before you go back. Someone should bring me a complete list of what was in all the drawers of her apartment and all identifying papers and documents you can possibly find. I want nothing left there that in any way associates her with the place."

"*Jawoll*, Herr von Kleinhoven. We'll be there shortly."

He slowly went back to the fourth floor and gave a complete report on his instructions to his colleague. After all, the standing orders to those assigned to collect Jews for deportation was to treat any one found dead in their apartment, either by suicide or otherwise, in the same fashion as if they were still alive and going through the formalities of their exodus. Papers had to be made out with all the belongings, and official documents of confiscation were to be filed. Keys were to be collected, and the front door of their residence was to be locked and sealed so that no one could reenter the room without permission.

Several families were left in shock and horror as they stood outside the house and watched the body wrapped in the white shroud being carried out and placed onto the truck. The two men raced off quickly and returned to the Gestapo compound at Lindenstrasse 27. They opened the garage door at the back of the driveway and transferred the shroud onto one of the small panel trucks parked next to the larger vehicles, covered it with a waterproof canvas that they tied down with ropes at the corners, closed the garage door, and quickly went into the office to report to their superior.

As they entered, the two *Unterscharfuehrer* saw von Kleinhoven, deadly pale, as he quickly lifted his head from between his hands, took a swig of coffee, and pretended to be in total command of all his emotions. They handed him the papers, documents, and forms they had found in her night table drawer and told him that they had packed up her things in several suitcases before leaving, which they still had on their truck. They wanted to know where to stack them before returning to the house to continue with their tasks. He told them to leave them in the garage on the floor next to the truck and go back to finish their job as quickly as possible. He then gave them additional instructions, which promised to make their day long and difficult.

"When you are finished with the houses assigned to you and have brought all of the travelers to the meeting point at the *Palmengarten*, come back here, eat something, and rest up an hour or so. By that time, it will probably be late afternoon. I want you to take the panel truck with its contents and drive out the Eckenheimer Landstrasse to the Old Jewish Cemetery. You have done this before, so you know where it is. But let me remind you that for the old cemetery you must make a right turn at Rat Beil Strasse and go into the entrance of the main gate.

"Having done that, you must pay very close attention because it is a matter of making an exact count from the point at which the graves assume a regular pattern on the left side of the road. You must count twenty rows up, stop, and walk in to the eighteenth headstone to your left. You should be able to read the inscription: Salomon Herxheimer and below it 1852–1911. That is the grave, and no other—you must be absolutely sure—on which I want you to work. As you have done before, you then go down one meter, which is exactly half the old and normal depth. Cut out a one- by two-meter rectangle and complete the burial at that level without removing the shroud.

"Make sure you restore the grave as per your prior procedures so that there is absolutely no sign of this plot having been disturbed. Wash out the truck thoroughly with the hose you usually use at the cemetery so that it is spotless and does not in any way reveal its mission. You're then dismissed for the day. In view of the fact that it will have been a long one, you can show up two hours later tomorrow at the Ostbahnhof to complete our dispatch of the people, who will then be waiting at the checkpoint stations."

"*Jawoll, Herr Obersturmbannfuehrer,*" they both responded in turn. They went outside to stash Carola's belongings in the garage next to the small truck and drove off, returning to continue their assignment at 167 and the other houses that had been given to them for check out.

When they were finished around two thirty in the afternoon, they returned to the office, had some sandwiches that were waiting for them, and sat around for two hours or so to wait until the end of the day. At 4:30 PM they got into the panel truck and drove off in the direction of the Old Jewish Cemetery. They turned right on Rat Beil Strasse, then through the gate, driving very slowly up the central path, and began counting the rows of the headstones on the left side beginning at the first complete line, as they had done a number of times in the past. At the twentieth row, they parked the truck and got out with spades, pitchforks, rakes and hoes as well as several bundles of old burlap, before proceeding to the eighteenth plot. There, indeed, they found the name Salomon Herxheimer engraved on the rectangular black granite headstone. This was the correct destination at which to finish their task. The grave was covered with ivy, thickly grown but well trimmed so as not to interfere with the ones on either side of it. Care might not be perpetual from here on in, but it certainly had been for so many years in the past.

As they had done before, they carefully spread the burlap around the three sides of the headstone and, using the spade with a straight and sharp edge, cut the ivy now by jamming the spade into the ground with their boots and loosening the first few inches of soil for subsequent removal. As the pieces were heavy, they cut exactly one meter by fifty centimeters by twenty centimeters down so that the two of them could lift a rectangular slice far enough to place it on the burlap next to them. They stopped, rested five minutes, and began to dig to loosen the dirt beneath. This was shoveled onto the other burlap on the right side into a neat conical pile so that it did not slip off onto other graves to give away what had been done. Of course, the loosened earth made a much higher pile than what was removed from the inside as it became fluffier, having been dug out. However, they did not stop until they had gone down exactly one meter in depth.

They were glad they had not hit anything indicating remains of a coffin or, worse yet, the bones of a body, so that they could feel comfortable in walking on the surface inside the dug out portion to tamp down what had been loosened up. They climbed out of the hole, walked back to the truck, and after lowering the back panel, carried the body back to the grave together. Once at the foot, they slid the shroud into the hole, placing what they surmised was the head end in the direction nearest the stone. They both then clambered out of the hole once more and, after a couple of more minutes' rest, began to shovel the earth back as quickly as possible to complete the burial.

When they reached the level of the grassy edge, there was a significant amount of the claylike mass left on the burlap because what they had newly dug out originally now had assumed a much lower density than it had remaining in the ground for the past ninety years. Hannes stuck his shovel into the pile, walked back to the path where he knew a long hose was carefully coiled up a few rows away, and attached it to a water faucet. Fortunately, it was long enough to reach the grave. He turned on the spigot while Franz began to water down the soil to eliminate the air so that they could ultimately replace the ivy rectangles in the same sequence as they had taken them out of the ground earlier.

Hannes continued to shovel in the remaining dirt while Franz ran a small flow of water to further eliminate the air so that eventually all the earth was back in place. The top surface was now fairly dry, and they both compacted it as much as possible, using rakes and hoes, as well as stomping on it with their boots. This left the rectangles of ivy, which they then carefully inserted so as to fit them in with the least disturbance in the same state they had found the grave when they opened it. They both sprinkled small amounts of earth in between the plants so that with somewhat more watering, it could flow between the cuts. They then sprinkled the plants themselves to give them a maximum chance for regrowing quickly and walked on them in tiptoe mode to finally smooth out the top. From experience, they knew that the hardiness of the ivy would make it regrow in a day or two and would leave the appearance pretty much in its original condition.

When all was done as well as it could be, they picked up their tools and burlap and brought them back out to the truck. After a last rinse under the faucet, they placed the tools on the burlap and covered them with the canvas so they would not show to someone walking by the vehicle. Both then went back and rinsed their boots, removing the heavy clay; washed their arms, necks, and faces; and dried them with towels they had brought along from the office. They rolled up the hose near the water faucet so that it did not look used and got back into the vehicle. By that time, about two hours later, the sun had begun to set. They drove out of the cemetery with headlights on, turning left at the end of the street back toward town. They had not talked to each other for the last hour of their work; this was not their first time, and they had no reason to make small talk or have a serious discussion about the task they had just completed.

As they were heading down the *Eckenheimer Landstrasse,* once more on their way back, Hannes Mueller finally spoke to Schrade.

"You know, Franz, it's getting kind of late. I must admit I am very thirsty. It is too late for dinner at home, and even if my wife left it for me on the table, I know she has gone over to our neighbors to play cards and spend the evening with the other women there. How about stopping at the Goldene Gickel and having a couple of beers and some food before we call it the day?"

"Sounds good to me," said Franz. "Let's do that, so we can cool off and relax; it's been a long day."

As they got near the *Marschnerstrasse*, they spotted the sign of the tavern, pulled up the truck, latched down the canvas to make it secure and totally innocuous looking, got out of the vehicle, and entered the pub.

"Heil Hitler and good evening, Elfriedsche. It's good to see you again. Let's have two liters of *Henningbrau* from the tap. We are both very thirsty and can't wait to get them down on our throats."

"Yes, but of course *meine Herren Unterscharfuehrer,*" she said in a chirpy voice, as there was only one other man sitting at the bar, brooding over a small glass of *Asbach Uralt.*

"Have a seat at your usual table, and I'll be right over."

She drew each of the liter kegs by tilting them at just the right angle so as to maximize their foam release and settle them as quickly as possible. Having drawn each and placing them one on each of her ample breasts to support their weight, she carried them eagerly to the table, put them down, and smiled sweetly at each man. Both men gulped the first half liter as if they were pouring it down a funnel and sighed with satisfaction once this first quantity had wet their innards.

After about ten minutes just sitting quietly and catching their breath, Hannes said to Franz, "You know, I'm really hungry. We worked hard today, particularly at the end of the afternoon. All that lifting and shoveling is something I'm not used to anymore at my age. I'd rather walk Jews to the Ostbahnhof any day. Let's have some food."

He waved Elfriede over and sat looking at his partner, who quickly acquiesced.

"Elfriedsche, let's have two times two Frankfurters, the big fat kind, nice and hot, with potato salad, cucumber salad, and your spicy mustard."

"Yes, but of course, Herr *Unterscharfuehrer*. They'll be out in just a few minutes."

When they arrived, they gulped their food down rapidly and with obvious gusto.

"Once more, another Frankfurter for each of us and a refill of the potato salad," Hannes said to her when they had finished, with which the waitress obliged them very readily with a sweet "Yes, but of course, right away." In fact, she brought them out within a couple of minutes because she had already anticipated the familiar refill they usually asked for. As they were brought over, both men dug in again with crude verve and asked for another two *Henningbrau* drafts in swift succession.

"Ja, aber naturlich, meine Herr'n: 's kommt wieder sofort."

As she promptly brought them over, having repeated the drafting process at the tap, carrying them across and subsequently unloading them from her mammary supports, she sounded out her "to your good health" in cheerful chant, *"Zum Wohl, meine Herr'n, Zu Ihr'm Wohl!"*

Both tipped their mugs again, but this time drank up more slowly to savor the pleasantly bitter liquid. After all, they knew they had to get home when they had drained the last of the brew.

It had indeed been a long and arduous day.

Breinigsville, PA USA
27 February 2011
256474BV00005B/53/P

9 781440 190391